Praise for the novels of Michelle Major

"A dynamic start to a series
with a refreshingly original premise."
—*Kirkus Reviews* on *The Magnolia Sisters*

"A sweet start to a promising series,
perfect for fans of Debbie Macomber."
—*Publishers Weekly* (starred review)
on *The Magnolia Sisters*

"*The Magnolia Sisters* is sheer delight,
filled with humor, warmth and heart....
I loved everything about it."
—*New York Times* bestselling author RaeAnne Thayne

"This enjoyable romance is perfect for voracious
readers who want to dive into a new small-town series."
—*Library Journal* on *The Magnolia Sisters*

Mistletoe Season

MICHELLE MAJOR

HQN

ISBN-13: 978-1-335-47702-6

Mistletoe Season
Copyright © 2021 by Michelle Major

A Carolina Christmas
Copyright © 2021 by Michelle Major

Recycling programs
for this product may
not exist in your area.

This edition published by arrangement with Harlequin Books S.A.

For questions and comments about the quality of this book,
please contact us at CustomerService@Harlequin.com.

HQN
22 Adelaide St. West, 40th Floor
Toronto, Ontario M5H 4E3, Canada
www.Harlequin.com

Printed in U.S.A.

Also by Michelle Major

The Carolina Girls

A Carolina Promise
Wildflower Season
A Carolina Christmas
Mistletoe Season

The Magnolia Sisters

A Magnolia Reunion
The Magnolia Sisters
The Road to Magnolia
The Merriest Magnolia
A Carolina Valentine
The Last Carolina Sister

Look for Michelle Major's next novel

Wedding Season

available soon from HQN.

For a full list of titles by Michelle Major,
please visit www.michellemajor.com.

CONTENTS

MISTLETOE SEASON

For all the readers who love Christmas books as much as I do. Thanks for letting me share this special season with you!

CHAPTER ONE

ANGI GUILARDI LET herself out of Il Rigatone, the restaurant her family had owned in Magnolia, North Carolina, for the past thirty years, and locked the door behind her. It was nearly eleven at night, and a brisk December wind whipped down Main Street. Although she should be wearing more than a white button-down, now stained with smatterings of red sauce, Angi welcomed the gust of air. At least it blew away the smell of sausage and tomato paste that clung to her like a barnacle.

Scents that seemed to be infused into her at this point, bringing back memories of years of a childhood spent in and out of the restaurant. It had been a long day, so she needed a shower and a glass of wine in equal measure.

She started toward her car, parked around the corner, but the sound of a door slamming nearby caught her attention. Downtown Magnolia rolled up the sidewalks early on a weeknight, so she didn't expect anyone else to be out and about. She arched a brow at the woman approaching.

"Are you stalking me?"

Emma Cantrell gave an impatient snort as she moved closer. "That's what it feels like, but it wouldn't be necessary if you'd return my calls or answer messages."

Angi turned to fully face her business partner—now former partner. "I've been busy," she said, trying to make her tone dismissive. Instead, the words reeked of desperation.

"How's your mom?" Emma asked gently, her annoyance with Angi temporarily put aside because, clearly, Emma was a good person. Too good for Angi to be ignoring her the way she had.

"Equally weak and ornery." Angi dropped the oversize set of keys into her purse with a jangle. "The doctor says two more weeks, and then she can slowly begin to resume her normal activities."

"Like running Il Rigatone?"

"We don't know yet if she'll ever return at the same capacity." Angi bit down on the inside of her cheek until she tasted blood. "It doesn't matter because I'm running it now."

"But only temporarily," Emma insisted. Or suggested, like saying the words out loud would make them true.

Oh, how Angi wanted them to be true.

She gave a small shake of her head. No more time for fanciful thoughts or big dreams about making her life her own. Unable to meet Emma's sympathetic gaze, she looked across the street to the storefronts decorated in festive holiday cheer.

Colorful twinkle lights danced in the darkened window of the hardware store, and she could make out the shadow of garland wound through the sign for the dance studio. Boughs of greenery with bright red bows hung from every light post on either side of the street. Magnolia had gone all out on the holiday cheer this year.

Too bad Angi didn't feel much of the holiday spirit. Sure, she'd gone through the motions of assembling the fake Christmas tree that had graced the corner of the restaurant's small waiting area each December for as long as she could remember.

During a lull in customers yesterday, she and one of the

waitresses had pulled out the totes of decorations from the storeroom, but nothing managed to conjure up the magic of the season. Not for her.

"I'm sorry I let you down," she told Emma, thankful her voice remained steady. "I've got calls in to a couple caterers in the area to see if they can—"

"I don't want another caterer." Emma stepped forward. "You're it, Ang."

"I can't…" She swallowed when a lump of sorrow lodged in her throat. "I should never have deserted my mom in the first place. If she hadn't been working so much and upset about me as well, maybe the heart attack wouldn't have happened."

"Sweetie, you aren't to blame for that."

"She almost died," Angi insisted, needing to make it clear. "Less than a year after my father. She collapsed in the restaurant's storeroom, and I wasn't here."

"You were at the inn."

"Having a grand old time, not a care in the world. My mom was fighting for her life, surrounded by employees until the EMTs got there, and I wasn't with her. When she needed me the most—"

"Stop." Emma held up a hand. "I remember that day, Angi. It was the McAlvey wedding, complete with the bride's niece and her tiny Irish dancer friends pounding away on the parquet floor we assembled in the backyard. You made food for over a hundred guests. Plus lunch baskets for the Thompson reunion and their picnic at the beach. Five of the six online reviews that came from those two events mention the food being a highlight. You care a lot, so don't pretend otherwise. Not with me."

Emma still didn't get it.

"I should have cared more about my mom. The way

she did when I needed her. She looked so pale, Em." Angi crossed her arms over her middle, squeezing tight. "I kept waiting for her eyes to pop open so she could start ordering me around or give me some kind of guilt trip, but she was still in the hospital bed with the monitors beeping and the smell of antiseptic permeating everything. She needs me now, and I can't let her down."

"What about letting yourself down? What about your happiness?"

Angi sniffed. "Doesn't matter."

"It should."

"I'm sorry," Angi said again.

She'd met Emma in the spring when the other woman bought an old mansion in town with a plan to turn it into a boutique inn. Emma had had her share of setbacks, but Angi admired her dedication to her dream. She also knew that leaving behind her old life had cost Emma her relationship with her mother.

Angi's mom had been outspoken in the way only Italian mothers can manage when Angi walked away from the restaurant to partner with Emma on the inn. But Angi assumed that her mom would get over her disappointment. That they'd find a way to bridge the emotional distance between them. She loved her mom, even if Bianca Guilardi could be overbearing and autocratic. The willful matriarch had good intentions.

But they never got the chance to mend their fences because, a month earlier, Bianca had suffered a massive heart attack that led to double bypass surgery. In an instant, all of Angi's plans changed.

She'd moved from her cozy apartment back to her childhood home, along with her ten-year-old son, Andrew, in order to care for her mom. She'd also stepped in at the restaurant, and in doing so, she'd left Emma in a pinch.

For that, she felt sick to her stomach with regret.

"If you can't find someone to take care of the holiday events, I'll still manage it," she offered now, absently thinking about ways to clone herself.

"You can't do both."

"I will."

Emma sighed. "My intention for tonight wasn't to guilt you into more work."

"Come on, I'm a master of guilt."

"I know." Emma gave her a pointed look. "That's why I don't want to add to it. I thought we were friends—business partners, as well. But you cutting me off as a friend is what hurts."

Cue the remorse, Angi thought. She didn't need anyone to lay it on her. She could do that very well for herself.

"It seems like all I'm doing lately is disappointing people. You and my mom." She hitched a finger at the restaurant. "The staff who can tell I don't want to be there. Andrew."

"Wait. What's going on with Andrew? I know you're an amazing mother. That kid thinks the sun rises and sets on his mommy."

Angi's throat tightened again at the thought of her sweet, awkward, lanky string bean of a boy. He was everything to her, and now he was struggling and she didn't know how to make it stop.

"He's being bullied at school," she confided. As difficult as it was to talk about, she appreciated the flash of supportive fury in Emma's dark eyes.

"Give me the kid's name." Her buttoned-up friend spoke as if she were some kind of avenging angel.

"I don't have it. Andrew won't say anything, and his classmates are keeping quiet, as well. But he came home with a split lip and scrapes on his hands. I talked to the teacher and met with her and the principal. They said all the right things, but kids can be such jerks. Maybe if we lived in a bigger town or someplace where differences were more accepted, it would be easier for him to find his way. I hated growing up in Magnolia, and now I'm doing the same thing to him."

Her nails dug into the fleshy part of her palms, and she welcomed the pain. At least it distracted her from the telltale scratchy eyes that foretold a bout of tears. She wasn't going to break down in the middle of the sidewalk, even if it was deserted.

"How is it possible to hate it here?" Emma shook her head. "It's idyllic."

"Not for the Italian cannoli princess," Angi muttered.

"Is that like a Midwestern Corn Queen at the state fair?"

"Not exactly. Never mind. My point is that I'm screwing up in every aspect of life. I'm sorry I ghosted you, Em. We are friends, but I didn't want to admit that I was ditching the inn. You gave me the new start I wanted, and I can't keep up my end of the bargain." She let out a humorless laugh. "Here comes the guilt again."

"I didn't give you anything. You earned your place in our partnership, which I refuse to believe is over. At least until your mom fully recovers and we see what happens next. I'll find someone to help with the nitty-gritty food prep and serving, but I'm going to take you up on your offer to manage things for the holidays. As long as it's not too much. We can reassess in the new year." She enveloped Angi in a gentle hug and couldn't have known how much it helped. "Either way, the friendship stands."

"Okay." Angi couldn't help but agree. She wasn't ready to let go of her dream, even though she knew she had to. She dashed a hand over her cheeks. "Do you believe in Christmas miracles?"

"Not really."

"Me neither," Angi agreed with a wry smile. "But I sure could use one."

ANGI HALF EXPECTED her miracle to materialize after the conversation with Emma. She'd gone home feeling lighter than she had in weeks, like there might be a glimmer of hope that she could control her own destiny after her mother recovered. The next morning dashed that hope like a late-season snowfall on a delicate spring bloom.

"Mom, I don't need a date. I don't have time for a date."

Bianca sat at the kitchen table, tapping one finger on the polished oak top as she glanced between her daughter and the laptop open in front of her.

"There's always time for love," she insisted, like she was imparting some deep wisdom.

"I have a date with the drop-off line at school," Angi countered, then glanced at the clock on the wall. "Drew, come on," she called as she glanced above her. "You need to eat breakfast so we can go, buddy."

"Don't call him that." Her mother tsked. "Such a ridiculous name."

Angi gritted her teeth. "It's not ridiculous."

"He looks like an Anthony," her mother said.

Where was the bottle of headache medicine when Angi needed it? She'd been having the debate about her son's name since the day of his birth. Bianca adored her grandson, but she couldn't understand why he didn't have a traditional Italian name, something to honor an older relative or dead ancestor. Angi had tried—for years—to explain to her mother that she liked the name Andrew and wanted her child to choose how much he wanted to embrace his heritage, not have his identity defined by a name. Luckily, Bianca never voiced her disappointment in front of Drew, but it was an ongoing, and useless, debate with Angi.

"Now, Andrew," Angi shouted, then turned her attention to her mom. "I'm meeting with Aldo Caferno to discuss our monthly order before we open, and then I'll be back to take you to the doctor after lunch. He's charging way too much for their meats."

"He's a good boy," her mom said. "We've been doing business with the family for years, so I'm sure they are giving us a fair price. How old is Aldo now?"

"He's married old." Angi dumped her coffee into a travel mug, cursing when it sloshed over the rim.

"His younger brother, Artie, is still single. Too much caffeine makes you jittery," her mother said. "We can talk about potential dates when you get back."

"No men." Angi said the words like a plea.

"I'm a man," Andrew pointed out as he came into the kitchen. He wore a striped sweatshirt and baggy jeans that she knew were hitched in at the waist by the growth buttons sewn into the fabric. His backpack looked like it might be heavy enough to make him topple over, but Angi knew her son was stronger than he appeared.

"My best little man." Angi made to ruffle his hair as he walked toward the table, but he ducked out of reach.

"I'm not that little."

Her heart stuttered at the sound of defiance in his tone. "Getting bigger every day," she agreed.

"Give your nonna a kiss." Bianca opened her arms wide,

shooting Angi an accusatory glance over Andrew's shoulder. "My strong Italian prince."

Next, Angi could just imagine her mother blaming Andrew's social issues on the name she'd given him.

She wondered if it was actually possible to grind her teeth to dust.

As Andrew ate his breakfast, Angi finished emptying the dishwasher, started a load of laundry and then kissed her mother's forehead, the scent of Shalimar taking her back to more innocent times. "What do you think about a hair appointment next week?" She finger combed her mom's curls. "Fresh highlights and a trim."

"That would be lovely," Bianca said, tucking a lock of hair behind her ear. "But I don't want to be too much trouble. I know you have better things to do than be burdened taking care of me."

Angi's cheeks hurt with the effort to remain smiling. "You're not a burden."

Before her mom could heap more passive-aggressive guilt onto the already overflowing pile, Angi herded her son out the door.

She tried to bring up the situation at school as they drove, but Drew kept steering the conversation back to his ever-growing Christmas list. His small hands gripped the straps of his camo-patterned backpack so tightly his knuckles turned white.

It broke her heart to see him hurting and not be able to help. Memories of her own struggles fitting in assailed her, and not for the first time she contemplated whether she could add homeschooling to her list of to-dos.

"I'm fine, Mom," he said as he opened the door, flashing a gap-toothed grin.

When had she become Mom instead of Mommy?

The hits kept on coming.

One of the few benefits to being pulled in a thousand different directions each day was that she didn't have much time to ruminate over all the ways she wasn't measuring up. She made it through the meeting with Aldo, refusing to allow him to mansplain supply costs to her and getting him to agree to a ten percent reduction in their monthly bill.

She greeted the regulars, along with a few new faces, who came in for lunch. The town of Magnolia had seen a recent resurgence in popularity after years of decline, and Il Rigatone should be reaping the benefits of the area's renewed popularity.

Unfortunately, visitors didn't seem to appreciate the old-school charm of the place, which hadn't been updated in decades. Angi knew online reviews for the restaurant were a mixed bag, some praising the classic dishes they served and others bemoaning the lack of innovation with the menu items.

Her mother's appointment was routine, so by the time she got back to the restaurant in the late afternoon, Angi felt somewhat calmer. Right now, checking in on her son topped the priority list, so she went looking for his dark head.

"Where's Andrew?" she asked Dominic Marcelli, Il Rigatone's longtime head cook. The elementary school was only a few blocks from downtown, so Drew walked to the restaurant after dismissal and did his homework or played video games in the back office until she could drive him home.

Angi had spent her childhood much the same way, although her son did a lot less pilfering of food from the storeroom and refrigerators than Angi had as a kid.

"Haven't seen him," Dom told her, not glancing up from his online poker game.

"His backpack is in the office," she said, trying not to let panic take hold. She knew he'd arrived safely from school, although normally Angi was waiting with a snack and a hug. Andrew knew not to go exploring around town without checking in with her first. Didn't he?

Neither of the waitresses on shift had noticed him, and it killed her that her son could be so overlooked by the people around him. Or that she hadn't been available when he'd arrived. What if something else had happened at school to upset him? What if he was hiding?

Calm down, she ordered herself. She wasn't going to do either of them any good by panicking. Magnolia was a safe town. People knew Andrew. They knew Angi and her mom. The freezer at home was stuffed to the brim with get-well casseroles, most of which her mom wouldn't touch because she was so particular about food. Plus, most of them didn't fit the new heart-healthy eating guidelines the doctor had given her.

"I'm going to walk the block," she told Annie and Lana, the two waitresses working the afternoon shift. "Maybe he went for candy at the hardware store or to check out Christmas trees." She'd promised him that this year they could get a real tree from the lot in the town square, and he had specific plans for what he wanted. "Please text me if he comes back."

"Will do. You and your brothers ran wild through the town at Andrew's age. I'm sure he's just following in your footsteps," Lana added, then went to wait on the one oc-cupied table in her station.

A terrifying thought.

Lily Wainright, who ran the hardware store her family

owned for generations, reported that Andrew had been in fifteen minutes earlier for a box of sour gummies. The knowledge calmed Angi somewhat. She couldn't imagine giving him a cell phone in fifth grade, but she sure would like one of those tracking apps made for parents.

After scanning both sides of the street with no sight of him, she made a lap through the square and then headed back toward the restaurant. A bright spot of orange on the ground caught her eye. A telltale gummy worm discarded just next to the coir welcome mat outside the In Bloom flower shop. Oh, no. What would her son want in a flower shop? Especially one now owned by a surly, cantankerous hulk of a man.

She glanced at the shop's picture window and saw a small head bobbing around displays of multicolored roses. As anxiety drained out of her, it was immediately replaced by irritation. Both at her son and the flower shop's owner.

Angi'd had a crap-tastic day, and an unavoidable confrontation with Gabe Carlyle would be the icing on the doo-doo cake of her life.

She pushed her way into the store anyway, ready to fling a bit of doo-doo around in Gabe's direction. Maybe that would help her mood. It certainly couldn't hurt.

CHAPTER TWO

How COULD ONE child produce so many questions in the span of a few minutes? Questions that seemed to tear scabs from old wounds as easy as ripping off a bandage. Gabriel Carlyle had tried to brush off the boy with no luck.

Andrew Guilardi was small in stature but big in curiosity.

Gabe didn't appreciate curiosity.

"How do you even breathe with all that yammering?" he muttered as the kid followed him toward the back of the store.

"I've been practicing holding my breath in the bathtub," Andrew answered, clearly missing the rhetorical nature of the question. "Did you know Navy SEALs can hold their breath for two or three minutes?"

The sound of the chimes over the front door gave Gabe an excuse to move past the boy. "A customer," he ground out, tossing a pointed stare at Andrew. "I have actual work to do."

"I'll wait." Andrew climbed onto one of the stools near the worktable. "I don't got much homework."

The kid couldn't take a clue if Gabe handed it to him.

He let out a soft curse at the woman striding toward him. "Where is he?" she demanded, like Gabe was holding the boy hostage or something.

"Hi, Mom," Andrew called as he heard his mother's voice. "Me and Gabe are hanging out."

One feathery brow arched as she glared at Gabe, her dark eyes flashing with temper. They often did when her gaze met his, which was complete bull because Gabe had done nothing to Angi Guilardi. After the hell she and her snotty friends had put him through when he was a goofy, misfit preteen, he didn't even want to look at Angi.

Especially based on how his body reacted to her. He chalked that up to having a pulse. No one could look at Angi, with her tall, willowy form, olive-colored skin from her Italian heritage, dark hair and eyes and not appreciate her beauty.

But looks could be deceiving, and Gabe had learned that the hard way with Angi. Since returning to town, he'd done his best to avoid her, although working with Emma at the Wildflower Inn had made that more difficult.

He managed. Managing was his specialty.

"He won't leave," he said under his breath. "Trust me, I tried."

She sniffed. "I can only imagine. Why is he here?"

"He wants me to tell him about my military career."

"What the…why… I don't understand."

After the initial shock, though, Gabe had a feeling she understood more than she was telling him about why her son had sought out Gabe. When he came to Magnolia in the spring, he hadn't made a huge deal about his career or the accolades he'd received throughout his stint in the army. He'd rather not think about that time, at least if he wanted to get more sleep. But it was a small town and people talked.

His grandmother was a popular resident and her store a fixture in downtown, even if it was somewhat musty and in need of a thorough cleaning. This was something Gabe hadn't bothered with over the past eight months because it had felt that admitting the store was a mess would only make him more culpable for not being there when his grandma had needed him.

"Talk to him," Gabe suggested with a shrug. "Preferably someplace other than in my store. I have work to do."

She glanced around the dingy shop. "Yes, I see."

He picked up a slip of paper from the counter. "An order." He held it in front of her face. "To deliver today."

"Andrew, let's go." Angi took a step toward the back room, then growled under her breath when the boy didn't materialize. "I mean it."

"Mom tone. Impressive."

She shot Gabe another look and, despite his desire to avoid her, he felt one side of his mouth lift into a smile. Gabe didn't have a lot of reasons to smile in life, so it felt unfamiliar. He liked the idea of getting under her skin the way she did to him, so when Andrew finally appeared in the doorway, Gabe shocked even himself by the words that came out of his mouth.

"If he doesn't have much homework, he can stay. I'll put you to work," he said to the boy, whose eyes lit up like sparklers on the Fourth of July.

"Yes. Mom, please."

Angi hissed out a breath. "You just told me you wanted to be rid of him."

True enough. "Changed my mind," Gabe told her.

"Because it bothers me that he's here?"

He narrowed his eyes. "Do I bother you, cannoli?"

"Do not call me that."

The golden flecks around the edges of her dark eyes

flashed in pain, and Gabe almost felt guilty for using the nickname he knew she hated. Almost.

"Listen to your mom, kid," Gabe told Andrew. "Go with her if that's what she wants."

She elbowed her way past and crouched down in front of her son. "You have to let someone know if you're going to leave the restaurant after school." Her tone had turned gentle, far softer than Gabe would have expected. "I didn't know where you were, and I was worried, Drew."

"You weren't there after school," he said, an accusation more than an observation.

"I'm sorry. I had to drop Nonna off at home after the doctor. But you can tell Dom or Annie or one of the other waitresses."

The boy looked down at his scuffed sneakers. "I hate going to the restaurant after school. Nobody wants me there, and it always smells like meatballs."

Gabe noticed the shift in Angi, the way her shoulders went rigid at Andrew's words. Leave it to a child to have the ability to gut his mother without even trying.

"Nothing I can do about the meatballs," she said with what Gabe guessed was fake cheer. "It's only temporary that you'll be at Il Rigatone. Remember that you chose not to go to the aftercare program at school."

"I hate it there, too."

Angi bowed her head, and Gabe suddenly felt he was witnessing a moment too intimate for the nature of their abrasive relationship.

"You know what a good remedy for hate is?" Gabe stepped forward. "Hard work. You can take out your anger on the dust bunnies in the corners."

"What's a remedy?" Andrew asked his mother.

"A solution," she answered. "Something I'm fresh out of."

"Gabe's got lots of dust bunnies." Andrew patted her shoulder as he looked around the shop. "Maybe even some dust rhinos."

Angi let out a small, tired laugh. But the boy's face cleared. Gabe knew the kid hadn't meant to upset his mom. He remembered what it had been like to try to coax smiles or an infrequent laugh from his mother, the effort made more challenging by the fact that she was usually nursing a hangover or halfway to her next buzz. His mom was a mean drunk.

His gran, in contrast, hadn't had a mean bone in her body. She'd been sweet and caring, always ready with a kind word or a hug for her grandson. Being back in Magnolia made Gabe miss those summers he spent with her with an intensity he hadn't felt in years. It also reminded him of the things about Magnolia that hadn't been good for him.

Angela Guilardi topped that list.

"I meant you can sweep up around the restaurant," he clarified. "Do some odd jobs for your mom to keep yourself busy when you finish your homework."

Angi straightened, shooting him a curious gaze, like she couldn't figure out why he'd be offering suggestions to make things better for her son.

She could get in line behind Gabe on that front.

"The restaurant's already clean," Andrew reported as he moved to the front of the store. "I'm just in the way."

"You're not," Angi argued. "Everyone there loves you, Drew."

The "yeah, right" look Andrew shot his mother was priceless. Gabe had to hand it to him. He might only be a tiny wisp of a kid, but he had one hell of a backbone.

"I can come here after school and work for you," Andrew told Gabe. "You need help."

"No, I don't."

"He doesn't," Angi said at the same time.

The kid rolled his big, guileless eyes. "You said you'd put me to work."

"Just for today if it's okay with your mom."

"I'll come every day," Andrew countered.

"No."

"Drew, if you want things to do after school, I can find stuff at Il Rigatone." Angi wrinkled her nose. "That's a better place for you, especially with your asthma. There might be things you're allergic to in here and definitely the…" Gabe followed her gaze around the shop, noticing the dead flowers decaying on a shelf and the general clutter in every corner. He had a tendency to overlook those kinds of details. His goal was to get through the trickle of orders as fast as he could so he could visit Gran at the nursing care facility he'd moved her to, or return to the solace of her house.

In truth, the florist part of running the flower shop wasn't the thing he liked best about returning to Magnolia. Instead, he loved his grandma's old greenhouse behind her house a few blocks away with the scent of fresh dirt filling the air. The intricacies of botany fascinated him, and he tended her garden and the living things she loved with a dedication he hoped would make her proud.

Maybe he needed to focus a bit more on the shop. It didn't seem to matter, though, when the bulk of the orders came from online sales. When it was just him in the store, he could do whatever he wanted.

Looking at it through Angi's judgmental eyes made him see the space in a different light.

"Listen to your mom," he repeated. He might be able to view the store with fresh eyes, but he wasn't going to change everything—or anything—just for her. Suddenly his offer for the boy to hang out with him seemed desperate, as if Gabe couldn't stand his own company. Ridiculous, because even when he'd been surrounded by a platoon of fellow soldiers he'd been alone in the deepest part of himself. "You're better off out of my hair. Take a hint and don't make a nuisance of yourself where you're not wanted."

Andrew's chin jerked up, and Gabe heard Angi's harsh gasp of breath. Maybe he'd gone too far with his words. So what? She didn't want her kid hanging out with Gabe, and Gabe didn't want it either. A clean break would be better for all of them.

"You're mean," Andrew said. "Just like everybody else." He pushed out the front door, and his mother hurried after him.

"I know you hate me," she said, glancing over her shoulder. "I probably deserve it. But Andrew didn't do anything to you. I hope you're proud of yourself."

Gabe realized his chest was heaving in and out when the store descended into silence once again. He stood there for a long moment tamping down the shame that threatened to overtake him, and then he returned to filling orders, knowing he hadn't been proud of himself for a very long time.

ANGI BURST THROUGH the back door of the Wildflower Inn on Friday night, her gaze darting between Emma and Mariella Jacob, the former famous wedding dress designer who handled most of the inn's marketing and branding. From the website to social media to selecting the aromatic diffusers in each bedroom, Emma rightly trusted Mariella to choose the best. Somehow, the cool blonde also managed to source amazing deals on everything from high thread count sheets to locally made toiletries for the bathrooms.

Plus, Angi had noticed the steady foot traffic in and out of Mariella's secondhand store a couple of blocks over from the restaurant. The dress designer might have left her society life and fast-track career behind in New York City when she'd moved to Magnolia, but there was no denying her talent for design and marketing. Some people were just built to be successful.

Too bad Angi wasn't one of them.

"What's wrong?" Angi demanded. Having responded to an SOS text from Emma, she expected to find some sort of crisis playing out with guests or the last-minute details for tomorrow's wedding.

Both Emma and Mariella had the good sense to look sheepish.

"We thought you needed a break," Emma said, then pointed a finger at Mariella. "I told you this was a bad idea."

"It's a great idea." Mariella smiled and handed Angi a glass of white wine. "Just one quick drink and you can go back to wallowing in your self-pity."

Emma nudged Mariella. "The idea was not to make her even more stressed."

"Can you get more stressed?" Mariella asked Angi, almost as a challenge.

"Perhaps if the local sheriff locks me up for beating the crap out of you," Angi answered with a sweet-like-candy smile.

Mariella shrugged. "I'm scrappier than I look. Have a drink and talk to us. We're your friends."

The words made Angi's irritation deflate like a popped balloon, but she still couldn't bring herself to admit how much she missed them and her work at the inn. "I'm sure Emma filled you in, so we're all on the same page." She downed the wine in two big slugs. "Nice seeing you both."

"What do you think about frozen puff pastry cups?" Emma asked suddenly. "Ham and cheese or spinach?"

"Neither." Angi glanced at the refrigerator that she'd stocked with appetizers for the reception. "I stayed up half the night last weekend making homemade stuffed mushrooms and spanakopita. What happened to them?" Her annoyance had returned full force.

"After the guests were asleep last night, I invited Cam over for a visit."

"A booty call," Mariella stage-whispered.

Angi rolled her eyes, although she really couldn't blame Emma. Cam Arlinghaus, Emma's fiancé, was tall, dark and handsome—plus he wore a tool belt better than any man Angi had ever seen. Unlike Emma, Cam had grown up in the area, but he'd become a recluse when his wife died in a car accident years prior. Through a strange twist of fate, he'd ended up helping Emma with repairs on the inn before its opening. Although they didn't seem like a match on paper, the two had fallen madly in love. Angi was glad for her friend and not the least bit jealous. Okay, maybe the teensiest smidgen jealous, but she let that go because she loved them both.

"I missed him," Emma said with a shrug. "I've been busy this week. He committed to work with Dylan Scott on the new headquarters for that sportswear company moving to town, so his schedule is just as packed as mine."

"What does Cam being here have to do with my appetizers?"

Emma cringed. "A few of the guests got the late-night

munchies and raided the fridge. Unfortunately, they left the trays on the counter and Cam's dog pulled them down."

"The dog ate my appetizers?" Angi felt her mouth drop open.

"Not all of them," Emma said quickly. "We heard the noise in the kitchen and came out. I thought he was closed in the laundry room for the night. I'm so sorry, Ang. They spilled all over the floor, and Toby got excited and…"

"He stress peed on them," Mariella finished with wide eyes. "Couldn't salvage a thing."

"We can't serve guests stuffed mushrooms that have potentially been peed on," Emma explained as if it weren't obvious.

"You also can't serve them prepackaged mini quiche." Angi spoke through clenched teeth. She tapped a finger on the rim of her empty wineglass. "Was the plan to get me liquored up to soften the blow?"

"No," Emma and Mariella said at once.

"The appetizers weren't even on the agenda." Mariella gave a pointed look at Emma. "You weren't supposed to mention them."

"I don't know which ones to go with," Emma argued, throwing her hands up before sending a beseeching glance at Angi. "It's just this once, I swear. We didn't want to upset you or stress you out any more."

"This must be what rock bottom feels like," Angi muttered, then dug in her purse for her keys. "I need to go get supplies. I'll have new appetizers here tomorrow—noon at the latest. What time is the wedding?"

"Two," Mariella said at the same time Emma stepped forward. "No, it's fine. You don't have to redo anything."

"Of course I do. My reputation is synonymous with the food the inn serves at its events."

"I thought you were done with our partnership," Emma said quietly.

"We seriously invited you over to make you feel better," Mariella added. "Not so you could swoop in and save the day."

"Sleep is overrated," Angi said with a weak smile.

"We'll help," Emma offered.

Mariella snorted. "Uh, I don't cook."

"You can chop or clean up."

Angi waited for Mariella to refuse. The former designer to the stars hadn't exactly lost her sophisticated edge. Angi couldn't imagine Mariella taking orders from anyone.

"Tell me what to do," she said, placing her still-full wineglass in the kitchen sink. "Give me a list and I'll do the grocery run. They're open until midnight on weekends, so I've got forty-five minutes. Surely we can knock out food for a reception of fifty in a few hours?"

"You're seriously going to roll up your cuffed sleeves and be my sous-chef servant?"

"Why is that such a shock?"

Emma leaned closer to her. "Because you avoid domestic work like you're allergic to it."

"I might be," Mariella admitted. "But my friend needs the help, so I'm going to give it to her."

"Thank you," Angi said quietly.

"Me, too," Emma added. "I know the whole situation was my fault, and I really am sorry. I'll stay up as long as you need."

Angi sucked in an unsteady breath. This was in no way how she'd planned to spend her Friday night, but both Andrew and her mom had gone to bed. Bianca was doing much better than even her doctors had expected after the surgery, and Angi knew her mother would call if there was a problem.

The truth was, she didn't want to go back home to the bedroom still decorated with her stuffed animal collection and posters featuring various boy band members. She should have updated the room, but changing things to reflect her adult taste felt too much like giving in and admitting she was right back where she started.

"Then let's get to work, ladies." Her shoulders relaxed as she stepped forward.

Maybe she'd have to give up her catering business and her work at the inn eventually, but not tonight.

CHAPTER THREE

THE WEDDING AND reception were beautiful, or at least that's what Angi heard from Emma and Mariella. They texted updates throughout the day and into the evening, several messages in all caps with quotes from guests praising the food.

Angi hadn't seen any of it. She'd stayed with her mother, who, after several weeks of improvement, had started feeling weak and dizzy midmorning on Saturday—right after Angi told her about the late night in the Wildflower Inn kitchen and her plan to stop by the event on her way into Il Rigatone that afternoon.

Her mom had gone quiet as she diced tomatoes for the lunch salads she complained about every day. Seconds later, the knife had clattered to the floor as her mom clutched the edge of the counter.

Angi had phoned the on-call cardiologist, but her mom insisted she just needed rest, and the doctor agreed that she should be monitored at home. So they'd gotten her to bed, and Andrew had climbed in next to her to watch the home improvement shows they both loved.

It had been simple enough to avoid a food catastrophe with the help of her friends the night before. Angi had actually had fun staying up into the wee hours remaking the appetizers for the wedding reception. She felt strong and capable while creating her own recipes and dishes in a way she never had in her family's restaurant. She refused to think about the timing of her mother's setback, although it was no secret that Bianca had been angry and hurt when Angi quit her job at Il Rigatone over the summer to work full-time with Emma.

Surely she wouldn't scare Angi half to death by faking not feeling well?

In truth, it didn't matter. Angi might have entertained the idea of returning to the inn after her mom was fully well, but she knew in her heart it wasn't going to work. Bianca needed her. Both Angi's brothers had their own lives, and after her father's death ten months ago, Bianca had come to rely on Angi even more.

She owed it to her mom for all the ways Bianca had supported her, even if it meant giving up her dreams to do the right thing as a daughter.

Neither Emma nor Mariella had responded directly when Angi messaged Sunday morning congratulating them on another successful event and reiterating the fact that, after the holidays, she'd be focusing solely on the restaurant. Emma had sent a blue heart emoji and Mariella a GIF of some reality starlet rolling her eyes.

But Angi had no other choice. None that she could see anyway.

"Angela?"

She hurried down the stairs from her bedroom at the sound of her mother's call. "What's wrong?" she asked as she rushed into the family room. Andrew glanced up from where he sat cross-legged in front of the coffee table contentedly building some sort of new Lego creation.

"You're going to be late for the planning meeting." Bianca tapped the oversize watch face encircling her wrist. Angi had gotten her mom a fitness tracker while she was in the hospital, although Bianca refused to use the complicated gadget for anything other than checking the time.

"I'm not going." Angi grabbed the hem of her battered sweatshirt as if to prove the point. "I need to be here with you."

Bianca sniffed. "I feel perfectly fine."

"Yesterday you could barely sit up without feeling like you were going to faint."

"That was then," her mom countered. "You took care of me because you're a good daughter. My best girl. Now I'm fine."

Angi counted to ten silently in her head as her mother offered a beatific smile. Had she been played yesterday so that she wouldn't go to the inn? She still couldn't wrap her mind around the idea that her mom would sabotage her on purpose. The heart attack and resulting bypass surgery certainly hadn't been deliberate.

"They don't need me at the meeting. I texted Carrie and told her I'd help with whatever she needs."

Bianca sat forward. "A representative from the restaurant needs to be there in person to show that we're leaders in this town. People think Il Rigatone isn't the same without your father..." She paused when her voice cracked. "We need to show everyone that we're honoring his legacy."

"Oh, Mom." Angi's heart ached for her mother. She and Angi's father, Vinnie, had been childhood sweethearts. His death after a sudden heart attack was a hole in the fabric of their family that could never be stitched, but the loss remained most difficult for Bianca. She put on a brave front, but Angi knew how much her mom missed her husband. "You don't have anything to prove. Dad would be proud of how you've carried on, but he wouldn't want the stress it's put on you. He'd want you to take care of yourself the way he took care of you."

"You will go." Her mother spoke gently, but there was no mistaking the steel in her tone.

"Yes," Angi answered with a sigh. "I'll go." She crouched down to Andrew's level and placed a gray brick in line with others that made up one wall of the structure he was building. "Hopefully, I won't be long," she promised him. "But if I'm not back by the time you go to bed, I'll come in and give you a good-night kiss when I get home."

"Can I stay up late with Nonna?"

"Not on a school night, bud. Nonna can tuck you in after your bath. Don't forget to wash behind your ears."

"My ears don't get dirty," he argued, pulling at one of them. "I wish the weekend could go on forever."

"Me, too."

After a kiss for her son and one dropped on her mother's forehead, Angi grabbed a jacket from the hook next to the door to the garage and started the quick drive into town. She loved the way the Magnolia community celebrated the season with colorful lights strung around windows or at the edges of gutters on the houses on both sides of the street, along with festive wreaths and cheery yard decorations.

It was still hard to believe her father wasn't here to enjoy it. He'd loved Christmas and all of their family traditions. He'd taken such pride in the ceramic nativity scene and ornaments that had been passed down from his relatives in Italy. She and Andrew had already put up a few things, but her mother wanted to wait on the tree and some of the more meaningful decorations.

As she got out of the car after parking in front of the town hall, Angi pressed her palm to her chest to try to stem the tight ache that collected there every time she thought of her father. A heart attack, similar to the one her mother had suffered, had taken him far too soon. She would not lose her mom, as well. What was a little personal happiness in a trade-off for her mother's health?

She hurried toward the town hall building, cursing softly when she realized she'd forgotten to change out of the faux fur–trimmed house shoes she wore at night and into regular boots or sneakers. Maybe the ragamuffin look would garner some sympathy from her fellow business owners, but more likely the gossip train would kick into high gear. She could imagine the barrage of texts and calls later tonight at how Angi Guilardi was losing her marbles.

Closer to the truth…they'd started escaping months ago, Angi had slipped and tripped on them on the way out the figurative door that led to her dream life.

The sound of someone retching stopped her in her tracks, and she saw a woman bent over the bushes at the far corner of the building.

"Carrie?" she asked when she recognized the willowy brunette. "Are you okay?"

"Not exactly." Carrie Reed Scott walked toward her slowly, dabbing a tissue at the corner of her mouth. "I can't seem to stop the nausea. It's a little out of control."

"How far along are you now?" Angi had heard about Carrie's pregnancy from one of the waitresses at the restaurant, although the artist and gallery owner hadn't been in for her usual \ order recently as far as Angi could remember.

"Almost five months," Carrie said with a wan smile. "I thought the morning sickness would end, but it's gotten worse and more along the lines of around-the-clock sickness."

"Can you drive? Do you need a ride?" Angi glanced at

the flight of stone steps that led to the building's entrance. "You aren't going back in there."

Carrie shook her head. "Dylan's on his way to get me."

Dylan Scott was Carrie's husband and the real estate developer who was helping his wife lead the charge on bringing the town back to its former glory. They'd dated in high school but had an ugly breakup thanks to the meddling of Carrie's late father, Niall Reed. The same man who'd owned the house that Emma had turned into an inn.

Angi had enjoyed watching as Carrie and Dylan went from sworn enemies upon his return to town last year at this time to a couple deeply in love. Carrie had always been kind to Angi and supportive of her parents, so she couldn't be happier for the other woman's happiness.

Too bad her pregnancy seemed so rough.

"My doctor is talking about hyperemesis gravidarum." Carrie didn't seem surprised by Angi's blank stare. "It's a condition that results in severe nausea and vomiting for the entire pregnancy term. Only a small percentage of women suffer from it, so I guess I'm one of the unlucky ones."

"That sounds awful. Didn't I hear about one of the royals having that?"

"Yep. At least I'm in good company."

"I'm so sorry, Carrie. The most important thing right now is to take care of yourself. If there's anything I can do—"

"I meant to talk to you before the meeting. I was hoping I'd feel better or at least well enough to coordinate most of the Christmas on the Coast events, but I'm not sure that's going to possible." She winced as the sound of a car peeling around a corner split the night air. "Or that Dylan won't fight me on it if I try. I'm not up for much of a fight right now."

"What can I do?" Angi asked, hoping Carrie only

needed assistance with some small piece of the month-long festival. Angi's plate was already full to running over.

"Could you stand in for me as chairperson of the festival committee?" Carrie asked with a hopeful—if slightly frantic—smile.

"Chairperson," Angi repeated, the blood pounding inside her head. "Are you sure I'm the best candidate? Maybe Josie from the dance studio or Lily at the hardware store. Even Stuart would be—"

"I've seen what you, Emma and Mariella have done with my father's former house and the success of the events you host there. You have a gift for putting things together."

"Not me," Angi protested, her hands held up like a shield. "Emma is the organizer and Mariella the creative genius. I just make the food."

"I don't believe that."

"You should. Maybe one of them would be a better choice."

"It needs to be someone who knows the town and the people here. The festival was a success last year because the business owners trusted me. They'll trust you."

Unable to come up with a decent refusal when Carrie looked so desperate, Angi was relieved when Dylan pulled in with a flourish at the curb. He hopped out of the sleek SUV and jogged toward Carrie.

"Let's get you home," he said with the same level of intensity as an ancient warrior rescuing some distressed princess from a battlefield.

Angi wondered what it would be like to have someone willing to go to battle for her.

"I'm fine," Carrie murmured, lifting a hand to Dylan's cheek. She glanced toward the bushes. "Unfortunately, I can't say the same for the stir-fry you made for dinner."

"Crackers and ginger ale," he told her. "We've got plenty at the house."

"In a minute." Carrie wrapped an arm around his waist, and Angi noticed that a bit of the tension eased from his stance. "Angi and I were discussing the holiday festival."

Angi gave a little wave to Dylan. He glowered for a moment before his features softened a touch. "You're going to take over the remainder of the planning."

Maybe he meant to ask a question, but it sure didn't sound like it.

"That's what we're working out," Carrie told him, her voice soothing.

It amazed her that Carrie could be so polished and serene minutes after puking her guts out.

"Angi has a lot going on already," Carrie explained to her husband. "I'm not sure—"

"I'll help," Angi said on a rush of breath.

Dylan nodded. "That's settled. Let's go."

Carrie whirled to face him fully. "Enough. I'll be ready when Angi and I finish our conversation. I threw up, Dylan. It's nothing new at this point." She pressed a hand to the small bump of her belly. "I'm going to take care of our baby."

"I know," he whispered, his blue eyes flashing with intensity. "I just worry about you. I need you to be okay."

Angi felt she was witnessing a moment of deep intimacy, and her heart squeezed in response to the palpable love and devotion radiating between the two of them.

After giving Dylan a quick hug, Carrie turned to Angi again. "Are you sure? You don't have to agree because Dylan is behind me glaring."

"I'm not glaring," Dylan muttered.

"More like a glower," Angi agreed, earning a chuckle

from Carrie. "I'm still not sure I'm the right choice, but I'll do my best. You go home to those crackers and ginger ale. I'll fill in everyone at the meeting, and we can discuss details when you're feeling better."

"Settled." Dylan stepped forward and tucked Carrie's arm into the crook of his elbow. "Thank you," he told Angi. "Avery and Meredith will help, too. Whatever you need so that Carrie can get the rest she needs."

Carrie opened her mouth like she wanted to argue and then clasped a hand over it. "Another wave is coming. We'd better go."

Angi hurried up the steps and into the town hall building, then down the main flight of stairs toward the meeting rooms. Thanks to her inability to say no, she was running her mother's restaurant, her own catering business and now she was adding holiday festival chairperson to her list of responsibilities. The new year couldn't come fast enough.

GABE STOOD AT the podium next to Magnolia's longtime mayor, Malcolm Grimes, wondering who he'd pissed off in a former life to warrant his current karmic kick in the pants.

As soon as Gabe arrived at the meeting, Mal had approached and requested Gabe's help coordinating the annual holiday festival. Plans were already mostly set based on the previous year's event. Carrie and her sister, Avery, had done a great job of marketing the month of holiday-themed events, so tourists and locals were already streaming into downtown for shopping, impromptu caroling and concerts. Over the next few weeks, they'd continue the traditions with a fun run to benefit Meredith Ventner's animal rescue organization and two weekends of arts and crafts fairs plus live music, as well as a performance of *A Christ-*

mas Carol by the local theater group and a *Nutcracker*-themed recital held at the dance studio down the street.

A calendar chock-full of Christmas spirit gave Gabe a splitting headache, but when he'd visited his grandmother earlier that afternoon, she'd been adamant that he represent the flower shop at the business owners' meeting. Gran still had more lucid days than not, but things were becoming fuzzy enough for her that he wanted to hold on even tighter than before to the woman he knew and loved.

If it had been solely up to him, Gabe would have said no to Mal in a heartbeat. He could imagine Gran's elation when he told her that the mayor had chosen Gabe to cochair the event with Carrie since she was having some trouble with her pregnancy. Gabe had missed so many opportunities in his life to make his grandmother proud. He couldn't pass one up now, not when he had no clue how much time they had left.

Just as Mal called the meeting to order and the room went silent, Angi burst through the door. Everyone turned to stare, and Gabe had to hide the smile that tugged at one corner of his mouth. She certainly knew how to make an entrance, even more so with her thick dark hair piled high on her head in some sort of *I Dream of Jeannie* topknot and her singular outfit, which consisted of a tattered sweatshirt under a thick flannel jacket, paisley-print leggings encasing her shapely legs and fuzzy slippers on her feet.

The slippers were a nice touch, he thought.

"Sorry I'm late," she said, her skin turning an appealing shade of pink.

"You're right on time." Mal grinned. "How's your mom doing?"

"Good." Angi nodded. "Better anyway. She had a little setback this weekend, but…" She drew in a shaky breath, and a shiver of sympathy rippled along Gabe's spine. "She's okay."

He rolled his shoulders to diffuse the sensation. Angi didn't need—or likely want—his sympathy.

Mal nodded. "We're sending her our best. She's a strong woman."

A few people called out words of encouragement, and somehow Gabe imagined them like bullets ripping through Angi's soft skin. He was used to thinking of her as tough and unflinching, so the vulnerability she couldn't seem to hide when it came to her mother unnerved him.

"Yeah." The smile she offered didn't reach her eyes. "I guess I should be up there with you." She frowned as she noticed Gabe, and he curled his lip out of habit. Mutual distaste was much easier to handle than the invisible connection that sometimes filled the space between them.

Mal inclined his head. "We're waiting for Carrie."

"Right." Angi nodded. "Carrie still isn't feeling well. I just saw her out front, before Dylan picked her up. She's asked me to take over her responsibilities for Christmas on the Coast."

"Ah, hell, no," Gabe muttered.

Mal turned to him with a quelling glance as the gathered crowd erupted into murmuring whispers. Gabe had no idea whether people were talking about him or Angi or the two of them. Either way, he didn't like it.

"Well, that will be perfect," the mayor said, his deep voice booming in the large room. "Because Gabe just offered to pitch in, as well."

"You asked," Gabe said under his breath. "There's a difference."

Mal ignored him and continued speaking to Angi. "The two of you can coordinate the events together."

"Just like Carrie and Dylan," Josie from the dance studio shouted with a throaty laugh.

"Not like that at all," Angi said as more people joined in with laughter and a smattering of applause. "I don't need help."

"Me neither." Gabe moved closer to Mal. "This is a bad idea," he whispered to the mayor.

"Why?" Mal turned to him as Angi joined them at the front of the room. The older man looked at each of them. "I understand that Carrie and Dylan had a history, but you two barely know each other. Unless you had some kind of secret dating life the rest of us don't know about."

"Who's dating?" Josie, who sat in the front row, leaned forward in her chair.

"No one," Gabe said through clenched teeth.

"Not even a little." Angi offered a patently fake smile. "I'd be thrilled to work with Gabe. I'm sure he'll have lots to offer as far as making this Christmas season in Magnolia the most festive ever."

The words seemed benign enough on the surface, but Gabe knew a challenge when he heard one.

"I have loads of time to devote to this town," he said solemnly, placing a hand over his chest. He glanced down at Josie and her cronies, and gave his most winsome smile. "I know it will make my grandma happy."

As expected, the women clucked and cooed over his devotion. Angi looked like she wanted to reach around Malcolm and scratch out Gabe's eyes, and it was strangely satisfying to get under her skin.

"Well, then." Mal grabbed each of their hands and held them above his head like some kind of referee calling a heavyweight boxing match. "We have our new Christmas on the Coast power couple."

tifully tried to arrange the wired pine strands in a more artful way.

"You're my best helper," Gran answered from the wheelchair she needed most days when she left her room. "You carried all those planters and baskets for the Carter wedding last weekend. They had more wisteria than any one event could ever need. I never thought you'd be able to haul them, but you did. My strong boy."

A sharp pain pierced Gabe's heart. He didn't remember the event in particular, but until his return to Magnolia after being discharged from the army, he hadn't worked in his grandma's shop since he'd been fifteen. "I think the Carters got married a while back, Gran," he said casually.

Her doctor had told him the confusion was normal. According to the medical team, it was still too early to know whether his grandma was suffering from full-on dementia or if she'd regain her lucidity as her body healed.

A mild stroke had complicated the recovery from her hip replacement. Her speech was still slightly slurred, and it took her longer to process the thoughts she wanted to say and speak them out loud. Her right hand lay close to her body, fingers curled in on themselves despite weekly physical therapy sessions. The doc assured him that she was making progress, and for the most part, she kept her sunny attitude despite the physical limitations that now plagued her.

Gabe wanted to move her back home, but she insisted she was settled in the nursing care facility on the outskirts of town. The building was a renovated former elementary school, with three wings coming off the main common area. He knew that they were each marked by the level of care residents needed.

His grandmother was in the middle unit, which meant

CHAPTER FOUR

"MORE BERRIES. And can you fluff the pine boughs a bit more, sweetheart?"

Gabe turned on the ladder and looked down into his grandmother's innocent hazel eyes. Eyes the same color as Gabe's and his mother's, although it had been years since he'd seen his mom in person. Poppy hadn't even come to Magnolia when Iris had the stroke, although Gabe had wired her money from where he was stationed in the Middle East to cover the plane ticket. Enough for a first-class seat and plenty of extra to cover miscellaneous travel expenses. He'd thought the idea of flying first-class from New Mexico, where his mom had lived for the past fifteen years, might be enough of an incentive to get her to make the trip.

She'd taken the money and then refused to answer his calls or respond to emails or texts. He could only imagine where his cash had gone. More upsetting than that was the fact that his grandmother had been alone with no family at her side until Gabe managed to get back. Of course, she had lots of friends in the Magnolia community, but it wasn't the same.

Gran had taken care of him when he'd needed her most, and he hated that he hadn't been able to do the same for her.

"I'm not much of a fluffer," he told her, although he dushe had full-time nurses available to her but still was considered mobile with some freedoms. It was also the wing that was designated for Alzheimer's patients, which broke Gabe's heart even as the doctor wouldn't commit to that diagnosis quite yet.

"I don't remember it specifically," he told her, stepping off the ladder and taking her hand. At her request, he'd brought a few boxes of greenery and bows to decorate her wing's community area. "But if you were in charge of the flowers, I'm sure they were amazing."

She studied him for a long moment. "A while?"

He rubbed his thumb against the paper-thin skin near the base of her thumb. "I bet you've lost count of the number of weddings you've provided flowers for," he told her.

"The shop used to be a lot busier," she said, her gaze suddenly unfocused and tinged with sorrow. "Nobody calls anymore."

"I've updated the website," he told her with a gentle smile. "And linked the store to a few national florist databases. We're getting more business again. When you come back, there will be plenty to keep you busy."

She laughed softly but didn't contradict him. At some level, they both knew she wouldn't be returning to the store, but Gabe didn't want to admit it. Not out loud. Who was Iris Carlyle without a flower in her hand? Certainly not the woman who'd made his life better during the summers he spent with her.

"I got the Christmas cactus in your bathroom at the house to bloom," he told her. "I'll bring it tomorrow when I come for the wreath-decorating class."

"A good boy," she told him, lifting her functioning hand to pat his cheek when he bent toward her. "Where is Poppy?"

Gabe tried not to wince at the mention of his mom. "Still in New Mexico. She likes the desert, you know."

"Running wild, no doubt." Gran tsked as Gabe straightened. "That girl can't stay out of trouble. She's like a loose seed with the wind carrying her in any direction. The principal called me last week to say…" She paused, shook her head, brows furrowed. "Not last week. A while ago. Years now."

"That's right." Gabe forced a smile. "Mom has been gone for a while. She's got her own priorities, but I'm here. For as long as you need me."

"You always had a way with the plants," Gran told him, and it felt like the greatest compliment he could have received. "Not everyone does."

"I know."

She lifted a gnarled hand to point to the pine boughs and ribboned greenery he'd hung in haphazard swaths around the perimeter of the common lounge. "But your artistic eye needs a bit of work."

He turned and grimaced. He'd done his best. After all, how hard could it be to decorate one simple square room, especially when Gran had rows of boxes of holiday supplies both in the shop's storeroom and the old house's basement? But as he looked at his handiwork, he realized the decorations were uneven and drooping, not to mention he'd completely missed one entire wall.

"That's why I need you," he told her honestly.

Her tired eyes filled with tears that she quickly blinked away when voices heralded people heading toward them.

"Wow, this is a different look for Christmas," Sharla, the Shady Acres activities director, said with a laugh as she walked into the room.

"It's a work in progress," Gabe answered. "Gran is going to help me fix it. She's the—"

He broke off as Angi Guilardi and her mother walked into the room.

"Hello, Iris," the older woman said, giving his grandmother a wide smile. "It's so nice to see you."

Gran darted a panicked glance toward Gabe.

"You remember Bianca," Gabe told his grandma with a slight nod. "She owns the Italian restaurant a couple of doors down from your shop."

"With Vinnie," Gran said, then looked toward Bianca. "He brings me a meatball sub every Friday for lunch. I love meatballs."

"Gran, Vinnie passed away earlier this year."

"Oh." Gran covered her mouth with her hand. "I'm so sorry."

Bianca bent to give her a gentle hug. "You were at the funeral, Iris. My Vincent loved how much you loved his meatballs."

"I really did," Gran said. "Do you live here, too?" she asked Bianca, who brushed a wisp of hair from his grandmother's forehead.

"No. My daughter, Angela, and I are here to teach a cooking class for some of the residents. Maybe you'd like to join us?"

"They took away my kitchen." Iris shrugged. "I like to bake my own bread, and I can't now." Her chin trembled.

"I'll bring you some bread from Sunnyside Bakery," Gabe offered. "Not as good as yours, but I'll make sure it's warm. Right now, we should get you back to your room, Gran." He looked over his shoulder at the jumble of unused ribbons and plastic ornaments still spread across the tables. "I'll clean up for today, and we'll finish decorating tomorrow."

Iris squeezed shut her eyes like she was in pain and nodded.

"I'll wheel her back," Sharla offered, "and get her settled. You can put away your things and then say goodbye."

No, that wouldn't work at all. Gabe could not be left with Angi and her mother and their sympathetic, pitying gazes. But the director had already taken the handles of Gran's wheelchair, talking softly to her as she pushed it forward.

"She's lucky to have you," Bianca said, placing her soft hand on Gabe's arm, just like a good mother would do. Something his mom hadn't ever done as far as he could remember.

"I'm the lucky one." He swallowed back the emotion that lodged in his throat. "She's still confused after the stroke," he explained. "The doctor says she'll be back to her normal self eventually."

The doctor hadn't said anything of the sort, and he had a feeling both Guilardi women knew it. He refused to look at Angi. It had been bad enough to see pity in her gaze back when he was the misfit wimp during those summer months spent in Magnolia. He'd grown out of that kid, and no way was he going back there now.

"Iris is a treasure in this town," Bianca told him with another squeeze of his arm. "You should stop by the restaurant for a meal. You know my daughter, yes? You and Angela played together when you were younger. She had a little more meat on her back then, but—"

"Mom, stop."

Now he did look at Angi. Her olive complexion had

gone bright pink in the cheeks as she glared at her mother. "I remember her," he nearly whispered.

"She liked to sneak food from the kitchen as if we wouldn't notice." Bianca gave a knowing laugh. "She could have taken anything she wanted. Her father, rest his soul, would have done anything to make his sweet cannoli happy."

"Enough with the cannoli nickname. Ma, please."

An unexpected chuckle burst from Gabe, earning a narrow-eyed glare from Angi. He couldn't help it. The only time she spoke like she was a member of some Italian mob movie cast was when something or someone got under her skin. Gabe wanted to get under her skin.

"It's cute." Bianca pinched her daughter's cheek. "She's cute, eh?"

Cute was a wholly inadequate word to describe Angi, but Gabe nodded because what else could he do?

"Also single," the woman added with a cunning glint in her eyes.

Gabe chose not to respond to that information.

Angi rolled her eyes. "Come on, Mom. We've got to get set up."

"It was good to see you," Bianca told Gabe. "You're a good boy. Also handsome."

Now it was Gabe's turn to blush, but Bianca wasn't finished.

"Come for a meal, and you can take my Angela out sometime. She has a date with Artie Caferno on Friday, but she's free another—"

"Mom, I don't have a date on Friday."

Bianca winked at Gabe. "I haven't told her about it yet, but she does. He's a couple of years younger, but Angela is as gorgeous as any girl out there. I talked to Artie's mom yesterday to confirm the details."

"Mom!"

"I had a heart attack," Angi's mother continued, her gaze focused on Gabe. "It helps me feel better—less stressed—to think of my beautiful girl settled. It's not too much to ask, right?"

Gabe blinked but was saved from answering as Angi grabbed her mother's arm and pulled her toward the door that led to the kitchen and dining area, muttering the entire way about appropriate boundaries.

"See you soon," Bianca called over her shoulder.

Gabe waved, then couldn't help but shout, "Have fun on Friday."

Angi lifted her hand like she was waving, but it turned into a one-fingered salute, which made Gabe laugh even harder.

ANGI DIDN'T REALIZE how difficult it would be to avoid Gabe Carlyle until she set out to try. After the humiliating interaction with her mother at the nursing care facility, the last thing she wanted was to see his inevitably smug smile or have him ask about her unwanted plans for Friday night.

She still couldn't believe her mother had arranged a date without Angi's consent. But when Angi had demanded that Bianca call Julia Caferno and cancel, her mother had pressed a hand to her chest. It had been subtle, and maybe she was faking, but Angi wasn't going to take the chance.

That was the number-one reason she didn't want to see or talk to Gabe, followed closely by the knowledge that he wasn't only the surly, angry man he appeared to her. It had been easy enough to write him off when that's what she'd thought. But the way he'd talked to his grandmother and the sadness that had filled his gaze at her obvious confusion added a facet to his personality that made Angi more than a little uncomfortable.

It made her remember the sweet and gentle boy she'd known during those long-ago summers. The boy who'd looked at her with an adoration she'd never before experienced, who hadn't cared that she was chubby or her hair was too black and her eyebrows too thick compared to a gaggle of blond-haired, blue-eyed Southern belles that seemed to inhabit the town. There had even been a runner-up for the Miss Junior North Carolina title in Angi's class. Angi had been different from every girl she knew. It hadn't mattered for her older brothers. They were athletic and swarthy. She was just an odd duck.

But not to Gabe. They'd been secret friends for three summers and then things had changed. Angi had changed, at least outwardly. She'd grown several inches and managed to curb her sweet tooth. One of her brother Marco's girlfriends had shown her how to use styling products to tame her frizzy black hair and taught her how to pluck her brows. Angi had gone from ugly duckling to swan over the course of a few months. The popular girls—queen bees by anyone's standards—had finally accepted her.

And she'd been a jerk of the worst sort to her summer friend.

He'd had the last laugh though when he'd revealed her desperation to be part of the in clique and had inadvertently managed to convince her not-so-true friends that Angi was just a hanger-on. It had taken her years to live down the reputation of a try-hard within the ruthless social circles of a small-town high school, and she had never quite regained her footing. She still wasn't sure where she fit in.

She'd thought they were even, wanted to believe it.

Needed to convince herself that she hadn't really hurt him back then, and he'd just been another callous boy, careless with the heart she tried so hard to protect.

But the pain she'd seen on his face when he looked at his grandmother had been almost visceral, and it had taken all her will not to reach out and try to comfort him the way her mother had done.

It also didn't help that for the past few afternoons, her son had sneaked away from the restaurant to spend time with Gabe at the flower shop.

Andrew was a wily one, and he'd left sweet notes to her, even though she'd told him not to go. Threatened him with losing his video game privileges and dessert for a week. Nothing seemed to deter him, and Angi was too busy to keep her eye on him constantly. Plus, it would make her look like a paranoid fool if she resorted to keeping Andrew under lock and key. After the first visit, Drew had assured her that Gabe had changed his mind and didn't mind the company.

Angi found it hard to believe, but the next afternoon, her clever son had come home with a note written in a scrawling, masculine hand.

Your kid is fine with me.
Unless you've got a problem.
One that you care to discuss.
If you aren't too busy with Artie.
G.

"See, Mom," Andrew had said proudly. "I'm welcome. I help him. Gabe needs a lot of help. Who's Artie?"

"No one," she murmured as she racked her brain to figure out why her son was so drawn to Gabe. Andrew had never shown much interest in plants or flowers, anything outdoors for that matter. But when she pressed her boy for answers, he went vague and evasive.

"It's not as boring as the restaurant, and it doesn't smell like spaghetti sauce."

A point she couldn't argue.

Between running the restaurant, working on menus for upcoming events at the inn, taking care of her mom and the new set of responsibilities she'd taken on with the holiday festival, the truth was Angi should be offering to pay Gabe babysitting money for keeping her son occupied.

Maybe it was guilt or the uneasy sense that she owed him something that led her to enter the flower shop just before noon on Friday. Il Rigatone was crowded with the usual lunch regulars, so it wasn't a big deal for her to sneak away for a few minutes, much like her son did after school.

"Be with you in a minute," the deep, familiar voice called out, and Angi had a few seconds to absorb the changes to the shop since her previous visit.

Instead of the dingy and dismal shelves filled with decaying flowers, the space had been transformed into something almost cheery. It was sparse and in need of some big-time design help, but the shop was clean.

"Can I help... It's you."

She whirled to find Gabe staring at her from where he stood in the doorway to the back room.

"Hey." She gestured around the store's interior, nearly knocking over a potted plant from one shelf in her fit of nervous energy. Get a grip, she commanded herself.

There was something about the weight of his unreadable gaze on her that made butterflies take flight across her middle.

"It looks great in here," she said on a rush of breath.

"Way better. I mean, more like a shop where someone would like to...well...shop. Or at least they'd want to buy the flowers instead of sending their old ones here to die. You know what I mean. Do you know what I mean?"

"That was a lot of words," he said slowly. "A few of them even sounded like a compliment. Andrew can take most of the credit. The kid works his butt off for me. He's also got ideas about ordering more merchandise."

"He does?" Angi didn't bother to hide her surprise.

"He's been talking to some girl in his class whose aunt owns a gift shop down along the Outer Banks. She's giving him the scoop, and he's relaying it along to me."

"I thought you didn't want him here."

"Told you, I changed my mind."

"Because it bothers me?"

"Not exactly, but that's a side benefit." He took a step closer to her, rubbing a hand over his stubbled jaw.

She would not react to that sound. A shiver passed through her anyway.

"Is that why you're here? To command me to stay away from your kid? Because he's the one who sought me out, not the other way around."

"Yeah, I just can't figure out why," Angi murmured more to herself than to Gabe. "I brought you lunch." She held out the white paper bag. "It's a meatball sub. The Friday special."

He took it from her and peeked inside. "Like your dad used to bring to Gran."

"I'm sorry she's struggling," Angi said.

Gabe shook his head, his gaze shuttering. "I don't want to talk about my grandmother."

"Okay, but if you ever need—"

"I don't."

She took a step back, the ferocity of his tone whip-sharp.

"Thanks for the sandwich," he said, his voice gentler. "Normally, I forget to pack anything and end up with popcorn from the hardware store."

"We're two doors down," she reminded him. "Lunch is served every day."

"I doubt you want me there."

She didn't contradict him, even though at the moment she couldn't decide what she wanted from Gabe Carlyle. "Really, though. Why do you think Andrew keeps coming over here?" She ran a finger along a polished wood shelf that held an assortment of colorful vases. Had the display been one of her son's ideas? "Is he that bored at the restaurant? Should I force him into an after-school program?"

"And give the little jerks at his school another opportunity to kick his ass? I don't think so."

Angi felt her mouth drop open. Blood roared into her head and her heart ached. "No. We took care of the bullying. His teachers are watching out for him, and he said it's fine. He's fine."

"Sweetheart, take it from someone who was just like Andrew as a kid. That boy is anything but fine."

CHAPTER FIVE

GABE WISHED HE'D kept his damn mouth shut as he watched emotions play across Angi's striking features. He didn't want to feel sorry for her. He didn't want to feel anything.

He closed his fist more tightly around the take-out bag because damn if he didn't have the urge to reach out and comfort her.

The woman was clearly holding it together by a frayed string of composure.

"You're wrong," she said, but there was no conviction in the words. "I'd know."

"My mom didn't know half of what I went through."

She gave him a pointed look, and he remembered that he'd once shared with her the struggles his mom had to be a decent parent. A decent human most of the time.

"You're not like her. I'm not suggesting that."

"But you are suggesting that my son is being bullied, and I'm clueless."

"He's good at hiding his issues." He placed the bag of food on the counter. "He doesn't want to worry you."

"My job is to worry," she practically shouted, and then ran a hand through her long hair, held back by an elastic band. She turned toward the window as she pulled it out and thick locks of hair fell over her shoulders. Gabe caught a faint whiff of citrus and tried to ignore his body's reaction.

He understood she was buying time so she could collect herself, and he at least wanted to honor that. He was grateful for it. The last thing he needed was a mommy breakdown in the middle of the store.

"It's the reason he sought me out," he explained as she looped her hair through the elastic again. "He heard about my military career and that I wasn't always a big guy. He's trying to convince me to teach him self-defense moves."

"Like you're his Mr. Miyagi?" she asked, disbelief clear in her tone.

Gabe bit back a smile. *The Karate Kid* had been his favorite movie when he was younger. He'd even watched it with Angi one summer, sitting on the floor in his grandmother's cramped office. The VHS tape had been his prized possession until the day his mom knocked it off the old dresser where the TV sat and then stepped on it.

He could have found the money to buy another copy, but at that point he'd learned all the lessons he needed from the teen flick. Instead, he'd gotten a job sweeping floors at a local gym near their apartment in Albuquerque and begun his transformation.

"I don't know karate."

"But you know lots of ways to defend yourself or even hurt someone, right?" She turned slowly. "I heard you were Special Forces or some kind of sniper or—"

"Something like that," he agreed noncommittally. He refused to discuss his time in the army with Angi. No way would he taint her with the violence he'd seen, the things he'd done.

"Are you teaching Andrew the techniques you learned?"

He shook his head and picked up a bolt of red velvet ribbon. He'd been using it to create lopsided bows for the front window. Gabe might not have the artistic eye or gift for design that his grandmother had, but he liked using his hands to create something instead of destroying what he touched.

"Mostly I have him clean up and pump him for tips from his little friend about how to display gift items in the store."

"An updated version of wax on, wax off?"

A chuckle bubbled up from his throat as he thought about the karate lesson from the movie, couched in everyday tasks.

"Sometimes dusting is just dusting," he assured her.

She studied him for a moment and then nodded. "I wouldn't be all that upset if you wanted to show him a few moves."

"You don't mean that."

"I do." She looked sad and desperate and a little wild. "You aren't the only one who knows what it was like to be bullied. I don't want him to be a victim."

"There are other ways for Andrew to defend himself than learning how to fight better than the kids who pick on him."

"Like what?"

"Walking away or talking to an adult or—"

"If you say turn the other cheek, I'm going to scream." She waved a hand in the general vicinity of his chest. "It's easy to go all pacifist when you're a big, burly ex-army stud with rippling muscles and badass vibes radiating off you like an electrical current. Andrew is just a small kid with a gentle heart who's been targeted by jerks who are stronger and meaner than him."

She continued to tell him about her son, as if Gabe hadn't spent enough time with the boy to understand his issues. But Gabe's mind had, unfortunately, snagged on a few of the words she'd used to describe him. A badass stud with rippling muscles. That couldn't possibly be how Angi Guilardi saw him.

No matter how many hours Gabe trained or how many missions he'd completed during his time in the military, he still looked in the mirror and saw the skinny dork he'd been.

He figured Angi, who'd known him better than almost anyone when they were kids, would be the same.

"Stop talking about him like he's a victim."

"He is a victim of those bullies." She pulled a cell phone out of her back pocket and jabbed a thumb against the screen. "I'm going to call that school and give his teacher a piece of my mind. It's ridiculous that they haven't dealt with those little hooligans."

Gabe took advantage of her discomposure to slip the phone from her hand. He held it above his head when she tried to grab it from him. At nearly five-ten, Angi was taller than most women, but he still had a good five inches on her. He might not have come into his full height until his late teens, but he took full advantage of it now. "Hold on to all the pieces of your mind. I said I wasn't teaching him to fight."

He waited until she settled, then added, "I'd never do that without your permission. You're his mother, and you call the shots. But those other avenues of dealing with confrontation are just as valuable. Remember that Mr. Miyagi believed fighting was a last resort."

"Thank you," she said quietly, "for the permission part."

He nodded. "Of course. He's a good kid, Ang. Stronger than he realizes and smart as a whip."

"He gets that from his father," she told him, seeming to begrudge the words even as she spoke them.

"Andrew said he's never met his dad."

She sucked in a visible breath. "He told you that?"

"He talks a lot."

"Not to me." She bit down on her lower lip. "His father was more of a sperm donor, although the pregnancy was accidental. No, I don't like that word. I don't like any of the words to describe it. Accidental, unintentional, a mistake. All of them give the impression that I would have chosen a different outcome if I had it to do all over again."

"Which isn't the case?"

"I wouldn't trade Drew for anything. I'm so much better a person because I'm his mom."

Gabe could see that. Her love for him shone from her like a spotlight, bathing everything around her in a golden glow. Whether she was talking sweetly to her son or gearing up for a battle on his behalf, that love infused every part of her. He didn't want to think of Angi in any sort of positive light, but she wasn't the insecure, social-climbing princess she'd turned into the last summer he spent in Magnolia.

"His father didn't feel the same?"

She shook her head, dark eyes going black like bitter espresso. "We'd only been dating a couple of months, and he was the owner of the restaurant where I worked. My boss's boss. You have to understand that I was living what I thought was my dream life. I'd gotten out of this town and was working in a restaurant where they served creative, innovative recipes. The head chef was a woman, still not as common as you'd think in the restaurant industry. She'd been a pioneer in the Manhattan culinary scene, and the fact that she hired me made me believe I'd made it."

"Sounds exactly like how you'd planned things to go," he told her.

She frowned as if she didn't remember that they'd

shared their dreams for the future back when they'd been summer friends. Gabe hadn't forgotten. He seemed to remember every detail of his time with Angi like her essence had been tattooed on his heart. Stupid heart.

"My pregnancy changed everything." She shrugged. "At first the chef, Monica, was willing to let me stay on. But I think she got pressure from my ex-boyfriend, her boss. She had a strict policy about dating coworkers, so we'd kept things hidden from everyone. It was a betrayal, and she fired me."

"Andrew's father had you fired?"

"Yeah. He made it clear that if I 'handled things' he'd reconsider. I handled the pregnancy by moving back to Magnolia."

"You made the right choice."

She didn't exactly smile in response, but there was a softening around the corners of her eyes that told him she appreciated his words. "It was an easy one to make, although the fact that my son is struggling breaks my heart. Maybe if I'd found a way to stay in New York, we would have had more choices for schools or finding a place where he could belong."

"He belongs here. This is his home."

"You aren't going to believe this," she said with a laugh and an eye roll, "but I'm glad he found you."

"You're right. I don't believe it."

"It's true." She placed a hand on his arm, and his skin burned from the contact. "We might be sworn enemies, but you've been through a lot. You can understand and help him." She leaned in. "You will help him, right?"

"Are we sworn enemies?" He shifted closer, so much so that he could feel her breath on his jaw.

"You hate me," she reminded him, her voice just the slightest bit shaky.

"I should," he agreed. "But when we're together, I keep forgetting why."

He hadn't forgotten, but when she was close the reasons didn't seem to matter. So much so that he leaned in and brushed his lips across hers. Something he'd wanted to do on so many summer nights back when they were young. She tasted exactly like he'd imagined—sweet and spice and like she could wreck him with one word or callous action.

Oh, yeah. This way led straight for a fall, and he wanted to pitch himself over the cliff without a second thought.

Luckily, Angi had more sense. She broke the kiss and stepped away from him, her gaze wary.

"That was unexpected."

Gabe gave a slow nod, not trusting himself to form a coherent sentence.

"And a mistake."

"Yep," he managed as if his heart wasn't about to pound out of his chest.

"I should get back." She edged toward the door, reaching for it as she pulled her jacket more tightly around herself. As if a few layers of fabric could protect her from the desire pulsing between them.

"It was the mistletoe," he said, pointing toward the ceiling. "It didn't mean anything, Ang. You don't have to worry I don't know that."

She followed his gaze to the sprig of berries and greenery that Andrew had encouraged him to hang. Gabe remembered his grandmother bragging about how she'd played matchmaker to more than one couple over the holidays by a well-placed bough of mistletoe.

In truth, Gabe hadn't given the fanciful idea much consideration until he witnessed Angi's reaction and had a sobering recognition of the line he'd crossed. He figured a mistletoe excuse was better than nothing.

She laughed, sounding only a tiny bit hysterical. "That stuff is dangerous," she said, then offered a patently fake smile. "Enjoy your lunch."

"I will," he promised. "I'll help your kid, too. Keep sending him over after school."

"I don't think he'd stay away," she said, and then disappeared with a wave.

As the door shut tight behind her, Gabe realized he was hoping Andrew wasn't the only one.

SUNDAY AFTERNOON, Angi sorted through a new rack of dresses in Mariella's store, A Second Chance. She still found it difficult to believe that one of the most famous wedding dress designers in the world—a woman who'd created custom gowns for Hollywood A-listers and even an actual European princess—could be happy running a small boutique in Magnolia.

But Mariella didn't seem to miss her former life and all the glamour that went with it. For the most part, she refused to talk about her past, although there had been a flurry of press after Mariella had designed a wedding dress for Magnolia native Holly Adams when she'd married Senator Brett Carmichael in an exclusive ceremony and reception hosted at the Wildflower Inn.

Mariella had left the fashion world in disgrace after making a scene at the wedding of a world-famous actress who had also been sleeping with Mariella's fiancé on the side. Angi had a feeling that if the sophisticated blonde wanted another chance, she could reinvent herself, a fashion phoenix rising from the ashes.

She also knew that Mariella had taken on a few select clients since Holly's wedding. Women she liked, not necessarily famous or rich, but brides whose stories of love and happily-ever-after appealed to Mariella's hidden romantic side.

"Do you think I should highlight my hair?" she asked as Mariella came out of the back room with two mugs of tea.

"Your hair is beautiful just the way it is."

"But it's so dark," Angi complained. "One dimensional. Maybe if I lightened it —"

"Blondes don't actually have more fun," Mariella interrupted, shaking her head. "Are you thinking about a new hairstyle for any particular reason?"

"Is it that obvious?"

"Just out of character for you to worry about your hair, especially with everything else going on at the moment. Now, if you want to do it for a distraction, I'm all for that. But let's do something fun like a blue streak."

"No primary colors. During dinner, Artie mentioned that his ex-girlfriend—also Italian—went blond," Angi admitted. "He said she got a promotion at work because suddenly she didn't look so ethnic."

"Ethnic?" Mariella sputtered out a disbelieving snort. "I hope you kicked him in the family jewels."

"I've known Artie since we were in diapers."

"Then you know where to find them. Probably tiny little walnuts."

"He meant well."

"No, he didn't. Tell me the rest of the date was better than that line would lead me to believe."

"Discussing my hair color was pretty much the highlight." Angi sighed. "Not that I thought it was going to be a love match, but he talked most of the time about his ex-girlfriend."

"The blonde with the promotion?"

Angi nodded. "I guess she also upgraded for a better boyfriend."

"Can't say as I blame her."

"Me neither."

"You didn't like this guy, right?"

"Not in the least. So why does it bother me that the feeling was mutual?"

"When was the last time you got busy with a guy?"

"That's gross." Angi focused on one of the dresses, running a finger along the scalloped neckline of a pretty yellow sheath. "Also private. Should I upgrade my wardrobe? Maybe start showing a bit more leg?"

"It's been almost two years for me," Mariella said without hesitation. "Since I found out my fiancé was shagging one of my best clients."

"I've got another year on you," Angi said with a sigh. "And it wasn't even that good, so I'm not sure it counts."

"It counts," Mariella told her. "But not a lot."

"I've kind of given up. How sad is that? My mother is more concerned about my dating life than I am. She's already got two more potential men lined up for me, and it's making me crazy. I don't want to go out with guys my mom picks."

She breathed out a tired laugh. "I barely have the energy to shave my legs, let alone worry about cute undies or whether I care about a man who knows how to kiss."

"Everyone cares about a man who's a good kisser."

A woman in her midthirties with two young girls walked into the store. Angi busied herself looking at racks of handbags while Mariella spoke to them.

She wasn't sure what was worse, the fact that she was seriously too tired to care about dating or that Gabe Carlyle, the last man on earth she wanted to feel attracted to, was the one who'd given her the best kiss of her entire life, and he hadn't even gotten around to using his tongue. Yes, he was handsome as sin and sexy in that quiet, brooding way he had. But she didn't like him. She shouldn't like him.

There was no time in her life for a man, despite what her mom believed.

"You might not want to date, but damn, girl, by the look on your face that must be some fantasy life."

Angi lifted a hand to her suddenly flaming cheek and tried to ignore Mariella's smirk. "It's nothing."

"It's something," Mariella countered. "Something we could both apparently use more of in our lives."

"Not me, not now. I came here to talk about the inn, and somehow we've gotten sidetracked by my nonexistent love life. I need to get my mom off the scent of a man for me. She's got way too much time on her hands since she's not busy at the restaurant." Angi checked her watch. "I haven't told her I'm still working at the inn, so she thinks I've got time, too."

"Make up a boyfriend," Mariella suggested as she straightened a display of colorful scarves.

"Lie to my mother?"

Mariella lifted a brow. "Are you saying you've never done that before? Because I'm fairly certain you just admitted to a lie of omission with regards to the inn."

Angi shook her head. "That's different. It's for my mom's own good."

"I'm not sure I agree." Mariella took a step toward the counter as the customers made their way there with several bath items and a set of matching earrings and a necklace. "Perhaps this is as good a time as any to think of your own good. You do a lot of living based on what will make other people happy, lady."

Angi couldn't deny it so she didn't bother. But to make up a boyfriend seemed needlessly complicated and like it would backfire on her in the end. Surely if she had someone, her mom would want to meet him. What kind of guy could Angi possibly come up with that would do the trick and not be too much work?

An image of Gabe once again flashed in her mind and she practically groaned out loud. He'd be the perfect pretend boyfriend. Hot, a great kisser, nice to her kid, and clearly interested in avoiding her as much as she wanted to give him a wide berth.

The idea of it was ridiculous. He wasn't made-up. He was an actual person, one who had every reason not to want to be involved with her.

He'd be a perfect choice.

The customers left with their packages, but before Mariella could make her way back over another group walked in. The store seemed to attract women of all ages and shapes, and Angi had yet to see someone leave without a bag and a smile. There was a market for retail in Magnolia these days. Looking around gave her ideas for home decor and small gift items Gabe could add to his inventory to attract a wider range of customers.

Maybe she could offer to help him update things in exchange for him pretending to be her boyfriend—strictly to give her a break from her mother's matchmaking. They were already going to need to spend time together for festival planning. It would be easy and uncomplicated for both of them.

"Give me a call later," Angi called to Mariella as she headed for the door. "I have a meeting at town hall, but I'll be around all afternoon."

Mariella waved and Angi headed out, a new spring in her step. She had a plan for her holiday fake boyfriend that just might work. At least she could get one aspect of her life under control before Christmas, and that was enough for her right now.

CHAPTER SIX

"Hı."

Gabe stopped in his tracks, holding up the garden rake like a weapon but almost immediately lowered it. He'd recognized Angi's voice in that one syllable. Somehow, he still felt shocked to see her standing outside the greenhouse.

"This is a gorgeous landscape," Angi said, waving a hand in the general vicinity of the property. He noticed she didn't make eye contact, despite seeking him out. He also took note of the hint of color that crept up her cheeks and didn't think the blush had anything to do with the brisk breeze that whipped through the backyard.

It had been colder than average in Magnolia recently, which only seemed to attract more visitors to downtown. The flower shop had seen a steady stream of foot traffic, although most people came and went quickly. He'd done his best to spruce up the place and had adorned the outside of the shop with just about every one of the decorations Gran had packed away.

No one could say he wasn't festive, although he also didn't seem to be fooling anyone into thinking he had any real Christmas cheer. He remembered the lessons Gran had taught him about arranging flowers, but that skill didn't translate into any sort of other artistic flair for him.

"It's seen better days," he answered, looking out to the lawn before returning his gaze to Angi. "If I'm still here next summer, I'm going to clean out the beds and plant a cutting garden plus some vegetables. Tomatoes, cucumber, pumpkins. The whole bit."

Heat burned along his neck as Angi stared at him like he'd just sprouted a second head. Why couldn't he shut up?

She wore slim jeans and a canvas jacket with a colorful patterned scarf double-wrapped around her neck. He would have liked to grab the end that whipped in the breeze and tug her closer but resisted the urge. She wasn't his to pull into him by any stretch of the imagination.

"Where else would you be?" she asked as if he'd lived in Magnolia all his life.

He shrugged. "Maybe Gran will get better and won't need me anymore."

"Do you believe that?"

"No, but it's what I want. The truth is I have an appointment set up next week to meet with her attorney. We need to think about what happens next."

"You're running the shop," Angi said, inclining her head.

"In order to help my grandmother," he clarified. "Not because it's what I plan to do with the rest of my life."

"When we were kids, you seemed so happy putting together the bouquets," she said quietly. "You'd bring me the bruised flowers, but they were arranged so beautifully I didn't even notice the flaws."

"I'm not as good at disguising flaws anymore." He sighed. "The shop isn't making money. It hasn't in several years." He gestured toward the greenhouse. "I'm doing my best to cultivate a variety of plants to sell as well as the bouquets, and I have ideas for how to incorporate a community garden into the business plan, but who knows if I'll get that chance."

"Why not?"

"My mom finally called. She wanted an update on her mother—basically she was asking if Gran was close to kicking the bucket. Mom intimated that she's going to inherit the house and the business after Gran dies and has made it clear that the first order of business will be selling the properties to the highest offer."

"But your grandmother isn't gone yet." Angi shook her head. "It feels morbid to even talk that way."

"I know." He said the words casually, like it didn't gut him that his mom would discuss his grandmother with such callousness. "But that's my problem, and I don't need to bore you with it. What are you doing here anyway?"

"Oh." She blinked. "Oh, right. I came to see you."

The flummoxed look she gave him made his heart feel suddenly effervescent, like he'd taken a big drink of soda and the fizz was making him light-headed. He didn't know what to think of the Angi who wasn't snarky or ignoring him, implying that he'd been the one to do something wrong all those years ago. When they both knew that wasn't the case.

"Yeah, okay. If it's about the nunchuck lessons I gave Andrew…"

"Excuse me?"

"Joking." He went to pat her on the arm but pulled back at the last second, not trusting himself with even the most innocuous touch.

"I'm here because I need a boyfriend," she blurted out of nowhere.

Or maybe out of left field was more like it.

Or outer space.

"What happened to your date on Friday?" Gabe asked, raising a brow. "I take it that didn't go well."

"Worse than not well," she admitted. "He was hung up on his ex."

"Which hurt your feelings?"

"Good Lord, no. I couldn't care less about Artie. I wish him and any potential Mrs. Caferno only the best."

"Why do you need a boyfriend?" he asked slowly, hoping that his frazzled brain could somehow catch up with her train of thought.

"Because my mom has a whole line of Arties waiting to take me out." She scrunched up her nose, rather adorably in Gabe's opinion. "I mean not literally more Arties. But more guys. Men I don't want to date. I'm not interested in dating."

So much for following her train of thought.

"But you want a boyfriend?"

"A fake boyfriend," she said, and when her chest rose and fell in a shuddery breath like it was tough to get the words out, awareness zinged through Gabe. He didn't want to be aware of Angi any more than he already was. "I want you."

Those three words didn't help.

"You don't even like me," he reminded her.

"My mom does," she countered. "Andrew, too. We have to work together for Christmas on the Coast."

"It seems to be running fairly smoothly without my involvement."

"That's because Carrie's amazing and set everything up, but as more events take place over the next couple of weeks, we'll have a lot to do. Organizing, working with the press, keeping things generally running smoothly. Plus making sure we keep bookstore Stuart away from Josie Trumbell."

Not helping his mental clarity. "What's the deal with Josie and Stuart?"

"He's had a crush on her for years, but she's still hung up on some guy from decades ago. Normally Stuart tries to kiss her under the mistletoe at some point during the holiday season, and it gets awkward for everyone."

He nodded. "Keep Stuart away from the mistletoe. Got it."

"Plus," she continued with a small smile playing around the corner of her mouth. "This year the proceeds from the special charity event each week are going to benefit anti-bullying programs at the school district. It's important that we have a record year."

"As important as you having a fake boyfriend?"

She tapped a finger on her chin, considering her answer. "Equally." The wind gusted again and she hugged herself, rubbing her hands up and down her arms. "Can we go inside for a minute to finish this conversation? It's weirdly freezing out here."

"I think we can be done now. I'm not going to be your fake boyfriend. It's a crap idea."

"Can I see the greenhouse?" she asked, clearly undeterred.

Send her away, his mind warned, like a flashing danger sign.

Always a glutton for punishment, Gabe turned and opened the latch and led her through. The door snicked shut behind her, and he breathed in the scent of dirt and mulch, only now it was mixed with the faint smell of citrus. Would he ever be able to walk into this refuge again without it reminding him of Angi?

"Look at all of this," she murmured in awe. At least the

greenhouse distracted her from the ridiculous business of roping him into a pretend relationship.

"Why don't you have more of these plants for sale in the shop?"

He shrugged. "My grandma wanted to concentrate on flowers. They were her happy place. I don't want anything to take away from that."

"But you'd be adding to the value the store brings to town, not detracting from it. To its reputation. It could be bigger, more. It could be amazing."

"I don't have a lot of experience with amazing," he said. Only with Angi. He might want to hate her and how she'd treated him when they were younger, but he couldn't deny that his life felt better—more—when she was a part of it.

"You need me." She nearly shouted the words, and Gabe couldn't tell which one of them she was trying to convince. "I'll help you make the shop magnificent."

"Andrew has already done that."

"I appreciate his effort, but you need more." She nodded, as if warming to the idea.

Gabe opened his mouth to argue, and then she said, "Think of how happy it would make your grandmother."

Talk about going for his soft underbelly.

"Why would it make her happy?" he asked slowly.

She turned to him, her dark eyes filled with an understanding that even he didn't have. "It wasn't just the fall and subsequent stroke that caused the struggle in the shop. Iris's business had been slowing down for years, Gabe. She'd been slowing down. It's part of why my dad brought lunch to her every week. He tried to keep her spirits bolstered."

He closed his eyes for a moment. "There were little hints as to that in the letters she wrote me while I was overseas, but mostly she supported me. I should have known or guessed."

"You know now," she said gently, "You're here and you're helping her. Don't sell yourself short."

"I appreciate the pep talk." He blew out a laugh. "Especially coming from you, but you aren't going to change my mind, Ang. I can't pretend to be your boyfriend."

"Just until the new year," she promised. "I'll help you at the shop in return. We can do some cross-promotion between you and Mariella. She's gaining a huge following. Beef up your online presence. There are all kinds of ways to improve sales at the shop."

"Why should I care?" Gabe gently rubbed a leaf between two fingers. "If all of this goes to my mom, it shouldn't matter to me."

"You're doing it for your grandmother. She's getting better, and think of how happy it would make her to see the shop bustling again. Iris and my mom are a lot alike in that way."

"Which is why you are burning the candle at both ends to help Emma with the inn while still running the restaurant? It's too much, Ang. You're going to wear yourself out."

"Who says I'm worn-out?"

He lifted his arm and traced the pad of his thumb under her eye. "You need sleep."

Once again, he was struck by her contradictions. Sassy mouth, sharp edges and the softest skin he'd ever felt.

"Did you just point out my dark circles?" She swatted his hand away. "Rude."

"I pointed out that you're doing too much."

"Another great reason I want to avoid going out on the

dates my mom is so determined to set up for me. I'm simplifying my life. Sparking joy and all that crap."

"You're not simple, Angi."

"Just consider it, Gabe. I promise I'll make it worth your while."

He lifted a brow, and she snorted in response. "Down, boy. I mean by helping with the store."

"The answer is no."

She glared at him. "I hate that answer."

"You have a million friends," he reminded her. "More than most people, I know how hard you worked at being popular in Magnolia. Surely one of your buddies would be a better choice than me. Pick someone else, Angi. I'm not going to fake it with a person I wouldn't even choose as a friend."

Even as he spoke the words, he recognized how harsh they sounded. But he couldn't help it. She'd been cruel to him at a time in his life when he was vulnerable. Yeah, he'd grown up and should move past that pettiness. But he wasn't quite ready to let it go.

"Thanks for the reminder of why this was a horrible idea," she said, cheeks once again flaming with color. "There's a choir concert in the town square tomorrow night. You can come and start carrying your weight as far as this partnership goes. Just do us both a favor and stay out of my way."

BY THE TIME the town square filled with people ready to sing along with popular holiday songs and carols, Angi felt dead on her feet. If Gabe had noticed she looked tired yesterday, she could only imagine what he'd think now.

No. She wouldn't imagine because she didn't care.

His opinion didn't matter in the least, despite the fact

that she'd stopped off at the local drugstore on her way into work to buy a new tube of concealer.

She'd stayed up far too late prepping a three-course dinner for the upcoming weekend reception at the inn and then tossed and turned as her mind spun with ideas for new menus and themes for future events Emma had booked. Events Angi would not be a part of because she was quitting her role as of the new year.

What else could she do?

She heard her name called across the faded green lawn in the center of town and turned to see her mother stalking toward her.

"That's not good," Emma, who was standing next to Angi, muttered. "I'll see you later."

"Chicken," Angi said under her breath, and Emma let out a few whispered clucks as she hurried in the other direction.

"Are you trying to break my heart?" Bianca demanded, wagging a finger in Angi's direction.

"No, Ma. Of course not. Emma and I were just visiting. We're still friends, you know." It wasn't exactly a lie. They were still friends, although moments earlier they'd been going over the timetable for next weekend. Guilt twinged along Angi's spine, but she reminded herself the situation was temporary. She was giving up her dream job of owning her own catering company no matter how it made her heart hurt.

"Why is Il Rigatone serving ravioli instead of the signature sausage ball?" Bianca threw up her hands. "I could hardly make it to the booth with the line of people waiting for service, and they aren't getting your father's recipe. Angela. That recipe was his Christmas pride and joy. You know that."

"There's a line?" Angi looked over her mother's shoulder but couldn't see over the people waiting for the concert to begin. "We don't usually get a line."

"They're waiting for your father's favorites," her mother insisted, but Angi knew that wasn't the case. Yes, her father's sausage balls were tasty, but they'd never been a unique draw at any of the local events where the restaurant served them. In contrast, she knew that her chicken and goat cheese deep-fried ravioli were mouthwateringly delicious and an easy food to take on the go.

She paired them with a drizzle of pesto aioli, and the staff had raved over them when she'd made a batch last week. Everyone from Dom to the longtime waitresses agreed that her ravioli was the right menu item to serve at the holiday events where regional food items would be available for purchase.

"Mom, this isn't a slight on the sausage balls. We wanted to try something different, to change things up."

"It's not your decision." Bianca crossed her arms over her chest. "You disrespect me and your father's memory with your selfishness."

"The restaurant isn't making money," Angi said as frustration bubbled up inside her.

When her mother glanced around wildly, Angi realized she'd nearly shouted the words and, of course, immediately regretted the outburst.

But she couldn't take it back.

"I know you understand how bad it is," she continued as she lowered her voice and drew closer.

"We're fine," her mom insisted. "A bit of a slowdown after your father passed away. But the town is turning around. Look at all these people. More visitors for every festival."

"People who are in line for ravioli."

Bianca's glossy lips compressed. "You have to honor the tradition," she said. "What are we without our tradition?"

"I miss him, too," Angi said softly, understanding that her mother was talking about Angi's father.

"Tradition," her mother repeated in a soft voice. She blinked rapidly, and emotion clogged Angi's throat.

"I'll serve the sausage next time, Mom. I'm sorry."

"People might like your food," Bianca said. "But Il Rigatone was your father's dream."

"I know."

Bianca reached out and wrapped her arms around Angi's shoulders. The embrace felt more suffocating than comforting. "You're a good girl, my sweet princess." She released Angi and patted her on the cheek. "Your pesto had too much oil. I can show you how to fix that next time you want to make it."

"Thanks, Mom," Angi said without bothering to look again toward the line at the restaurant's booth. What was the point? Her mother waved at one of her friends and then left Angi alone. No need to discuss things further now that the guilt trip had been fully meted out.

Unfortunately, Angi wasn't alone for long. Dabbing at the corner of one eye—it must be dust because she certainly wasn't going to cry in the middle of the festival—she heard a loud whistle behind her. "Hey, RPC."

"Swallow me, please," she whispered, tapping her booted foot against the grass.

"Remember when we sneaked away from the Christmas parade they used to do down Main Street? It must have been seventh-grade year," Brandon Mitchelson said, leading her former best friend, Sara Weathers, toward her.

Brandon had been the star center of the high school

basketball team, and she'd had an enormous crush on him for most of middle school. Mostly he acknowledged her to get free food. Once she lost weight and grew breasts, he'd tried to get lucky in the empty school gymnasium after homecoming. His breath had smelled like stale beer and cheese puffs.

"I remember." Sara nodded, her blond hair shimmering under the twinkle lights strewn around the square. It killed Angi that she'd ever thought this grown-up mean girl was her friend. "When Ang ate her weight in cheesecake in the back of her dad's restaurant."

Brandon laughed like Sara had told the funniest joke on the planet. They'd married right after high school, their son only a couple of years older than Andrew. Not once had any of them gotten together socially since Angi had returned to town, and she planned to keep it that way. "The cannoli princess was the master of shoveling it in."

Angi rolled her eyes. "Don't go there, you guys. Come on."

"It's all fun and games," Sara said. "By the way, your mom came into the salon the other day and spilled the beans that you were going on a date with Artie."

"No way." Now Brandon laughed so hard he started wheezing. "No way would RPC go out with that loser."

"There's nothing wrong with Artie. He's a decent human being, which is more than I can say for some people." She narrowed her eyes at Brandon. "And enough with the nickname. It was obnoxious when we were kids. It's offensive now." Of course, she hadn't had the greatest time with Artie. She didn't think of him as more than a friend, and even that was a stretch.

"Roly Poly Cannoli and Artie Caferno." Sara scoffed. "Come on, Ang. Even you haven't sunk that low."

Angi blew out a breath as her temper spiked. How could she have been friends with people like this? In truth, she'd worked her butt off in high school to worm her way into the popular clique. Sara had been the undisputed queen bee of their grade. Angi had literally worked her butt off, losing nearly thirty pounds between freshman and sophomore year so that she could finally try out for the cheerleading squad.

And she'd done it. Just like some retro teenybopper movie, she'd made herself into what the cool kids wanted her to be. She'd dated a guy on the football team and been nominated to homecoming court. Everything she'd thought she wanted.

She'd lost other things in the process, including her special summer friendship with Gabe Carlyle. Now she realized what a bad judge of character she'd been. When she'd returned to Magnolia, her old friends had wanted very little to do with her and the feeling was mutual.

In many respects, she was as much a misfit now as her son. Or as she used to be. But there was a difference. She'd stopped giving a damn about the so-called popular cliques and their indiscriminate judgment.

"Artie is a great guy. He's smart and funny, and the woman who ends up with him is going to be lucky. It's just not me."

"It's embarrassing, Angi." Sara scrunched up her pert little nose and gave a mock shudder. "Even for a woman in your situation."

Angi opened her mouth to offer some brilliant retort. Instead, the backs of her eyes stung with the telltale sign of potential tears. She could not let these jerks from her teenage years reduce her to tears. But it wasn't just them and their petty cruelty. It was the guilt her mom dispensed like holy water on a Sunday morning in church mixed with the cold splash of disappointment at the way her life was unfolding, worry over Andrew and plain old exhaustion.

Her gaze caught on Sara's, and her former best friend's crystal-blue eyes took on a sharp glint, like a shark that smelled blood in the water and was primed for the kill.

The worst part was Angi saw it coming and couldn't get out of the way. She couldn't move, couldn't speak. It was as if she'd been worn down to such a nub that not even her self-preservation instinct would kick in.

Then a heavy hand landed on her shoulder, and she was pulled close into the warmth and heat of Gabe's strong chest. "It's time," he said, seemingly talking to her but keeping his gaze on Sara. "I know we agreed to keep this on the down-low, sweetheart..." He placed a gentle kiss on Angi's temple, just where a headache was beginning to pulse. "But it's Christmastime and I'm sure your friends will be happy for you."

"They aren't my friends," she muttered.

He chuckled at that, low and slow, the vibration of it reverberating through her.

"Wait a minute." Sara stepped forward. "You two aren't a couple."

Duh, Angi wanted to blurt out. Gabe might kiss her like a man possessed, but with their history she knew nothing would come of it. She just couldn't figure out why he was at her side now, but before she could agree with Sara, Gabe answered.

"It's new." He said it like that was the most normal thing in the world to say. "We're both busy and private. No need to give the gossips around town with nothing better to do something to talk about."

Sara frowned, as if she wasn't sure whether he was talking about her as one of the town gossips.

"You two should meet us over at Champions later for drinks and a round of pool," Brandon suggested. Angi hadn't been to either of Magnolia's local bars since she'd needed a fake ID to get in. "It'll be like a regular seventh-grade summer reunion."

Seventh-grade summer, when Brandon had pushed Gabe into the dirt or off his bike every chance he got. When Angi had been too embarrassed to go to the pool or the beach because she'd developed breasts and hips and dimples on the backs of her plump thighs. The summer when she and Gabe had watched movies at his grandma's house during the heat of the day and taken long walks on the beach at sunset, talking about everything and nothing.

Those were the memories she wanted to focus on. The sweet ones, not what came after.

If Gabe thought it was strange to so casually be invited to hang out with his former nemesis, he didn't show it. Not outwardly, although Angi felt the slightest ripple of tension cascade through him.

"We have plans for later," Gabe said with another kiss to her head. The words were innocent enough, but the way he said them gave a different message. One that made goose bumps erupt along her skin. "We're not exactly advertising what's going on between us," he told the couple. "Appreciate if you don't spread the word."

Brandon and Sara both nodded, although Angi noticed the other woman's hand dip into the pocket of her leather jacket like she was already reaching for her phone.

The music cued up, and they all glanced toward the stage. "The concert is about to start," Angi said, as if that wasn't obvious.

"Catch you later, RPC," Brandon said with a wave, and led away his wife.

"What's the RPC about?" Gabe asked, immediately releasing her.

She stood there for a second, too stunned to move. "Roly Poly Cannoli," she told him, then immediately wished she hadn't. It was a horrible nickname, left over from a childhood of being plump and having a sweet tooth.

"Jackass," Gabe muttered.

"What was that?" she demanded as emotions rushed through her. "You kissed me. You told them we were dating. You know that asking those two to keep quiet is like posting the whole thing on social media. This *whatever*—" she flicked a hand between the two of them "—is going to go viral in minutes."

The choir started singing the first stanza of "Santa Claus Is Coming to Town," but Angi couldn't even appreciate the way the crowd enthusiastically sang along.

"I know." Gabe shrugged and turned toward the stage. "That's the point."

"You said no."

"I changed my mind."

"You can't do that," she whispered.

"Break up with me," he countered.

She let out a groan.

"I thought this was what you wanted."

"Yes, but…" How could she explain that what had seemed straightforward in theory was so different in practice? That when she'd come up with the brilliant plan for him to be her fake boyfriend, she hadn't considered how it would feel to be close to him, her body not paying one bit of attention to the fact that it was a charade. "Why?"

He continued to watch the concert for a few more seconds before turning to her. "I saw my grandma earlier today. She was crying, which the nurse told me is normal around this time of year for people in her condition. She seemed confused and upset, and kept talking about going to work and taking care of her business." The stark pain in his gaze gutted Angi. "You said you'd help with the shop, to get it back to what it once was. I need that. Gran needs that, or at least I need to give it to her."

Angi nodded. "Okay." She wasn't going to push him for more. They were both too close to the edge. A pretend boyfriend was what she wanted, and with Gabe she knew things wouldn't get confusing.

She closed her eyes for a moment. That was a lie because everything about this man befuddled her. But it was only until the new year, and he'd certainly distract her mom so Angi could also spend time at the inn.

"Okay," he repeated without glancing at her. Then her new boyfriend turned and walked away.

CHAPTER SEVEN

"INVITE HIM TO DINNER."

"Mom, no."

"He's your boyfriend. I want to get to know him."

Angi inwardly cringed at the excitement in her mother's tone. "We're dating. It's new. He's not exactly my boyfriend."

"Of course he is. He kissed you in the middle of the town square."

"On the head, Mom. He gave me a quick peck on the head."

"A kiss is a kiss."

As she'd predicted, news of her so-called relationship with Gabe Carlyle spread like melted cheese oozing from an overcooked mozzarella stick.

Before the final notes of the last song of the holiday concert had been played, Mariella had tracked her down in the crowd.

"When I told you to make up a boyfriend, I meant from your imagination," she'd said in a low voice. "Not to pick the man who irritates the hell out of you and call him your dream guy."

Angi had yanked Mariella away from the crowd to the quiet of a copse of fir trees. They were adorned with strands of white lights and helped give the impression of that section of the square being some sort of magical fairy garden.

"I didn't say he was my dream guy." Although other than the fact that he didn't like her, Gabe came pretty close. Hot as sin, hardworking, dedicated to his grandmother, kind in his unique way to her son. "He's not."

"Are you trying to convince me or yourself?" Mariella had asked with a knowing twinkle in her eyes.

"I asked him, and he's willing to do it. I'm going to help around his grandmother's shop. You're going to help me help him, and this will get my mom to stop setting me up with every not-so-eligible guy around these parts and to use as cover when I'm really at the inn. I can't use her home kitchen, and she'd hear about it if I was at Il Rigatone after hours."

"I still think the imaginary boyfriend would have been safer," Mariella had told her.

"Gabe is plenty safe," Angi had lied.

She'd been telling far too many lies lately. It was getting difficult to keep them all straight. She took a deep breath and placed a hand on her mother's arm. "I don't think it would be a great idea for Gabe to come over right now."

"Gabe is coming over?" Andrew asked as he walked into the room. "Cool. I can show him my *Minecraft* world."

"Even my grandson wants him here," Bianca said with a sniff. "It seems odd that you're the only one who doesn't."

"It isn't that I don't want him," Angi muttered. In fact, just the opposite. She wanted him far too much.

"Then invite him."

She grabbed her phone from the back pocket of the corduroy pants she wore and punched in a text. "He's probably tired or already has plans."

"You don't know?"

"Mom, we're dating. I'm not his parole officer. There's

no ankle monitor that keeps me apprised of his where-abouts."

She let out a little yelp when her phone dinged.

"You're nervous," Bianca said with a satisfied smile. "It's cute."

Hardly.

But her pulse thrummed when she read his response. "He's coming for dinner. What time?"

"Six. We always eat at six. You know that, my sweet cannoli. Nervous. So cute."

As Bianca studied her, Angi pasted on a smile—not a nervous one either. But her finger trembled slightly as she texted him the time and told him he didn't have to worry about bringing anything. Her mother had sat at the kitchen table and was furiously scribbling on a pad of paper, prob-ably coming up with questions she planned to ask Gabe that would no doubt embarrass Angi to no end.

She hadn't talked to him since the concert, although she'd emailed him several ideas for updates to In Bloom from an exhaustive internet search of successful small-town flower shops. After tonight, she was going to owe him a lot more than sage advice on stocking the right in-ventory.

Neither Angi nor her brothers brought dates to the fam-ily home very often. The last time Marco had invited a girlfriend to a family dinner, the poor woman had left in tears after their mother had grilled her about why she re-fused to eat bread if she could handle gluten.

It was a lesson learned for all three of Bianca's children.

Sure, her mom had made an offhand comment about Gabe and Angi dating, but now it was real. When her fa-ther was alive, he'd made it clear that few men could ever live up to the standards he'd set for his daughter.

"Here is my list," Bianca said, ripping off a piece of paper. "You'll need to go to the store right now so the cheesecake has time to set and I can get started on chopping the mushrooms for the marsala sauce."

"What marsala sauce?" Angi asked, gazing at the list of items her mother had requested. "I defrosted an enchilada casserole overnight."

"We aren't feeding your new boyfriend a reheated taco pie for his first time having dinner with us. You have to show him what an amazing cook you are. You know what they say about the way to a man's heart."

"I'm not trying to impress him with my culinary skills," Angi argued. "Besides, he knows I can cook."

"Gabe says Mom's spaghetti and meatball tacos are his favorite thing."

Bianca narrowed her eyes. "What is this spaghetti taco? We don't serve tacos at the restaurant."

Not exactly true since Angi had put the popular recipe she'd developed for the inn as a special on the Il Rigatone menu last week. She felt a familiar sense of guilt wash over her.

She'd specifically chosen to feature the dish on a night when her mother had gone in for a checkup earlier. Bianca was always tired after her doctor's appointments so Angi knew her mom wouldn't make a surprise visit to Il Rigatone.

But after the fiasco with the sausage balls and her mom's reaction at the concert, she wasn't going there again soon. "I made dinner at his house a while back." She shrugged. "It was just a weekday night when you were at book club and Andrew had practice."

"So this thing between the two of you isn't exactly

new?" Bianca nodded slowly. "You've been holding out on me, Angela."

"No, Mom." At least not in the way her mother thought. "But your menu sounds amazing." Before Bianca could ask her any more questions, Angi grabbed her purse and headed for the door. "I'll be back shortly."

She only briefly considered driving past the grocery store turnoff and continuing down the highway out of Magnolia and into parts unknown. She'd always done the same thing when times got tough—imagined fleeing to a new place with Andrew in tow. But she understood that trouble could, and most likely would, follow her anywhere. Better to face it head-on.

At the store, she added everything her mom had asked for to the cart, plus a pint of rocky road ice cream—appropriate for her mood—and a bag of chocolate-covered espresso beans. If she was going to face life head-on, might as well do it with a bit of sugar and caffeine in her system.

The rest of the afternoon passed quickly as she and her mom made homemade gnocchi to accompany the chicken marsala, Andrew helping to form the little U-shaped pieces of yummy goodness. The familiar steps calmed her frazzled nerves as the scent of potato filled the kitchen. She'd often resented the way her family's tried and true recipes overshadowed her culinary creativity. Il Rigatone sometimes felt like a lead weight around her neck. But in her mother's kitchen, with the warm yellow walls and the vintage gas stove where Angi had first learned to love cooking, it was different.

Her mother seemed happier, as well. It reminded Angi that as much as she didn't want to take over the restaurant, her mom also didn't want to necessarily give up her role. They laughed and then poured two glasses of wine, harmonizing along with Frank Sinatra and Bing Crosby as they sang about their white Christmas dreams.

She lost track of time so completely that shock pulsated through her when the doorbell rang. A glance at the clock on the stove showed her it was nearly six. "He's here," she whispered, wondering why butterflies danced across her stomach and how to best tamp them down for good.

"Answer the door," her mother suggested with a knowing smile.

"Look at me." Angi brushed her hands across the apron she'd tied around her waist. It was still dusted with flour. "I'm a mess. I meant to stop early and change clothes."

"You're beautiful." Bianca cupped Angi's cheeks between her palms. "You're always most beautiful when you're in the kitchen. It's your place of joy, sweet cannoli girl. Just like it was your father's."

Tears clogged Angi's throat. She loved the thought that she shared this passion with her father. Despite her current situation, so many of her happy memories involved him and food.

"Gabe's here," Andrew announced.

Her mother patted her cheeks and then turned to welcome their guest.

Angi stirred the sauce as Bianca clucked over Gabe, taking his coat and offering him a glass of wine. The good thing about having been occupied in the kitchen was that she hadn't had time to get nervous. The bad thing was she was sweaty and flushed, and smelled like flour and butter.

Andrew bounced up and down, more animated than Angi had seen him in ages. Her son really did have a connection with Gabe. Andrew ran out of the room to collect some toy he wanted to show their guest.

"Smells delicious." Gabe's voice was soft at her side,

and she turned, not wanting to appear as flustered by his presence as she was.

"Thanks for coming over." She glanced around him to find that they were alone in the kitchen, at least for the moment. Her mother had gone to hang up his coat in the front hall.

"Thanks for the invite." He lifted his hand and brushed a thumb across her cheek. "You have a bit of flour here."

"I'm as coated as a Sunday chicken," she said, her cheeks flushing when the words came out breathy. "I meant to get cleaned up, but my mom was so happy in the kitchen. I was happy hanging out and just having fun. Slowing down has been tough for her and..." She drew in a slow breath. "I'm babbling."

"I don't mind." His eyes were bright with amusement. "The babbling or the flour."

"We can talk about ideas for a big event to cap off the festival." She took a step back from him, and it felt like pulling herself away from a magnet drawing her closer. "It doesn't have to be a complete waste that you came over here."

"A home-cooked meal is never a waste."

"That's what I told her," Bianca practically shouted as she walked back into the room. "A man likes a woman who knows her way around the kitchen."

Angi rolled her eyes. "Mom, we aren't in the nineteen fifties anymore. I don't have to impress anyone with my domestic skills." She narrowed her eyes at Gabe. "I hate to vacuum, in case you were wondering."

He held up his hands, amusement still dancing in his gaze. "I wasn't. Promise."

"She knows how to vacuum," her mother said, like she had to cover for her daughter's domestic deficiencies. "I taught her to back out of the room as she goes so there are no footprints in the brush pattern."

Gabe looked between the two of them. "Is that a thing?"

"No," Angi muttered.

"Of course it is," her mother countered. "Give him a taste of your sauce, cannoli. He needs a sample. I'll set the table in the dining room. We'll eat on the good china with our guest."

"Don't go to any trouble on my account," Gabe said, looking vaguely terrified.

"No trouble," Bianca assured him, and bustled into the next room.

Angi grabbed a wooden spoon from one of the ceramic containers on the counter.

"Is it just me, or did that business about me tasting your sauce seem to have a double meaning?" he asked.

"Ignore her," Angi advised as she dipped the spoon into the pot of simmering sauce. "But you still have to try it."

Keeping her gaze trained on his mouth, she gave him a taste. She refused to think about how soft his lips had been when he'd kissed her, at odds with his rough exterior.

A low moan of appreciation hummed out of him, and Angi felt pride flush through her.

"It's so good," he said. "Different than how it is at the restaurant, though. A little tangier."

She nodded and glanced over his shoulder. "I put in a dash of vinegar. My mom doesn't know, but I think it adds a richer complexity to the sauce."

"You don't make that change for your customers?"

"Il Rigatone uses my great-grandmother's recipe, the one that she passed down to her daughter who passed it down to my father. It's our family tradition."

"And you want something different?"

"Yes." She knew he was speaking about the sauce, but the gentle manner in which he asked the question made her want to tell him more. To share that for years she'd dreamed of making her way in the world. How leaving Magnolia had been hard but necessary. The fact that she'd locked away every selfish desire she had when Andrew came into the world. Her son was her whole world, but now she feared she'd convinced herself of that because she didn't have anything else. Emma had given her a chance for something new—pushed her into believing she could have more.

And now she was back to making the recipes that were part of her history and sneaking in ingredients while her mother's back was turned or throwing new specials on the menu when they wouldn't be discovered, as those were her only ways to assert her independence. And hiding wasn't any kind of freedom.

"Who would win in a fight?" Andrew asked, and Angi startled and took a step back. "Deadpool or Wolverine?"

"That's a tough one," Gabe said without taking his eyes off Angi. Once again, she knew he wasn't just talking about action heroes. He turned to Andrew and held out a hand to take one of the figurines from her son. "Now if I was going to choose a guy to have at my side in a fight, I'd pick Captain America. He's not always running his mouth and he avoids violence as a rule, but you know he's got your back when it counts."

Andrew studied the two plastic men, clearly processing everything Gabe had said. "I'd pick Wolverine."

Gabe quirked a brow at Angi. "Want to weigh in with an opinion?"

"I'm going with Wonder Woman," she said. "She's still the best."

"Mom." Andrew groaned. "It's not even the same universe."

"Then I want to live in the universe with Wonder Woman."

"I think you already do," Gabe said, and then proceeded to engage in a detailed discussion about superheroes with her son.

Had he just subtly compared her to Wonder Woman? Oh, boy. She needed to keep her head on straight around this one and remember that nothing that happened between them—or anything she felt for him—was real.

They ate dinner in the dining room with Angi regularly cringing or groaning as her mother shared embarrassing details about her childhood with Gabe. As if he cared to hear any of that.

To his credit, he played along like a champ. He laughed at the right moments, asked for seconds of the marsala and gnocchi. If Angi wasn't smitten at that point, her mother certainly seemed so.

So much so, that as they cleaned up the plates, Bianca turned to Gabe, grabbed his hand and said, "I have a favor to ask you."

He looked mildly fearful yet nodded. "What can I do for you?"

"I'd like you to bring up the Christmas tree from the basement."

"Mom, no." Angi flipped off the water and turned from the sink.

Gabe's eyes went wide. "I…if you want… I mean…"

"Vincent carried it up every year the day after Thanksgiving. It was tradition. Cursing and muttering the whole time about what a pain it was. But he loved that tree. Our house is empty without it. Do you have a Christmas tree in your grandmother's house?"

"Uh, no."

Angi stepped forward. "Mom, seriously. You and I can bring up the tree."

"I'm not sure my heart could take the strain of the stairs." Bianca patted her chest.

"You walked two miles yesterday after your water aerobics class. If you can't manage it, Andrew will help me."

"But Gabe is here." Bianca moved her hand up his arm and squeezed his biceps. "A strapping young man and he doesn't mind." She turned to him, literally batted her eyes. "You don't mind, right?"

"I'll get the tree."

"I'll show you where it is." Irritation and embarrassment warred inside Angi. She wagged a finger at her mother as she walked by. "This is why Marco and Luca don't bring their girlfriends home."

"There are no girls good enough for my boys."

There were times Angi wished she'd paid more attention to the Italian lessons her grandmother had tried to give her when she was younger. She could have used a rant in another language at the moment. She settled for throwing up her hands and stalking toward the basement, far too aware of Gabe on her heels.

"SHE MEANS WELL."

Angi rounded on Gabe as she hit the bottom step in her parents' unfinished basement. "You have got to be joking. That wasn't a mother with good intentions." She pointed to the ceiling. "That was out of line."

"You're the one who wanted a boyfriend for the holidays."

"To get her off my case. Not so she could start picking out china patterns."

"I never understood good china," Gabe said conversationally, wanting to distract her. He'd had a great time at dinner, better than he'd ever expected. He didn't think being asked to carry a Christmas tree was the worst thing that could happen to him. "I was in a friend's wedding last spring, and they got so many plates. A million different sizes of glasses and two gravy boats. What does anyone need with two gravy boats?"

Her mouth formed a small O, and he bit back a smile. At least he'd gotten her mind off the irritation with her mom for a few moments. He took the opportunity to place his hands on her arms and move her to one side so he could get down the last couple of steps. The basement was small but neat, with rows of shelves along two of the walls. A washer and dryer took up space in one corner, and there was an abandoned exercise bike currently being used as a drying rack.

"You were in a wedding? Like as an attendant?"

He frowned. "Best man, actually. One of my army buddies."

"That's so strange."

"You think so?"

"Did you smile for pictures?" She studied him as if he were a puzzle to solve. "And dance and make a toast? Like an actual human being."

"Tell me what you really think about me." He shook his head. Maybe this plan to distract her was working too well. The last thing he wanted or needed was someone dissecting his habits or personality or where he was lacking in either area.

"You just don't seem like the wedding-party type."

"My actual friends would tell you I'm not the fake-boyfriend type either, but your mom seems to be on board with it."

"She likes you," Angi murmured, still in puzzle-solving mode.

"She likes the thought of you settled."

That drew an unexpected laugh from her. "I'm a single mom living in my childhood bedroom and working the same job I had when I was sixteen. Not exactly living the wild life here."

She pointed to an overly large plastic bag stuffed between two shelves. "There's the tree. It's a behemoth, but luckily my dad updated to one with pre-strung lights a couple of years ago. I have so many memories of him shouting and swearing at the burned-out bulbs."

"Why is your mom so interested in finding you a guy? Does she do the same thing with your brothers?"

Angi shook her head. "Luca has been dating the same woman for five years, even though it's been nearly that long since he brought her to visit. They're bound to get engaged one of these days. Marco is a serial dater with no intention of settling down."

"Neither of them wants to work in the family restaurant?"

"Oh, Lord, no. They both hightailed it out of Magnolia as soon as they were able. For some reason, my mom doesn't worry about them like she does me. Maybe because they're doing well and I'm—"

"You're raising a great kid, taking care of your mom, running the family business and making a go of your own business at the same time. Give yourself a break, Ang."

"I never thought I'd get a pep talk from you." She dragged out the tree bag, sneezing once when a cloud of dust puffed into the air.

"I didn't anticipate giving one," Gabe agreed, and took hold of the edge. "You're not the same person who treated people like dirt on your shoe back in the day."

"Not a flattering assessment, but I guess it's a win that you think I've changed."

He heard the pain in her voice and stopped moving until she looked at him. Her gaze was solid on his, and if he didn't know better he'd swear he saw understanding in it. "People make mistakes," he told her.

"Does that mean you forgive me for mine?"

"You don't need my forgiveness," he told her. "I'm just the pretend boyfriend." He made the words casual and focused on maneuvering the tree up the narrow staircase. He didn't know if Angi truly wanted his forgiveness or if he was in a place to give it to her.

In a lot of ways that would only confuse things, and his life was already complicated enough.

But as he set up the tree under her mother's watchful eye, Gabe realized that his version of complicated didn't have to be the only one. Angi had a lot to deal with, but the love she felt for her mother and vice versa was palpable. They hung ornaments and her mom told a story about almost each and every one, with Andrew continuously asking for more details. So many memories of happy Christmases, memories Gabe didn't have.

His mom hadn't cared much about the holidays, other than when it came to whatever lavish gift she wanted from her boyfriend of the moment. There hadn't been decorations, and some years she'd forgotten to buy presents altogether until the last minute. Gabe had gotten used to receiving random gifts obviously purchased from the chain drugstore that was open late on Christmas Eve. Gran had always sent something perfect, but more often than not, her thoughtfulness only seemed to infuriate his mom.

The more he compared Angi's family traditions with those of his own, his gut began to clench. He was the worst option for a fake boyfriend because what did he know about what normal people did or acted like?

She'd been right to question his ability to have friends or act human. He hadn't made friends easily as a kid, and his time in the military had just about pummeled the desire to connect with people out of him. He'd transformed himself from the wimpy kid who was a target for bullies far and wide to a hard and honed soldier, but the cost was too great.

He watched Andrew as he hung each ornament his nonna handed him with care and precision. Gabe mentally made a plan to show up at the elementary school the following morning and beat the snot out of those little punks who were tormenting Angi's son.

Okay, he wouldn't hurt a kid, but he was ready to scare them enough so that they'd be motivated to leave Drew alone.

The kid was valiant in his dedication to learning self-defense or karate or any kind of fighting moves in order to be tougher, but Gabe knew from firsthand experience that wasn't the answer. Andrew was perfect just as he was, and Gabe wanted to protect that innocence. The way he'd wanted a protector.

As Angi met his gaze across the room, her eyes warm and filled with a gentle sentimentality, his heart leaped in his chest. He wasn't fit to be the boy's protector or her knight in shining armor or even a decent fake boyfriend. But damn if he didn't want all three.

Gabe had learned at an early age that it was the wanting that led to heartache. Wanting made him vulnerable. Wanting made him an easy target. He'd crafted a life devoid of hungering for things he shouldn't hunger for, and he wasn't about to change it now.

He stood abruptly. "I've got to go," he muttered, and

stalked from the room and out the front door before anyone could argue.

Angi followed him, and he held up a hand as she caught up to him halfway to his car. "No more family dinners," he said, grounding out the words and hoping she couldn't hear the emotion behind them.

"Okay," she agreed immediately. "Although you did pretty well—better than me—up until the last few minutes. What's wrong?"

"I don't like Christmas," he said without thinking.

"Yet you didn't walk away from the festival cochair role even though it meant working with me."

"I wanted to piss you off."

"How's that working for you?"

He glanced toward her as he reached the truck. "I'm the one who's pissed off."

"Give me a minute," she promised, squeezing shut her eyes with a grimace. "I can conjure anger with the best of them."

He didn't want that. He liked seeing her smile, making her smile. The fact of it pissed him off even more.

After a moment she opened her eyes again. "Thank you for coming over tonight."

"You don't sound angry." He didn't bother to hide the accusation in his tone.

"I hide it better than you," she admitted.

"That's the problem," he told her as he climbed into his truck. "I'm not good at pretending."

He started the engine and drove away before she saw what he needed to hide most of all. The fact that he'd never stopped wanting her.

CHAPTER EIGHT

ANGI FOLLOWED HER mother into the Shady Acres later that week, thinking that Gabe would have been thrilled with her current mood. Anger, frustration, self-pity—a veritable cocktail of negativity poured through her.

"Mom, I think you can handle a dance class on your own," she said as they stopped in the lobby to sign in. The woman at the reception desk greeted her mother like a long-lost friend.

"I want you here with me," Bianca said with a sweet smile. "This is the first class I've gone to since the heart attack. What if it's too taxing?"

"It's ballroom dancing for seniors," Angi pointed out. "How taxing can it be?"

"The restaurant is slow this time of day, and Andrew won't be finished with school for a couple of hours. You have nothing else to do, right?"

"Right." Actually, Angi should be at the Wildflower Inn, prepping for a Rotary Club luncheon they were hosting the following day, and she was fairly certain her mother knew it. She'd seen Bianca glancing at Angi's phone when a text came through from Emma about a produce delivery that had arrived at the inn.

Her mom had denied reading anything when asked about it, but she'd suddenly become adamant that Angi go with her to the dance class.

Angi wasn't about to reveal her commitment to helping Emma through to the end of the year, not after she'd promised her mom that she was going to give up the partnership.

It was one more example of Angi failing in multiple areas of her life.

They walked into the large dining area, where the tables had been shifted to the sides of the room to make space in the center.

Josie Trumbell, who owned the dance studio in downtown Magnolia, welcomed her mother. The other class participants crowded around Bianca with murmurs of how great she looked. Angi waved to Josie and headed toward the residents who sat on one side of the room to watch the class.

Iris Carlyle was in a wheelchair, her hands clasped together tightly. She stared blankly at a place in front of her while the other residents carried on a conversation around her.

"Hello, Mrs. Carlyle," Angi said as she lowered herself into the empty seat next to the older woman. It took a few seconds for Iris's gaze to focus, and then she smiled gently.

"Angela?"

"Yes, it's me."

The woman's frail shoulders relaxed a bit, as if she'd been worried she might get Angi's name or identity wrong. "I remember when you used to take the old blooms from the compost bin in the alley and make them into necklaces."

Angi reached out and wrapped her hand around both of Iris's, which were cool to the touch. "You were so nice to me. I loved the smell of your shop and all of those flowers. I'd breathe in the scent and imagine I was someplace else, like a beautiful field in the French countryside."

"Flowers are a thing of beauty," Iris said softly. "I miss my shop and the feel of the petals between my fingers. Gabe brings me a fresh bouquet every week. He's a good boy."

Angi sucked in a quick breath but didn't answer.

"Have you met my grandson?"

"I have. He loves you very much."

"He spent too many years in the army. It changed him." Iris's feathery brows drew together. "Or maybe it's just what happens in life, but I don't think so. He was always a serious boy, but now he's harder and sadder. Still a good boy. He came to Magnolia when I fell and is running the shop. Do you know my shop? It's downtown. The name is…" Her eyes squeezed shut as she obviously searched for the name in her mind.

"In Bloom," Angi supplied. "It's a wonderful shop. I'm sure it's been difficult to not be able to visit the store, but Gabe is taking good care of it."

"He said he's going to bring me downtown to see the lights for Christmas." Iris gave her a watery smile. "I don't like getting old."

"You're still beautiful." Angi leaned in and placed a kiss on Iris's cheek. The dancers took to the center of the room.

Her mother had been paired with Stuart from the bookstore, a longtime friend, and a man who was definitely participating in this class because of his longtime crush on the dance instructor. Josie gave a few initial instructions and then the music started.

"No," the woman denied. "I'm letting myself go in here. The hip surgery slowed me down, and I haven't even gotten my nails done." She stretched out her fingers to reveal nails with just a few specks of polish left on them.

"I'd be happy to do your nails," Angi said, tracing a thumb over Iris's nails. "What's your favorite color?"

"I'd like red for Christmas."

"I'll be here tomorrow at this time."

"Thank you, dear." Iris squeezed Angi's hand. "Have you met my grandson, Gabe? He's a good boy and quite handsome. The two of you would make a lovely couple. He needs a nice girl in his life. Needs to smile more."

"I smile plenty."

Angi startled at Gabe's deep voice. She started to turn, but he stepped in front of her. "See me smiling," he said to his grandmother, then offered a maniacal-looking leer.

"That's terrifying," Angi muttered, earning a chuckle from Iris.

"Hello, my sweet boy," she said, and lifted her arms toward Gabe. Without hesitation, he bent and kissed her forehead as she gave him a gentle hug. "Have you met Bianca?" Iris asked when he pulled back. She frowned and turned to Angi. "No, that's not right."

Angi's heart tightened at Iris's obvious distress. It must be so difficult to lose track of the details. To still be lucid enough to recognize the loss but not to do anything about it.

"I'm Angi." She pointed to the dance floor. "Bianca is my mom, the one currently dancing with abandon." Her mother looked over and gave a little wave, then beckoned Angi to join the class.

"Do you dance?" Iris asked.

"Not like that." Angi shook her head. "I never learned anything beyond the Electric Slide."

"Gabe is a wonderful dancer." Iris beamed at him. "I taught him back when he was just a little squirt. He stepped on my toes something awful at the start, but he learned.

Do you remember, Gaby? Those nights dancing to Tony Bennett."

His smile softened into something so sincere and genuinely sweet it took Angi's breath away. "You always were a fan of Tony. It's a good thing Grandad found you first."

How could this sweet man be the same crusty man who blew hot and cold so fast Angi felt like she had both frostbite and third-degree burns in response? Would Andrew someday be that dedicated to his grandmother or even to his mother? Angi could only hope.

"Your grandad was the only man I had eyes for," Iris said, none of the uncertainty of earlier in her voice. "He did basic training down in South Carolina, and we met when he and some friends came up to the Outer Banks. In his uniform, he was the most handsome soldier I'd ever seen. My grandson is his spitting image." She leaned into Angi and whispered in a voice that wasn't a whisper, "Gabe is a handsome devil, don't you think?"

Angi wondered if the older woman remembered making almost that exact comment minutes ago. How often did Iris circle back through a conversation, loops on repeat?

"I'm sure many women find him handsome," she said instead of her earlier agreement. She sure wasn't going to stroke his ego, even for his grandmother's sake.

The song changed to a mid-tempo waltz, and Iris grinned. "Oh, this is the perfect song. Gabe, be a gentleman and ask this beautiful young woman to dance."

Gabe looked as shocked as Angi felt at the suggestion.

"I can't. I really don't know how to dance."

"The man leads. Gabe will take care of you."

Didn't those words just send an unwelcome thrill skittering along her spine?

Gabe looked like he'd rather stick his hand into a nest

of pit vipers than offer it to her, but he dutifully held it out, palm up. "May I have this dance?" he asked like some broody Austen heroine. Mr. Darcy the florist, as her friends had dubbed him months earlier.

Heat rose to Angi's cheeks. She tried to ignore her body's reaction to him and her heart's stammering pitter-patter inside her chest. "I don't dance," she mumbled, like that would make a difference.

Since when did what she wanted to do change what she did?

"You might surprise yourself," Iris said, undeterred by the weak protest.

So Angi placed her hand into Gabe's, acutely aware of the warmth of his skin and the scrapes on his fingers and his calloused palm. She'd always appreciated a man who had work-roughened hands, although the same didn't apply to her own.

She had the classic beat-up hands of kitchen workers everywhere. Red from being washed so often and her nails in sore need of tending. She could give herself a manicure at the same time she gave one to Iris, she supposed.

The myriad of thoughts she tried to distract herself with disappeared as Gabe led her to the edge of the circle of dancers.

"A youthful couple," Josie exclaimed, clasping her hands together in front of her generous bosom. "How lovely."

Bianca beamed. "My daughter is as lovely as they come."

"Breathe," Gabe advised as he pulled Angi closer.

"I'm breathing," she ground out, then realized she was holding her breath.

"There's no pressure." He lifted her hand to his shoulder and placed his on her waist. "We're guaranteed to look good in comparison. You could face-plant a dozen times, and the fact that you could get back up would make you the envy of everyone in the place."

"I don't want to dance," she told him as she glanced up into his dark eyes. She hadn't been so close to a man, held for any length of time, for far longer than she cared to admit. She blamed her heightened awareness on that fact and tried to ignore her body's response to Gabe in particular. This close, the flecks of green in his hazel eyes were obvious, and the fine lines fanning out from the corners of his eyes made her want to trace a finger over them.

Had he gotten those because he'd been deployed to deserts with harsh sun and cruel wind? Or had there been a time when he'd laughed freely—maybe with a woman—and that past joy was now constantly reflected on his face?

"You and I have more in common than either of us probably cares to admit." He spun her in a wide circle. "We're both living our lives for other people at the moment."

The words hit her like a sledgehammer, and she nearly tripped as they pummeled into her. Gabe's arms tightened around her as he steadied them both.

Gabe will take care of you.

Iris's words fluttered through her mind. Angi didn't want anyone to take care of her. Since returning to Magnolia, pregnant and out of options, she'd been trying to prove that she could manage her own life. Yes, she'd made a colossal mistake in falling for a man who loved his career more than he could ever care for her, and she'd vowed not to repeat it.

But that mistake had resulted in Andrew, the best part of her life. There were no regrets on that front.

Others, yes, but better not to focus on what she couldn't change.

"That's not true," she argued when she felt steady enough to say the words without her voice cracking.

Gabe lifted a thick brow. "You're at a dance class in a retirement home, surrounded by people who think a rousing game of bingo is the highlight of their week."

"Don't underestimate the lure of bingo," she said. "Both for improving cognitive function and the fun of covering that last square."

Gabe stared at her.

"I'm here because I want to be," she murmured.

"Me, too," he agreed. "Because it makes my grandmother happy. Your mom depends on you for her happiness."

"I'm fine with that."

"It's not what you'd choose for yourself if you didn't have to."

His voice was soft, but the words chafed like sandpaper across her skin.

"You can't always get what you want," she said, letting sarcasm drip from her tone.

One side of Gabe's full mouth curved as he led her in an elaborate spin that ended with her facing away from him, her back pressed to his chest. "But what do you need, Ang?" he asked into her ear.

She was saved from answering by the end of the song. "Next we're going to move to the Electric Slide," Josie told the dozen participants. "It's a wedding reception staple, and now that the Wildflower Inn is putting Magnolia on the map for discerning brides everywhere—" she winked at Angi "—we need to make sure you can cut a rug with the best of them."

Bianca, who was standing a few feet away with her partner, dropped Stuart's hand and stiffened. "I'm feeling slightly light-headed," she said with just the right amount of breathiness. "I'll sit this one out."

Angi took a step toward her mother but paused when Josie held up a hand. "Bianca, stay with us." She leveled a stare at her longtime friend that Angi would imagine had struck fear in the hearts of many a tiny dancer. "We'll go slow and make sure you're okay. You're strong, my friend. Your heart is strong. It can handle this."

A multitude of emotions flitted across her mother's face. Irritation, defiance and, finally, resignation. To Angi's surprise, her mother nodded. "Fine," Bianca agreed. "But I'm not going to like it."

"We'll see," Josie said, and then turned on the music.

"I agree with your mom," Gabe said a few minutes later as he turned the wrong way again and bumped into Angi. "Can't we just stick to the chicken dance?"

Angi chuckled and executed a perfect turn. "This is more my tempo. I love a good line dance."

Josie led them through several more dances, including the cha-cha and the foxtrot. Angi found herself paired with Gabe as well as several male residents of the facility. For men who shuffled back and forth to their rooms most days, they moved with surprising grace in the dances.

"I remember USO dances," one of the men told her as he led her in a swing dance. "It was always the best part of the holidays on base. We might be homesick, but for a few hours dancing to the music we could forget how far away we were from the ones we loved."

Angi's heart melted at the nostalgic sentiment. She glanced over to see Gabe dancing with her mother, and her heart softened even more at how relaxed he appeared.

Her mom had seemed to recover from her claim of light-headedness at Josie's goading. Not for the first time, Angi wondered at the coincidence of her mom claiming to feel bad whenever the inn or Angi's work outside the restaurant was mentioned.

But now everyone in the group was laughing and having fun, and the residents watching, including Iris, seemed to be enjoying the music and dancing just as much as the class participants.

So much so that when the class had finished, Angi pulled Gabe and Josie aside. "I think we should do a holiday dance as our big fundraiser event for the festival. It would be something unique and fun. We can rent a big tent to put up in the square and find a DJ who can play a variety of music. People can buy a special ticket to attend a class taught by Josie at the start." She glanced at the other woman. "If you'd be willing to donate your time?"

"Of course." Josie grinned. "We haven't had a community dance in town for decades."

"Because people don't want to come to something like that." Gabe shook his head. "Dances are for high school kids—homecoming and prom or whatever."

"Not true," Angi argued, wondering why he would fight her on this. "As Josie said, everyone loves dancing at weddings. This would be an easy way to raise money for..."

Gabe scowled at her. Josie looked expectant.

"A veterans' program." The idea came to Angi on a flash. "Meredith and Ryan were in the restaurant the other day, and they were working on plans for an emotional support pet program for former soldiers. We're almost at our goal for funds to donate to the school. What if the money we raise at the dance goes toward that?"

"It's an amazing idea," Josie told her.

"Seems like more work than it's worth." Gabe shrugged. "We don't have a lot of time until the final weekend, and most of the advertising and marketing budget has already been spent."

"I'm sure we can talk to Avery in the mayor's office," Josie said. "I'll personally call Malcolm and get his buy-in."

Bianca approached at that moment. "What's going on?"

"Your daughter had a fantastic idea for a fundraiser to do as a culmination of Christmas on the Coast."

"Of course she did." Bianca wrapped an arm around Angi's shoulder. "She's the best. And with her wonderful boyfriend at her side, my girl can do anything."

"Mom, stop," Angi grumbled.

"What boyfriend?" Josie demanded. "What did I miss?"

"You didn't know that my Angela and Gabriel are a couple." Bianca grinned at Gabe. "They are gorgeous together."

"I…didn't realize… I mean…yes." Josie looked between the two of them. "Since when have the two of you been dating? As I remember it, there's some history there."

"We can't rely on good weather," Gabe said, ignoring Josie's question and comment. "And there isn't a big enough space in the square for the size tent you'll need."

"What about at town hall?" Josie suggested, then shook her head. "No, even in the basement there are no rooms large enough." She sighed. "It's a great idea, sweetheart." She patted Angi's cheek. "But I don't think there's any place big enough in town to hold a dance."

Angi smiled even though tears stung her eyes. It shouldn't matter. It was one idea, and she'd figure out another one. But she liked the idea of a dance to finish the town's holiday celebration. People wanted to feel like part of the community, and it meant something to her to be able to give them that. To make the event her own.

She felt Gabe studying her and purposely looked away.

"I have an idea for a location," he said in that low, gravelly voice.

"You don't even think it's a good idea," she reminded him with an eye roll.

"Your sweetheart is being nice, sweetheart." She couldn't miss the warning in her mother's tone. "Don't be irritable."

Bianca reached around Angi to squeeze Gabe's arm. "She didn't have much for lunch, so she's probably hungry. She gets cranky when she's hungry."

"I'm not cranky," Angi said, then turned to Gabe. "I'm not."

"You're allowed to feel however you want," he answered simply, defying every one of her expectations.

Then he shocked her even more by leaning in for a quick kiss, earning approving clucks from both Bianca and Josie. Like a miracle, Angi's anger disappeared, replaced by a tingly feeling rushing through her veins.

"Um…thank you. What's your idea?"

"Dylan Scott is working on redeveloping the old mill outside of town. I heard he's got a sportswear company interested in leasing the space."

"Mal mentioned that at our last city council meeting," Josie confirmed.

"But it's still empty as far as I know. It might be a good option for the dance, and I'm sure if Carrie likes the idea that Dylan will make it happen."

Josie nodded. "That boy is over the moon for her."

Angi thought about what it would be like to have someone in the world who was so dedicated to her happiness.

"I'll call Carrie when we leave here." She reached up and wrapped her arms around Gabe's neck. "Thank you," she repeated, trying to convince herself that his display of physical affection was all for show.

Even if that wasn't how it felt inside her body.

CHAPTER NINE

GABE PULLED UP in front of the old mill the following morning and parked next to Angi's small hatchback. A sleek black SUV turned into the parking lot shortly after. Dylan Scott and Avery Keller Atwell climbed out.

He gritted his teeth against the burgeoning tightness in his stomach. Somehow, instead of getting less involved in the town, he was now in the thick of holiday festival planning. Yes, he'd agreed to it, but once he knew Angi was involved, it had been more a way to get under her skin.

Sort of like dancing with her had gotten under his. Holding her close and having an excuse to press his body against hers as they swayed to the music. He shouldn't have liked it as much as he did, but there was no denying it.

Everything about the encounter with her yesterday had thrown him off his game. Shouldn't there be some internal barometer that prevented a man from getting turned on in a nursing home? And with his grandmother watching, no less. Walking in to see Angi talking to his grandma had been the first chink in his armor. He had a soft spot for anyone who showed kindness to his grandma, and the way she'd smiled at Angi made him understand that the woman who should remain his nemesis wasn't an enemy in the way that counted the most to Gabe.

"How's it going?" Dylan asked as he walked forward, hand outstretched. "Gabe, right?"

"Yeah." Gabe shook his hand. "It's fine. Thanks for being willing to open up the mill for a holiday dance."

"It's the perfect location," Angi added as she appeared at Gabe's side.

"I appreciate the two of you taking over for Carrie," Dylan answered.

"We all do," Avery agreed. The slim blonde wore a pair of tailored trousers and a fitted sweater that looked like it was made of some expensive fabric. Cashmere probably. She seemed like a woman who'd wear cashmere, but the warmth of her smile calmed his nerves.

Angi nodded. "Of course. How's she feeling?"

Dylan's gaze clouded. "It's been rough, but she's getting through it. Yesterday she didn't throw up once, so that's an improvement."

The worry in the other man's eyes was evident, and Avery put a calming hand on his arm. "She's going to be fine. Why don't we take a look inside? I think people are going to love the idea of a dance."

"Do you think we have enough time to get the word out and sell tickets?" Angi asked as they started toward the entrance.

"Absolutely," Avery answered, and Gabe smiled as Angi threw an "I told you so" look at him over her shoulder.

He fell into step next to Dylan. "Heard you've got a big company interested in leasing this space."

"As a matter of fact, we sign the final papers later this afternoon." He shielded his eyes against the bright winter sun as another black SUV pulled into the parking lot. It was like a rich-guys club, Gabe supposed. "I invited the CEO of one of the new tenant companies to join us today. They're interested in getting more involved in the community, so I thought this event would be a great way to introduce them to people."

"Is that Alex?" Avery paused at the front door.

"Yep." Dylan tossed her a set of keys. "You all go ahead. I have a few quick things to talk through with him and then we'll meet you inside."

Avery opened the tour and led Angi and Gabe through. He could see how nervous Angi was with Avery and didn't understand it. She was alternately quiet and then almost aggressively chipper as Avery showed them around the place. The building had been cleared out and cleaned up, obviously left as a blank slate for whatever business might come in next.

"What happened to the condos and micro-retail shopping mall Dylan originally planned?" Angi asked Avery after a few minutes. "I thought once he decided not to take over downtown, he'd turned his attention to this place."

Gran had written to Gabe of her fear over losing the flower shop last year when she'd sent him a Christmas care package. He'd been stationed in the Middle East, and every day was a loop of sand, sun and endless training drills. He hated to admit how little attention he'd paid to his grandmother's words at the time.

She'd glossed over her upset by telling him that no matter what happened, she knew things would work out for the best. Looking back, he wondered if her letters were as much for herself as for him. A catharsis of sorts and a way to work through some of the issues she had because there was no one in her life she felt comfortable confiding in. In that way, he was an easy outlet.

Now he wished he'd done more to support her. He could have made a bigger effort if only he'd realized how uncertain her future had been.

"That was his intention," Avery agreed. "But this town has a way of helping people see what's really important. Obviously, Carrie was a big part of that change in direction, as well. Dylan mellowed out quite a bit and decided that he wanted to develop his properties in a way that added to what we were already doing to revitalize Magnolia instead of competing with it."

"Mom says he's a way better landlord than the last guy who owned the restaurant's building. Dylan's property manager is responsive and keeps everything maintained." She turned to Gabe. "Don't you agree?"

He shrugged. "I cut a rent check once a month. No other maintenance needed." As far as he was concerned. Until Angi had come back into his life, he'd resisted getting involved with anyone.

"Downtown is doing great, and we're on track for a record tourist season this month." Avery inclined her head as she studied Gabe. "A few people have talked to me about the fact that the In Bloom storefront isn't exactly looking festive. Your grandmother always did such a lovely job with her holiday displays."

"A few people?" Tension knotted in Gabe's gut. He did not want to know that people were talking about him when he was barely holding it together. Particularly if they implied he wasn't doing the best he could for his grandmother's legacy or the store she loved so dearly.

But that morning he'd received a voice mail from his mom demanding he shut down the store sooner rather than later and send her the proceeds for the display shelving and supplies he managed to sell. How could he still work hard knowing her plan to destroy everything Gran had built?

It might be convoluted, but Gabe couldn't help but believe that if he ignored the business for a period of time his mom would lose interest. She didn't like hard work. If In Bloom wasn't making money, she'd have no reason to come back now and cause his grandma more pain.

"It would be nice if you could get something up before this weekend." Avery gave him an encouraging smile. "If you need help—"

"He doesn't," Angi interrupted before the blonde could finish her thought. "I'm going to help him." She moved closer and slipped her hand into Gabe's, the touch soft and reassuring.

He shouldn't let himself depend on her for anything because he knew their relationship was fake. She was using him to placate her mother, and he was letting it happen because he wanted to make his grandmother proud when she came to the shop.

"We've both been busy." Angi nodded and leaned toward Avery as if conveying a secret. "You know Iris is still recovering in the nursing home? And with my mom's rehabilitation, we both are juggling a lot of balls."

The blonde frowned, clearly as confused by Angi's behavior as Gabe. Where was the nervous, stammering woman of a few minutes ago?

Avery nodded. "Of course, I wish a full recovery for your grandmother."

"Thank you," Gabe said quietly.

"He's at the nursing home almost every day, you know," Angi added. "Things may have fallen behind at the store, but we're going to fix that. The two of us. Together."

"Please let me know if there's anything I can do to help," Avery told Gabe, her tone so sincere it made him wish he was truly a part of this kind of community where people genuinely seemed to care. "We're featuring several of the downtown businesses on the Magnolia website and our social media accounts. I'd love to do a feature on In Bloom." She switched her gaze to Angi. "Or on Il Rigatone. I hope your mom is feeling better, as well."

"She's fine," Angi muttered.

"How's it going?" Dylan asked as he approached their little trio along with the man who drove the Land Rover. "Do we have everything planned to turn this place into a holiday dance hall extravaganza?"

He colored slightly when they all stared at him. "Those were Carrie's words," he explained quickly. "She said I wasn't allowed to ruin the vibe by being moody or awkward during this meeting." He laughed. "As if."

"Oh, we're well past moody and awkward," Avery told him, her blue eyes lit with humor.

"Then I'm missing all the fun." Dylan flashed a mischievous smile, then introduced his companion as Alex Ralsten, the new CEO for The Fit Collective, an athletic wear company moving their corporate headquarters to Magnolia. "Alex is single-handedly going to put this town on the map."

"We're already on the map." Avery gave him a playful swat on the arm. "Thanks to me and your wife."

"I couldn't agree more," Alex said. "The reason the company is moving to Magnolia is because I had such a great impression of the town when I was here over the summer."

"Are you Brett Carmichael's friend?" Angi studied the CEO. "I remember you from the wedding."

Alex's eyes suddenly lit with recognition. "You're the chef who created the amazing menu for the reception. And the food we had during the planning weekend at the Wildflower Inn?"

Gabe tried not to react as Angi slipped her hand from his. "That was me."

"I swear to God, I've had dreams about your scallops and cream sauce. You are immensely talented."

The transformation in Angi was once again nothing short of confusing as hell. She dipped her chin and looked at the ground like she was embarrassed or unworthy of the compliments. "Holly and Brett were easy to please. I enjoyed working with them. I'm glad your time in Magnolia left such a positive impression."

"It did. I might need to schedule our company kickoff retreat at the inn just so I have an excuse to enjoy your fabulous culinary skills again."

"Angi runs the Italian restaurant in town," Avery told Alex, earning a glare from Angi. "What?" The blonde held up her hands. "You do run Il Rigatone."

"But those aren't my recipes," Angi muttered.

"I'm sure anything you're involved in is amazing." Alex offered a wide grin that somehow didn't sit well with Gabe.

Or maybe it was Angi's reaction—a sweet smile, the kind she never gave to Gabe—that he didn't like.

"What are we thinking for music?" Gabe asked suddenly. "A DJ can play more variety, but the energy of a live band would be festive and fun."

Angi gaped at him. "Did you just use the words *festive* and *fun*?"

"Those are perfect descriptions." Avery beamed at him, and he moved a few steps away from Angi. He had to get a little distance in order to tame his tumbling emotions.

"The acoustics of the space would work well for a band," Dylan agreed. "And we've got the power to handle any of their AV needs."

As they continued to discuss specifics, Angi's phone

rang. Her features tightened. "Sorry, I have to take this. It's the school."

She stepped away, and Gabe managed—just barely— not to follow. Stupid, he chided himself. Angi didn't need him hovering like some unnecessary guardian angel, and he had no business worrying about her son.

But he had to admit the boy had wormed his way into Gabe's heart. Every day without fail, he showed up at the flower shop and begged to learn something new. Gabe had finally broken down and hung a punching bag in the back room and put light weights there for the kid to work on his reflexes and coordination. Gabe knew from experience that being the weakest would only add to his social misery. Kids could be merciless.

"So you and Angi?" Avery asked with a raised brow as Alex and Dylan moved toward another room.

Gabe blinked and then realized what the other woman was talking about. "Yeah, um. It's new. She's amazing."

Avery scrunched up her pert nose. "She definitely doesn't like me."

"That's not true." Or at least Gabe didn't understand why it was true.

"Sure it is. I don't mind." Avery shrugged. "I got used to people not liking me in my old life. Apparently, I'm an acquired taste. I'll win her over. I'm a big fan of her mom's chicken piccata."

"Angi doesn't exactly love being back at the restaurant full-time," Gabe explained. "It makes her a little grumpy. The inn is her dream. I know it was your dad's house, although I don't have many memories of him from when I spent summers in Magnolia."

"I didn't even find out about Niall until after he was dead." Avery smoothed a hand over her hair. "I beat you on the memories front, but I met my sisters thanks to him, so Niall's memory and I are good at this point."

Gabe chuckled. "Fair enough. Give Angi a break, though. She's going through some stuff."

"But she's got you to support her."

Gabe started to shake his head. He wasn't in a place to be a support to anyone. "Yeah," he said, after a moment. "She does."

"Have you met my husband?" Avery asked, in a quick pivot of subject matter. "Gray Atwell? He's a local firefighter."

"I don't think so."

"He's a good man. The best." Her smile turned tender. "The best for me, even when I didn't realize it."

Gabe scratched the back of his neck. "I'm not much for subtleties or secret meaning. If there's some message you want to give me, then—"

"I've got to go." Angi came rushing back to them, agitation clear in her tone.

Dylan and Alex moved toward the group as well, clearly alerted by her voice that something was wrong.

"Is everything okay?" Avery took a step forward.

"It's my son. Andrew. He—"

"What happened?" Gabe gripped her arm. "What happened to Andrew?"

"I'm not sure. I've got to go," she repeated, looking stunned. "There was a fight and he's… I don't know. He hit his head on the concrete. Maybe a concussion."

"Oh, no," Avery murmured. "What can we do?"

Angi shook her head. "I've just got to get to him."

"I'll drive you," Gabe told her.

"You should finish the meeting."

"The meeting is done." He looked to Avery, who nodded. "Let's go."

He led Angi out of the building and toward his truck. She paused before climbing in. "I can drive myself."

"I know," he said, nudging her into the seat. "But I've got a lead foot. Learned to drive like a maniac when I was barely fourteen and honed those skills in the army. I'll get you to him, Ang."

She bit down on her lower lip like she was holding herself together by a thin thread. "Hurry."

Gabe didn't waste any time. He drove like a madman toward the elementary school. It was only a few blocks from downtown, so he knew the location.

"What did they tell you?" he demanded as he took a corner so fast that Angi gripped the door handle to prevent herself from sliding toward him.

"Just that there was a fight, and he hit his head."

Gabe muttered a curse and then another. "What the hell kind of school is this that lets something happen to a ten-year-old kid? He's supposed to be safe in school. Things were bad enough for me, but my mom never got called because I'd been hurt."

"I made things bad for you," she said quietly, then turned to him. "Is this some kind of karmic payback for how mean I was as a girl?"

"Don't." He reached out a hand and covered hers. Her skin felt cool, almost clammy, and he wanted to pull over and haul her into his arms, but that wouldn't help anyone at the moment. "This isn't about you." He squeezed her hand. "There's plenty of time to rehash the stupid mistakes you made. I'd be happy to help you. Just not now."

"Wow." She blew out a small breath. "Did you ever consider going into the life-coaching business?"

"Did I take your mind off being terrified for your kid for a few seconds?"

"Yes," she admitted. "Because I was thinking about how annoying you are."

"My work here is done."

He pulled into the school lot. It was a cheery one-story redbrick building with paper snowflakes hanging from the classroom windows, even though it almost never snowed in this part of the country.

Angi was opening the door before he'd even come to a complete stop. He threw the truck into Park but didn't move. He had no dog in this fight, even though his heart disagreed with that assessment.

She paused before slamming shut the door. "Thank you," she said softly. "For being here."

He gave a small nod. "I'm not going anywhere." He just wanted to know they were both okay.

CHAPTER TEN

THIRTY MINUTES LATER, Angi walked out of the school with a sullen Andrew next to her. Anger pumped through her like someone had just turned on a garden hose, ready to explode out in a torrent of temper.

She was angry at herself for not realizing how bad the situation had gotten for her son. Angry at the school for not doing enough to protect her sweet boy. Those two outlets should be enough, but she had plenty of temper left over for the man waiting for them in the truck.

The one who'd set her sweet boy on this path to the current deluge of problems.

"Hey, bud," Gabe said as Andrew got into the back seat. "You okay?"

"No," Angi snapped before Andrew could answer. "He's not okay. Do you know why he's not okay?"

Gabe gave her a sidelong glance. "Guessing it has something to do with that cut above his eye." He turned to Andrew again. "How's your head?"

"Fine," the boy muttered.

"Do not speak to him," she commanded, all the anger that she hadn't been able to let loose on the well-meaning principal coalescing into a heavy ball of frustration. One that she could now level at the man sitting next to her. "He's not okay because he just got suspended for fighting. A three-day suspension. You should see the other boy." She sucked in a quick breath. "In fact, there he is." She pointed to the kid walking down the steps of the school with his obviously furious mother. His face was red from crying and his right eye was already developing a massive bruise.

"He's twice Andrew's size," Gabe said on a harsh breath. "Looks mean as the day is long."

"But this one—" Angi jerked a thumb toward the back seat "—beat the tar out of him from all accounts. It was a regular pummeling."

"I thought Andrew was hurt."

"I slipped when the teachers pulled me off him," the boy explained. "Hit my head on the ground. It's fine. Even the school nurse said so. That's Johnny, and he's a bully. But I took care of him."

"Violence doesn't take care of anything," Angi said, frustrated that things had gotten so out of control. She lifted a hand when Gabe would have spoken. "Not a word from you."

"I was going to agree," he said under his breath.

"Not a word," she repeated. "Please take us to my car. I called the pediatrician's office, and Andrew has an appointment for concussion testing this afternoon."

Gabe shifted into gear and headed back toward the mill. He'd given her so much comfort on the way to the school when she'd been anxious and frazzled. But she didn't know how to deal with this new side of her son.

Andrew was a sweet kid, a little awkward but with such a big heart. Now he'd been suspended for fighting, of all things. What had changed in his life? She rolled her lips together as guilt tumbled through her. Everything. She'd sublet her apartment so they could move back into her mother's house after the heart attack. Andrew had lost his grandfather this year, the only father figure he'd ever known.

Angi was burning the candle at both ends as she tried to balance her responsibilities at the restaurant with the ones she had yet to give up at the inn.

But the biggest change—or at least the one she could control with a few well-chosen words—was Gabe's involvement in their lives.

"Mom, I don't need the doctor," Andrew told her, his voice brimming with enthusiasm. "I feel good. I stood up to Johnny. He's not going to bother me again."

God, she hoped that was true. The warrior mother in her still wanted to throttle the little jerk who'd antagonized her son, but she hadn't admitted any of that in front of the principal or Andrew's teacher.

"According to Johnny," she reminded Andrew, "you came after him unprovoked."

"That's a lie," Andrew said, his voice losing its fervent edge.

"Then tell me why." She adjusted the seat belt so she could turn to face him. "It doesn't help your case with the principal that you wouldn't give details as to what he said to upset you, Andrew. All she knows is that you started a fight with a boy on the playground."

"I didn't start it," Andrew insisted. "I finished it."

Angi set her jaw and darted a look at Gabe. "I assume you taught him that bit of wisdom."

"No," the infuriating man answered. "But I respect the hell out of him."

"No swearing," Angi warned.

Gabe nodded. "Right. Sorry."

"I learned it on YouTube," Andrew offered. "But Gabe

taught me not to tuck my thumbs when I make a fist. That way I can punch harder."

To his credit, Gabe had the good sense to look chagrined. "Your mom is right, Drew." He looked at her son in the rearview mirror. "Violence doesn't solve problems."

"It stopped Johnny from saying mean things," Andrew countered.

"What mean things?" Angi demanded. "What on earth could that boy have said to make you react in that way, Andrew?"

"He said my daddy didn't want me which made me a stupid little..." His voice cracked as he finished, "Crap bastard."

Gabe turned into the mill's gravel driveway at that moment, taking the speed bump too quickly. Angi let herself be jostled, like she was riding a violent wave after the ocean had been turned up by a storm. That's how she felt— as if she were being pulled under and then thrown again. Her emotions pitched back and forth, tossed this way and that before finally being dragged under into the darkness.

The truck jerked to a stop, and Gabe threw it into Park and turned fully to face her son. "That boy at your school—Johnny, right?"

"Yeah."

"Johnny is a jerk, Drew. He's a piece of dog poop on your shoe, and nothing more."

Again with the life coaching, Angi thought, but that was the only coherent idea that registered. She should take over. As the mom, this was her issue. As the single mom who'd walked away from Andrew's father without a word or any attempt to make him own up to his responsibility, this was completely on her.

She was afraid to speak. Afraid all that would come out

was a keening wail because that little piece of dog poop had given voice to her biggest fear for her sweet child. That he'd be judged for her mistakes.

It had been a mistake to let herself trust a man who was perfect on paper but not in reality. That was all she would admit to because the rest of it had led to Andrew. Her son was the best part of her.

The very best part.

And now he was tainted by her past when she'd worked so hard to be everything for him. It felt as though all of that effort had been turned to nothing with a few callous, cruel words.

"I knew kids like this Johnny," Gabe continued, filling the void when she still couldn't speak. "He's going to grow out of his meanness or not, but picking on you is about his problems. You are a great kid. You're smart and clever and persistent to the point of being annoying."

Angi sucked in a breath, which Gabe must have recognized as the admonishment it was because he ran a hand through his hair and said, "I mean that as a compliment. You're not afraid to go after what you want, buddy. You don't do it by tearing people down. You get to work and make things better. That's a skill that a dumb fu—"

He shook his head. "A fool like this Johnny can never understand. Trust me. One thing I learned in the army was how to read people. I can tell you within thirty seconds of meeting a person all I need to know about their character. You have incredible character."

"What's a bastard?" Andrew asked, another knife driven into Angi's already bleeding heart.

"It means a person whose parents weren't married when he was born." All the fury Angi felt was written across Gabe's face. "It doesn't mean anything about you, kid.

That's on the guy who was stupid enough to let your mom walk away."

While she appreciated his valiant effort to put a positive spin on this for both of them, she had to fight her own battles. So she swallowed back her anger and guilt at what her son had experienced, dashed a hand across her cheeks and turned.

"Gabe is right," she told Andrew with as much reassurance as she could muster. "And trust me, I don't say that lightly. I'm not sure where this Johnny character learned that word or why he's chosen to taunt you with it. But it's mean and ugly, Andrew."

"It's true though." Her son's sweet rosebud mouth had turned into a prickly pout.

"You are loved," she said, instead of responding directly. She wouldn't lie to him, but she needed to focus on what was essential at this moment. "You know I love you. And Nonna does, too. You were so loved by your papa, and your uncles think the sun rises and sets by you."

"I'm partial to you despite my best efforts," Gabe added.

To Angi's great surprise, that revelation was the one that made Andrew's stiff shoulders relax the tiniest fraction.

"Your..." Angi hesitated, her breath catching in her chest. She didn't even want to give her ex the honor of using the word *father*. To her, that was earned not by a few minutes of pleasure but by showing up in a child's life. Something that man had not done even once. "He's the one who's missing out, sweetheart. He has no idea how much, and I doubt he ever will. But that's on him. Not you."

She reached out and placed a hand on his knee. "It's also on me for choosing so badly, but it brought you to me so I'll always be grateful. Even if he's a complete idiot."

"Okay," Andrew agreed, and she wondered if part of his

acquiescence was just to shut her up before she lost control and started blubbering all over the place. He shouldn't be dealing with this sort of stuff at his age, and she thought she'd protected him from it by returning to Magnolia where he was part of the Guilardi family, well-known and well loved in town.

But small towns didn't let anyone off the hook, a fact she understood better than most.

"Why didn't you tell the principal or your teacher?" she demanded as Gabe drove forward slowly.

"Dunno," Andrew muttered, and she saw him gazing out the back window.

Gabe gave her a "duh" side glance, and her heart pinched again. Of course, a boy wouldn't want to repeat those awful words out loud. Even in the privacy of the truck's cab, it was as if speaking them made them somehow truer. Real.

She didn't want any of this to be real. The first Christmas since her father had died, and with everything else on her plate, to add this one more heart-wrenching thing was almost too much. What was her tipping point? Or more accurately, her crumbling point—the moment when she just couldn't deal with any of it any longer and she gave up? Gave in.

She opened her mouth to give another lecture on how violence wasn't the answer but snapped it shut just as quickly. She was all out of smart words of advice.

They stopped next to her car and she turned to Gabe first. "Thank you for the ride," she said. "We'll talk about your fighting lessons another time."

"Self-defense," he clarified.

She only arched a brow in response and then shifted to face Andrew. "Let's get this visit to the doctor over, and then we'll stop by Sunnyside Bakery. I'm sure Mary Ellen has some of her famous holiday hot chocolate and ginger-bread cookies."

"Can Gabe come with us?" Andrew asked as he un-buckled his seat belt.

Visits to the bakery were a treat, their special mother and son time. Now her baby wanted to include someone else like it wouldn't change everything. Death by a thou-sand small cuts, Angi thought. Sometimes she wondered if all mothers felt that way.

"Sorry, bud." Gabe spoke the words without inflection. "I've got orders to fill this afternoon. I'm going to be too busy. Take care of your head and leave off the fighting. Johnny Rotten isn't worth it."

Ignoring Andrew's heartfelt sigh, Angi got out of the truck and closed her door without meeting Gabe's stormy gaze again. He pulled away, and she hugged her boy and then led him to the car.

Angi almost texted Emma and canceled their meeting later that night. Although the walk-through at the old mill had filled her with promise, the day had gone way down-hill from there. She thought nothing could be worse than picking up her son from the principal's office after that frightening call. Then she'd had to deal with her mother.

Bianca was incensed at the fact that someone—anyone—had laid a hand on her grandson, and she'd launched into an angry tirade, mostly spoken in Italian. After Andrew had been sent to his room, she'd stomped back and forth across the living room as she wrung her hands and grunted between litanies. Angi had understood about half of what her mom said. She could follow along only when Bianca spoke slowly, but she did catch something about wishing for a plague on the bully and all of his descendants.

If only it were that easy.

In the end, her restlessness and a sense of duty she couldn't seem to shake propelled her out the door while her mother and Andrew settled in to watch their favorite Christmas baking show. She told her mom she was stopping by Gabe's to work on some details for the weekend's shopping extravaganza. Bianca had winked and given Angi a knowing nod of approval, which only added to her guilt.

She drove through the dark town, marveling at how time could pass so slowly even with the shorter days. Neighborhoods were decorated with cheerful lights on houses, some white and others colorful, as well as wire reindeer and blow-up Santas and snowmen. Part of her wished she could fast-forward through all of this—the festivity and cheer so at odds with her mood.

The Wildflower Inn had pride of place in the center of Fig Tree Lane, the prettiest street in town. The house, which was one of the largest in Magnolia, had been transformed into a picture postcard of holiday nostalgia. Although it was difficult to make out in the darkness, large swaths of pine boughs framed the front door, and wreaths with bright red bows adorned every window.

Emma and Cam Arlinghaus had strung lights along the roofline and front porch so that the whole inn glowed like some kind of Christmas beacon ready to welcome guests.

Angi parked in one of the spaces designated for guests and walked around to the back. She knew Emma was hosting a family reunion for a few nights, and Angi was in no mood to play nice with strangers.

Some of her tension dissipated as she entered the inn's

kitchen. Emma had redone the space with granite counters and white cabinets with stainless steel appliances and a six-burner stove plus double ovens on one wall. In many ways, it was the kitchen of Angi's dreams.

It had taken so much to walk away from her family's restaurant this past summer and forge a partnership with Emma. She'd been terrified that she wouldn't live up to expectations. After all, she'd been in her first year of culinary school, after scrimping and saving for tuition money, when she'd gotten pregnant with Andrew. Yes, she'd learned a lot about basic techniques and even more during her time working in a fast-paced New York City restaurant kitchen, but she didn't have a formal degree. Emma hadn't cared. She'd taken a chance on Angi just like she'd taken a chance on the property, and the excitement of truly getting a chance at her dream job had propelled Angi forward.

But it hadn't been enough, not when she owed so much to her mother, and to her father's memory.

She ran a hand along the cool countertop and opened the refrigerator door, smiling slightly as she took in the neat containers of food on the shelves. The Wildflower Inn was a bed-and-breakfast, but Angi also knew it could be a culinary destination for guests.

With a happy whine of greeting, Emma's dog, Ethel, came padding into the kitchen from the front of the house.

"Have you been entertaining guests, sweetheart?" Angi bent down to scratch behind the labradoodle's fluffy ears. Drew had been asking for a dog—or a pet of some sort—for months now, ever since he met Meredith Ventner, the woman who owned and operated the local rescue, Furever Friends.

Angi had said no without hesitation when they'd been in the apartment, not sure how she would add one more responsibility to her already long list of duties. Now it was an even less likely prospect since they'd be living with her mother for several more months. One more option taken out of her hands. A grown woman, and she couldn't even choose whether to adopt a pet.

"Are you and Ethel coming up with a plan for world peace?" Emma asked as she walked into the room. "Looks like a serious conversation between the two of you."

Angi straightened and the dog headed over to her bed in the corner. "I can't get a dog because I live with my mother."

"Based on how I've heard you talk before, you don't want a dog."

Angi scrunched up her nose. "A cat isn't an option either."

"Do you want a cat?"

"That's not the point." She blew out a breath. "The point is I'm thirty years old and I live with my mother."

"Because you're taking care of her," Emma reminded her.

They both turned as Mariella entered through the kitchen door. "Why so serious?" she asked, glancing between the two of them.

"Angi is lamenting the fact that she's currently staying with her mom."

"Not exactly lamenting," Angi said with a sniff.

Mariella nodded. "It's kind of pathetic on paper even if it's for a good reason."

Angi inclined her head as Emma bit back a laugh. "Did you just call me pathetic?" she asked Mariella, horrified to discover tears stinging the back of her eyes.

"She didn't mean it," Emma said quickly.

"I was joking," Mariella confirmed, looking at Angi in shock. "You and I trade jabs. It's what we do."

"Yeah." Angi turned back to the refrigerator and pretended to study the contents. "It was a good one. A joke. Right now, my whole life feels like a joke."

She stiffened as Mariella grabbed her shoulders and turned her. "Um, nope. You aren't a joke. I was making one, apparently badly. I was funnier back when I was drinking. Or at least I thought I was funny. You're handling more right now than most people deal with in a decade. Give yourself a break, sis. If anyone deserves one, it's you."

"You being nice makes me want to cry more," Angi said with a watery laugh. "I must be pretty bad off if you're not throwing verbal jabs."

"What's going on, Ang?" Emma came to stand next to Mariella. "Is it the workload between here and the restaurant? As much as we need you—"

"Drew got suspended today," she said, the words sounding no less awful now than they had when she'd shared them with her mom earlier.

"Not *your* Drew." Emma shook her head.

"No way," Mariella agreed. "That kid is pure as the driven snow."

"For fighting," Angi said with a sigh.

Emma opened the wine fridge tucked under the counter on the edge of the island. "We need to sit down for this."

A chime dinged as the innkeeper pulled out a bottle of pinot grigio. "Start without me. I think the rest of the guests are back from dinner in town. Let me just check on them."

She handed the bottle to Angi and hurried from the room.

"Would it be bad if I started drinking straight from the bottle?" she asked Mariella.

"Been there done that," Mariella answered, grabbing three wineglasses from a cabinet. "Definitely don't recommend it."

The bottle had a screw-on top, and Angi had to admit at that moment she appreciated not having to work for something. She poured the wine and carried two glasses to the kitchen table.

"I didn't mean to upset you," Mariella said with more emotion than she usually displayed. "I know what it's like to have people kick you when you're down."

"Speaking of that…" Angi sipped the dry white. "Can't you petition to have that video of you taken down or something? It doesn't seem right to have one mistake haunt you."

Mariella shrugged and brushed a lock of pale blond hair away from her face. "I don't care at this point. Plus, it's a good reminder of a person I don't ever want to become again."

"Do you watch it?"

"Oh, no. God, no."

Before coming to Magnolia, Mariella Jacob had been one of the biggest names in the fashion world. She'd created a bridal empire and, from what Angi understood, was in the process of inking a deal to expand into ready-to-wear fashion. Then she'd discovered that her fiancé was having an affair with one of her clients. Mariella had shown up to the woman's wedding and made a huge, destructive scene. One that had been recorded by several guests at the ceremony and quickly picked up by tabloids and uploaded to various sites online.

The wedding had been ruined, right along with Mariella's reputation. The following day she'd been fired by the board of directors from the company she founded.

"What would have happened if you hadn't left?" Angi asked the question she'd wondered about since hearing Mariella's story. "What if you'd stayed and fought for your business?"

The blonde traced a finger along the rim of her wineglass without taking a drink. Angi had never seen Mariella finish a full drink.

"I watched it once." Mariella's voice was raw. "The video. And I hated that woman making a spectacle of herself, even more than I hated Joshua for his betrayal."

"The cheating fiancé?"

Mariella gave a tight nod. "I chose to leave. I sold everything of value that I personally owned, and walked away. It wasn't difficult. What has been harder is coming back into the world in any kind of meaningful way, even on a small scale."

"You mean designing dresses for brides who seek you out."

"And working with the brides who've contracted with the inn to plan their weddings."

"Do you need the money?" Angi placed her glass on the table. "Is that why you're doing it?"

"I don't need money. I saved enough to get by. I like weddings. I've been fascinated by brides since I was a kid, and I feel like with the inn there's a certain woman—or couple—who chooses this place as a venue. The type of people I want to help. The Wildflower is special."

"I know," Angi murmured. "That's why I can't quite let go of it yet. Why I'm a grown woman sneaking around like a teenager so my mom doesn't bust me."

"For following your dream?"

Angi looked at the ground. "For not wanting to follow hers."

Emma burst through the swinging door that led to the dining room at that moment.

"Problem?" Mariella asked, arching an eyebrow.

Emma looked between the two of them. "Honestly, I was afraid you two might be at each other's throats."

"We're like peas and carrots," Mariella told her, and Angi laughed in response. It felt good to laugh despite everything. She appreciated these two women. She might have grown up in Magnolia, but it wasn't until meeting Emma that she felt she'd found a true friend. Mariella, too, despite their differences and the friction that sometimes arose between them.

"What have I missed?" Emma asked as she picked up the glass Angi had left for her on the counter.

Angi glanced at Mariella. "Nothing," the blonde said. "We were waiting for you." She met Angi's gaze, her cool blue eyes giving away nothing of the vulnerability she'd just revealed. "Let's figure out how to help your boy," she said, and Angi felt immensely grateful not to be alone.

CHAPTER ELEVEN

THE PHONE ON the shop's counter rang for what felt like the hundredth time that morning. Gabe stared at the ancient rotary dial, wishing his grandmother at least had a device with caller ID installed. Who didn't have caller ID in this day and age?

Not that Gabe needed it to know who was so incessantly trying to get a hold of him.

His mother had been calling nonstop for the past three days, and he'd grown tired of arguing with her. Two older women who'd stopped in on the rainy morning quickly let themselves out of the shop after he cursed out loud at the ringing telephone. He wasn't sure whether to applaud or groan. He'd promised his grandmother a visit to the shop, but he couldn't seem to stop himself from letting it fall to ruin just to piss off his mother.

The phone was blessedly silent for a few seconds and then began to ring again. He grabbed the receiver and barked a terse "What?"

"You can't ignore me, Gabriel." His mother's husky voice, deepened by decades of chain-smoking, was like sandpaper across his soul.

"There's nothing to talk about."

"The bills," his mom said before he heard the deep inhalation of her taking a drag. It was a sound so familiar to him that he could envision the thin plume of smoke rising to the ceiling of her cramped apartment. Plenty of his friends had smoked overseas, but Gabe never took up the habit. Too many bad memories of his childhood, back when he'd been worried about his mother's health. When he'd pour water over her precious packs of Marlboro Lights, risking her wrath in some unrequited hope that she'd finally stop with the cancer sticks.

"I'm taking care of upkeep on the store and Gran's house," he answered, keeping his tone neutral. "Plus paying for the facility. There's no frivolous spending going on." No way would he give her the satisfaction of knowing how much she upset him.

"You're paying her bills with my money."

"With Gran's money."

"Put her in a cheaper place."

"No."

He wasn't going to explain again how Shady Acres was the best facility within fifty miles of Magnolia. Or the fact that Iris had friends who lived there and people she knew in the community who visited. He knew his grandma hadn't planned to remain long-term in the nursing home, yet he couldn't see a way that would change.

When he'd first arrived in Magnolia, she'd told him that she expected to be released at any moment. But it had become apparent that she wasn't in a place to take care of herself or the shop, and although it was clear she struggled with the decision, Iris had agreed to become a long-term resident. He still held out hope she'd recover enough to return to her house.

"Do you know how much Shady Acres costs per month?"

"Insurance covers most of it," he countered. "Gran's savings are good for the rest."

"She's going to drain it so there's no inheritance left for

me other than that stupid flower shop, the one you're supposed to be taking care of. I called Mary Ellen Winkler, Gabe. She told me you haven't even decorated for Christmas and that sometimes you scare away customers. Are you trying to run the place into the ground so the business fails before I get it?"

"I've made a few updates. Besides, you don't want it, Mom."

"I want the money I can get from selling it."

"Gran doesn't own the building."

"The business is worth something," his mother insisted.

That was true, and Gabe had been determined to rejuvenate it when he'd first come to town. At that point, he'd felt he was making it better for his grandmother's benefit. So she would return to a thriving storefront. He'd filled the place with plants and flowers because he knew Iris would be happy surrounded by so much flourishing green.

Then his mother had called for the first time. He'd thought she wanted to check on Gran, but he should have known better. After all, this was the woman who'd accepted money from him, wired when he was abroad still on active duty, to travel from her home in New Mexico to Magnolia in order to be with his grandmother after her surgery.

But she'd never come to Magnolia. Iris had been alone, first in the hospital and then in the rehabilitation wing of Shady Acres until Gabe had finally arrived almost a month after her fall.

Okay, it might be an exaggeration to say she was totally alone. She'd lived in the small town for over half her life and had many close friends. People loved her. But there had been no family. Gabe and Poppy were her only family.

Now his mother was hinting that she anticipated her

own mother's death so she could claim an inheritance and that the money coming to her was more important than Gran's quality of life.

"I'm going to go, Mom," he said flatly. "If you want me to keep the business going so it's worth something to you, I need to work."

"I want her moved to another facility," his mother told him, and his stomach churned with acid. He'd met with his grandmother's attorney, Douglas Damon, shortly after arriving in Magnolia but still knew very little about Iris's will. He'd been granted power of attorney, but if his mom decided to challenge him, it could get messy.

Gabe didn't have time for messy.

"Let's get through the holidays," he said, forcing fake cheer into his tone. "I'll talk to the people at Shady Acres about the money, and if we can't work something out, I'll look at other places." That was a bald-faced lie. If his grandmother was happy at the home, he'd do anything to keep her there.

He also wanted to get Poppy off his back.

"We used to be a team," his mother said.

We were never a team, he thought.

"I love you, Gaby."

Yeah, now that she thought he was giving her what she wanted.

"Goodbye, Mom."

He hung up and fisted both his hands in front of him, trying hard to resist the urge to punch his fist into a wall or hurl a ceramic pot across the store. Anything to get rid of some of the tension curling inside him.

Except he'd just have to clean up the mess, and he had more than his share of those at the moment.

A feminine throat cleared behind him, and Gabe whirled to find Angi standing just inside the shop's entrance.

"You didn't hear me come in," she said, as if that wasn't obvious.

"How much did you hear?"

She lifted one shoulder. "Enough from your end to understand why you've let this place go the way you have." She stepped forward, one long finger trailing over the leaf of a poinsettia. "I don't remember ever meeting your mom during the summers you stayed with Iris."

"Probably because she barely pulled to a complete stop before pushing me out the door." Angi was in her normal uniform from the restaurant—a crisp white button-down and slim black skirt. He imagined she'd left the green apron that completed the ensemble back at Il Rigatone. "Trust me, I'm not complaining. I loved summers here with my grandma and dreaded the day my mom would return to collect me. Sometimes I wished she'd just kept traveling. Why do you look like a waitress today?"

She sniffed. "Because I am one today. Annie took the day off to take her daughter shopping up in Raleigh."

"Is there anything you can't handle?" he asked, feeling his mood lighten ever so slightly.

"This list is long," she answered. "Can you fight your mom for ownership of the shop?"

Cue the return of the black emotions. "I don't know that I want to. The whole purpose of me taking care of things was to make them better when Gran returned. I'm still hoping she can, but the problems with her memory since the accident concern me. Some days it's good, but others are a struggle."

"I saw you here in the summer, Gabe. You were having fun with the shop and that didn't have anything to do with your grandma. What changed other than your mom's interest in the store?"

"That's plenty."

"You promised your grandmother that you'd bring her here for the holiday shopping event."

"I know."

"So…" She gestured around the shop's drab interior. "You have to decorate. That's why I'm here." She glanced at the oversize watch that encircled her wrist. "Only for a minute, actually. I wanted to tell you I'll come by after the lunch shift ends. Well, after lunch and after I check on Andrew."

He lifted a brow. "Is he with your mom for the suspension?"

She gave a tight nod. "He wanted to come to the restaurant, most likely so that he could sneak over to hang out here. There's nothing that feels more like a punishment to a ten-year-old boy than being stuck at home with his grandma with the job to clean the baseboards."

"I'd argue the grandma part, but the baseboards are a nice touch."

"Thanks."

A charged silence fell between them, and Gabe's heart suddenly felt like a flock of birds were fluttering against his rib cage. It was stupid to be so aware of Angi, but he couldn't stop it.

He tried to remember that she didn't belong to him. He didn't want her to be his. He just wanted her help with the store, but no part of him was buying it. Still, he forced himself to remain where he was. "You could have texted me about the decorating date."

Color bloomed in her cheeks, and an answering heat pooled low in his belly. "It's not a date. It's an appointment."

"Still."

She glanced past his shoulder like she couldn't bring herself to make eye contact. "I also wanted to apologize for how I acted yesterday. I know Andrew's suspension isn't your fault."

"It's okay. I understand you were upset."

"Don't let me off the hook," she said, her tone raw with an emotion he couldn't name. "It's like when we were younger, and I was cruel because I wanted to be part of the popular crowd."

"We're not kids anymore, Ang."

She took a step toward him, her dark eyes flashing. "I know, which is why I need to do better. I need to model better behavior for Andrew so he knows he has options other than flight or fight. I don't want him to feel like he has to run away from his life. The way I did."

"You're a good mom," he told her. "Trust me, I know the difference."

He had started to reach for her, unsure which of them needed comfort more, when the bells over the front door chimed.

"Oh, I must have the wrong place," an older woman said, her face falling as she took in the shop's drab interior. Andrew had done his best to help Gabe, but the interior needed more. Way more.

When Gabe didn't answer, Angi gave him a quelling look and then smiled at the potential customer. "What were you looking for?" she asked.

"I thought this was the same little flower shop I stopped in last year at this time." The woman took off her gloves. "I'm driving down to Charleston to see my grandkids, and I bought the cutest ornament and holiday arrangement. My daughter was so tickled by it, I thought I'd make it an annual tradition." She frowned. "But this can't be the same shop."

"It is," Gabe muttered, guilt spiking at him because he'd let his animosity toward his mother change how he treated his grandmother's precious flowers and plants. What could he do about it now?

"We're behind on getting our Christmas stock on the shelves," Angi explained, like the store belonged to her as much as it did him. "The owner had a bit of crisis." She flicked a glance toward Gabe. "The store will be transformed by this weekend."

The customer perked up. "That's good to know. I'm visiting my girl for a few days, then driving back. I could stop in on my way home at the beginning of next week."

"We'd love that," Angi assured her.

Gabe would love no such thing but didn't argue.

"You might even consider bringing your daughter for a visit and staying overnight in town." Angi pulled a business card out of the pocket of her skirt. "The town is having an art walk and shopping event on Friday. All of the shops will be offering promotions and specials. You can do your Christmas shopping right here in Magnolia. Plus, there's a new inn, the Wildflower, that opened this past summer." She handed the woman the business card. "It's amazing."

"She should know." Gabe placed an arm around Angi's shoulder and squeezed. "She's the in-house chef and is fantastic. She's even gotten praise from a US senator."

Angi's body went rigid. "Well, there's no pressure to stay, but at least stop back in to shop."

"I will." The woman nodded, studying the card. "I may even make a reservation."

"That was unnecessary." Angi stepped away as soon as

the door closed behind the customer. "No point in talking up my part in the inn when it's going to end at the beginning of the year."

"Not if you explain to your mom that you're going back."

"You aren't exactly in the best spot to be doling out advice on setting boundaries with mothers."

He inclined his head. "True."

Angi frowned as if she'd expected him to argue. When he didn't, she blew out a breath. "You're annoying, but I'll be here after lunch."

She held up a hand before he could answer. "No arguments, and I'm bringing you a meatball sub."

The relief that flooded him was as strong as a river's current after the spring thaw. "I wouldn't dare argue with meatballs," he told her, earning a small smile as she walked out.

That smile made him feel like he'd accomplished something monumental, which made him a massive fool.

IT WAS NEARLY three before Angi made it back to In Bloom, and she half expected that Gabe would have closed early just to avoid accepting her help.

Instead, she walked into the shop and did a quick pivot as she took in the transformation that had occurred in a few hours.

He'd cleaned up the mess in the corners and on the shelves, and strewn handfuls of tinsel across most every horizontal surface. Several large bins of decorations sat in front of the counter as if they were waiting to be placed.

"Where did all of this come from?" she asked as Gabe straightened from wiping a spot of dried dirt on the floor.

Something about the look in his eyes made her heart

skip a beat. "Also, I brought you a sandwich," she added, holding up the brown bag in front of her to draw his attention.

"Gran's attic," he said with a smile. "After you left this morning, I went to see her. I needed to remind myself why I was doing this and to distance myself from that call with my mom." He straightened. "I admitted to my grandma that I'd let things go with the store because taking care of it felt like I was helping my mom."

He picked up a snow globe only half filled with water and studied it like it offered answers to the great mysteries of life. "I wasn't raised with any sort of religion, but I'm guessing it's what recalcitrant kids feel like going to confession. I stole two cookies from the cookie jar and all that business."

Angi was bowled over by the sincerity in his tone, and also equally amused. "Have you never admitted to any wrongdoing in your life?"

"Not to anyone who mattered."

"Seriously? What about as a teenager? No sneaking out or stealing your mom's liquor." Her voice trailed off as he gave her a "for real?" look.

"You knew me back then. Not only was I not getting into any trouble, my mom wouldn't have cared if I did. Hell, I might have actually made her proud of me."

"Gabe, you served our country. Of course she's proud of you."

"Not even a little. I would have been better off aspiring to a career as a grifter if I'd wanted to impress my mom." He held up a hand when she would have argued. "Let me be clear, I never wanted to try. Gran is a different story."

"Did she offer you absolution and assign penance in exchange for a promise of Christmas decorating?"

"You've got the lingo down."

"Italian on both sides," she said with a laugh. "It's in my blood."

"Gran was sweet and also lucid today, which helped. As far as penance, she wants to come for the downtown shopping event on Friday night. So I have four days to turn the store around and make it the best Magnolia has to offer."

"Tall order," Angi said, whistling under her breath. "Did you see the cute Christmas tree Stuart made out of books?" She stepped closer. "And Lily at the hardware store is doing holiday craft demonstrations that night. Avery and Meredith are helping with the art gallery since Carrie can't be there."

He blinked. "How do you know all of this, and is it your version of a pep talk?" He placed the globe on the counter. "Because you aren't going to be giving Tony Robbins a run for his money anytime soon."

"I'm the festival chairperson. I take my duties seriously." To Angi's immense horror, a yawned stretched her lips, and she quickly tried to stifle it. "Sorry. You didn't see that. Let's get going on these decorations."

"We're the festival *chairpersons*," he reminded her, then reached out and took her hand.

She was so shocked by the gentle touch that she allowed herself to be led around the counter and into the back room.

"You're supposed to share the responsibility with me," he said. "Not take on everything by yourself."

"You found the space for the dance. That's plenty."

"That was nothing and we both know it. Dylan Scott is to thank for that. Or really Carrie, since he'd do anything for her."

"They're a cute couple."

"So are we," he said. "Everyone thinks so."

"We aren't a couple." Heat spiked through her, followed quickly by a cold rush of anxiety because her body reacted to those words, even though she knew he meant them as a joke.

"We're still cute." He released her hand and pushed her down onto the small love seat that was shoved up against the back wall of the office.

"What are you doing?"

"Giving you a break," he said conversationally, as if it were the most normal thing in the world. "When was the last time you had one?"

"I take breaks," she argued.

"Tell me the last time."

"I took a break when my mom had her heart attack," she said, then wrinkled her nose.

"What did you do on that break?"

"I took care of her," she admitted. "No need to gloat."

"I'm not gloating." He pulled up a wooden stool and sat in front of her. Then he lifted her foot into his lap.

Angi had already started to relax into the small couch's soft cushions but immediately stiffened and tried to jerk away her leg. "What the—"

"Relax," he told her, and flipped off the clog she wore during waitressing shifts. "Let me take care of you, just for a few minutes."

"Don't you have boughs of holly to—" She broke off with a moan of pleasure as he pressed his thumb into the bottom of her stockinged foot, kneading the arch. "Oh, that's nice."

"Relax," he said quietly and, despite her misgivings, she did. How could she do anything else when his hands worked their magic on her sore feet. There was nothing overtly sexual about the touch, but it felt intensely intimate just the same. "There was an issue with Gran's decorations."

"She has too much mistletoe?"

Gabe's gaze took on a wolfish gleam, and Angi did her best not to squirm under it. "Just the right amount of mistletoe. But she had most of her newer decorations in the garage in cardboard boxes, some of which have water damage. I'm guessing that corner flooded during the huge storm this summer. I was so busy shoring up the house that I didn't realize it. So now I'm left with the older stuff I found in the attic. Most of the decorations look like they date back to circa nineteen seventysomething or even older. I guess I can drive up to one of the big-box stores in Raleigh and load up on decorations before Friday. I don't think kitschy retro is the theme most businesses in Magnolia focus on for the holidays. Hell, I'm not sure what people do with strings of silver or color wheels."

Angi smiled. "That's tinsel. My mom always complained that it multiplied worse than Easter grass."

"I understood about a tenth of what you said there." Gabe paused in the act of lifting her other leg into his lap.

"You just keep up with the massage." Angi rubbed her hands together. "I think we can work with what your grandmother has on hand. A retro Christmas theme with all of her vintage stuff. Think about how happy it will make her to step back in time and see all decorations she's collected over the years."

He stared at her for a long moment, then looked down at her feet again. She noticed that his fingers trembled as he massaged.

"Gabe, what is it?" She pulled her legs off him and slipped back into her shoes. "What's wrong? If you want to get new—"

"She'll love it," he said gruffly, and she could hear the emotion in his voice. Despite his size, the scruff covering his jaw and his obvious strength, she suddenly had a memory of the sweet, sensitive boy she'd met all those summers ago. The one who seemed uncertain about everything other than how much he loved his grandmother.

"Then we'll make it perfect for her." Angi reached forward and cupped his face in her hands. She held steady until he finally met her gaze. "This isn't about your mother or the future. It's about you and your grandmother."

"Thank you," he whispered, and Angi realized there was no place she'd rather be than in this moment, decorating for the holidays with Gabe Carlyle.

CHAPTER TWELVE

BY THE TIME Friday night came, Angi was running on adrenaline, caffeine and very little else. The week had been a whirlwind of activity.

The afternoon at the flower shop, she'd spent several hours helping Gabe with his grandmother's vintage Christmas knickknacks and trimmings. He'd turned the shop's sign to Closed, put on a classic holiday playlist, and they'd unloaded all of Iris's decorations—from families of plastic snowmen to an original color wheel to boxes of tinsel—to transform In Bloom into a retro festive extravaganza.

Time had flown by in the blink of an eye. She'd gotten used to the hours dragging at the restaurant, a thought that left her unsettled and a little melancholy. Unpacking boxes of glass ornaments had brought back memories from when her dad used to close down the restaurant for a few days over Christmas and drive up the coast in the old minivan to visit her nonna in Connecticut.

She remembered her parents laughing and singing carols—alternating between English and Italian—while her brothers played on their Game Boys in the third row of the big Suburban. Angi loved to look out at the houses she could see from the interstate and draw designs on the car windows when they frosted over.

At that point, she couldn't have imagined living anywhere other than Magnolia.

Sorrow lanced across her heart at the memories of how much her father had loved this time of year. She added one more item to the list of ways she was failing. She'd been so busy subtly resenting having to return to the restaurant full-time and the burden of taking care of her mother that she hadn't considered how her mother was dealing with this first Christmas without her beloved husband. Angi missed her father and his calming presence in all of their lives.

She wished she could talk to her mom about her feelings, to share in their grief and also hopefully grow closer by looking to the future.

Unfortunately, the only future Bianca seemed to care about when it came to Angi was seeing her married. In that respect, her mother would be disappointed when Angi and Gabe broke up in the new year, as was the plan.

A plan she was quickly coming to detest.

"Everything looks beautiful," her mother said. She came to stand next to Angi looking out the front window of Il Rigatone as shoppers began to crowd Main Street. The weather for the evening was perfect, with temperatures hovering in the midforties and clear skies that showed off a swath of stars above them. Angi had asked Malcolm if the town would cordon off the streets so that the shops could spread their displays onto the sidewalk and leave more room for pedestrian traffic.

The business owners and town council had loved the idea, so she, Gabe, Emma and Cam had brought folding tables that the inn used for wedding receptions and positioned them along the center of the street. Now people not only had more opportunity for shopping but also a place to gather in front of each shop or restaurant.

"Thanks, Mom." Angi squeezed her mother's shoulders.

"Dad always loved this time of year. I remember how excited he got when out-of-town visitors would stop in, like he was the official Magnolia welcome committee."

Her mother sighed. "It was hard for him when things slowed during the years of economic downturn, and not just because of trying to keep the business afloat. He missed talking to new people. I'm glad he understood, before his heart attack, that the restaurant was going to survive. I like to think it gave him a sense of peace in his final moments."

"Oh, Mom." Angi's heart pinched as her mother's voice cracked with emotion. "I know you miss him. I do, too." There was something in her mother's tone, a hint of painful acceptance. "Are you sure the restaurant is still your dream?"

Her mother broke away, swiping a hand across her cheek. "Why would you say that, Angela? Your father and I built this place together. It was his dream—our dream— from the start. Now the town is flourishing again and I should just give it up?"

"I'm not saying that." Angi chose her words carefully, not wanting to upset her mother more than she already was. Especially not tonight when there was so much excitement in the air. "I was thinking about those holidays when we drove to Nonna's house. I used to listen to you and Dad talking, and you were always planning for the future. For some distant day when you'd have time to travel. Remember how you wanted to take an Alaskan cruise? It got so bad that Luca bought you bear spray for your birthday as a joke. What about those plans?"

Her mother's eyes went wide. "That was a different time. Yes, I had plans for when your father and I retired. But things changed. The restaurant struggled for several years, and your dad made some investments that..." She sighed. "Taking time off wasn't an option when he was alive, and he worked so hard to bring the restaurant back from the brink of failure. When Dylan Scott threatened to shut us down, it was like a knife to the chest for your dad. Then things changed, but he didn't get to see all of the success. I can't just walk away from it."

"Mom, working so hard is what killed him. I don't want to see the same thing happen to you." Angi didn't mean to say the words out loud. Yes, she'd thought them count-less times since her mother's heart attack. There was no way she could bear the thought of losing both of her par-ents. But if her mother came back to the restaurant as she planned, how would Angi prevent the stress?

"That's why I have you," Bianca said, as if it were that simple.

Angi looked away, out to the street where Emma and Mariella happened to be walking by. She was supposed to go to the inn later for another round of prepping the food for a Sunday baby shower. Emma had installed a small-scale gourmet kitchen in the cottage she'd renovated that sat on the edge of the inn's property, and Angi had been sneaking over late at night to manage her culinary duties.

She didn't want to keep Emma or her guests awake, but she also couldn't use her mother's kitchen to test recipes for the upcoming weddings she was catering. Two events, two weeks in a row. The first was the Saturday before Christmas and the second would take place the following weekend just before the new year.

Of course, Bianca thought Angi was leaving at night to visit Gabe. How much different it would be to spend her nights in a handsome man's warm bed being creative in a totally different way than with food? She nearly sighed at the thought.

"Yes," Angi said, because how else could she respond? "You have me."

Her mother frowned and studied her again. Angi pasted on a bright smile. "I'm going to head over to In Bloom to check out Iris's reaction to the shop."

At the end of the night, Mayor Grimes would announce the winner of the voting for the best-decorated shop. That winner would receive special ad placement on the town's main website and social media sites for the remainder of the holiday season.

"I'll see you there," her mother said, glancing over her shoulder. "I want to check in with Dominic."

"Mom, you're supposed to be enjoying this night, as well. Not trying to come back to work."

"Dom has been with us for over a decade." Her mother tsked softly. "He's a friend as well as an employee. I'm going to visit with my friend."

Angi walked out of the restaurant and took a deep breath of the cool December air. She could smell the popcorn from the machine the hardware store had set up just outside its entrance and saw a line already forming in front of Sunnyside, where she knew Mary Ellen would be serving her famous hot chocolate and s'mores cookies.

There was a cheer to the air, an excitement that made Angi almost want to turn and run the other way. She didn't want to dampen anyone's spirits, and it was getting harder to keep up her energy on all fronts. Every moment she spent at the restaurant felt heavy, like the checked tablecloths were going to suffocate her with the weight of responsibility.

She pulled her jacket more tightly around her and commanded herself to get it together. Since returning to Magnolia and returning to work at the restaurant, she'd felt the silent judgment of the people she knew who thought she'd shamed her family by getting pregnant and coming back to her hometown. But in the past few weeks, she'd been on the receiving end of a new kind of respect. Part of it came from how she was helping her mom, but it also resulted from her ideas and stepping in for the Christmas on the Coast festival.

Carrie had set the bar high last year, but Angi was both balancing it and adding her own twist to things. She wasn't sure why something as inconsequential as a few weeks of festive holiday fun meant so much, but they did.

With a deep, cleansing breath to rid herself of her melancholy, she headed across the street and toward the bakery. Mary Ellen always gave cookie samples, as well as chai tea latte shots during the holidays, and Angi figured the little liquid pick-me-up couldn't hurt.

She'd only made it a few steps before she was wrapped in a warm hug from behind.

"This is amazing," Emma said, resting her chin on Angi's shoulder as she turned both of them so that they were facing the lit street, bustling with shoppers and small crowds of friends. "You are amazing."

"Carrie did most of the work to set it up," Angi answered automatically. It's the line she'd been using all week whenever someone tried to compliment her. It didn't feel right to take credit that shouldn't belong to her.

Emma only hugged her harder. "This is me. I know better than anyone how many last-minute details there are to make an event like this look so effortless."

"It does look good." Angi sighed. "Maybe there's one area of my life that isn't falling to pieces."

"We can find someone to help with the inn over the

holidays," Emma offered without hesitation. "Not as good as you, but—"

"No." Angi turned to face her friend. It didn't matter if she had to mainline caffeine for the next several weeks. She wasn't giving up. "It's fine. I'm fine."

"Fine isn't good enough," Emma said softly.

"It is for now, and tonight I'm amazing. Let's get some sugar."

"A quick stop at In Bloom first?" Emma asked. "I want to pick up a few sprigs of mistletoe for the inn. We have some honeymooners coming in this weekend, and I thought it would be a fun touch for them."

"Sure," Angi agreed, her gaze snagging on a group of kids she recognized from Andrew's school as they headed toward the flower shop. Her son wasn't among the group, but she saw the boy he'd fought earlier that week. The kid still had bruising under his eyes, a fact that made Angi wince. No doubt Johnny's mom was regaling her friends with tales of the fatherless Guilardi boy who needed someone to rein him in.

"Still better than fine?" Emma asked with a sidelong glance.

Angi shook off thoughts of bullies and town gossips. Tonight was about a successful event. "Amazing," she confirmed.

"Just like In Bloom." Emma flashed a grin as they approached the shop, which was adorned with snow-flecked garland and bright red ornaments. "It looks like how my grandma used to decorate." Her smile widened. "My grandma on my dad's side anyway. My mom's family always had professional people to take care of the holidays, but my Grammy did it all herself, just like this."

"These are Iris's original decorations." Angi could see

the people passing the shop pointing and smiling at the bright storefront. Although the kitschy vintage trimmings weren't the traditional decorations someone would expect from a florist, they were unique and unexpected. Much like Gabe, she mused.

Her heart picked up speed as they entered the shop, which was as crowded as she'd ever seen it. In the center of a group of locals, Iris sat in a wheelchair that had been decorated with ribbon and boughs of holly. She wore a red sweater with three festive trees stitched on it, her silver hair pulled back into a neat chignon. She looked so joyful as she spoke to friends and customers. Behind the wheelchair, Gabe stood like a sentry, but even he seemed surprisingly relaxed.

"Hey, Mom," Andrew called from where he stood next to a table of iced cookies from the bakery, a few crumbs dribbling from his mouth.

"Hi, Gabe's mom," the pint-size girl standing next to him shouted.

"Close your mouth when you chew, Violet." Avery sidled over to Angi and Emma as she spoke to the girl. "Your stepmother is raising you with better manners than that."

The girl gave Avery a big thumbs-up and continued to gaze at Andrew like he was her own personal superhero as she took another bite of cookie.

"She's got sass for days," Avery told Angi as Emma greeted a couple who Angi guessed were guests at the inn for the weekend. "It's what I love best about her."

"I'm guessing her stepmom has taught her that, as well." Angi knew the little girl was Gray Atwell's daughter from his first marriage, which made her Avery's stepdaughter.

"I think she was born that way." Avery grinned. "But

I support it wholeheartedly, although remind me of that when our kids are teenagers. I might regret it then."

"I can't imagine Drew as a teenager." Angi's heart flipped at the thought of her boy at that age and then fluttered for a different reason as Gabe waved to her. There was no mistaking the warmth in his gaze, and it made her toes curl with pleasure.

"Andrew's going to be a great teenager, I'm sure. Just like he was this week. It's a bummer about the punishment, but I'll tell you Violet has a regular case of hero worship at the moment."

Angi turned to face Avery more fully. "What are you talking about?" She guessed it had something to do with the scene on the playground earlier that week, but she couldn't imagine how Drew fighting another boy who teased him about his lack of a father could make him a hero to Avery's girl.

"That stupid Johnny kid takes great pleasure in terrorizing the younger kids, but he's sneaky about it. He's got that whole Eddie Haskell vibe going with the teachers, so they don't realize what a snake he is."

She shook her head. "Gray has been coaching Violet on how to handle herself, but I think after Andrew stood up to him, the kid is going to think twice about picking on the other children again. And maybe the teachers will pay more attention, too."

"I don't condone fighting," Angi said even as her mind whirled. Andrew had confessed the ugly comments the other boy made about him, but her son hadn't mentioned other kids being involved. Was it possible she'd missed a key portion of the story?

"Oh, me neither." Avery nodded and then shook her head as if unable to decide which side she fell on. "It shouldn't have come to that, but Violet said Andrew did his best to first use his words to diffuse the situation. I don't know why there are still these unwritten playground rules about not getting teachers involved. They wouldn't stand for it, I'm sure. But that boy said awful things. Violet wouldn't even share some of them, which makes me know they were bad. She did say that it wasn't until Johnny pushed one of her classmates that Andrew stepped in."

Avery wrinkled her nose. "I know fighting isn't right, but your son defended not just himself but several kids who couldn't stand up for themselves. I think he deserves a little hero worship at this point." Her expression cleared as she gestured to some of the decorations. "You deserve a bit of worship, too. Not only have you been a lifesaver with Carrie out of commission, but you just about performed a miracle in this shop. Everyone is talking about it, and Iris is beyond thrilled."

"Gabe did the bulk of the work," Angi said immediately.

"You suck at taking compliments." Avery was far blunter than Emma had been, but the message was the same.

"I'm coming to understand that." Angi shrugged. "Thank you. I've been working my butt off this week, but it's worth it."

"Angela, come over here, dear."

Angi started forward at Iris's gentle command, and it was like the Red Sea parting as people cleared a path.

"I wanted to thank you," the older woman said, reaching out to take Angi's hands. "And not just for my gorgeous nails."

Angi made a show of studying the older woman's gnarled fingers. She'd stopped at Shady Acres earlier to give Iris a manicure that included cheery red polish and a paraffin massage from a kit she'd bought at the local drugstore.

After Gabe's attention to her feet earlier in the week, Angi thought about Iris and how it must feel not to be touched by people other than for clinical purposes.

Not that Angi had a lot of physical attention paid to her, but even at the ripe old age of ten, Andrew would sometimes snuggle up on the couch to watch a movie and he always wanted a good-night kiss and hug from both his mom and his grandmother.

So Angi had spent an hour she didn't really have massaging Iris's hands and then painting both of their nails. She'd hoped it would make Iris feel special.

"Your nails are as festive as you tonight," Angi told her. "Your grandson did an excellent job with the shop, as well."

"With your help," Iris said, glancing up at Gabe and then back to her. "The two of you make a wonderful team."

Yes, they did, she thought. More than she would have liked.

"I was honored to help." She squeezed Iris's hands once more and stepped to the side, aware of everyone's attention on her. Should she move closer to Gabe or keep her distance? She had to remind herself that they had a pretend relationship to maintain and her feelings weren't supposed to be real.

Heat crept into her cheeks as she smiled at Gabe and moved closer to him. He studied her for a long moment, like he was as unsure as she was about how they should handle this very public moment. Then he took her hand and linked their fingers together. The touch both energized and grounded her.

"You're under the mistletoe," Iris said as she pointed toward the ceiling.

Angi glanced up to see a sprig of mistletoe dangling above the two of them. She should have realized it was there. After all, she'd helped to hang it and she'd delivered similar boughs to other stores along Main Street, spreading a bit of holiday cheer from In Bloom.

It had been nearly a week since he'd kissed her. All that time they'd spent together decorating, and he hadn't made one move to draw her close.

The worst part was she'd wanted him to. Oh, how she'd wanted that. Even though it was stupid and pointless and would only lead to complications down the road. At least one of them was mindful of keeping their relationship on a level where it was only on display when it mattered. When they had something to prove.

Which Gabe apparently did now because he released her hand and lifted both of his to cup her face. His gaze was the color of an angry sea tonight, proof that his mood was just as stormy.

"You can't argue with mistletoe," he said with a secret half smile, and then he pressed his lips to hers. It was as if the people in the store disappeared in an instant and only the two of them remained. Angi couldn't have focused on anything else if she'd tried. Gabe took over—his touch an assault on her senses. His mouth was warm and gentle. He didn't go overboard with the kiss, but it was more than a simple peck. It was a kiss that gave a message, and the message was clear enough in Angi's mind.

Mine.

He ended the kiss too soon—it was just for show, after all—and Angi locked her jelly knees before she did something stupid like stumble into him.

"Blame it on the mistletoe," someone called out, and

Gabe offered a smile that looked suspiciously like one of a cat who'd just feasted on the canary.

Angi forced a breezy laugh, then turned away to talk to some of the locals she knew in the store. After a few minutes of fielding questions about her mom's health and the plans for the holiday dance, which apparently was already generating great interest within the community, she excused herself and made her way to where Andrew still stood near the cookie table, Violet Atwell glued to his side.

She thought about the details Avery had shared regarding the circumstances of Drew's fight at school. Why hadn't he told her those specifics? Would it have mattered?

"I only ate two cookies," he announced as if he knew she was coming to admonish him. The universal role of a mother—setter of limits, destroyer of fun. Angi had never had the option of taking a break from that duty. There was no one else to step in.

She wondered if she'd feel so much pressure to be on all the time if Andrew's father was in the picture. If she had someone to share the responsibility—the endless worry of parenting.

Giving his shoulder a tiny squeeze, she smiled at Violet. "I bet if you and Violet head over to the restaurant, Nonna will find the extra wedding cookies for you. Dom made a special batch for tonight."

"They're even better than the ones from the bakery," Andrew told his new friend, clearly enjoying the idol worship he was receiving from her.

"I'll ask Avery," Violet said, then disappeared through the crowd.

"So you know Violet from school?" Angi asked, picking up a corner of a cookie that had broken off and popping it into her mouth.

Andrew nodded. "She's not a baby or anything."

"She seems to like you a lot."

Andrew looked up, his big brown eyes clearly conveying a "duh" sort of message.

"I heard the situation with that boy earlier in the week involved a couple of the kids from Violet's class."

"Johnny is a butthead," Drew muttered.

"You can't use that word."

"Nonna calls him that."

Angi hid her smile. "I'm telling your grandmother the same thing."

"You kissed Gabe."

She blinked. Should have seen that one coming. "It was the mistletoe," she explained. "It's tradition. I'm sorry if it upset you, sweetie. I—"

"I like Gabe," he told her. "It's weird to see him smile so much."

Angi followed her son's gaze to the front of the shop where Gabe was ringing up a purchase and, indeed, smiling at the customer.

"It's a nice smile," she said, more to herself than Andrew.

"Yuck." The boy made a face. "That's so mushy."

"I'm not mushy." She bent down and tickled his belly. "You're mushy."

His laughter rang out, a balm to her weary soul. It had been too long since she'd heard him laugh.

Maybe this night could be a new start. Hope bloomed like a delicate flower in the shadowy corners of her heart. Was tonight's success proof that Angi was on the right track and taking the first step toward living up to the potential she believed she possessed? And what would the next few weeks bring?

CHAPTER THIRTEEN

MINE.

The word haunted Gabe for the rest of the night. He'd kissed Angi under the mistletoe at his grandmother's urging after he'd spent the better part of the week resisting the desire to do just that.

Every time he was near Angi, he wanted to draw her into his arms. So many things made her irresistible to him—her beauty and the way she cared so much for the people around her. The scent of citurs that enveloped her like a warm, sunny day.

The kiss shouldn't have meant anything. They were pretending to date. Did that kind of public display of affection even count? It was mistletoe, after all. But pressing his mouth to hers after so many instances of holding himself back had felt like coming home.

How was it possible that after holding on to resentment for most of his adult life—the sting of how she'd turned on him when their friendship had meant the world to him—now it was as if all of the years had disappeared? He was back to where he'd started. Gabe a lovesick schoolboy and Angi the bright star of whirling activity shining her light on everyone she met.

But they weren't kids anymore, and he'd do well to remember that. Whatever their connection, he had no doubt she'd sever the cord once the holidays were over and she no longer needed him as a diversion. It made his heart ache, which made him feel like the biggest fool on the planet.

Tonight had been the first time he'd seen Andrew since the day the kid had gotten in a fight at school. Gabe hated to admit how much he missed the boy's chatty presence at the shop in the afternoon, the way Andrew's energy was so similar to his mother's. Angi hadn't talked any more about the incident or asked what exactly Gabe's lessons to her son entailed. Her silence spoke volumes. He wanted to ask, but it wasn't his business. A stark reminder that their relationship was just for show.

Still, she'd helped him in the shop, and, without even telling him, she'd gone to the nursing home to make his grandmother feel special with the mini spa day. How was he supposed to resist that kind of inherent sweetness?

He'd hoped to have a few minutes alone with her after the event ended, but she'd kept herself busy and made sure there were always people around them. The other business owners were ecstatic at the turnout, and he'd heard lots of talk about anticipation for the upcoming dance. He'd made sure to stay in the background as Angi received the praise she deserved, and he hoped this shot of confidence would make her see her true worth.

The doorbell rang, and his gaze flicked to the clock on the cable box that sat below the TV. Two minutes to midnight. He couldn't imagine who would be at his grandmother's door at this hour, but he got up and padded down the hall.

There were plenty of places he'd been in the world where he wouldn't dare open his door without confirming who stood on the other side.

Magnolia wasn't one of those.

Still, his heart seemed to pummel his rib cage as he took

in Angi standing on his porch. She'd changed out of the navy sweater dress she'd worn to the shopping night. The one that had smoothed over her gentle curves and dipped in the front, revealing only a modest amount of skin but managing to take his breath away just the same.

Yet here she was in a pair of baggy camo print leggings and an overlarge sweater with the words Good Vibes Only stitched across the front, her dark hair piled into a messy bun on the top of her head. His breath hitched in that familiar way. He didn't think his reaction to her would ever change.

"Were you asleep?" she asked, crossing her arms over her chest like she was gearing up for an assault.

He shook his head. "Watching an old movie."

She rose on tiptoe to glance past him into the house. "What movie?"

"Die Hard." He ran a hand through his hair. "It's a Christmas movie."

Her mouth twitched. "Yippee-Ki-Yay."

Just the hint of her smile could melt his heart. "Is something wrong?"

"No. Can I come in?" She looked ten kinds of uncomfortable making the request, and he realized he was showing a subtle lack of manners by leaving her standing there in the first place.

"It's nearly midnight," he said, but stepped back to allow her to enter.

She looked at that oversize watch she always wore. "A minute past now. I've never been in your grandma's house."

He flipped on the hall light he hadn't bothered with when answering the door. Standing in the intimacy of a darkened house with Angi might be too much of a temptation, even for Gabe.

But the light didn't help at all because she was so close that he could see the smattering of freckles across the bridge of her nose and a bit of white powder—flour, he guessed—near her jawline.

His fingers itched to brush it off, but he kept his hands to himself.

Mine.

The word ricocheted through him again, but he ignored it.

Angi Guilardi did not belong to Gabe.

"Do you want a drink?" he asked, because that's what people did when a guest arrived.

"No, thanks." She followed him down the hall and into the cozy den situated off the kitchen. His grandmother's house had been built in the 1940s and had the small, choppy rooms indicative of architecture in that decade. In the months he'd spent living there, Gabe had come up with an imaginary plan for updating the house that involved knocking out walls and redoing the plumbing and electrical.

Ridiculous musings because the house didn't belong to him. Not to mention that it would be easier and probably less expensive to buy something that was more in line with his taste anyway. Gran's decorating style consisted mainly of floral wallpaper and delicate lace doilies covering every surface.

Still, if he had the opportunity, he'd make this house his own. It was the only place that had ever felt like home to him. Plus, the greenhouse and gardens out back were incredible.

The television glowed blue in the darkness and then burst into a bright yellow shine when Bruce Willis blew up something.

Gabe reached for the lamp on the side table, but Angi's hand on his arm stilled his movement. "Leave it," she said, then took a seat on the sofa, patting the cushion next to her. "I haven't seen this movie in ages. Look at how handsome he was back in the day."

Unsure what to make of her appearance at his house, like they were old friends who'd made a plan to hang out in the wee hours of the night, Gabe lowered himself next to her, careful their bodies didn't touch.

He'd learned plenty about self-discipline during his years in the military, but even he had his limits.

They watched the movie in silence for several minutes, but Gabe wasn't paying a bit of attention. He was hyper-aware of Angi next to him...her heat, the scent of citrus, and the soft rhythm of her breathing. Without trying, he matched his breath to hers. Slowly his heart stopped feeling as though it was attempting to fling itself out of his body.

Maybe this was what normal people did.

"I'm supposed to be here tonight," Angi said during a lull in the action.

He kept his gaze on the TV. "Yeah?"

"When we finished downtown, I had to go to the inn and prep food for a bridal shower tomorrow," she explained. "My mom thinks I leave at night to come over here."

"How often does that happen?" It wasn't exactly a surprise. She'd told him that part of the benefit of a fake relationship for her was to have an excuse to work on the Wildflower Inn events without drawing suspicion.

"Three nights this week." She shifted, tapping a finger on the top of her thigh.

He commanded himself not to look at her shapely leg.

Not to think about having her wrapped around him, heat and desire. No desire. Desire was bad.

"No wonder you're exhausted," he said, and now he did look at her. "Wait. Did you come over here for another foot massage?"

Out of the corner of her eye, he saw her shake her head. And he waited. There was something more. The air around them crackled with anticipation, like a tree in the early-morning hours of Christmas before even the most dedicated of children had woken from their fitful dreams.

"The kiss in the shop tonight…"

His breath hitched. She was going to tell him to keep his grubby paws to himself or at the very least to limit their public displays to a few perfunctory kisses that would make people believe the ruse. He'd had no right to—

"I liked it," she continued. "Probably more than I should have."

"Is there a limit on how much a person can like a kiss?"

She turned to him with a soft laugh. "It felt like you liked it, too."

"Yep." He kept his eyes glued to the television.

Anticipation infused his veins with a heat he couldn't deny. He thought that if he allowed himself to look at Angi in this moment he might actually burst into flames of need.

"I guess I'm here because I was wondering if you'd like to do it again, more even."

Now he couldn't resist shifting to face her. "More?"

"You know," she insisted. "Doing more, only with fewer clothes."

"Does this have anything to do with proving something to your mother?"

Angi made a face so disgusted he almost laughed. "Lord, no. The stuff I want to do with you…" Her voice grew husky. "To you...has nothing to do with anyone except us."

"Why?"

"Because I'm not a sicko."

He chuckled even as a voice inside his desire-addled brain gave the imperative command to shut the hell up. "I mean, why do you want more than what it will take to keep people convinced that we're an actual couple?"

Her gaze dropped to her lap. "I just... I like you."

Well, as declarations of desire went, it was fairly simple, but it made Gabe feel like he'd just won the lottery. He shouldn't care if Angi Guilardi liked him. He'd gotten over his silly crush on her years ago.

But it mattered. She mattered.

"It would only be for now," she added quickly. "During our arrangement. I don't expect... There are no expectations beyond what we've already agreed upon. I just thought—"

He leaned in and claimed her mouth, giving some of that frenzied need an outlet for escape before it burned him to ashes. "No more thinking," he murmured against her lips, and she seemed more than happy to oblige.

There was none of the hesitancy he'd felt from her when they had an audience. She met him stroke for stroke, her elegant fingers raking through his hair and pulling him even closer. Pulling him down as she lowered herself to the sofa.

SHOWING UP AT Gabe's house might have been the best decision Angi had made in months. Chances were she'd regret it tomorrow morning. But morning seemed like a long, distant, faraway place.

What mattered now was the moment and the way her body was zinging to life with every kiss, every touch of his hands. She needed something to take her mind off all the things weighing on her, and trading those worries for the comforting weight of Gabe's body over hers was the best way she could think of to achieve just that.

No more thinking.

Just the moment.

He slid one hand up and under her shirt as he trailed kisses along her jaw. To her surprise, Gabe was a talker, and she loved the little murmurs about her beauty and what she made him feel that accompanied his attention to her body.

She trailed her fingers over his broad shoulders and the muscled planes of his back, but it wasn't enough. The thin fabric of his shirt and her sweater suddenly felt like ten layers of fabric and she wanted more of him. Needed his warmth to heat all her cold, forgotten parts.

As soon as she tugged on the hem of his shirt, he levered himself off her and yanked it over his head. Oh, yes. That was much better. The muscles of his arms bunched as he held himself over her once more. She'd known he was fit and had guessed at his muscled physique, but seeing it with her own eyes made her limbs grow heavy with desire.

His mouth quirked at one end, and at the same time his cheeks colored a brilliant shade of pink.

"You're blushing," she told him, using her elbows to prop herself up on the cushion behind her.

"I don't think anyone has ever looked at me the way you are." His grin widened. "I like it."

Maybe Angi should feel embarrassed that she'd been caught ogling him, but at this point she could not have cared less. She might not be the most confident in her life choices, but she was no shrinking violet. It had been a long time since she'd been with a man, and she couldn't remember ever wanting someone the way she did Gabe.

There was no apology or shame in that desire, and she knew he was telling the truth. He liked her asserting control, and she liked him even more for that.

She pulled off the sweater, leaving her in just the simple black bra she wore under it. If she'd planned better, she'd be wearing some lacy confection meant to entice her partner, but by the intensity of Gabe's gaze on hers, he was plenty enticed.

He moved toward her again slowly, like he wasn't sure if he would scare her away.

But her fear had been drowned out by desire and had no place in what was between them now. He trailed kisses along the length of her neck, and she moaned low in her throat when his hands cupped her breasts, thumbs grazing over the hard nipples. Her head fell back against the cushion. It took too much strength to hold it up. Strength she was using to keep herself in check so she didn't fall over the edge from just the simple touch of his hands on her breasts.

Clearly, she was more desperate than she'd even realized.

Or maybe it was Gabe and the way he seemed to intrinsically know how to touch her in a way that made her want to writhe with pleasure. She tried—and mostly failed—to stay patient and let him go slow with her.

A part of her appreciated that he seemed content to take his time. Slowly drawing his tongue across her bare skin before peeling the bra strap down her arm and drawing one hardened peak into his mouth. His tongue swirled around her and her core pulsed with need.

Now, she wanted to shout. *More. Right now.*

But she was no green girl, and she'd had enough sub-par experiences with the opposite sex to savor a man who knew what he was doing.

He was still talking, more to himself than her, she thought. Words of praise and explicit whispers of what he wanted to do to her. With her.

She was a big heck yes to all of it.

"This couch is too narrow," he said suddenly, and she wanted to protest aloud when he released her.

Apparently, she waited too long to answer, because Gabe took her hands, pulled her up off the couch and then lifted her into his arms. He kissed her as he moved, and it was a wonder he didn't trip over anything.

"I can walk," she told him, tearing her mouth from his as he started up the stairs. Angi was tall and solid, not in any way the kind of woman men carried around like some kind of romance novel heroine of old.

"If you think I'm letting you go now," Gabe said, taking the stairs two at a time like he hefted women into his arms all the time, "you haven't been paying attention to the last few minutes."

"I was distracted," she said, and leaned in to nibble on his ear.

He let out a hoarse grunt and wrapped his arms more tightly around her.

She liked being held by him way too much.

The hallway was dim, lit by a flickering night-light at the end of the hall, but she could make out some kind of floral-pattern wallpaper, and the scent of baby powder and butterscotch hung in the air. It reminded her that this wasn't his house. It belonged to his grandmother, and Gabe was here temporarily.

That should have made her feel better. She'd told him

she wanted something temporary. Somehow, the thought dimmed the light glowing inside her ever so slightly.

Gabe paused just inside the bedroom door. "Are you okay?" he asked, shifting her so she had no choice but to meet his gaze. Angi hated the flicker of doubt she saw there. Hated that he could probably see the same thing reflected in her eyes.

She blinked it away and kissed him again, letting his spicy scent remind her of why she wanted this. But it wasn't just his smell or the heat of his body enveloping her. It was Gabe and the fact that he could pick up on the slightest nuance of her emotions. And that he would pause—and stop if she needed him to—to ask her about it. To make sure she was still with him.

That made her all in with him.

"I'll be better when we're both naked," she said, letting the need rise to the surface again.

The look of outright adoration that flashed in his gaze made a shiver pass through her.

He drew back the comforter and sheets and lowered her to the bed. What in the world was wrong with Angi that the fact that he made his bed meant something to her? In truth, too many things involving Gabe meant something. As he straightened to unbutton his jeans, she hooked her thumbs into the waistband of her leggings and pushed them down over her hips.

His stormy hazel gaze never left hers as he stripped off the jeans along with the boxers, putting the evidence of how much he wanted her on full display. The way her core seemed to ache in response had her breath catching in her throat.

He took a condom wrapper from his wallet and tossed it onto the nightstand. She automatically lifted her arms as he bent toward her, wanting to draw him closer. Needing his weight on top of her like she was a ribbon in a hurricane-force wind and he was the anchor that could tether her to this moment.

He kissed her—or she kissed him—it was difficult to say who led this charge. All she knew was she was ready to lose herself, and she knew without a doubt that she could hurtle over the edge and Gabe wouldn't let her fall.

She ran her fingernails along the taut muscles of his back, and he groaned in response. His calloused palm smoothed a path down the length of her and then up again until one clever finger dipped into her center.

"Yes," she said on a small cry and then pressed her lips together, embarrassed at the need in her voice.

Gabe, who was trailing wet kisses along her throat, lifted his head. His hand stilled, making her want to groan out a protest. "Don't stop," he urged, his voice rough with desire. "Tell me what you want, Ang."

"You seem to know what to do," she answered. "More of that."

His mouth quirked. "Tell me anyway. I want to hear it from you, sweetheart. I want to give you exactly what you need."

She squeezed shut her eyes when tears threatened. So silly to get emotional at a time like this. But when was the last time anyone had given her total control? When someone in her life had been completely focused on her needs and wants?

She couldn't remember ever feeling so powerful.

It gave her the freedom to do exactly what he asked. In murmured commands she told him how she wanted to be touched. She set the pace—more, yes, there, faster—and Gabe seemed eager to obey.

He drove her to the edge of reason and then over to a release more powerful than anything she'd ever felt. And just as she expected, he was there to catch her, holding her steady and pressing his mouth to hers as if he wanted to capture every one of her moans.

Then he ripped open the condom wrapper, but she covered his hand, plucking the condom from his fingers and wrapping her other hand around his length. She stroked it once, twice, and felt a tremble shiver through him as his head dropped to her shoulder.

"We're not going to get to the good stuff if you keep that up," he told her, his voice raw.

She liked that she had that effect on him.

"It's all good," she said. She rolled the condom onto him and then pushed him onto his back, straddling his lean hips.

He looked up at her with those stormy eyes, and she lifted herself enough to take him inside her. He was a perfect fit.

They began to move together, and it felt better than anything she could have imagined. His thumbs grazed over her nipples again, driving her wild with need.

It could have been minutes or hours as she lost herself in the way this man made her feel.

She tumbled into another release, stars exploding behind her eyes. Gabe's hips bucked again as pleasure claimed him. Then he wrapped his arms around her and whispered her name like it was the most beautiful word he'd ever heard.

Angi wasn't sure what came next, but she curled into his embrace while he placed gentle kisses on her head like she was precious to him. She understood that whatever was between them would change her—had changed her. From this moment on, Angi would never be the same.

CHAPTER FOURTEEN

LATER THAT WEEK, Angi waited near the loading dock at the old mill. Gabe had found a rental company about an hour away that was willing to donate a portable stage and parquet floor they could use for the big dance.

She appreciated his dedication to the cause, although she felt strangely nervous around him again after the night spent in his arms. Neither had talked about the intimacy, and she was unsure where it left their relationship. All she knew for certain was she liked him way more than she should.

The latest donation was a huge savings and would mean nearly a thousand more dollars could be donated to the local charity instead of using ticket revenue to cover their costs for the event. She'd visited Carrie yesterday to go over their progress on all of the Christmas on the Coast activities and felt so proud when the soon-to-be mom had cried happy tears at everything Angi and Gabe were accomplishing.

That almost made up for the fact that she was relying even more this week on caffeine and sheer willpower as she continued to try to balance all of the things on her to-do list.

A car door slammed, and she stepped to the edge of the open door, waving Mariella to that side of the building. The shop owner had offered to meet Angi today to help put together the stage and make a plàn for decorating the large space. She had an intrinsic eye for design, and Angi appreciated not having to handle every last detail on her own.

"This place is creepy," the cool blonde commented as she approached, pulling the sides of her camel-colored trench coat more closely around her. It amused Angi that Mariella thought she blended in with the small town of Magnolia. To Angi, her friend gave off big-city fashionista vibes for days with her wedge-heeled boots and trendy tattered jeans.

Although they still liked to tease and banter, for the most part the animosity that had bloomed between them like an aggressive weed when they'd first met had all but disappeared. At this point, Angi couldn't even remember why the hostility had started, but she was relieved not to deal with it any longer.

"Are you sure it's the right place for a holiday event?" Mariella mock shuddered. "I'm getting definite horror-movie vibes."

"Dylan said they've just about inked the deal to lease the space to a sportswear company. This time next year, it will be unrecognizable. And with your help, we're going to transform it into a Christmas on the Coast winter wonderland."

"What company?" Mariella came to stand next to Angi, obviously examining the empty mill with new eyes.

"It's called The Fit Collective," Angi told her. "We met the new CEO. I think he's a friend of Dylan's or something."

"Interesting. I know that brand. They make a quality product, but the founder went off the rails at one point. More out of control than me, even. She made a big deal about being a woman-owned business and then said some awful things about her female clients and whether they actually deserve to wear Fit Collective apparel. Capped off with a tone-deaf remark about needing thigh gap to wear her leggings."

"Oh, that's bad." Angi made a face. "I didn't hear any of the history."

"The brand took a hit." Mariella tapped a finger on her chin. "I guess they're trying for a new start or at least a second chance. I can appreciate that."

"Does it give you any ideas?" Angi asked. "You design the most beautiful wedding gowns I've ever seen. You made women feel beautiful."

Mariella's gaze took on a faraway look. "I liked that part of it. Women should feel beautiful." She bit down on her lower lip and glanced around before turning to Angi. "Can I tell you a secret?"

"Absolutely."

"I've started making dresses again," she said quietly, as if the words might echo off the walls if she spoke in a normal tone.

"You're going back to the fashion business? Your studio in New York City?"

"No," Mariella said almost aggressively. "I'm a one-woman shop."

"Is there money in that?" Angi asked.

"Not exactly," her friend admitted with a frown. "But there's more satisfaction than I would have guessed. I like designing, but I forgot how much I like the sewing part, as well. My social life isn't exactly thriving, so working on one dress at a time gives me something productive to do at night."

"Because vegging in front of the television isn't an option?"

Mariella shook her head. "Not for me. It's hard to be still. The only time I was good at it was when I was high or drunk, and I'm not going back there again."

"Oh, well, I guess that's a positive."

"I guess," Mariella agreed with a harsh laugh. "Not all of us can be as perfect and strong as you."

Angi made a show of glancing around. "Who are you talking about? I'm not perfect. Far from it. You've seen me at some of my worst moments. Hiding behind a door at the inn to avoid my mom. Sneaking out of her house at night even though I'm a grown woman. You have a pretty messed up version of strong and perfect if I'm your benchmark."

"Maybe *perfect* wasn't the right word," Mariella admitted. "But I stand behind *strong*. You're a fantastic mom—"

"Debatable."

"And a wonderful, dedicated daughter."

"Did you miss the part about me sneaking around because I'm too cowardly to stand up to my mother?"

"You're a good person," Mariella said, her tone going somber in a way that had the little hairs on the back of Angi's neck standing on end. "I hated you for it at first."

Angi wasn't sure how to respond and so asked the first question that came to her mind, "Is that why we didn't get along? I probably shouldn't have played into that narrative, but it was kind of nice to have an outlet—even misguided—for all of my anger."

Before Mariella could answer, her eyes went wide with alarm like she'd seen a ghost. "No, no, no, no," she whispered, color draining from her face.

Angi reached out a steadying hand and then turned to see Alex Ralsten, Dylan's friend or at least his soon-to-be tenant, walking toward them from the back of the building.

She knew from Dylan that the native New Yorker had been spending more time in Magnolia in preparation for The Fit Collective's big move. He'd even gotten the company to agree to make a sizable donation to the dance as a sponsor when she'd explained the goodwill it would foster within the community.

He was looking down at his phone, punching in something on the screen with his thumb. As if he could sense the tension coming from Mariella, he looked up with a start, and the device clattered to the concrete floor.

Angi cringed as she glanced down and saw that the screen had shattered.

If Alex noticed, he didn't react. He bent with stiff movements to pick up the phone, and when he straightened again his features were devoid of any emotion.

The same could not be said for Mariella.

"What's wrong?" Angi asked, shifting toward her enemy-turned-friend like she was the other woman's protector.

"I can't…this isn't…he shouldn't be…"

"Well, this is a small world," Alex said with a sardonic smile. "Or a small town at least."

"Why is he here?" Mariella spoke to Angi, but her gaze remained locked on Alex.

"He's the CEO of the company I told you about."

"No," Mariella repeated. "Why?" she demanded.

"I needed a change," he said with a dismissive shrug. "I assume you can understand my motivation for that."

"You had to know I was here." Mariella lifted a hand to her throat, gripped the scarf she wore like it was choking her. "I spent most of the wedding weekend avoiding you."

Angi studied the handsome man. His features remained neutral, but there was a flush of pink across his cheeks and the bridge of his nose, and she noticed he gripped the shattered phone so tightly his knuckles had turned white.

He'd been a guest at the first wedding hosted at the Wildflower Inn, the best man of the groom, a US senator from a lauded political dynasty. To be honest, Angi hadn't paid much attention to Alex. He was undeniably handsome but far too polished for her. Mariella hadn't mentioned knowing him or what their shared background was, but Angi did not like seeing her usually unflappable friend in this kind of state.

"Are you suggesting this town isn't big enough for the both of us?" Alex demanded, his full mouth curled into a slight sneer.

Angi took a step forward and held up a hand. "I don't think we need to resort to a Wild West standoff. I'm sure whatever—"

"I'm saying I want you to pick somewhere else." Mariella's tone had gone from upset to outright desperation. "Please."

"You can't always get what you want. I definitely wouldn't have chosen for an angry, unhinged drunk to interrupt my wedding and reveal my fiancée's infidelity in front of two hundred of our closest friends and family." He inclined his head. "You did it anyway, Mariella."

Suddenly the strain between the two of them made complete sense. Angi hadn't watched the viral video of Mariella storming into the church during a famous client's wedding to confront the woman who had been conducting an illicit affair with Mariella's own fiancé.

The scandal was bad enough, but the obscenity-filled speech Mariella had delivered while clutching the neck of a wine bottle had been caught on camera. Although the bride was guilty of cheating, she'd launched a media blitz to ruin Mariella's reputation and erode the trust her clients and potential customers had in her. Mariella's company, Belle Vie, was one of the premier wedding dress design studios in the world. She'd just taken the company public, and the new board had wasted no time in firing her.

"I sent you a note of apology," Mariella answered, looking away as Alex's eyes narrowed.

"Apology not accepted," he muttered. "I don't particularly give a rat's ass whether you want me in Magnolia or not, and I could give even less of a care about your feelings. I've become an expert at avoiding things I don't like since my wedding day, and trust me, you're at the top of the list. As far as I'm concerned, we can go back to being strangers."

Mariella squeezed shut her eyes for a long moment, and Angi's heart ached when a single tear leaked out. She knew her friend wouldn't want to break down in front of Alex—or anyone—but sometimes trying to hold back the emotions was impossible.

"You should go," Angi told Alex, facing him fully.

His dark brows lowered. "You realize I'm running the company that's sponsoring your little town dance."

The tone he used expressed clearly that Alex Ralsten wasn't a man who was used to being told what to do.

"Yes," she said slowly, trying to tamp down her temper. "I also know my friend needs you gone right now. Magnolia may be big enough for both of you, but it's going to get uncomfortable quickly if you make it hard on her."

Alex shook his head as he glared at Angi. During the first meeting at the mill, he'd been charming and affable, but it was clear the man had his own demons to contend with, and many of them involved Mariella.

Still, he didn't argue. "I'll go for now, but you can't get

rid of me or shame me into leaving. I picked this place, and I intend to stay."

As he turned on his heel and stalked away, the sound of his boots on the concrete echoed in the ensuing silence.

Angi gave Mariella a moment before turning back to her. The blonde still looked like she'd just been sucker punched in the gut, but her eyes were clear of tears. "How can he be here?" she asked, her voice just as miserable as it had been earlier. "I left my past mistakes behind."

"No," Angi said, shaking her head. "You can never really run from the past, hon, even in those fancy heels you like to wear. If you don't deal with things, the past lives inside you, which is almost as damaging as having it come for you outright."

Mariella dashed a hand across her cheeks, as if she could still feel the tears there. "I'm not sure anything could be worse than the thought of having to see Alex on the regular."

The sound of a truck engine had them both looking toward the edge of the parking lot. Gabe drove in, pulling a trailer loaded with supplies for the stage. Angi could see Cam in the passenger seat. The local furniture maker had offered to help on the construction end of things.

She glanced at Mariella. "If you need some time, we can handle this without you. I can get things in the basic locations, then you can come back when—"

"I'm here now." Mariella took a deep breath as she stared at the far end of the space, where Alex had disappeared. "I might not want to deal with Alex, but he's not going to chase me away. Not yet."

Angi reached out an arm and hugged Mariella to her. "Never, if I have anything to say about it."

"You're better at this friend thing than I would have thought," Mariella told her with a muffled laugh.

"I like you as a friend more than I would have guessed," Angi answered with a wink.

Mariella flashed a smile, which felt like a victory, and they headed toward the front of the building together.

GABE WALKED INTO the flower shop that afternoon and heard the telltale sound of grunting and smacks against the punching bag he'd hung in the back. He exchanged a glance with Maybelle, the young woman he'd hired to help run the shop when he couldn't be there.

"I told the kid he should wait until you came back," she said by way of an explanation.

"And yet…"

"He's stubborn for such a little squirt." Maybelle held up a printed order form. "Good news, though. I've got another stack of orders. This vintage Christmas thing you've got going is a hit."

Gabe smiled as warmth infused him. He thought about how his grandmother would react when he told her, and his smile grew. Until he heard a guttural yell from the back room. An older couple, browsing for gifts in the corner, gave him an alarmed stare.

"All good," he said. "He's rehearsing for the Christmas pageant and those are some voice exercises."

Maybelle snorted, and then schooled her features and came around the counter. "Let me show you the collection of ceramic angels that just came in," she told the couple as Gabe headed for the back room.

The door to the utility closet where Gabe had hung the punching bag was ajar, and he could see Andrew's small fists encased in bulky boxing gloves pummeling the leather. Conflicting emotions warred within Gabe. He'd missed the boy's afternoon visits, which had been curtailed by Angi after the incident at school.

And they hadn't talked more about the situation or his thoughts on how to help Drew. He didn't bring it up because what right did he have to intervene in her parenting choices? Hell, he had little experience with kids other than having been one. Plus, she was under enough pressure, and he didn't want to add more to it. But the kid was still struggling, and if Gabe could help with that, he wanted to.

The urge to intervene didn't make sense. The boy was simply one more complication that Gabe would have argued he didn't want, but he couldn't deny the connection he felt with Andrew. Different but no less important than his relationship with Angi.

A subject he hadn't broached since they'd had the best sex of his life. He was too damn scared to take the risk of hearing her say it had been a mistake.

"Hey, Rocky," he said as he pushed open the door. "I thought we talked about working with the bag after the shop closed. You're scaring the customers."

Andrew stopped moving and gave Gabe a mulish glare. "I needed to let off some steam."

"Try push-ups," Gabe suggested. "Or meditation."

"I tried meditating like you said." Andrew pushed a lock of hair out of his eyes with one oversize boxing glove. "It didn't work. I just had all the same stupid thoughts running through my head."

Gabe nodded. "We talked about that. The point of meditation is to quiet those thoughts. Notice them and let them run through. Your job is to let them come and watch them go."

The kid looked doubtful. "Does that really work?"

"Surprisingly, yes," Gabe told him. Another thing for

which he could thank his gran. It had been a low point in his military career, when he was stationed in some godforsaken desert in a hostile country. He'd sent a letter to his grandma late one night when he couldn't sleep, telling her how close he felt to the edge. When her next care package arrived, the box had included not only his favorite rice cereal treats but also a book on mindfulness and meditation.

Gabe hadn't planned to read it, but the insomnia had been almost debilitating. He'd spent so much time working on his body, making it strong and powerful because he'd hated the weakness of his childhood. But he'd done nothing to shape his mind, and the emotions swirling around inside him had been dragging him down. The mindfulness practices and meditation he'd made a daily part of his life had helped calm his brain.

When Andrew had first come to him, Gabe had focused on the kid's body because that was where he'd started. After the suspension, Gabe realized that he was doing the boy a disservice by not also helping him to train his mind. So he'd done some research on teaching mindfulness practices to kids and introduced several of the concepts to Drew.

"Tell me what has you needing to beat the tar out of the bag today," Gabe said, making his tone purposely casual. "And does your mom know you're here?"

Andrew scowled. "She's too busy to notice where I am."

"Not true, and we both know it." Gabe took a step forward and reached for the boy's hand. He tugged on the boxing glove until it came off. "Give her a break, buddy. She's balancing a lot right now."

"She doesn't understand." Andrew sniffed and wiped his sweaty brow on the sleeve of his *Iron Man* T-shirt. "She doesn't care that I don't have a dad."

"You have a dad, he's just too stupid to want to be a part of your life."

Andrew's mouth pursed into a thin line, and he blinked rapidly like he was trying not to cry.

Holy hell. Gabe couldn't take it if the kid cried.

"For the record, my dad wasn't a part of my life either. I never even knew who he was. My mom wouldn't tell me."

"Then you don't know if he would've liked you or not." Andrew went over to the water bottle he'd placed on a table and took a long drink.

Gabe just waited, understanding the kid needed a moment to collect himself.

"My dad told me he didn't want anything to do with me," he said, studying the top of the water bottle like the orange plastic held the secrets of the universe. "I might as well not know him."

"What do you mean he told you?" Alarm bells clanged in Gabe's brain.

"I got the number of the restaurant where he works from the internet, and I called him."

"I'm assuming your mother doesn't know that either."

Andrew shot him a "duh" look.

"Why?" Gabe asked, rubbing a hand across his jaw, trying to ease some of the tension. He was seriously considering catching the next flight he could get to New York City and pummeling Angi's ex.

"He said it wasn't a good time," Andrew told him. "It's busy at the restaurant and he's opening a new location in Vegas so it won't be a good time for a while."

The guy was a bigger dolt than Gabe had even imagined.

"Why did you call him?"

Andrew sniffed. "Because I want to go on the scout overnight trip, and stupid Johnny says I can't because it's a stupid father-son thing and I don't have a stupid dad or even a grandpa this year." The boy's voice cracked on the word *grandpa*, making Gabe's chest clench.

Was this how Scrooge felt when faced with adorable and pathetic Tiny Tim?

"What's so important about this overnight?"

Maybelle peaked her head into the back room. "Gabe, I'm heading out. Can you watch the front of the shop?"

"Yeah," Gabe called, then gestured to Andrew. "Let's finish this conversation with a snack. I have some leftover bear claws from the bakery."

"I guess," came the downtrodden reply from Andrew. The kid must be really bad off if Sunnyside pastries didn't put a spark in his eye. Gabe knew they were his favorite, which might have been why he'd started stocking them. Not that he was going to come right out and say it.

They walked to the front of the shop, which was empty of customers at the moment. Gabe didn't worry about that. He'd had more foot traffic since putting up the decorations than he'd had in the previous couple of months. Add that to the online orders and his new association with a national florist registry, and the store was going to be in the black for the month of December.

He was both proud and conflicted, as he didn't want to do anything that would please his mother. But Gran was so happy with the changes he'd made that he couldn't regret them.

Andrew climbed up on his normal stool behind the counter, and Gabe put out a plate of pastries and a juice box. The boy looked at them with a longing sigh, but didn't reach for one.

Tough times, indeed.

CHAPTER FIFTEEN

GABE'S HEART MELTED for the kid, and he decided in that moment, no matter what it took or how hard he had to work to convince Angi to let him help, he'd do it. At least to get Andrew through this rough patch. There had been so many times Gabe could have used someone to guide him. His grandma had done her best, but he'd only come to Magnolia for the summers. School years had often felt like a field of land mines with one wrong step sending his world into chaos.

"You were about to tell me why this activity is such a big deal."

"The scouts in my troop need hours to get the community service badge each year. Everybody goes to the forest thing because it's the best way to get them. We do trail cleanup and cut down Christmas trees to donate to families who don't got money to buy 'em."

"Can't you just do something else? Volunteer at Furever Friends scooping poop or feeding kittens or something?"

"I guess," Andrew said after a long pause. "But the woods are the most fun. We have lunch at a cool cabin with a big moose head on the wall, and we get to use axes."

"Very smart on the part of your troop leaders, by the way. Sending a bunch of boys into the woods with sharp tools. Wait until you read *Lord of the Flies* in school and you'll understand what I'm talking about."

"We also get extra points toward awards at the end of the troop year," Andrew explained. "Each boy gets credit for his hours and his dad's. My grandpa used to go with me, although he usually just brought lunch and didn't do much chopping. That counted though, and it was fun. And now I can't go because I don't have anybody."

Cue the violins, Gabe thought, but he understood Andrew's dilemma. Gabe might never have known his father or been rejected outright, but he remembered how it had felt when other kids had dads and he didn't. At school functions or summer baseball games or generally hanging out.

As a kid, Gabe had sometimes daydreamed about his dad showing up out of the blue on one of his birthdays with two broken-in baseball mitts. He'd hand one to Gabe and invite him to a neighborhood park to toss ball.

Other kids talked about trips to Disney World and the Grand Canyon. Gabe had just wanted to toss ball.

"Do you have a baseball mitt?" he asked Andrew.

The boy blinked and then frowned, clearly trying to figure out the abrupt change of subject. "No," he said after a moment. "I play soccer, but I'm kind of bad at that, too."

The door to the shop opened with a jingle from the bells overhead. Angi entered, her face a mix of frustration and acceptance. "I thought I'd find you here," she said to her son, flicking an exasperated glance at Gabe. "We talked about leaving the restaurant without telling me."

"Drew and I were just discussing the scout holiday hike or whatever they call it," Gabe said, willing her to understand the implications for her son.

"It's this weekend," she said with a nod. "There's an event at the inn, but I told Emma I can't be there because I'll be collecting pine cones."

"We don't collect pine cones." Andrew looked understandably horrified. "And you can't come with me, Mom. It's a father-and-son thing."

She scoffed, redoing the low ponytail that held back her dark hair. Gabe was momentarily distracted by her beauty. She wore the usual restaurant uniform of a white blouse and fitted black skirt, which to his mind was sexier than frilly lingerie. As she tipped up her chin to run her fingers through her hair, his gaze caught on the tiny beauty mark on the side of her throat. She had a smattering of similar spots across her body, and he'd spent a satisfying hour the other night cataloging as many as he could find.

If Angi truly belonged to him, he'd go to her now and brush his lips across her neck. A quick kiss, but one that would remind them both of things to come.

"That's ridiculous," she said now as she lowered her arms again. The beauty mark disappeared under the collar of her shirt. "I can tromp through the woods as well as any man. If those troop leaders want to discriminate on the basis of sex, I'll just have to channel my inner Ruth Bader Ginsberg and—"

"No, Mom." Andrew hopped off the chair with fisted hands. "No. I don't even know who your Ruth friend is, but it doesn't matter. You can't go. And I can't go. Because I don't have—"

"I could take you," Gabe said before the boy could finish his rant. Angi was sensitive to her status as a single mom, and a glance at her suddenly pale face suggested she realized now why this mattered so much to her son.

Her dark eyes met his, and the pain in their depths pierced his heart in the same way Andrew's upset had minutes earlier. He gave a subtle nod and focused his attention on Andrew. "I know I'm probably a poor substitute for your grandfather. The troop will get no lunch from me, but Maybelle is looking for extra hours. She's saving up to buy wireless headphones for her boyfriend this Christmas. It won't be a problem for me to take off a whole day."

Although Andrew's chest still rose and fell with ragged breaths, he no longer looked like he was about to burst into tears. A little victory but a good start.

"Don't get me wrong," he told the boy. "I agree with your mom. Troop members should be able to bring whoever they want on this little outing. But if they're so insistent on participants being of the variety who stand up when we use the facilities, I fit that bill."

"I guess that would be okay," Andrew said after a moment, clearly contemplating the reaction of his friends to showing up with Gabe. "Last year, Brett's dad was out of town so his older brother came. He spent most of the day on his phone, but Brett still got credit for his hours."

"I'm not going to be on my phone," Gabe promised the boy.

"You don't have to do that," Angi said, her voice subdued. "It's a ridiculous tradition, and time that it changed. I can—"

"Mom, please no." Andrew wrapped his arms around her middle, gazing up into his mother's face with pleading eyes. "Gabe can go. He said he doesn't mind."

"I don't mind," Gabe echoed.

Andrew gave Angi a fierce hug. "Please, Mom."

Well played, kid, Gabe thought.

"Fine," she murmured, stroking a hand through her son's thick mop of hair. "But I'm going to volunteer to provide lunch, just like Papa used to do. I'm sure the troop won't mind a mom bringing food to the event."

Andrew nodded. "Sure. Maybe I'll even get extra credit for that. Thanks, Mom." He turned and looked at Gabe. "Thanks."

"Go do your homework," Gabe told him with a nod. "And remember that you have to tell your mom that you're leaving the restaurant before you do."

Andrew grabbed two big pieces of bear claw from the plate on the counter and then hurried out the door like he was worried Angi might change her mind.

"It's not right," she said when they were alone again. "He shouldn't be made to feel bad because his father isn't a part of his life."

Gabe thought about whether to tell her that Andrew had reached out to the piece of trash who shared his DNA and decided against it for now. She looked fragile and fatigued, and he figured he'd wait to drop that little bomb.

"I've been there." He reached for her, tugging her closer. "He'll be fine eventually. It's crap that whoever is running this troop still plays into those stereotypes, but you can find another time to fight that battle. Once Andrew gets his bonus hours for the tree we're going to chop down."

She rested her forehead against his chest, and he was grateful for her warmth and to have her fresh scent surrounding him once again. "It's my fault. I was the one who made him join scouts and the soccer team and almost every activity he's been a part of. I just didn't want him to be left out, but now it looks like I've added to his issues instead of making them better."

"You're a wonderful mom," he reminded her. He cupped her face in his hands and tipped up her chin. "You're also under the mistletoe." He raised his eyes to the strand of berries hanging above them.

"We don't have an audience," she said with an arched brow.

"I think this week proved that we're better off without one," he answered, and kissed her.

ANGI RUSHED INTO Il Rigatone on Saturday just after noon and headed to a booth in the corner, loading her arms with dirty plates and glassware before she'd even deposited her purse in the back or taken off her jacket.

The restaurant was at capacity, with groups waiting on the benches in front of the hostess stand. Dom had called and left several messages for her asking for help because they were down a waitress with the flu and two of the busboys hadn't shown up for their shift.

Unfortunately, Angi had been busy feeding a high-maintenance bride and twenty-five of her closest friends and family when the SOS calls had come in. It hadn't been until a break in the action at the inn that she'd realized Dom needed her.

In fact, the only reason she'd checked her phone was to make sure she hadn't missed a call from Gabe. He'd picked up Andrew early that morning for the scout adventure in the national forest about an hour west of town. She'd sent enough food for the entire troop and had no reason to believe things wouldn't go well for her son and his stand-in grown-up, but she worried just the same. It's what mothers did best, she sometimes thought, even when there was no cause for concern.

Would Gabe get along with the actual dads on the day trip? Would he and Andrew make a good team as they worked on trail maintenance and tree cutting? What was going to happen to her son's relationship to the surly and surprisingly sweet flower shop owner when their fake romance ended along with the holidays? For that matter, what was Angi going to do?

Whether better or worse, those questions would have to wait for another time. She didn't have a second to contemplate the state of her life, which might be a blessing in disguise.

As she turned from the booth, Angi's breath caught in her throat as she realized her mother stood a few feet away, glaring at her.

Her body went slack with guilt for a split second, long enough that the plates and glasses she held clattered to the tile floor. Customers from nearby tables gasped at the noise, then politely looked away as she quickly bent to retrieve the broken dishes.

When she straightened, her mother had moved closer, a wet rag and bottle of cleaning solution in her hands.

"What are you doing here, Ma?" she asked as she started to move past. "I thought you had a Zumba class at Josie's this afternoon."

"Dominic called me when things got out of hand and he couldn't reach you."

Angi paused, inwardly cringing. "I'm sorry. I—"

"Save it," Bianca said, her mouth pulled into a tight frown. "We'll have time to talk when the restaurant clears after lunch. Right now, I'm focused on keeping my customers happy."

Angi knew what that emphasis on the possessive pronoun meant. It was no accident that her mother had used "my" instead of the "our" that had become standard.

She also didn't argue because her mom was right.

A quick glance around the restaurant showed a cluster

of tables unbused and several patrons with empty water glasses. Angi wasted no time in depositing the dishes in the back and then taking care of business up front.

She left her mother to seating people or talking with customers who were waiting for tables. Angi refilled drinks and water glasses. She brought complimentary baskets of bread to each of the tables along with personal recommendations from the menu, pausing to talk with each group.

Lana gave her arm a grateful squeeze as she brought a family of six their food, and it was then Angi noticed that a number of the items being served were specials she'd put on the menu over the past few weeks. Alarm thundered through her as she glanced over her shoulder at her mother. Bianca had already lectured her about switching up her father's recipes, so Angi knew her mother would be upset if she realized many of the orders included the new dishes.

During her next trip to the kitchen, Angi observed the line cooks preparing her signature menu items. She caught Dom's eye and gestured to the food, then shot him a questioning glance, which was answered by only a wink and smile.

Not good enough. "What's going on?" she asked in a frantic whisper, coming to stand close at his side. There was no need for the staff to witness her panic attack.

He picked up a single sheet of paper and handed it to her. "I put these in each of the menus. With all of the weekend visitors in town for the festival, today was bound to be busy. It seemed like a perfect time to give the customers options from our new and improved menu selection."

"Not improved," she insisted. "Dad's recipes are completely fine."

"And ordinary," Dom added. "You know it, Ang. Why else would you experiment with these new items?"

Her heart constricted as she studied the specials list. When her father and mother ran the back and front of the restaurant, there had been no need for Angi to put her culinary creativity on display. That hadn't stopped her from reimagining some of the more staid options and thinking about new twists on Italian classics.

Since her mother's heart attack, Angi had slid a menu item in here or there just to please herself. She loved trying new things with regular ingredients. By and large, customers had appreciated her attempts to reinvigorate the offerings, but she knew her mom wouldn't.

"Has Mom noticed?"

Dom frowned. "I don't think so. We were slammed by the time she got here, so she's been occupied with waiting on customers."

"She can't know what I've done."

"Angela, you're saving the business she's dedicated most of her adult life to building."

"The restaurant was fine," she lied.

"Your father was my best friend. I know that's not true."

Angi blinked, unsure how to respond, not knowing what to do next. The adrenaline that had propelled her through the morning seemed to drain away in an instant.

From getting Andrew ready for the day with the scout troop to the bridal shower to the lunch crowd frenzy, she'd hurtled through the day on autopilot. Now she couldn't move forward. She couldn't seem to move at all. Her limbs felt heavy with fatigue. How was she supposed to deal with all of the different people relying on her? Needing different things from her.

Expecting more than she could give.

"I'm glad customers like my food."

"They do."

"Why was your father's food not good enough?"

Angi whirled at the sound of her mother's voice.

"Mom, that's not what this is about."

"He put his heart and soul into this restaurant. Il Rigatone was his life. Our life. We made our home in this town. Raised you and your brothers here. Now you want to change everything?"

"Mom, please—"

Bianca's hand cut through the air like a knife blade.

"You disrespect me and your father's memory. His legacy."

Angi could feel the eyes of every employee in the kitchen watching the scene unfold. She'd spent so much time taking care of her mother and her mom's feelings. Giving up her apartment and her freedom in order to make sure her mom was taken care of.

"Can we talk somewhere else, Mom?"

Bianca's eyes narrowed. "Perhaps we could take a short field trip to the Wildflower Inn since that's where you're still spending so much of your time."

"I… You can't… I don't…"

"You think I haven't known?" Her mother gave a sharp shake of her head. "I see the shadows under your eyes and watch you downing coffee and then diet soda like it's your lifeline."

"Mom, I'm sorry." Angi looked between her mother and Dominic. He gave her a sympathetic nod.

"You're sorry," Bianca repeated, her voice reed thin. "But you're lying to me. You're lying to all of us."

Heat infused Angi's cheeks. "I'm sorry," she repeated, and tried to blink back the tears that flooded her eyes.

Dominic cleared his throat. "We still have more customers to serve." He leveled a pointed glance at Bianca. "People who are happy with the current offerings on the menu and the specials I chose to serve."

"Fine," Bianca said with a dismissive shrug. "I guess I'm not needed, then."

"Of course you are," Angi told her mother. But as she reached for her mom, Bianca pulled away, sending a nail into the coffin that encased Angi's heart. She'd done so much to try to not hurt her mom and had ended up doing it anyway.

The thought broke her heart.

Her mother offered a sincere smile to the employees still watching their interplay. "Thank you for all you do. We appreciate you and your dedication to Il Rigatone. To my husband's dream. My dream."

Angi's phone began to ring in her back pocket, effectively ruining the sensitive moment between her mother and the staff. With a murmur of apology, Angi pulled it out and immediately accepted the call.

"Brad, what's wrong?" She'd put in the number of the scout leader in case of emergencies. "Is Andrew okay?"

"What happened to Andrew?" her mother demanded, reaching for Angi's arm.

The kitchen had gone momentarily silent as everyone seemed to wait for her to speak. She listened to Brad for a few moments and then gave a thumbs-up to her and the staff members. "Andrew is fine," she whispered, cupping her hand over the phone's speaker. But, as the dad on the other end of the line continued to speak, her heart plummeted.

"Thank you for the call," she told Brad, walking to the

far side of the kitchen. "And for bringing Andrew back. My mother is at the restaurant if you could drop him off here?"

She disconnected and clutched the phone to her chest as tears clogged her throat.

"What's going on?" Bianca's voice had softened slightly. "I thought Gabe had taken Andrew to his activity today. Why is another father giving him a ride home?"

Angi turned to her mother. "Gabe's grandma died this morning. The nursing home was just able to reach him now."

The tears she'd tried to hold back slid down her cheeks as she thought of how Gabe must feel. He was alone, and all she could think of was how soon she could get to him.

CHAPTER SIXTEEN

GABE WALKED OUT of the front entrance of the nursing home an hour later, the bright winter sunshine overhead mocking him and his dark mood. Gran was gone, and he hadn't been there with her or had a chance to say goodbye before she passed.

The whole reason he'd come to Magnolia in the first place was to take care of her, and he'd failed when she needed him most. Just like he hadn't been able to get to her after her fall and subsequent surgery, although during that time at least he'd had the excuse of his military career.

Today there was no reason he shouldn't have been available, other than the fact that he'd allowed himself to get distracted from his purpose in this town. His heart ached and his throat felt tight with guilt.

The director of the facility had met him at the door to Gran's room. He'd failed her. The thought drummed through his mind like rainfall on a tin roof.

He noticed the small sedan parked next to his truck in the lot as he approached, and his pulse gave a now expected leap as Angi climbed out.

His reaction to her might be familiar, but his inability to control it remained a source of frustration. Another distraction and an unwanted pull on his heart.

"I'm sorry," she said as she came toward him. "I got

here as soon as I could. I figured you'd want a few minutes with her."

"With her body," he muttered, shame making his gut clench painfully. "She died with no family at her side. She died alone."

Angi enveloped him in a soft hug. He didn't deserve anyone's comfort at this moment, but he greedily took it anyway. Another mark against him.

"She knew you came," Angi said against his jacket. "Her spirit was still there."

"I don't need you to placate me." He should have pulled away but couldn't bring himself to release her.

"Can I at least offer support?"

"It won't help," he told her, determined to wear his theoretical hair shirt for as long as possible. Other than his own guilt, what could he offer his grandmother as retribution for not being with her?

She leaned back enough to look up at him. "I'm going to give it to you anyway. I can be stubborn like that."

"She shouldn't have died alone," he whispered, and squeezed his eyes shut when a flood of tears pricked the back of them. He couldn't remember the last time he'd cried.

"Gabe, your grandmother knew how much you loved her. Think about her face that night in the shop. She was surrounded by people who cared about her, and the business she'd dedicated her life to was flourishing again. You did that. You put your life on hold to dedicate yourself to making her happy and taking care of her. She knew she was loved."

"I don't want to feel better," he said, another round of guilt plaguing him. "I need to be sad right now, Ang."

"Grieving is normal," she told him. "But you don't have to do it alone."

Wasn't that just the kicker? Here she was offering him comfort and he couldn't even allow himself to take it.

"I should go," he said, and forced himself to step away from her. "I need to start with funeral arrangements and call my mom."

"Will she come to Magnolia for the service?" Angi's face looked pained as she asked the question.

Gabe could imagine the same emotion reflected in his eyes.

"I don't know." He gave a humorless laugh. "Although I'm sure she'll be here to take over the shop and house once the estate is settled."

"What will you do?"

"Move on, I guess." He shrugged. "This was always temporary."

He refused to acknowledge the disappointment in her chocolate-colored eyes. He refused to consider that he didn't have to walk away. There was no possibility Gabe could live in the same town as his mother, or watch as she sold the shop and house he loved.

And he couldn't ask Angi for something more than a pretend relationship when he had nothing to give her other than himself. He didn't deserve her.

A part of him wanted her to argue, to fight for their connection. But he couldn't bring himself to do it.

She nodded. "If there's anything you need, please let me know. And thank you again for taking Andrew today. I'm so sorry that it meant not being there for your grandmother."

His insides felt raw, scraped out with a dull knife until

there was nothing left but empty space. "Me, too," he told her, and then turned toward his truck.

"THIS IS A bad idea," Angi said as she followed her mother up the front walk to Gabe's grandmother's house later that night. Andrew followed behind them pulling a wagon that held an assortment of holiday decorations.

"Why?" her mother asked. "He shouldn't be alone tonight, and you said he doesn't have Christmas decorations. There are so many memories in Iris's house for him. It should be a festive place."

"But he wants to be sad," Angi argued weakly.

"We'll be sad with him," Andrew offered, and her heart melted at the sweetness in her son's tone.

Angi had returned to her mother's after Gabe walked away, feeling both helpless and hollow. Bianca and Andrew were already home, and he took great pride and pleasure in regaling her with stories of his adventures with Gabe from the morning. Apparently, Johnny Rotten, as Andrew now referred to his tormentor, had come to the event with another dad and son, which he'd expressly told Andrew was forbidden by troop rules.

She would have called the little bully out on that but hadn't needed to since Gabe had offered to be Drew's stand-in. Johnny's dad had left town because he and Johnny's mom, one of Angi's former friends, were in the midst of a nasty divorce. She had a feeling the kid hadn't wanted Andrew to see him without a dad at his side after making such a big deal about the lack of masculine influence in Drew's life. As if that would have mattered to her son.

The more Andrew talked, the more she realized what a huge debt she owed Gabe. Her dad had taken his grandson to the event for the past three years, but Andrew never had the kind of fun he did with Gabe.

It was a toss-up whether she felt guiltier that taking care of her son meant Gabe hadn't had those last moments with his grandmother or that she'd put Andrew in the situation of not having a father in the first place by picking such an absolute loser for a boyfriend years earlier.

Andrew had been the one to suggest they come to Gabe's tonight, bringing dinner and as much holiday cheer as they could manage with only a week until Christmas. As much as he'd clearly loved the event, she could tell he hated that Gabe had gotten the news about his grandmother that afternoon.

The idea had resonated with Angi's mother, as well. It was obvious Bianca still harbored tremendous anger and disappointment in Angi for lying about her work at the inn but she had a soft spot for Gabe Carlyle.

For better or worse, Bianca didn't seem to realize that her daughter's biggest deception involved the relationship with Gabe.

How was Angi supposed to admit to that now when her mother already had so many reasons to be upset? Maybe she should feel relieved that at least Bianca hadn't done more heart clutching in the wake of discovering Angi had been lying. That felt like progress.

As Angi's palms went sweaty, Bianca knocked on the door. Gabe opened it a second later, as if he'd been standing on the other side or watching them approach from the front window.

Then Angi noticed that he wore a jacket like he was on his way out. Where would he be heading on a night like this?

"Your grandmother was a wonderful woman and will

be dearly missed by everyone who knew her." Bianca wrapped Gabe in a tight hug, rocking back and forth with her arms around him like she was comforting a small child.

He met Angi's gaze over her mother's shoulder, his eyes both stunned and strangely shiny with emotion.

Not for the first time, she'd wished he had grown up with a mom like hers. Angi might have issues with how overwhelming her family was, but she'd never once doubted her mother's love or dedication.

Every child—young or adult—should have that.

"We brought dinner," she told him, somehow understanding that he needed her to lighten the moment.

"And Christmas decorations," Andrew added from behind her.

Angi nodded as Bianca released Gabe. "But it looks like you were headed out? We can just leave—"

"I was coming to see you," he said, scrubbing a hand over his jaw. "To apologize for being rude earlier."

Angi's heart seemed to skip a beat, and she couldn't quite form a response.

Her mother had no such trouble. "Don't be silly," Bianca told him, patting his arm. "You're grieving. When we're at our lowest, the people who care about us are the ones who hold us up. Without question or apologies. You and my daughter are in a relationship. She's your person, and we're here for you as well, Gabriel. Now you should invite us in."

He stared at Bianca for a long second, and Angi had the fleeting fear that he might divulge the truth. Instead, he gave a small nod and stepped back to let Angi's mother pass.

"Thank you," he said quietly. "I guess it's good not to be alone right now."

THE NEXT SEVERAL days went by in a whirl of activity. Gabe had felt paralyzed as far as making arrangements for his grandmother's service. It was still inconceivable to him that she was gone. No matter where in the world his career had taken him, knowing his beloved grandma was sending her love to him was like a tether to a version of home.

Without her he felt like a million snowflakes floating through the air with no place to truly land.

In the months he'd been in Magnolia, the town had come to feel like home. But the shop and Gran's house didn't belong to him. His mother had shown little sadness at losing Gran; nor had she given any inkling about her plans now that she stood to receive her inheritance. It might take a few weeks or months to work out the details, but his mom would come for what was now hers.

Leaving Gabe with nothing.

Except that his life in this small town didn't feel like nothing, even without a purpose. Angi's mother had slipped into an easy maternal role with him, and he took more solace than was right from Angi given the temporary nature of their arrangement. She, Emma and Mariella had stepped in to help him make arrangements, even hosting a reception at the inn after the funeral.

He stood in the Wildflower's dining room, which was laden with food that Angi had made, receiving sympathetic hugs and words of kindness from people he knew, as well as complete strangers.

"Since when have you become a hugger?" Mariella asked as she came to stand at his side.

"I'm not," he muttered under his breath. He took a long drink of the rum and Coke he'd been nursing since the function started.

"Seems to me you're getting reinvented in this town."

Out of the corner of his eye, he saw her throw a glare at one more well-meaning neighbor who approached, causing the older woman to veer off in another direction.

"Thanks." He gave Mariella a gentle elbow to the arm. "Pretty sure you're the queen of reinvention around here."

"Not anymore," she said with a bitter sigh. "I can't exactly continue with my fresh start when the past has followed me here."

"That sounds dramatic, like some sort of made-for-TV movie."

"Reality is often stranger than fiction. What are the chances that a man I never wanted to see again decides to move to Magnolia?"

"In Alex's defense, I think he needs a fresh start even more than you."

"Why?" She turned to face him fully. "He's the sympathetic scorned groom. I'm sure everyone he knows feels terrible for him."

"Quite a desirable situation for most men."

"He's rich, smart and handsome as sin." She rolled her eyes. "If you're into smoldering gazes and chiseled jawlines."

"My favorites," Gabe answered, feeling his lips pull into a small grin despite his grief. It was the first time he'd managed a smile all day. "What are you going to do? Start over someplace else?"

Her winged brows lowered. "Hell, no. I'm not giving up my life here. If he wants to tangle with me, then so be it. I've atoned for my mistakes. As much as I'd like to not have the reminder of the past, I'm done running away. I like it here."

"Me, too," he whispered before he thought better of

it. Then he shook his head. "But sometimes that's not enough."

"It is if you make it enough."

He glanced toward the swinging door that led to the kitchen. "Have you told that to your friend Angi?"

Mariella's gaze followed his, then tracked to Bianca, who stood with Dominic in the corner, glaring at the spread of food on the table.

"She told me her mother found out that she was still working here. I thought Mrs. Guilardi might realize how much it means to Ang. That it would make her see she doesn't belong at the restaurant. This is where she needs to be."

"Because she likes it?" Gabe asked, not bothering to hide the skepticism in his tone.

"It's more than that. It makes her happy. Having something that she's created on her own fulfills her in a way the restaurant never will. That's important."

"I'm not arguing."

"You're important to her, too."

He blinked.

"Only until the new year," he said, ignoring the ache in his chest at the thought.

"Only if you screw it up."

"I screwed up by agreeing to it from the start. We are what we are now."

"Change it," Mariella told him.

"Make peace with Alex Ralsten."

"There's a difference. I don't care about him."

"You care more than you let on. Unfortunately, we have that in common."

Bianca approached at that moment, giving Mariella a

glaring once-over, as if she were the ringleader of a biker gang that had led unsuspecting, innocent Angi astray.

"That's my cue," Mariella said under her breath. "Nice to see you again, Mrs. Guilardi."

Angi's mother only sniffed and looked away.

"We are what we make ourselves," Mariella said to Gabe, and she moved toward where Emma and Cam stood near the head of the table.

"I don't like that girl," Bianca said as she glared after Mariella. "She has bad energy."

Gabe shrugged. "She's had some tough breaks in life, but she's a talented designer and a good friend to your daughter."

Another derisive sniff. "If those two were true friends of my daughter, they wouldn't ask her to continue working when she's needed at the restaurant."

Gabe placed his drink on the buffet situated to his left. "She likes her work at the inn."

"It's a distraction," Bianca insisted. "One she has no time for."

He was a distraction as well, but he didn't bother to bring that up.

"Thank you for everything you've done this week, Mrs. Guilardi. It's meant a lot to me."

"You're like family, Gabriel."

He inwardly cringed.

"I'm sorry your mother wasn't able to make it to the service."

"Yeah," he agreed, his gut churning. "Mom works retail, so it's difficult to take off right before the holidays. We'll do something to honor Gran's memory when she arrives."

He assumed she'd show up once the contents of the will were made public. In truth, he had no idea what his mother was thinking about the future. She'd been terse and defensive when he'd called to tell her about Gran's passing. The bit about her working retail wasn't a lie, but he had no idea if she could have gotten time off or not. She'd simply told him she couldn't make the trip, and he hadn't questioned her.

He didn't want her there anyway.

The point of the service was to honor his grandmother's memory, not to entertain his mother's stories about how awful her childhood had been because of so many made-up infractions.

He wouldn't claim his grandparents had been perfect. No family was perfect, but his mother lived in a house made entirely of glass, so she was the last person who should be throwing stones.

"If there's anything you need, please let us know. Of course you'll spend Christmas at our home."

"I don't know—"

"I insist," Bianca told him. "We have a traditional Italian feast, and my Angela makes the best panettóne you've ever tried."

"I don't even know what that is," he admitted, smiling at the affronted look he received. "But I know Angi is amazing in the kitchen." He gestured to the table. "Have you tried the chicken samosas? I think they're becoming one of her signature items at the inn. Emma told me guests request them when booking events."

"I haven't taken a bite of anything here." Bianca said the words almost proudly or like a challenge. "Angi will soon be done with this place. Perhaps we'll add panettone—which is a traditional Christmas bread—to Il Rigatone's menu."

"I'm going to check on her," Gabe said, taking a step

away from Bianca. "You should try some of the food. Give it a chance. One thing I learned from this week is not to let any moment pass you by."

Bianca eyed the table like it was covered with slithering snakes. "Thank you for the suggestion," she said, not sounding appreciative in the least. "I'm simply not hungry."

Why did families have to be so complicated? Gabe wondered about the dynamics he'd never noticed before as he made his way past sympathetic guests toward the kitchen. His mom had been negligent bordering on abusive, and as a kid he'd thought he had it worse than anyone else he knew.

But maybe that was just an immature perspective. A lot of kids didn't have anyone to give them unconditional love the way his grandmother had. And other children had expectations placed on their shoulders by well-meaning parents like Bianca.

In some ways that was almost worse. At least he could do his best to cut his mother out of his life and certainly out of his heart.

Angi loved her mom, even though their relationship taxed her nerves and heart.

"You've outdone yourself once again," he said as he came through the swinging door into the kitchen. The smell of garlic and fresh herbs was heavy in the air. "I think you can take a break. The guests are starting to leave, and there's still plenty of food left on the table."

"I'm prepping for an office holiday party Emma's hosting early next week. They want heavy hors d'oeuvres and a variety of cookies. I've been researching recipes that can be made and frozen ahead of time." She placed a tray of something in the oven and then wiped her sleeve across her forehead. "If my mom forbids me to come over here again after today, I want to make sure Emma has what she needs."

"Angi, your mom shouldn't be able to forbid you to do whatever makes you happy."

"I'm too tired to even think about happy at the moment," she shot back, and then grimaced. "I'm sorry, Gabe. Today isn't about me or my problems. How are you holding up?"

He swallowed. "It's easier because of you."

Her features gentled, as if she could hear all the things he wasn't saying. "Who would have thought we'd end up as friends in all this?"

Friends. A simple word but more powerful than Gabe could have imagined. He might want more from Angi than friendship, but he wouldn't deny how much it meant to have that from her.

He went to the prep sink and started to wash his hands. "Put me to work," he said over his shoulder. "How can I help?"

"You still have guests," she reminded him, pointing to the swinging kitchen door.

"They'll entertain themselves." He grabbed a towel that hung from the oven door and turned. "I want to be here with you, Ang."

CHAPTER SEVENTEEN

ANGI ENTERED MARIELLA'S store a few days later, a stack of flyers promoting next week's holiday dance in her hand. She'd already distributed one batch to local business owners, but several had called and texted asking for more.

Avery was handling online ticket sales through the mayor's office. She'd reported that they'd already sold enough to cover their expenses and it seemed promising that they'd be in a position to make a hefty donation after the event. Angi appreciated that at least one area of her life seemed to be on track.

She smiled at two customers perusing a rack of dresses—a mother-and-daughter duo based on the family resemblance. If only her relationship with her mom could be that simple. Other than family trips to visit relatives along the eastern seaboard, Angi couldn't remember ever doing something with her mom just for fun.

Oh, they'd had the requisite shopping trips during Angi's teen years for clothes and prom dresses. Her brothers and dad had ensured that the energy in the house was predominantly masculine, but her mom made sure the boys grew up knowing they had to give Angi her privacy and, more importantly, put down the toilet seat after their time in the bathroom.

But even shopping with her mom had been a lesson in efficiency instead of a fun bonding time. The restaurant and Bianca's responsibilities there had always been a factor. She'd have an hour or two between the lunch crowd and dinner rush during Il Rigatone's heyday. No time to stop for ice cream or to browse for something other than what was essential during any particular excursion.

If Angi wanted quality time with her mother or to have a real conversation, it had to happen in the kitchen. Maybe that's why cooking was such an inherent part of her now. She couldn't imagine a life that didn't revolve around food, despite her concern about missing out on things with Andrew because of her job. Her multiple jobs.

Mariella approached from behind the counter after ringing up a customer. "If you tear that to shreds, I hope it means you're going to buy it."

Angi looked down, surprised to find a scarf from a nearby display held tightly in her hand. She'd placed the promotional flyers on a shelf so she could try on one of the flowery prints as she waited for Mariella to finish the sale. Now her fists were clenched around the silky fabric.

She sighed and gentled her hold on the scarf. "I might need a stress ball instead of a scarf," she admitted.

"Unfortunately, not something I keep in stock." Mariella's gaze clouded for a moment. "I should think about ordering some. For myself more than anyone else."

Angi smoothed out the scarf and hung it back on the hook. "Maybe you won't even notice Alex Ralsten is in town." She picked up the stack of flyers.

"You grew up here," Mariella observed as they walked toward the counter. "Are there people from your childhood that you try to avoid?"

Angi snorted, then tried to hide it with a cough. "Almost all of them," she said after a contemplative moment. "I don't like the person I was back then, and a lot of the people who were my friends haven't changed much over the years."

"How's that going for you?" Mariella arched a brow. "The avoiding old friends in a town this size."

"I work at a restaurant on Main Street. Not only do I have to see those people, I have to wait on them and make small talk and act like their petty digs about what I've done with my life don't bother me."

"But they do?"

"I let them," Angi admitted.

"Now imagine that the people you didn't want to see weren't jerks. You were the jerk, and you ruined their life and your own in a very public manner."

"Do you remember how I acted toward Gabe when we first started working with him last summer?" Angi's face heated at the memory.

"You weren't kind."

"I was embarrassed and defensive," Angi clarified. "He's the person I humiliated in a very public way. He thought of me as a friend and I turned on him because the little jerks I wanted to impress expected me to."

"That's rough." Mariella took the flyers from her hand and placed them next to the cash register. "And now you're fake dating." She gave a harsh laugh. "Or maybe it's real dating by this point. Either way, I don't see that happening with me and Alex."

"You don't have to fall in love with him. But take a lesson from my failure. Don't be a jerk. You made a mistake that impacted both of you. He doesn't have to forgive you for it, but don't take out your humiliation on him."

She'd been fiddling with a pair of earrings hanging on a turntable, her gaze glued to the little gold hoops because it was too difficult to look at her friend and admit how she'd failed so miserably. When Mariella didn't answer, Angi finally looked up, unsure what had caught the other woman's attention.

"Are you in love with Gabe Carlyle?" Mariella asked in a hushed tone, staring at Angi with wide eyes.

"I didn't say that."

"That's not an answer." Mariella waved and called goodbye to the mother-daughter duo.

"We have an arrangement. Mutually beneficial through the holidays."

"Still not an ans—"

"Yes," Angi said on a hiss of breath. "It's ridiculous and stupid and bound to lead to a broken heart, but I have totally fallen for that man." She squeezed shut her eyes, again bracing for Mariella's reaction.

Silence.

Finally she peeked out of one squinted eye.

Mariella was smiling at her.

"Stop," she muttered.

"You're in love."

"With a man who is leaving town as soon as his mom gets here."

"Because he doesn't know how you feel. You have to give him a reason to stay."

Angi shook her head. "I'm not a reason to stay. I'm a thirty-year-old woman doing a job I hate and living with my overbearing mother while raising my son, who is still struggling and I have no idea how to fix his problems or mine." She pressed a hand to her stomach. "I'm a reason to run the other direction as fast as he can."

"You love him," Mariella said. "You make him happy. That's a reason to stay and fight. For both of you. All the other stuff will work itself out."

"How can you be so optimistic about my life and so down on your own?"

"Because I'm a recovering train wreck," Mariella answered immediately. "You're a good person, Ang. You have a great kid. You deserve happiness. Why shouldn't it be with Gabe?"

"I was horrible to him when we were younger. He knows the worst part of me. And I'm sure he won't stay in Magnolia once his mother arrives. As far as Gabe is concerned, what's between us is for show in town and so that we can mutually scratch an itch in the bedroom."

Mariella leaned forward. "You've had sex with him."

"Yes," Angi said, looking away.

"You're blushing. I bet it was great. Was it great? Hot? Was he amazing? Let me live vicariously through you. Please just tell me something so—"

"The sex was amazing." Angi yelled the words like an accusation.

At that exact moment, the door opened.

"Welcome," Mariella called cheerily, then grimaced at Angi. "Maybe they didn't hear."

Meredith Ventner walked around a shelf of candles and bath products, a medium-sized mutt following close at her side. "Who's having amazing sex?" she asked with a grin. "Carrie and Avery always get the town gossip first. I'm going to scoop them on this."

Angi whirled to face the pixie-sized dog rescuer. "You can't tell anyone."

"Is the dude married?"

"Of course not." Angi shook her head. "I wouldn't do that."

"It's Gabe," Mariella volunteered.

"But why is that news?" Meredith gave a little tug on

the leash when the dog hesitated. "I thought you two were dating."

"Fake," Mariella said with a wink.

"Big mouth much," Angi muttered.

"To appease her mom and his grandma." Mariella looked up toward the tin tile ceiling. "Rest her soul."

"Can we talk about something else?" Angi crouched down to pet the dog. "Who's this little guy?"

"That's Princess," Meredith said, humor lacing her tone. "She belonged to an older gentleman who wasn't able to care for her. When she came to us, her fur was pretty matted and her teeth were in bad shape. She's almost eight, which isn't especially old for a Yorkie mix, but she needed some TLC and work on her manners."

The dog turned her head and politely licked Angi's hand, as if thanking her for the attention. "I think she has wonderful manners," Angi said. Andrew would love a dog like this. He'd love any dog. When Emma had adopted her labradoodle, Ethel, over the summer, Andrew had spent hours playing with the sweet animal in the inn's big backyard.

Every kid should have a dog or cat or something to love and help take care of. Angi's old apartment hadn't allowed pets, and her mom had never wanted animals in the house.

Her son was stuck wishing and hoping for something he'd never get.

Just like Angi.

Except she could have a dog. Her mother might not like it, but there were plenty of things her mom didn't approve of in Angi's life at the moment. And if Bianca was so against it, Angi could rent a place of her own, one that took pets.

As she continued to stroke the animal's small head, her

heart seemed to expand in her chest. "Is she available?" She glanced up at Meredith to find the woman staring at her with a speculative stare.

"When I brought Ethel around the first time, you were riding on the no-pet bandwagon," Meredith reminded her. "Remember that dogs are a big commitment, even a mature one like Princess. Yorkies can live into their teens. This isn't something you do on a whim."

Angi's face heated. She knew Meredith's job was to protect the animals that came to her shelter, but it stung to be told outright that she might not be a good fit. "It's not a whim."

"It's a distraction," Mariella offered, not very helpfully in Angi's opinion. "Do you have a question about sizes?" she called to a younger woman who'd walked in while Angi was petting Princess. "I can help with that."

Angi straightened as Mariella moved toward the customer. "It's not a whim," she repeated, meeting Meredith's assessing gaze. "Or a distraction. I haven't shown much strength in making my own decisions or acting like an adult lately."

Meredith's features gentled. "You're taking care of your mom, rocking the single mom deal, running the family business and helping at the inn. Tell me what's more adulting than basically holding down four full-time jobs?"

"Not a lot, but I'm kind of failing at all of them. I'm letting what other people want or need dictate my choices. I'd like to choose something for myself." She smiled down at the animal. "I choose Princess."

"Is she soft? What's her favorite toy? Do you think she'll like me?"

Angi turned to smile at Andrew, trying not to let her

nerves show. "I'm sure Meredith will give us all the details. Of course she'll like you. But remember that owning an animal is a big responsibility, Drew. A dog isn't a toy that you can put up on the shelf when you get tired of her. It's a big commitment."

"I know," the boy answered. "Can she sleep in my bedroom?"

"We'll see." Angi looked out the window again as they came to the Furever Friends sign, decorated with garland and a bright red bow.

"Was that speech more for him or you?" Gabe asked quietly as he steered the truck down the long, gravel drive that led to the local animal rescue.

"I'm not sure." Angi clasped her hands together in her lap.

Gabe's mouth curved at one end, but he didn't say anything more.

"Goats," Andrew called out excitedly as they approached the red barn with large pens on either side. "We saw the goats when I came here for the school field trip. The one named Darcy was my favorite. Do you think he's still here?"

Gabe parked the truck next to a silver station wagon. "Why don't you take a look?" he told Andrew with a nod. "Your mom and I will be there in a minute, and then we can go meet this lucky Princess dog."

Andrew scrambled out of the truck with lightning speed, like he was afraid Angi might tell him to stay.

In truth, Angi was too riddled with anxiety to say much of anything.

"It's a dog." Gabe reached across the console and covered her hands with his. "You can handle a dog."

His skin was warm, especially since she felt chilled to

the bone. Andrew had been the one to ask Gabe to join them on this trip, and Angi was grateful for his steady presence. It had seemed easy enough to commit to an animal when Princess had looked at her with those big brown eyes, but the reality was a little different.

"What makes you think that? I'm not handling anything right now with any success. Making a hash of my own life is bad enough. But this is a living, breathing animal. I can't screw it up."

"You won't," he promised.

"How do you know?" She turned her hand over in his and linked their fingers. "Even Meredith seemed to have her doubts. The only thing that's going well for me right now is that I have a great boyfriend." She gave him an arch glance. "And our relationship is pretend."

"Our friendship isn't fake."

"You're leaving," she reminded him, unsure why that mattered at this moment. Somehow it did.

He didn't deny it, and oh, how she wanted him to deny it.

"You'll be so busy with Princess that you won't even notice."

It felt as though her heart was cracking, a small fissure but one that would let in the damp and cold until she was nothing other than a freezing speck in the night wind. She wouldn't let Gabe see that sad, pathetic part of her. He owed her nothing. They'd made no promises beyond the season. And he had become her friend in the past few weeks, one of her best friends.

It didn't matter that she wanted more. When the magic of Christmas was packed away, she'd put her love for him up on a high shelf, as well. It would stay in the dark gathering dust until she forgot how much it meant in this moment. Until she could ignore the rest.

She swallowed hard and pasted a smile on her face. No point in even responding to his comment, not when trying to make a witty comment might reveal too much. It was easier to ignore the inevitable. "The one bonus is that my mom is so mad at me for telling Andrew about the dog before checking with her that she hasn't mentioned the Wildflower Inn or the changes I made to the Il Rigatone menu once in the past twenty-four hours."

"Small favors," he said gruffly. Something in his tone gave her pause. Had he expected her to respond in a different way? Gabe didn't seem like the type of guy who'd take pleasure in a woman pining after him for no reason. He was too honorable. Maybe he finally realized she truly was a big heaping holiday mess. But the new year was coming, and Angi was going to make some changes, even if the things she wanted most were out of her control.

"And I put in an application to rent a small house a few blocks from the elementary school. Meredith told me about it. She's friends with the owner, and it's pet friendly."

"Then let's go meet your new dog."

She got out of the truck, flexing her fingers which were still cold despite the temperate weather. Normally it hovered in the low fifties during December in Magnolia, but this week had been unseasonably warm. At first, Angi had worried that people wouldn't continue to come to events downtown. She'd only spent a couple of winters in New York, but bundling up and braving snow and ice had been a December tradition she'd quickly grown to enjoy.

Christmas on the Coast felt different, but instead of shoppers and visitors shying away, the warm weather brought out the crowds in droves. Avery had called yesterday to report that they'd sold out of tickets to the dance. The event would be full capacity, a mix of locals and visitors from neighboring towns.

Angi knew from Emma that the inn was booked through the new year, and Angi had made enough profit on the events she'd catered so far this month to have plenty to give Andrew a magical Christmas morning plus pay the deposit on a new place.

So maybe things weren't as dire for her future as they seemed.

"Mom, can we get a goat when we move?"

She gawked as Andrew ran up to her, his eyes shining and his cheeks flushed with excitement. "You're kidding, right?"

"I'd take care of it. Come on, Mom. Please."

Okay, maybe not dire. Still, she was hanging by a thin thread because all she wanted was to let out a scream, turn and walk to the beach, only a couple of blocks from Meredith's property, and hurl herself into the pounding winter surf. Was it possible the waves could wash away some of the stress she couldn't manage to let go of on her own?

She was trying to do the right thing. To make Andrew happy. Her mother happy. Prove her worth to the town beyond her identity as Bianca's daughter. Would it ever be enough?

Did any mother feel like they were doing enough?

"You haven't proven yourself as a pet owner yet." Gabe placed a large hand on Andrew's shoulder and gave a squeeze. "Let's give your mom a break, buddy. She's really going out on a limb. Princess is going to be a transition for all of you, and you know dogs are pack animals."

"Yeah," Andrew agreed, turning to gaze up at Gabe. "What does that mean?"

"Well, every pack has an alpha. The leader. A person that all the others look up to."

Gabe darted a glance at Angi.

"Princess is going to be the one to decide where she fits in, and she'll choose her person. The one she's most loyal to and bonded with. Often, dogs pick the person who does the most training with them or sees to their needs. Food. Walks. Making sure they have fresh water."

"I can do those things," Andrew offered.

"I know you can," Gabe answered. "The question is whether you will. If your attention is caught on every shiny new goat that crosses your path, Princess might sense that. She might know you aren't completely devoted to her the way she wants to be with you."

"I am devoted. I promise."

"A good place to start is meeting her, and paying close attention when Meredith goes over her training."

"Welcome," Meredith called from the open barn doors at that moment. "Andrew, are you ready to meet Princess?"

"Yes," the boy whispered, and then gave Angi a hug so fierce it made her eyes sting with tears. "Thank you, Mom. I'll take care of her. I'll be the alpha, and I won't bring up goats again."

"Princess is going to love you," Angi said as she hugged him back. "You can run ahead with Meredith and we'll be right there."

The boy ran toward the rescue owner with an excitement Angi hadn't seen in him for a long time. She clutched a fist to her chest and smiled at Gabe. "You forgot to mention scooping poop."

"We'll cover that on the way home, once he's fallen in love."

"How do you know so much about bonding with animals?"

"My mom got me a dog for my birthday one year, but her next boyfriend hated animals and made me give it away."

"I would never do that."

"I know," he said as if he were soothing her. "You're a good mom, Ang. You'll show Andrew how to take care of the dog and you'll both fall in love."

Angi laughed, although it came out sounding more like a choked sob. Handling the hard parts after falling in love. Wasn't that just the way of it, and not limited to cleaning up after an animal? Angi would happily take all of Gabe's tough stuff at the moment if only he'd be willing to share it with her.

He knew so much about her, and maybe that was part of the problem. What man in his right mind would sign up for the mess she'd revealed to him from the start? A part of her—the girl who'd played make-believe with her dolls as a kid, where Barbie had always ended up married to her perfect Ken—wanted a do-over. She'd shave her legs and curl her hair and spritz a subtle scent on her throat and wrists. He'd take her out to dinner at some fancy restaurant, and she'd smile and flirt and find excuses to touch his arm.

Any excuse to touch him.

But the part of her—the biggest part—who lived in reality knew that even a do-over wouldn't make it better. And she didn't really want that kind of better anyway. If she wanted to live the life she craved and step fully into herself, there was no point in playing pretend. Her reality was complicated and messy. No amount of expensive perfume would change that.

Just like no amount of wishing or hoping would change the fact that Gabe would leave Magnolia in the new year.

Taking her heart with him.

"It meant a lot to Andrew to have you come with us today," she said, giving at least a slice of the truth. "Thank you."

He studied her for a long moment, as if trying to decipher some hidden meaning in those words. Then he nodded. "I'm glad to be here."

"Mom. Gabe." Andrew's voice called from the barn. "Come on. I've already taught her to sit. You have to see. She's the smartest dog ever."

Angi let the happiness in her son's voice soothe the ache in her heart. "We're coming," she answered, and led Gabe toward the open barn doors.

CHAPTER EIGHTEEN

GABE LOCKED THE door to the florist shop the following evening and turned to survey Main Street. He'd stayed last to catch up on orders and update inventory. It was nearly nine so the storefronts around him were darkened, although the sidewalks still glowed with the twinkle lights that had been strewn across windows and wrapped around light posts for several blocks.

At first, he hadn't appreciated the effort business owners and community leaders put into making the town a coastal holiday paradise. Not that he considered himself a grinch. He just didn't see the point in going all out for only a few weeks of the year.

A lot had changed. The lights had become a sort of beacon, representing the hope and magic he hadn't even realized he craved in his life. On nights when he couldn't sleep, he'd drive around and look at the lights that people had forgotten to turn off for the night, imagining happy stories for the families behind the bright facades.

Angi had helped him see how important that magic was. As much as he missed his grandmother, he'd be eternally grateful that he'd had this precious time with her and that she'd seen her shop filled with people once again before she passed away.

Gabe might have lessened Angi's struggle with her mom by agreeing to their pretend relationship, but he'd been the one to benefit the most. And this was despite the fact that she saw him as a temporary arrangement and nothing more.

He wasn't going to be her *more*.

Even after he left Magnolia, he'd see Christmas lights each year and think of her warm brown eyes and the way she hummed off-key when she was focused on a task. The scent of citrus would evoke memories of her soft skin or the way she'd hold him more tightly when he slid into her in the quiet hours of the night.

A couple holding hands came out of Il Rigatone at that moment, laughing about some casual story or private joke. Gabe wished he'd taken Angi on some real dates while they'd been together. Maybe then she would have seen that they could be more than just pretend.

Maybe he'd have the guts to tell her how he felt.

Probably not.

Old habits died hard, as the saying went, and Gabe wasn't good at talking about his feelings. Every time he'd opened up, it felt like he'd been hurt. His grandmother had been the only exception to that rule.

Even Angi had turned on him when they were younger. He'd trusted her when they were kids and told her she was his best friend.

A week later she'd humiliated him in front of her friends.

She wasn't that person now. He understood that. He also wasn't the awkward boy he'd been.

But that kid was still part of him, and his past prevented him from claiming the future he truly wanted.

All he could hope now was that Angi would find her happily-ever-after without him.

He knew she wasn't at the restaurant still. She and Andrew had stopped by the shop earlier while they were taking Princess for a walk. The dog sported the most ridiculous holiday sweater, and Gabe had been shocked to hear that Angi's mom had bought it for the animal.

Apparently, it had only taken Princess a day to win over Bianca, who'd been staunchly against an animal in her house.

Both Angi and Andrew had seemed happy and relaxed in a way Gabe envied, and he didn't doubt that despite the troubles both of them had faced recently, mother and son would find their way through it. They had each other for support, after all.

While, with Gran gone, Gabe had no one.

He walked down the quiet street and stopped in front of Champions, the local bar around the corner from the hardware store. It felt pathetic to have a drink alone, but he couldn't face returning to his grandmother's house yet.

Angi hadn't visited him since the dog's arrival in their lives. She'd told him she didn't feel comfortable leaving in case the dog was restless or woke overnight, and Gabe had no reason not to believe her. But the insecurity he couldn't quite release reared its ugly head in the wee hours, whispering that the animal was an excuse. He was no longer necessary since Angi had stopped working at the inn. She didn't need him, or perhaps she could sense that he needed her too much.

Either way, he was damn lonely. Normally being alone wouldn't bother him, which was another thing that had changed since coming to Magnolia. He now craved interactions with people.

Even strangers, he thought as he entered the bar. The bartender, an older man with grizzled features and a full beard, called out a friendly greeting, and Gabe walked forward, wondering if he looked as pathetic as he felt on his own.

He ordered a draft beer, but before he could take a seat, a heavy hand landed on his shoulder. "This one's on me, Mike," the stranger said to the bartender.

Gabe blinked. "Appreciate the holiday spirit of giving, but do I know you?"

The man, who was tall and broad with a dark head of cropped hair, offered a slow smile. "Gray Atwell," he said, extending a hand. "I think you know my wife."

"Avery," Gabe supplied. "Right." He shook Gray's hand. "You have a cute kid, too," he told Gray, who he knew to be a firefighter for the local department.

"Violet is something special," Gray agreed.

Mike placed two pint glasses on the scuffed oak bar. "I'll put it on your tab," he told Gray.

"It's nice to meet you," Gabe said as he lifted his beer. "But you don't have to buy me a drink. Unless this is a first date and I don't know it."

"I'm spoken for," Gray said with an easy laugh. "Although I've been meaning to stop by your grandma's shop and thank you in person."

The beer was cool on Gabe's throat. "For what?"

He didn't mean for the question to come out as rough as it sounded. He'd gotten a lot better at managing small talk with customers, but he still had a ways to go with being able to function socially in any sort of successful way.

Gray didn't seem to notice or care, which could be a result of being married to Avery. She was a straight shooter as far as Gabe could tell.

"A couple of reasons." Gray took a pull from his beer. "First, my wife is over-the-moon relieved at how well you and Angi are managing the holiday activities in town. The festival means a lot to her, but not as much as Carrie does. The fact that her sister is able to relax and take care of herself because everyone trusts the new dynamic Christmas on the Coast duo is huge."

"Then you should be buying Ang a drink." Gabe tried not to let any telltale emotion sneak into his voice. "She's the brains and creativity behind everything."

"She's not here, otherwise I would." Gray blew out a long breath. "I also owe you both a debt of thanks for encouraging her son to stand up to those little jack holes at the elementary school."

Gabe arched a brow. "I'm not a parent, but pretty sure you're not allowed to call other kids names."

"Then those other kids shouldn't mess with students who are younger than them. I don't tolerate bullies."

"We have that in common."

"I heard as much. Violet is a big fan of Andrew, and he told her that you're the one who taught him how to stand up for himself."

"A lesson I learned the hard way at that age," Gabe admitted. "In fact..." He glanced toward the back of the bar where several guys from Angi's old group of friends surrounded one of the bar's large pool tables. "There were a few little jack holes in this town when I was younger and came to visit my grandmother. Seems like it's nothing new around here."

"Unfortunately, yeah. I appreciate what Andrew did, and I'm sorry he got in trouble for it. I put a call in to the principal to report what Violet told me. I know a lot of kid problems go unnoticed, especially when bullies are sneaky little jerks."

"Jerks," Gabe echoed. "That might be an improvement over jack holes. Not that this makes the behavior okay, but I guess the main culprit's father has left town and they don't know whether he's coming back. Went on a business trip and hasn't returned."

"That sucks for the kid," Gray said, "but it's not an excuse. Either way, thanks for your part in making both the women in my house a lot happier than they would have been otherwise. That makes me happy."

Gabe tipped his beer toward Gray and they both drank. He liked the firefighter. He exuded a natural confidence, like he'd always been sure of who he was and where he fit in the world. Gabe envied that ease and wondered if he'd ever achieve it for himself.

"Do me a favor in return," he told Gray. "Chances are good that I'm going to be heading out of Magnolia myself after the holidays. With my grandmother gone, there's nothing keeping me here."

Gray arched a thick brow but didn't argue.

"Keep an eye on Andrew, would you?" Gabe's chest tightened as he thought of the boy. "He needs all the support he can get and deserves a decent man to be a part of his life."

"Aren't you that man?"

"Not when I won't be here."

"You don't like running the shop?"

"I was taking care of things for my grandma. I haven't talked to the attorney yet, but now that she's gone, I imagine my mom is going to inherit In Bloom. She and I don't mix."

"Got it. The fire department has an opening," Gray said, and gestured to a group of men and women at the back of the bar. "The reason I'm here on a weeknight is because our captain is retiring. They're promoting me, so I'm going to be the one doing the hiring. There's training and a long list of requirements, but if you change your mind about heading out of town, give me a call."

"Thanks," Gabe said, the thought of staying like a shiny gold object just out of reach. "But I doubt that's going to happen." And he wasn't about to admit how much he wanted it to.

ANGI'S PHONE VIBRATED on the kitchen table, and without looking at the home screen, she grabbed the device and shoved it into a drawer of the hutch that sat next to her chair.

"Do you think you should answer?" her mother asked, sipping her morning coffee.

"No." Angi smoothed a hand over her hair, ignoring the trembling of her fingers. Trying her best not to think about how she was letting down her friends when they needed her most. "I'm going to make a smoothie for breakfast." Maybe the noise of the blender would drown out the pounding in her head. "Would you like one?"

"Angela."

She recognized the tone with which her mother said her name. The one that communicated clearly her disappointment and frustration. She'd heard it far too many times in her life.

"It's fine, Mom."

"Based on the way that drawer is vibrating, something is happening this morning that is not at all fine." Her mother rose from the table. "Tell me."

"I don't know," Angi said as she took the blender out of a cabinet under the island's counter. "I haven't answered any of the calls or read the texts."

"If you had to guess…"

She closed her eyes and counted to ten in her head.

Why was her mother doing this? Bianca had wanted her to end her partnership with Emma and Mariella. To walk away from her work at the Wildflower Inn. So Angi had done it. But the only way she could manage it in her mind was a clean break. The plan had been to end the partnership at the end of the year, but managing everything had proved to be too much.

"They're hosting a wedding today, the final big event at the inn before Christmas."

"How many guests?"

"Around a hundred and fifty," she said, drawing in a painful breath. It was the biggest event Emma had hosted this season. "The bridal party is staying at the inn. Over a dozen people."

"And you were supposed to handle the food?"

Of course she'd been expected to handle the food. That was her part. The kitchen at the inn, with its granite counters and clean white cabinets, belonged to her. She'd helped create the design, and Emma had chosen the upgrades to the stainless steel appliances based on Angi's preferences. She loved working in that kitchen.

"They know I'm not coming back," she told her mother now. "I prepped as much as I could, and I hired Sarah Beth Catering to take over for me."

"Her chicken tastes like rubber," Bianca said with a sniff. "If I'm going to something where she's catering, I'm sure to eat before I arrive."

"Thanks, Mom," Angi muttered. "That makes me feel a lot better about my decision."

"No need for the sarcasm and sass, young lady."

Angi threw a bag of frozen berries onto the counter with a thwack. "I'm not a young lady," she said through gritted teeth. "Or a girl. I'm a grown woman, and if I don't try to deflect with humor or sarcasm, then I'm going to burst into tears because I'm letting down people I care about. I'm letting myself down."

Her mother's lips thinned. Without a word, she went to the hutch, pulled Angi's phone out of the drawer and brought it to her. "Figure out what's wrong at the inn," she said resolutely, "and then we'll go fix it together."

Angi's fingers felt numb as she took the device. "I already walked away."

"But before that, you made a commitment." Bianca smoothed a hand over the Christmas sweater she wore. Angi noticed that her mother's nails had been painted in a sparkly red with a delicate silver ring on her right hand. Instantly she thought of Iris and how happy the woman had been to have Angi give her a manicure. How much it meant for Iris to have that connection.

Connection was what mattered. She thought about how scared she'd been when her mother suffered a heart attack so soon after they'd lost Angi's father.

Everything else was insignificant.

"Emma and Mariella understand," she said quietly, even as she glanced at her phone. To her surprise, the missed calls and texts weren't from either of her friends. The number belonged to Sarah Beth. That did not bode well, but she still didn't unlock the home screen.

"You committed to this," her mother said again. "As a grown woman, I would have appreciated you not lying to me or sneaking around like some kind of rebellious teenager, but that's in the past. The inn might not be your future…"

Her mother paused when Angi winced at those words.

"…which doesn't mean you have to relinquish a promise. I hope your father and I raised you better than that, Angela. We raised you to be a person of honor."

Angi didn't bother to argue even though sometimes it felt as though she'd been raised solely to dedicate herself to the family business and the family's honor. Her mother was giving her a chance to make things right in this moment, and Angi was going to take it.

"Thank you, Mom," she said as she hit the voice mail button and listened to the frantic voice mail from the stand-in caterer. Already she was moving toward the coatrack. She called Sarah Beth as she slipped into a pair of clogs.

"I'm on my way," she said when the other woman answered. "Take all of the containers out that are on the top shelf of the freezer and start a pot of water boiling."

"Can you salvage this?" Sarah Beth demanded, panic clear in her voice. "I haven't even told Emma yet, and—"

"I'm going to make it right," Angi promised, and disconnected the call.

"What's wrong?" her mother asked.

"The power in Sarah Beth's company kitchen went out last night, and all the food ended up at room temperature by the time she realized it." Angi blew out a shaky breath. "Emma and Mariella don't know they have an entire reception to feed and only crackers and uncooked pasta to serve them. Can you watch Andrew and Princess? I have to go."

"Wait. What's your plan?"

Plan. Right. Angi wished she had more time to come up with an acceptable alternative. "I'm going to turn the menu into a full-blown feast of my Italian favorites—and hope that the bride and groom are understanding if I give them a big discount."

"How do you feel about my pierogies as an appetizer?" her mother asked. "I always have ingredients on hand."

"You don't have to do that, Mom. I can figure it out on my own."

"I know you can, sweetheart. But I want to help."

"Why?" Angi couldn't help the bitterness that seeped into her tone. "This is perfect for you. Even though I asked Sarah Beth to cover for me, I'm still the name on the contract. If Emma ends up with an irate bride on her hands, that's on me. A fitting end to my attempt to do something on my own."

"You'll find a way to make it right," her mother answered. "And I don't want you to fail, Angela. I never wanted that."

Emotion made Angi's throat raw. That's how it felt. Or at least it felt that her mom only wanted her to succeed with the parameters she set. She could succeed if it was safe and small, but not if it meant she might really fail. She'd tried to go big with her life, a disaster by any standards. How could she ever take that kind of chance again?

Now wasn't the time to take a moral stand or allow her pride to get in the way. Saving the food for the reception meant she'd be saving Emma, so Angi couldn't afford to refuse help from anyone. "The pierogies would be a huge help," she said with a nod. "I'll swing by the res—"

"You go on to the inn and start working things on that end. I'll wake up Andrew, and we'll meet you there." Bianca picked up the landline that still hung next to the refrigerator, harkening back to a simpler time in communication.

"You don't have to come. Who are you calling?" Angi pulled on her jacket.

"The more people you have to help, the better it will go. At least if they're people who aren't incompetent." Bianca rolled her eyes and muttered in Italian. Mostly complaints about the stand-in caterer. "Dominic? Hello, *tesoro*. I know it's your off day, but can you meet me at the restaurant? We need to help Angela with an event at the inn."

Angi felt her eyes widen as a blush crept into her mother's cheeks as she smiled at the longtime cook's reply. Had her mother just referred to Dom as "treasure" in Italian?

That was a quandary for another day.

"Thanks, Mom," she whispered as she headed for the door. She drove to the inn, her heart hammering in her chest. She couldn't let her friends down, but it was difficult to return knowing that it would only be to fix the mess she'd inadvertently created. Her mom had been right about Sarah Beth. The woman might own the only other catering business in Magnolia, but that didn't mean she cooked innovative or even edible food.

But Angi had been desperate for a way out of this final event after her mother's reaction. Another thing Bianca had been right about. She had no business getting on her high horse about being treated like a grown-up when she'd been sneaking around like a child.

Heck, even Andrew was brave enough to face his troubles. It was simple, if not easy, to blame her family—and her mother, in particular—for what was going on in her life and the things she'd missed out on. What if that wasn't true? What if Angi's fear of failure or unwillingness to risk herself again had caused her to blame her mom? A simple excuse for a complicated tumble of emotions.

Good thing the new year was coming, because Angi was piling up resolutions like snow on a sledding hill.

There were cars parked along the street and in the inn's lot. Emma had done an amazing job of transforming the old mansion to a gorgeous boutique hotel, and Angi had no doubt its business would continue to grow and thrive, as well. There was no question that she'd always miss being a part of it.

She quickly walked around the house to the kitchen entrance. The ceremony was scheduled for just before sunset, when the golden light of the setting sun would infuse the whole backyard in a warm glow. The benefit of being in a temperate climate in North Carolina was that if the weather cooperated, Emma could hold outdoor events all year-round. She'd also invested in a large tent to use for those times when it was too cold to be outside.

The whole setup was perfect—exactly what Angi saw for her future, and also not an option when her mother needed her.

Emma and Mariella faced Sarah Beth across the kitchen island as Angi entered the space.

"You can't be here," Emma said, pointing at Angi.

"We need her," Mariella jabbed an elbow into Emma's rib cage.

"It's fine," Emma said tightly. She gave Angi a smile that looked slightly feral around the edges. "We're fine."

"It's a disaster." Sarah Beth threw up her hands. "You were the one who just called it a disaster."

"Not Angi's disaster." Emma's eyes narrowed. "What are you even doing here?"

"Sarah Beth called me. I'm here to help."

Mariella nodded. "We need all the help we can get. At least she realized it had gone bad before we served it. Bad reviews are one thing. Headlines for giving the entire event food poisoning are quite another."

"We're going to fix this," Angi promised.

"You quit," Emma reminded her.

Angi turned. "I thought you said we were still friends."

"Of course we're still friends." Emma sniffed. "This

has nothing to do with friendship. It's the fact that serving a wedding reception whatever food we can pull together from the grocery freezer section might not help our reviews."

The tightness around Angi's chest loosened ever so slightly. It had been so long since she'd had friends like Emma and Mariella—women who mattered to her. Growing up, her insecurity had caused her to put more emphasis on superficial relationships, and she'd picked friends who weren't kind. Who made her unkind.

The idea that even if things continued to go horribly wrong today that Emma would still be her friend... Well, it made her want to fix the mess even more.

"We're not going to rely on the grocery," she promised. "My mom is picking up food from Il Rigatone," she told Emma and Mariella. "We're going to have to change the menu around a bit, but I promise it will still be amazing. I'm not sure when to tell the bri—"

The air rushed from her lungs in a whoosh when Emma grabbed her and hugged her close. "Thank you," her friend whispered. "I don't know what you did to convince your mom to help or why you answered the distress call in the first place."

"She misses us, obviously," Mariella said, leaning in to join the hug. "Also has some superhero complex where she wants to save the day."

"I wish I could offer more," Angi said honestly. "I still feel horrible for walking away. I'm letting you down and myself." She pulled in a shaky breath. "But not today. Today we're going to avert a catering catastrophe."

"I'll go talk to the bride," Emma said, pulling back.

"Put me to work," Mariella told Angi. "I have no skills

and I hate being told what to do, but I'm making an exception for you."

All three women turned as the kitchen door opened again. Angi's mom, along with Dom and Andrew, entered.

Dom carried a large box of various Italian staples, and Angi breathed a sigh of relief.

"It's going to be fine," her mother said when their gazes met.

"Thank you, Mrs. Guilardi." Emma came forward and took the cooler from her mother's hand. "Thank you for your help today."

Tears lodged in Angi's throat as her mother offered Emma a small smile. "I will do anything to help my daughter."

Mariella leaned into Angi and said quietly, "Do you know how lucky you are?"

"Yes," Angi answered. "Right now, I do."

CHAPTER NINETEEN

GABE SAT IN the darkened living room later that night, the only light coming from the tree Angi, her mother, and Andrew had brought to him earlier that week.

The wind whistled around the windowpanes and down the chimney of the fireplace original to the house. If he was staying in Magnolia and his grandmother's property belonged to him, there were so many things he'd do to modernize and update it.

He wished he'd made time to visit Gran and take care of some of those tasks. Although Magnolia stayed relatively mild, drafts seeped from under the doorways and through the corners of windows on colder nights, and the furnace in the basement should have been replaced years ago.

How had his grandma kept warm here at night on her own?

She'd never complained or given him any reason to think she needed help.

He should have known anyway.

Now it was of no consequence because it was only a matter of time before his mother showed up.

Even if he could buy the place from her—and he had no doubt she'd inflate the value if she had any idea how much he wanted it—he didn't want to live in the same town. She tended to suck him in with her dark judgment, and he'd always been afraid he might turn as bitter and miserable as her if they spent too much time together.

His phone dinged, and he grabbed it from the coffee table.

He smiled at Angi's face on his home screen. He'd taken the photo of her at one of the holiday events downtown, capturing her easy smile at a candid moment when she hadn't known he was looking.

Are you home?

Yes. Enjoying the tree.

Do you want to build a snowman?

He chuckled as he glanced out of the window to the dark night. It might be cold and windy in Magnolia, but the sky was clear. No chance of snow.

Is that a trick question?

Come out front.

Anticipation squeezed his chest as he levered himself off the couch. He opened the front door to reveal Angi at the curb next to her car, surrounded by several grocery bags.

"You know the doorbell works," he called.

She beckoned him to her. "I didn't want to unpack the car if you weren't home."

He walked forward, not bothering with shoes. His feet stung as they hit the cold concrete of the front walk, and he thought about the physical discomfort he'd dealt with in the military. How that had been easy compared to the way his heart now seemed to constantly ache.

"Where else would I be?"

She studied him for a moment, brushing her long hair away from her face when the wind whipped at it. She wore a knee-length corduroy skirt with boots and a heavy canvas jacket with a bright red scarf tied around her neck.

"I don't know where you might be spending your time," she told him. "Because you've been avoiding me."

"The dance is tomorrow night, Ang. We've both been busy."

Something like disappointment flashed in her dark eyes, and he felt a chill chase through him that had nothing to do with the outside temperature.

"That's why I'm here." She smiled so broadly he thought maybe he'd mistaken the previous emotion. "We have one more project to finish."

He glanced at the grocery bags. "The mill looks amazing. I stopped by this afternoon. There's not a thing that could be added."

"Snowmen," she said. "You can't have a winter wonderland dance without snowmen."

"I think you could," he said, even as he leaned over the trunk and pulled out two large shopping bags. "We'll have a very successful dance without snowmen."

"Except it would be like a sundae with no cherry on top." She shut the trunk and picked up the bags she'd left on the ground. "Cherries are the best part."

"You seem especially happy tonight."

"I'm glad you think so," she answered, which wasn't exactly the same as agreeing with him.

"Am I wrong?" He glanced over his shoulder as he led

the way toward the house. "How did Sarah Beth do the other day? I'm sure you left her with detailed instructions. I dropped off the flowers early that morning, but she wouldn't let anyone into the kitchen."

"Because she was trying to figure out how to get rid of the food that had gone bad. It was all ruined."

Gabe stopped on the bottom step of the porch. "What are you talking about?"

"Let's get this stuff in the house and I'll tell you. It's freezing out here."

He led the way toward the kitchen and listened as she explained the near disaster of the last big wedding they'd hosted. "You had to swoop in and save the day once again?"

She placed the bags on the table. "I wouldn't exactly call it saving since the fact I walked away caused the mess in the first place."

"You did what you had to do," he said quietly.

"Yeah," she agreed with a sigh. "We all do. But I fixed it, along with my mom and Dom."

"Your mom helped cater an event at the inn?"

Angi wrinkled her nose. "I was as shocked as you, but she said she didn't want me to feel like I'd failed Emma. I know she loves me and wants the best, even if we don't agree on what that is. I was secretly freaking out, so I'm grateful to her."

"You should have called me," he told her, frustration settling over him that she'd needed something and he hadn't been there for her.

"We had it covered," she told him, another lance to his heart. "But I need your help with snowmen, so here I am."

"Okay, then." With how he'd been acting lately, he supposed he should be grateful she was willing to let him in in any way. She pulled out her laptop and they watched an instructional video on making homemade snowmen while he poured two glasses of wine.

As he began to assemble the crafts, something he never imagined himself doing, Gabe felt a sense of contentment wash through him. The exact reason he'd avoided Angi in the first place. It was one thing to want her physically, but his feelings for her went way beyond desire.

They continued working in easy silence until the entire counter was filled with a line of various sizes of snow people staring at them. The biggest were nearly two feet tall, with smaller ones, as well. They all had bright orange noses cut from felt and cheery red scarves around their cotton batting necks.

"I'll bring them over to the mill bright and early," he told her as they cleaned up the leftover supplies. "They turned out better than I thought."

"I think they're perfect," she said with a proud smile, like she was looking at her own children.

He shifted closer to her and spoke into her hair. "Kind of like you."

She didn't pull away as he'd expected with how distant he'd been since his grandmother's death. Instead, she turned and wrapped her arms around his neck. "What if I told you the snowmen were a ruse to have an excuse to see you alone?"

He stilled. There was no way she'd make an effort like that, not for someone like him.

"Alone," she continued, leaning in to place a gentle kiss on his jaw. She breathed deeply, as if she craved the scent of him. "And with a big bed just up the stairs."

"What about Princess?" Gabe remained completely

still, afraid to break the connection between them or remind her in some way that he didn't deserve her attention or her affection.

"She's settled in. Sleeps every night at the foot of Drew's bed. He's her person," she told him with a small smile.

"You're mine," he said, his voice hoarse.

She laughed low in her throat. "You just compared yourself to a dog."

He made a growling noise and then lifted her into his arms. "I'll be whatever you need," he told her as he carried her up to his room, hoping that would be enough.

ANGI STOOD IN the center of the old factory and spun in a slow circle, hardly able to believe what they'd pulled off in the space. It truly looked like something even Santa would be proud of—colorful lights, boughs of holly adorning the walls, along with the snowmen families placed as centerpieces on the tables that surrounded the dance floor. The band stood on the stage that Gabe had found, tuning instruments. She could see people crowding around the hot chocolate bar and enjoying steaming bowls of chili and soup from the food truck that had set up shop in the parking lot.

They had created a winter wonderland.

She turned at the sound of a joyful squeal. Carrie and Dylan stood near the entrance, the graceful artist's big gray eyes wide with wonder.

"It's better than I imagined," Carrie said as she rushed toward Angi.

"Slowly," Dylan said, placing a gentle hand on her arm.

"You came." Angi was shocked and delighted. "I thought…"

"Just for a few minutes," Carrie said. Color infused her cheeks, but there were still dark circles shadowing her eyes. On the few occasions Angi had seen or talked to the other woman, Carrie downplayed her illness, but Dylan wasn't shy about making sure everyone knew that his wife should be called only in an outright emergency due to her focus on staying healthy.

"I'm fine, Dylan." She looked at the haughty developer with such tenderness it made Angi's breath catch in her throat.

That's what she wanted in a relationship. Someone she could look at with unabashed adoration. A man she didn't have to make up excuses—like an entire snowman craft project—to see.

"I think you've started a tradition," Carrie said, turning to Angi. "The town is going to expect a holiday dance every year."

"We're raising money for a great cause," Angi answered. "And it wasn't too much trouble."

Dylan threw back his head and laughed, which seemed more than a little out of character. "How much time did it take you to make all of the snowflakes?" He pointed to the flurry of paper cutouts fluttering above them. "It's a regular blizzard of paper snowflakes."

Angi felt color creep up her throat. The snowflakes, like the snowmen, were a somewhat last-minute addition to the decor. She'd needed something to keep herself occupied once she had the falling-out with Gabe. Knowing he didn't feel for her what she did for him somehow only made her yearn for him more.

So she'd spent far too many sleepless nights cutting out snowflakes at her mother's kitchen table to prevent herself from reaching out to him. To dull the ache in her heart that had only seemed to ease when she'd finally gone to his house and he'd taken her into his arms.

Now she could at least take comfort that her silly way of passing the time had resulted in something magical. There was a lesson in that somewhere, but at this point Angi was too frazzled to discern it.

"I had fun with it," she said, which was somewhere between the truth and a big fat lie.

"We appreciate you." Carrie gave her a gentle hug, and Angi felt the delicate bones of the other woman's shoulders. "The festival wouldn't have been the same without your help."

"I was glad to help," Angi said. "Gabe and I both were."

"You make a shockingly good team," Dylan told her with another chuckle, which died instantly as Carrie winced. "What is it?"

"I'm fine." Carrie smiled, but the corners of her mouth looked tight. "In addition to everything else, I have sciatica. It's all worth it, but I'll be happy when this baby arrives." She cradled her still-flat stomach. "We should go before more people arrive. I'm not up for a lot of socializing tonight."

"Thank you for coming by." Angi squeezed Carrie's hands. "I'll take lots of pictures and text them to you. It will be like you're here, only without people stepping on your toes or having to hear the Macarena."

"You're not seriously doing line dances?" Dylan made a face.

"Meredith requested it," Angi said.

Carrie laughed and took her husband's hand. "Of course she did. Merry Christmas, Angi. I hope all your holiday wishes come true."

Angi kept the smile on her face even though she was afraid none of her wishes would come true. She supposed it was time to start wishing for other things.

TWO HOURS LATER, the dance was in full swing, and Angi felt as if her heart might burst from a combination of happiness and pride, mixed with just a touch of melancholy. She'd done it—along with Gabe.

It seemed like nearly the whole town had come out for the event. Couples young and old mixed on the dance floor, everyone smiling and laughing. Angi Guilardi, who had only ever waitressed in her family's restaurant, had finally stepped out of the long shadow of her last name.

That accounted for the pride and the happiness from finally feeling like she had a place in this community. The melancholy...well. Her gaze sought out Gabe, who stood on the other side of the room talking to Cam Arlinghaus and Ryan Sorensen, who was Emma's brother and Meredith's fiancé.

Gabe smiled at something Ryan said, although even from this distance Angi could see it didn't reach his eyes. He ran a hand through his thick hair, and she wondered if she was the only one who saw the lines of tension bracketing his mouth or the faint shadows under his eyes.

Who would look after him when he left Magnolia? Would he easily find another woman to make him smile and to push him so he didn't revert to his loner habits?

She forced herself to look away. What Gabe did when he left town was none of her business. Christmas was drawing nearer, and after that they would stage a fake breakup and go their separate ways.

The thought made her chest burn.

"Why does this scene remind me of all of our high school dances?"

Angi suppressed a groan as Sara and her bestie, Abigail Johnson, the mom of Johnny Rotten, approached wearing twin sneers. From what she'd heard from Andrew, Johnny had left him and the other kids alone since the scout activity. Maybe the boy had learned something from his father leaving, and although Angi wouldn't wish sadness on a child, she was relieved to have her son not being a target.

"Watered-down punch and the smell of sweat?" she asked conversationally, in no mood to take a trip down memory lane with these two former friends.

"Ew," Sara muttered, pursing her glossy lips. "It's familiar because you're standing alone with no one to ask you to dance." Sara gave a snide little giggle as she patted Abigail on the arm. "Remember how we let the cannoli princess tag along with our group because her parents always gave us free dinner beforehand?"

Angi drew in a deep breath. She remembered how it had felt to know that the people she considered her best friends were using her for their gain. She'd always been aware—even when she couldn't admit it out loud—that the popular group kept her around because she was useful. Even after she'd lost the weight and grown into her looks, they'd still seen her as a means to an end.

At that point, it had seemed worth it. Oh, if she could go back and make a different choice—to be able to give the knowledge and experience of the person she was now to the girl she'd been.

"God, I loved your dad's meatballs," Abigail said, the words suffusing Angi with another layer of bitterness. Her parents had been so generous with her group of friends, thrilled to see their often awkward daughter fitting in. Too bad it had all been fake.

"I hope you both are having a good time tonight," she said, deciding not to rise to Sara's bait. The woman had always been as mean as a snake, and a master at hiding her cruelty behind soft words and a few well-chosen bless-your-hearts. "Abigail, I was sorry to hear about your divorce."

"Temporary separation," Abigail muttered immediately. "Jack will be back. He just needs to sow a few oats. You know how that goes."

"Not really." Angi shook her head. "But I understand that issues within the family can be difficult for kids. I hope Johnny is past his acting out. Andrew wants to get along with everyone in his class."

Abigail's complexion mottled with ugly splotches of color. "I hope that you aren't comparing my son to your strange little boy. Johnny has a father and friends. He's not a misfit."

Strange. Misfit. Angi swallowed back her anger. "Andrew is kind and has a big heart." She took a step closer to Abigail, her patience at an end. She'd tried turning the other cheek and encouraging her son to do the same. Now she realized that part of wanting Andrew to fit in or try to play nice was left over from her own childhood insecurities. She felt bad about her situation and hadn't wanted him to make waves.

It was past time she stop playing small. "I don't give a damn if Jack sows his oats from here to Pensacola. Nothing about the situation excuses you or your son or anyone in your family from being mean. It ends now."

"Calm down, Ang," Sara said with a nervous laugh. "People are starting to stare. I know that Italian temper is cute, but…"

"This isn't my temper talking." Angi cut a glare to Sara that had her taking a step back. "I should have stood up to the two of you years ago. Just like Andrew stood up to your son when he was behaving like a bully. I don't give a rat's behind what happened when we were in high school or what you think you know about me. I'm not the same girl I was back then, and it's pathetic that grown women still play the sort of petty popularity games you tried to win as kids. Grow up, both of you." She leaned in toward Abigail. "Keep your kid away from mine. This is our issue now, and you don't want to take me on."

"You promised me a dance, Angi."

She rolled her shoulders and turned to Gabe, who was standing just behind her, his eyes dancing with amusement.

"RPC is overset at the moment," Sara said smoothly. "She might need a breather to collect herself. Perhaps you'd be a gentleman and dance with me, Gabriel?" Her smile turned sickly sweet as she held out a hand. "My husband, bless his heart, had a late meeting tonight so I'm here all on my own."

As Abigail sucked in great gulps of air, obviously trying to calm herself, Sara turned her back fully on her friend. Clearly Abigail was a liability at the moment, part of the scene Angi had created. She could feel the weight of curious gazes but couldn't quite bring herself to care. What she did care about, however, was the thought of Gabe choosing Sara in this moment.

Angi forced her chin to tip up and met his gaze, hoping that none of the rioting emotions swirling through her could be seen in her eyes. Of course he would walk away with Sara. It was the perfect revenge for the way Angi had turned on him all those years ago.

The amusement was gone from his storm-cloud eyes, replaced by a bone-deep knowledge of what this moment meant.

The worst part was she couldn't even blame him. She deserved to be left behind with a whole crowd to witness her humiliation. This would be the perfect and most believable way to end their fake attachment, because there was no way—for all the Christmas magic at the North Pole—Angi could pretend after Gabe danced with Sara.

She lifted her brows ever so slightly in silent challenge. *Do it*, she wanted to scream. *Turn on me the way I turned on you.*

His broad shoulders rose and fell in a slow breath, and then he flicked a glance at Sara and her outstretched hand before offering his to Angi.

"I believe this dance is ours," he said, his voice a low rumble. As if everyone around them wasn't listening. As if she was the only person who mattered.

Angi only realized she'd been holding her breath when it blew out on a shaky exhalation. She barely registered the gasp of disbelief and subsequent whispered cruelty that Sara dispensed. It was as if she'd been plugging a dam of emotions and Gabe's words and actions had yanked her finger out of the hole.

Love poured through Angi like a wave, and she placed her trembling fingers in his hand. "Every dance is ours," she told him.

Right then she decided to hell with pretend. She had fallen for this man with her entire heart, and she wasn't going to let him go.

As he led her onto the dance floor, the music shifted to "I'll Be Home for Christmas," crooned by the female vocalist's smooth alto.

The past few weeks had changed Angi and her idea of home, what it could mean to her. To a woman who'd learned a hard lesson about not being able to count on a man, Gabe and his steady presence in her life—in Andrew's life—had been a revelation. She could count on him in the most important way possible. She could count on him with her heart.

"Thank you," she said as she wrapped her arms around Gabe's neck.

He pulled her close, and they swayed to the music along with dozens of other couples. The scene with the two other women was ostensibly forgotten by the onlookers since it afforded no juicy town gossip.

Angi would always remember that Gabe had chosen her.

"It would put a damper on the festive mood if the creative genius behind the event got in a fistfight as the main attraction. Can't have you hogging all the attention."

She leaned back enough to look into his eyes. They were once again bright with amusement, but Angi wasn't going to let him make light of what was between them.

Not anymore.

"You're a better person than I was back in the day," she admitted. "The moment that I turned away from you is still the biggest regret I have." She gave a small laugh. "And it's a long list."

"No regrets," he told her, brushing a thumb over her cheek and leaving a trail of sparks in the wake of his touch.

"Will you come to my mom's for Christmas?" Angi asked. They hadn't spoken about plans for the holidays or the future in general. Other than specific arrangements for the town's holiday events, most of their time together was spontaneous or when she couldn't stay away or to appease her mom.

Angi wanted Gabe to know she was choosing him in the same way he had her. She wanted him to know how much he meant to her, even if she couldn't say the most important words just yet.

"I don't want to intrude on your family time," he said, looking past her shoulder.

"Gabe, I want you there." She leaned in and kissed the edge of his jaw. "You belong with us. I want you to know…"

She broke off as his entire body went stiff. Was his reaction a result of her offer? Even if his feelings weren't as deep as hers, they were friends now. Surely that meant—

"I can't believe it."

She frowned as she realized his attention was miles away from her. The color had drained from his face and a change had come over him, like all the light had been snuffed out by a hurricane of darkness.

"Gabe, what's going on?" She tried to turn but his arms held her still, almost painful in their tightness. Angi doubted he even realized the way he was grasping onto her. "Is it Sara? If she's making a scene, I'll—"

"No." He dropped his arms suddenly. His jaw went slack and he gave a sharp shake of his head. The dancers continued to move around them, several couples adjusting their steps to avoid bumping into them since Gabe was now like an unmovable mountain in the middle of the dance floor.

Angi followed his gaze and saw an older woman staring at him from near the bar on the far side of the room. She had black hair, clearly dyed, pulled back into a severe knot on the back of her head. She was small but not frail and looked oddly out of place amid the joy of the crowd attending the dance. After a moment, the stranger turned her attention from Gabe to Angi, lifting the small silver flask she held in her hand as if in a toast.

"Who is that?" Angi asked even as Gabe moved to block her view.

It seemed endless minutes passed before he answered, although in truth it was only a quick second.

She felt the change in him. A systemic shift as if everything between them was gone.

"That," he said slowly, his voice as cold as she'd ever heard it. "Is my mother."

CHAPTER TWENTY

GABE WOKE ON Christmas morning to the sound of Patsy Cline blaring through the house.

He stifled a groan and rubbed two fingers against his temples. He knew what that music meant. His mother had always gravitated toward music about broken hearts when her mood was down, and her mood was always bad during the holidays.

It was as if every slight or loss she'd had throughout the year—even her lifetime—was compounded at Christmas. As an adult, he'd learned it wasn't unusual for people to be depressed at this time of year. Despite all the magic that Angi and her family seemed to find in the holidays, plenty of people struggled with unrealistic expectations or comparisons of their own imperfect life to the cheery images on Christmas cards or endless social media posts.

Hell, before this year, he'd been one of them.

But he'd been given a huge gift, one that no money could buy. The gift of hope and joy. And love. Most importantly love. Even though he missed his grandmother, he knew she'd want him to find happiness.

Her love was truly unconditional, and she'd always wanted him to focus on the good moments in life. In the end, he'd been able to offer a bit of that back to her. As awful as it was to have his mother in the house now, he tried to remember the joy that had surrounded him when he'd been working to make his grandma's dream come true again.

Although the noise from the first floor seemed intent on drowning out whatever Christmas spirit he could muster.

He threw off the covers and glanced at his phone as it vibrated on the nightstand.

A text from Angi.

With a sharp ache in his gut, he cleared the home screen without reading her message. What the hell was there to say at this point?

They hadn't spoken since those final moments when he'd held her in his arms on the dance floor. He knew she'd been surprised that he hadn't taken the opportunity to embarrass her in front of those grown-up mean girls.

How could she believe he'd do anything other than choose her? Even when he'd been holding on to his anger and bitterness like a lifeline, she'd had his heart. He understood that was why he'd been so bitter in the first place. It was the only defense mechanism he'd had. The only way to keep his heart safe.

But she'd managed to move past his defenses like they were made of jelly instead of the brick walls he'd tried to build. There was nothing he could deny her when she looked at him with those soft chocolate eyes.

At least not until his mother had arrived back in town, reminding him that he didn't belong in Magnolia. This place wasn't his home.

Gabe dressed, brushed his teeth and headed downstairs. "Mom?" he called as he entered the kitchen. "Can you turn down the music?"

The only answer was a dull thumping sound. He eyed the mess of dirty dishes and leftover food in the kitchen with a sigh, and then headed toward the front of the house, following the banging and swearing.

Had one of his mother's usual loser boyfriends followed her to Magnolia?

Gabe's breath caught in his throat as he came to the threshold of his grandfather's office. The room had remained largely untouched for decades. He knew his grandma hadn't been able to bring herself to use the large cherry desk that had belonged to her late husband.

Instead, she'd set up a smaller, delicate writing desk in one corner of the room. Gabe had gone through it when he'd first arrived in Magnolia, although most of her paperwork for the business was kept at the store.

He took in the scene before him with a clawing sense of frustration. Papers and books were strewn across the floor along with several empty beer cans and a jar of peanut butter with a dirty spoon lying next to it. He quickly walked over to the old amplifier and cassette player on the bookshelf and flipped it off.

"Mom, what the hell?" he demanded as Poppy looked up, the sudden silence alerting her to his presence.

"She kept all my old cassette tapes," his mom told him, as if that was the answer to his question. "My parents hated my music, so I can't believe she didn't relish tossing them to the trash just like she did me."

"Your revisionist history isn't going to work with me," he said, setting his jaw so he didn't yell the words. His mother would love nothing more than a big, dramatic argument and the ability to turn him into the bad guy, the way she had her parents. "Gran took care of you, and she took care of me. She kept a ledger, you know. Every payment she made to you, Mom. She was sending you money up until her fall. So let's not pretend otherwise."

His mother's eyes narrowed. "Not the money I needed. She saved that for her precious town and business."

"What are you doing?" He took a step forward. "Did you sleep at all, Mom?"

Her lip curled and she swiped a finger under each eye. His mom had always favored coal-lined eyes, which seemed strange given the fact that she didn't seem to care about taking off her makeup at night. As he remembered from so many mornings of his childhood, she had the appearance of a hungover raccoon, only now the lines at the corners of her eyes were deeper, the day-old liner sunk into them like tar on a cracked driveway.

"How can I sleep when I feel your hatred toward me? It's hard to breathe in this place between your judgment and my mother's lingering disappointment."

"She's gone," Gabe reminded his mom. "Can you give her a break now?" *Give me a break*, he wanted to add but didn't bother. When he left home at eighteen to join the army, he'd made a vow that he'd never ask his mother for another thing.

A vow he had no intention of breaking.

"Are you hiding the will?" she asked, eyes narrowed. "Trying to cut me out of what's rightfully mine?"

Her accusation stung, and he hated that he let any of her verbal animosity affect him. This was why Gabe had cut himself off from feeling anything. There was too much hard that could come in with the good. By not feeling anything, he protected himself from feeling the things that were too difficult. Unwanted.

The way his mother hadn't wanted him. And still didn't, apparently.

"Merry Christmas to you, too." He rubbed a hand over the back of his neck, trying unsuccessfully to loosen the knots that had formed there. "I'm going to shower and make breakfast. I don't suppose we have much to do in the way of exchanging presents."

"Gabe, answer me."

He wanted to ignore her. To walk away, pack his bag and leave this house. The happiness that he'd found in Magnolia was like a distant memory at this point. All he could see was the mess his mother had made, and not just of this room. She'd made a mess of his life. The life he hadn't realized he wanted but that now meant more to him than anything else.

But his sense of duty wouldn't allow him to. Despite knowing he'd never make her happy, why was it so difficult to turn his back on the parent who'd rejected and demanded from him in equal measure?

He'd learned that happiness was a choice, and one his mom would never make.

"I haven't seen an actual will," he said, his tone flat. Barren like the way his heart felt. "But I'm sure it's here somewhere. I can give you the number of her attorney in town. That's my gift to you, Mom. I'm walking away having added value to the house and the business, and you'll reap the benefits." He started to turn but looked at her again with the cool detachment he'd give to a stranger. "As a bonus, I'll be gone tomorrow. It's all yours. Merry Christmas, Mom."

ANGI RANG GABE's doorbell later that night, holding tight to the plate of leftovers she carried and trying to keep her heart from beating out of her chest.

An old sedan with New Mexico plates, dented on one side with the fender loose, sat in the driveway in front of Gabe's truck.

She hadn't talked to him since his mom made her appearance at the dance. The irritating man had left Angi on the dance floor as he'd stalked over to Poppy Carlyle, exchanged a few heated words and then taken off.

No return calls or texts, even though Angi knew how hard it must be to have his mom finally here.

He'd dreaded that moment, although they both knew it was coming.

Selfishly, Angi had hoped that Poppy would arrive after Christmas. That she'd have a chance to spend the holiday with Gabe and finally ask him to reconsider ending their pretend relationship, the connection all too real for her. She wanted a do-over on the past few weeks, one where she would have told Gabe how she felt about him.

The fact that she'd fallen in love with him.

It took a few minutes for the front door to open, and she found herself face-to-face with Poppy, who gave her a long, assessing once-over that might have made Angi cringe at some point. But she was past caring what anyone thought of her. Although this was Gabe's mother, Angi had little interest in playing nice.

"You're the one he was dancing with the other night," Poppy said, her fingers clasped tightly in front of her bulky sweatshirt.

"I'm Angi Guilardi." Angi held out a hand because that's how she'd been raised. "A friend of Gabe's."

Poppy didn't take it, which told Angi everything she needed to know, confirming her suspicion about the kind of person Gabe's mother was.

With a sniff, the other woman turned and hollered up the stairs, "Gabriel, you have a visitor." She said the last like it was the worst of all swear words. Then her sharp gaze flicked to Angi again. "My son never had many friends."

"He does in Magnolia."

"A change from when he spent summers here as a kid." Poppy shook her head, but the corner of her mouth curved into an almost smile. "Such an awkward, odd boy. I thought he might be touched in the mind. Turns out the army did more with him than I ever could."

"Maybe you should have tried harder," Angi said before she thought better of it. "Or at all."

"Snippy one," Poppy murmured as heavy footfalls sounded on the stairs behind her. "Interesting choice for him."

"What are you doing here?" Gabe asked as he came to stand next to his mother.

"Merry Christmas," Angi answered with a smile. One he didn't return. "I brought you some food." She looked at Poppy. "There's a plate for both of you."

His mother shook her head. "I got Chinese carryout earlier. Ate my weight in moo goo gai pan." She patted Gabe on the arm, and Angi would have sworn he had to make an effort not to flinch away from the touch. "It's our family tradition."

"We don't have family traditions," Gabe said quietly, his voice like a razor cutting through the awkward tension.

His mother just laughed like he'd made a great joke, turned and walked away.

"How are you?" Angi reached for him once they were alone, but Gabe shifted away from her.

Warning bells clanged in her brain, and she did her best to ignore them. The new year wouldn't dawn for another week, but it was past time she worked on being brave.

"I missed you today. We all did."

His eyes darkened for an instant, and then he grabbed the wrapped plates from her hand, placed them on the side table in the entry and pushed her a step backward out the door.

The door slammed shut behind him, and Angi swallowed against the rising panic in her chest. This was a Gabe she'd never seen before. It was more than disdainful, as he'd been when he first arrived in Magnolia. It was as if he'd turned to ice, and a shiver rippled through her in response.

He moved to the edge of the porch steps like he might bound off into the darkness. She could feel the agitation radiating from him, and she wrapped her arms around her waist to shield her from whatever was coming next.

"You shouldn't be here," he said. "Go home to your family, Ang. It's over."

"I don't want you to be alone on Christmas."

"You met my mother," he said with a derisive laugh. "Clearly I'm not alone."

She wanted to argue. It was clear as the night sky that he was as lonely as he'd ever been, maybe even more so because of his mother's presence in the house.

"Not just today," she said before she lost her nerve. "I miss you in general, Gabe. It's more than just the holiday and I refuse to believe we're over."

"Of course we are," he said. "That was the agreement."

"No." She stepped forward, praying that he wouldn't bolt on her. "Or maybe it was, but everything changed."

"You're right." He turned to her, his jaw tight and color high on his cheeks. "My grandmother died, and my mom is here now to take what belongs to her. I don't have to pretend in order to make anyone happy."

"I'm not pretending," Angi said, opening her gaze and

hoping she could get through to him. Praying it wasn't too late. "I love you, Gabe."

"Don't say that."

"It's true." She breathed out a soft laugh. "I've known it for a while. But at the dance when you took my hand—"

"That was part of the act."

She shook her head, ignoring the way his words stung like the lash of a whip.

"I told you I'd keep it up until the new year," he said, his voice just as icy as his demeanor. "But it ends now."

"I don't want it to end." She held out a hand but gathered it to her body before he could take it. She didn't know how to reach him when he was like this. "I know you feel something for me, too. Something real."

"Pity," he said, and she sucked in a breath. "You're grasping at me because you're too afraid to go after what you want in life. I feel sorry for you, Angi. And for Andrew, because he deserves a mother who knows how to stand up for herself and what she wants."

"I want you," she whispered, desperate to make this work even as she felt her heart splintering.

"I'm leaving town tomorrow." He closed his eyes and shifted his gaze to the front yard, like he couldn't even stand looking at her. "I won't be back."

"You can't mean that." Her voice cracked and she felt tears sting the back of her eyes. She dug her fingernails into the soft flesh of her palms, needing the physical pain to drown out everything else. "This is your home."

"I don't have anything here," he said. "No business. No house. No—"

"You have me," she whispered, then cleared her throat. "You have Andrew and friends. Choose me. Choose us, Gabe. Don't let your mom win."

He snorted. "She already has. I'm done. You deserve better. The younger version of you knew it. Current you just has to remember."

"I love you," she repeated because what else could she say?

"You're wasting your time. I don't know how to give you what you want. I can't be that man."

You already are, she wanted to tell him.

She wanted to scream and yell and beat on him until she broke through that frosty exterior to the tenderness and vulnerability she'd discovered he hid deep inside.

What was the point? As he'd just told her, she was wasting her time, and that was something she'd promised herself she would no longer do. She was too valuable for that, and if Gabe couldn't see it then that was his loss.

Even if hers was the heart shattering.

"I took you for a lot of things, Gabe." She drew in a deep breath as she stepped away from him. The first of many. "A coward wasn't one of them."

Without waiting for his reply, she bounded down the porch steps, needing to get away before she crumpled into a million pieces.

CHAPTER TWENTY-ONE

"I COULD HIRE YOU."

Gabe returned the gas pump to its holder and offered Cam a disbelieving stare over the rims of his sunglasses.

"A pity job," he said on a laugh, although there was no humor in the sound. "Gray Atwell said almost the same thing. As much as I appreciate the offer, I'm going to have to pass."

"Who says I'm making it out of pity?" Cam shook his head. "Maybe I'd do whatever it took to get you to stay in Magnolia." He took a step closer. "Somehow I doubt Gray and I are the only ones."

Gabe swallowed hard and tried not to let any of the emotions swirling through him show on his face. It was the day after Christmas, and he'd sent Cam a message saying he was leaving town. It would have been easier to sneak away with no one the wiser, but that felt like a cowardly move.

Angi had accused him of being a coward last night, and the label still stung. He knew she'd thank him eventually. He was doing them both a favor by leaving when he wasn't sure he'd ever be able to give her the life she deserved. Not when it was so hard for him to truly open his heart.

"It's better this way," he told the other man. Cam had asked to see him on his way out, so Gabe had agreed to meet at the gas station near the water tower on the edge of town. The morning was cold and quiet, most residents probably still tucked into bed or kids playing with the toys they'd received for the holiday.

The erector set he'd bought for Andrew sat under the tree in his grandmother's house. He'd gotten it over a week ago, hoping the classic building toy would spark the boy's imagination the way it had Gabe's back in the day. But that had been before. Before his mom came back. Before Gabe woke up and realized he was living and loving on borrowed time. Before he'd known he couldn't possibly stay.

"What does Angi have to say about that?" Cam asked softly.

"She agrees with me." At least she must after he'd been such a jerk last night. "I'm sure Emma told you our whole relationship thing was a pretend arrangement to keep her mom and my grandma from playing matchmaker all through the holidays."

"Bull." Cam spit out the word like it tasted rotten on his tongue.

"It's true." Gabe took his receipt when it printed. "We were going to break up after the new year anyway."

Cam inclined his head as he studied Gabe. "Did you get dropped on your head as a baby?"

"What the hell is that supposed to mean?" Gabe crossed his arms over his chest. "Did you ask for a face-to-face goodbye so you could hurl insults at me on my way out?"

"I want to talk some sense into you. You have a good life here, Gabe. Why walk away? You know as well as I do how hard happiness is to come by." He held up a hand when Gabe would have spoken. "And don't expect me to believe for a second that you weren't happy with Angi. I don't care how the relationship started, the two of you are the real deal."

"We aren't anything at this point," Gabe said, keeping

his voice steady. "She's better off that way. Does happiness count when I was living a life that didn't belong to me? I came here for my grandmother, and took care of her house and her business. Neither of which I can claim at this point. I have nothing to offer Angi, even if I wanted to."

"That's not true," Cam argued. "Stay. Just stay and try to make it work."

Gabe wanted to agree. He wanted to turn his truck around as much as he wanted his next breath. But that was the problem. Where was he supposed to go? He had no home. No job. He'd made a place for himself in Magnolia, but his mom's arrival wiped it all away. She'd always treated him like he was worthless, and there was no way he was going to stick around and let her go after him again.

He didn't have it in him.

Maybe that made him a coward after all.

"Keep an eye on Ang and Andrew," he told Cam. "That kid has a heart of gold, and I hate to think about some jerkwad boy with his own daddy issues bullying it out of him."

"He needs you," Cam answered.

Gabe gave a sharp shake of his head. "I wish I could be the kind of man that kid needs, but I've even managed to screw that up at almost every turn. They'll both be better off without me."

Before Cam could argue, Gabe reached out a hand. "You're a good guy, Cam. Just please keep an eye on the boy."

"I will," Cam said quietly as they shook. "If you ever need anything…"

"Appreciate it." Gabe forced a smile. "I'll figure something out. I always do."

And with those words, he climbed into the truck and pulled away. He kept his eyes on the road ahead of him, despite not having a single idea of what direction he was headed. It didn't matter. He was leaving everything important behind him, but to glance in the rearview mirror would only cause more pain.

He rolled down the window and tossed his cell phone into the trees that lined the two-lane highway. He focused on what was coming and tried his best to begin to rebuild the walls around his heart.

ANGI SAT IN the darkened living room on New Year's Eve. It was five minutes to midnight, and Andrew was fast asleep, curled into a ball on the sofa with Princess snuggling next to him. Her mother had gone to bed an hour earlier, claiming that she honored the new year best with a good night's sleep.

They'd been invited to a party at the Wildflower Inn by Emma and Mariella, but it was too difficult for Angi to be there knowing their partnership was at a distinct end along with so many other things that had become essential to her.

Emma was hosting a New Year's Day brunch for the inn's guests and a few close friends, but Sarah Beth wouldn't be helping to prepare for it. After the near disaster of the wedding, Angi had contacted a smaller operation on the south side of Raleigh. The kitchen that she loved now belonged to someone else.

Instead of preparing her own recipes, she'd open Il Rigatone tomorrow, serving the special Alfredo lasagna her father had always prepared to usher in a new year. There was a group of loyal regulars who came to celebrate the start of a fresh calendar each year. Angi knew them by name and had no doubt they'd pinch her cheeks and tell stories of the girl she'd once been as they laughed and gossiped in the same way they had for decades.

Maybe there would be new people this year. Visitors who'd come to Magnolia for a holiday getaway or locals who appreciated some of the changes she'd made in the menu and wanted to try something new.

Her mother wouldn't like it, but Angi would keep pushing to expand and curate the menu to her culinary preferences. If she was going to be the one to carry on the family tradition, at least she would fight to put her spin on it.

Princess lifted her head as Bianca walked into the room, her slippers a soft shuffle across the hardwood floor. The dog sighed, then settled again. Angi's heart tugged at how dedicated the animal had become to Andrew.

Perhaps she should have added a dog to their small family sooner, but she wasn't going to wallow in regret about something so small. Princess was the perfect pet, so she had to believe that the timing of adopting her had happened just as it was meant to be.

If only it were that simple to release her regrets about other parts of her life.

"He's going to miss the ball dropping." Bianca gestured to the muted television, which showed split-screen images of happy revelers on both coasts.

"I'm recording it," Angi answered with a shrug. "He can watch it tomorrow, and I'm sure it will be just as exciting."

Her mother lowered herself into the chair across from Angi's. "If only it were that simple to go back in time. The changes I'd make…"

Angi frowned. She'd never heard her mother express regret for the way she'd lived her life. Bianca was steady and steadfast like the ticking of the grandfather clock in the formal living room.

"What would you do differently, Mom?" she asked, almost afraid to hear the answer.

"I would have told your father I loved him more often. I would have found a way to take time off and travel the way we'd planned to." She sighed. "Always planning for the future but never making those big dreams come true. Your father worked too hard, Angela. Maybe if he'd had more rest…"

"Dad loved working," Angi said. "The restaurant meant so much to him. The two of you built it together, and that meant the most."

"Yes, we had a good life. I shouldn't wish for things from the past. A new year is for looking forward."

Angi sat upright when her mom pressed an open palm to her heart. "Mom, are you okay? Is that why you're awake? Let me help you back to bed, and you can sleep in tomorrow. I'll handle—"

Bianca waved her to sit down when Angi started to rise. "I'm fine, sweet cannoli." She shook her head. "I suppose I shouldn't call you that any longer. I know the nickname caused you too much distress with those nasty kids you insisted on calling your friends."

"It's okay," Angi assured her. "I don't mind."

Her mother arched a brow.

"You're right, I hate it," Angi said, and then wrinkled her nose when her mother chuckled.

Andrew stirred and both women were quiet for a moment.

When her mother spoke again, her voice seemed to come from miles away instead of a few feet across the room.

"Just like you hate running Il Rigatone."

Angi's heart pinched, and she tried to decipher her mom's tone, squinting to read her expression. Bianca had sat back, her face in shadows, giving away nothing.

"I don't hate it," Angi said carefully. It would have been so easy to lie or gloss over the truth the way she'd done for so many years. But a glance at the television told her there were only thirty seconds left in the current year. And she'd made a vow to be different.

Maybe Gabe hadn't believed her, but this was her chance to prove it to herself.

"The restaurant was your dream, Mom. Yours and dad's. I know how much you both sacrificed, and I appreciate the life you gave us because of it." She glanced at her sleeping son. "I understand that you wanted something dependable and solid. We had a good childhood. It was a wonderful way to grow up."

"Even if you always smelled like tomato sauce," Bianca added. The way the aroma of the restaurant clung to her had been the bane of Angi's existence as a teenager. She'd doused herself in scented body lotion and way too much perfume in order to mask it.

"There are worse things to smell like," she admitted. "Mom, I know you need me to take over the restaurant so you can focus on staying healthy. That's most important for both of us. I don't want to lose you like we did Dad." Her voice broke, and she dragged in a steadying breath.

"I'm not going anywhere," her mother promised, then shook her head. "Actually, that's not true. I might be going to Florida."

Angi blinked. "Okay," she said slowly. "Do you want me to look at tickets?"

Bianca shook her head. "A couple of friends from the exercise class at the senior center are planning a trip. Marcie and Jim have a house on the beach in Naples."

"That sounds nice. How long will you be gone? When are you leaving?" Angi's head spun. She couldn't remember the last time her mother had gone on a vacation that wasn't to visit family.

"They left just before Christmas to open the house for the season. I might need a few weeks to get ready with—"

"I can help you pack."

"Angela…" Bianca sat forward, her eyes glistening with tears. "I'm going to sell the restaurant."

Angi was up and out of the chair in an instant. She crossed to her mom and knelt before her, taking Bianca's trembling hands in hers. "Mom, no. You don't have to do that. I'll make it work. I'm sorry if—"

"*Cara*, hush." Bianca shook her head gently. "I'm the one who owes you an apology, Angela. For making you believe that you were tasked with making my dream yours. Of not seeing that you had your own life to live and allowing you to choose your path."

"I don't need a path, Mom," Angi insisted, keeping her voice low so as not to disturb Andrew. With the emotional tide rising inside her, it was difficult. "I want to honor you. To do what's right for Dad's memory."

Bianca squeezed Angi's fingers. "What's right is for our daughter to be happy. I didn't realize you weren't, and I'm most sorry for that."

"I can be," Angi said. "I will be again. I don't need something outside myself to make me happy. Not disappointing you makes me happy."

"You've never been a disappointment." Bianca leaned forward and brushed a gentle kiss across Angi's forehead. "To be honest, I thought this business about the inn was just a rebellion, and I understood that. I didn't like it, but I understood the need for it. At your age, I had three young kids, a husband who worked seven days a week, and the need to work almost as much myself. It wasn't a happy time for your father and me."

"I never knew."

Bianca smiled. "You were barely out of diapers. It wasn't your place to know. But it was a dark time for me, and there were moments I thought about walking away."

"From Dad?" Angi sat back on her heels. She couldn't even fathom her devoted parents not being together. "From all of us?" Her mother had been a constant presence in her life, no matter the ups and downs they'd had over the years.

"I don't know at this point." Bianca shrugged, looking unsure and unlike herself. "I was desperate, and desperation causes us to do strange things." She patted Angi's cheeks. "Things like lying about work and partnerships." She paused and then added, "About relationships."

Angi felt color rise to her cheeks. "I have plenty to apologize for," she said with a grimace.

"I hate that you felt like dishonesty was the best choice."

"I didn't want to upset you, Mom. Your heart—"

"Is strong and sure. I'm going to be here a long while. Long enough to see you succeed with your friends at the inn. Watching you in that kitchen was a revelation. Your father's legacy isn't Il Rigatone. It's you, Angela. I saw the same joy in creating and serving food to people in your eyes that I remember in his. That's what I want for you, and if you've found that at the Wildflower Inn, then you have to make it work."

"I walked away," Angi said, swiping a hand across her cheek when a tear escaped. "I found someone to take my place."

"Call Emma tomorrow," her mother said with a knowing wink. "I think she'll be expecting to hear from you."

Angi's breath caught in her throat. "But you love the restaurant."

"I do," Bianca agreed. "And I love the life I had with your father. Things change, though. We've had interest from buyers on and off over the years, but now that the town is thriving again, I've had solid offers. I want the space to be run by someone who loves it the way your father did. It's time for both of us to move on, Angela."

"What about Dom and the rest of the staff?" Angi frowned as the wheels started turning in a different direction. "If Emma stays busy with the events or I expand my catering business, I might be able to hire a couple of the waitresses."

"If things work out with the offers I have on the table," Bianca said, "you'll have a good-sized nest egg to start. Since Dylan Scott owns the building, he's helping me with negotiations. I much prefer having him as a partner than going up against him."

"You're serious about this." Angi still felt dumbfounded.

"I am." Her mother looked toward the television. "I wouldn't worry too much about Dominic if I were you. I'm trying to convince him to take that Florida vacation with me."

Angi's jaw dropped open. "Mom. You and Dom?"

"We're friends," her mother said, although her cheeks bloomed with color. "At least for now."

"He's a lucky guy," Angi said softly.

"So was Gabe Carlyle," her mother answered.

"There's no point in pretending that was anything more than a ploy to avoid you setting me up with every single man in Magnolia."

"It was more."

Angi opened her mouth to argue, but what was the

point? Her mother knew her better than that, and it was now officially the new year. Her year of being brave.

"For me," she admitted. "But not him."

"He cares about you."

Angi straightened and brushed a hand over the front of her sweatshirt. Thinking about Gabe was difficult. Too difficult for the emotions already tumbling around her chest. She would most likely lose it completely, and that's not who she was going to be this year.

"I loved him," she told her mother. "Whether or not he cared for me doesn't matter now. He wasn't willing to take a chance on us. That's on him."

"Stupid boy," Bianca muttered.

"Yeah," Angi agreed. "But I'll be okay."

"You're amazing," her mother said with the conviction of devoted mothers everywhere. Angi wished Gabe's mom had possessed one whit of maternal instinct. Maybe then he wouldn't have felt that closing himself off was the only option.

"It's going to be a wonderful new year, Mama." No matter what, it truly would be a time of new beginnings.

CHAPTER TWENTY-TWO

GABE EXPECTED MAGNOLIA to look different.

He couldn't explain why. It had been only two weeks since he'd driven out of town. But he had changed in that time.

Or at least had pulled his head out of the proverbial hole where he'd buried it.

Which was what he should have done from the start.

The past, his doubts, and the regrets he couldn't control had held sway over his life. Fear had ruled the day, and there was a chance he wouldn't be able to make things right.

He had to try.

He'd hurt Angi. There was no doubt about it. He only hoped she would find a way to forgive him. He'd spend the rest of his life earning his place at her side if only she'd let him back into her life.

He had thought about calling, although that was a bit of a challenge given he hadn't replaced his cell phone. His was probably smashed into a million pieces or buried deep in the woods that bordered the highway where he'd thrown it on his way out of town.

That was an excuse and a lame one at best. He'd spent the past two weeks on a buddy's farm outside of Memphis. Hours of helping with chores and far too much time ruminating over the mess he'd made of his life. At first, he thought he could walk away. He convinced himself it was better. Better for Angi. Easier for him. Yet she'd never been far from his thoughts, and the walls around his heart simply refused to be rebuilt.

She was a part of him. Magnolia was a part of him. This town had become his home. Maybe it had always been that way since those summers spent here with his grandmother and he'd just been too bullheaded to realize it.

Away from this place, there was no happiness or contentment. The idea of peace was like a song stuck in his head, but he couldn't quite remember the words. Being with Angi was what made the song of his life complete.

He turned onto Main Street, knowing he'd have to pass In Bloom on his way to see Angi at the restaurant. It was Saturday midmorning so he knew she'd be there prepping for the lunch crowd.

Seeing his grandmother's shop when he was no longer a part of it wouldn't be easy. Based on his mother's vitriol and the way she'd taken apart the house so quickly, for all he knew she'd already closed up this storefront and sold off the inventory just to make some quick cash.

Even if Poppy chose to stay in Magnolia, Gabe wasn't going to be run off. He'd let the relationship with his mom—her negligence and outright hostility—define his life for too long.

He was a grown man and it was time to start acting like it.

As he passed the grassy center of town, he noticed a group of kids playing soccer. One dark head stood out among the boys. Gabe winced as Andrew kicked at the ball and missed. But true to form, Drew didn't give up. He simply turned around and kicked again, this time passing to one of the other boys on the team.

"You keep kicking," Gabe murmured into the truck's quiet interior.

Without thinking too much about it, he parked near the curb and got out, slowly approaching the action. The kid Andrew had passed the ball to dribbled down the make-shift field and took a shot, the ball sailing up and into the goal.

Gabe let out a whoop of congratulations, drawing the attention of several boys, including Drew. The kid's shoulders stiffened and his smile disappeared instantly.

Damn.

Gabe had expected a potentially icy reception from Angi, but he'd figured Andrew would be happy to see him return. Not so much, based on the glare the kid was currently shooting in Gabe's direction.

In fact, after an almost imperceptible shake of his head, Andrew turned on his heel and stalked toward the far end of the field where his friends were currently gathering.

His chest aching, Gabe stopped. He wouldn't force Drew to talk to him, especially not before he knew whether Angi was willing to forgive him.

Then, as quickly as Andrew had whirled away, he spun around and jogged toward Gabe.

"That's my boy," Gabe whispered under his breath.

Only Andrew still clearly wasn't happy to see him.

"I hate you," the boy ground out as he got closer. "My mom hates you, too. You made her cry."

"I'm sorry." Gabe felt like he'd been punched in the gut. Of course he knew he'd hurt Angi by leaving, but hearing the raw emotion in her son's voice tore him apart in a way he wasn't expecting.

"What do you want?"

Nothing. The word was on the tip of Gabe's tongue.

What the hell had he thought would happen upon his return? In truth, he hadn't given much thought to the messy reentry into the lives of the people he loved. The understanding he'd gained about being willing to risk his heart to have the future he craved had trumped any doubt.

It was simple enough to give lip service to the idea that it wouldn't be easy. Having a kid who'd adored him shoot visual daggers in his direction brought home the reality of what he truly faced.

He fisted his hands at his sides and forced a deep breath. He'd told himself that nothing would stop him from fighting for Angi and Drew. If he gave up so easily, what would that say about him?

Andrew continued to glare, and Gabe could hear the boy's panting breaths like he was having trouble controlling his upset. Gabe knew about that, and he understood using temper and emotional distance as a shield because those were less scary than fear of rejection and vulnerability.

And Andrew had plenty to be scared about, as much as Gabe had at that age. But the boy kept at it, and Gabe almost smiled realizing that Drew had already mastered a skill Gabe was still struggling to learn.

"Nice assist on that goal," he said, hoping to distract Andrew long enough to figure out how to make this better. If nothing else came from his return, Gabe wanted Andrew to know that he would be there for him no matter what.

"Thanks," the kid muttered because his mother had raised him with good manners. "Why are you here?" he asked.

"Because I screwed up, and I want to make it better." Gabe ran a hand through his hair and hoped Andrew hadn't heard the catch in his voice. "I'm sorry I hurt your mom and I'm sorry I hurt you, Drew. I was selfish and stupid."

"You didn't even say goodbye."

"I know." Gabe crouched down in front of the boy. "It's because I didn't really want to leave Magnolia. I love it here. I love you and your mom very much, and it killed me to drive away from the two of you."

"But you did," Andrew reminded him.

"Yeah, I was scared, buddy. Terrified of admitting how much you both mean to me." He bit out a harsh laugh. "In my experience, when someone knows I love them, it makes me weak. It makes them able to hurt me."

"My mom wouldn't hurt you. She's nice."

"More than nice." Gabe nodded. *Nice* was wholly inadequate to describe all the amazing things about Angi, but he could tell that to the boy it was high praise.

"Johnny's dad isn't coming back," Andrew said, as if the situations were the same. "He's gonna stay in Florida, but Johnny'll get to visit him for spring break."

"I'm not moving," Gabe said simply. "No matter what happens, Magnolia is my home."

"Even if Mom doesn't want to be your friend anymore?"

Friends. Gabe sighed. Angi was his best friend, and he had no idea what the hell he'd do if she refused to give him another chance.

At least he knew what wouldn't happen. He wouldn't run away again.

"Even if," Gabe confirmed. "Although I hope I can convince her to try." He flashed a tentative smile. "I hope I can convince you, as well. I'm sorry I messed up so badly, Drew. I missed you a ton while I was away, and I'd like to earn a place as your friend again."

The boy inclined his head as he considered that. "Johnny

has mostly stopped bullying kids since we've been back from winter break."

"That's good." Gabe was impatient to know how Andrew felt about him but understood he needed to give the kid time. There might not be an easy answer to moving past the pain he'd caused, but he refused to give up. "Are you and Johnny friends?"

Drew made a face. "Heck, no. Somebody said Johnny doesn't even change his underwear but once a week. That's gross."

"It sure is."

"But we're not enemies no more either." The boy's brows furrowed together. "I guess I'd like to be your friend again if you're staying in town."

"I am," Gabe said. He reached out and squeezed the boy's arm. "And no matter where you go in life or what happens with me and your mom, I'll be here for you, Drew. You're a special kid."

"You first told me I was annoying."

"That was also a mistake." Gabe grimaced. "Let's stick with special, okay?"

"Yeah." Suddenly Andrew grinned, and to Gabe it felt like the sun popping out from behind a dark cloud, bright and warm on his skin. "I taught Princess to roll over."

"I'd like to see that."

"Only if Mom says it's okay that you come over. If not, I'll have to bring Princess to visit you 'cause Mom was real sad after you left. I don't want her to be sad again."

"Me neither." Gabe pushed down the regret that rose in him like a noxious weed. He had to focus on making things better with Angi, not all the crap he'd done wrong. That was a sure road to ruin. "I was actually on my way to Il Rigatone to see her." He straightened. "Maybe you want to come with me so she knows you and I are square? That might get me some points with her, you know?"

Andrew shook his head, and Gabe did his best not to be wounded. Baby steps. The boy didn't seem to hate him anymore, so that was at least a win.

"Mom's not at the restaurant," Andrew explained. "She isn't working there anymore."

"What?"

"Nonna's selling it and going to Florida, although she's not gonna see Johnny's dad. I asked her and she called him a bad word in Italian."

Gabe blinked, his mind reeling from all the information he'd just received. "Where is your mom?" he asked, focusing on what was most important.

"The Wildflower Inn. It's some girlie baby shower today with lots of pink food and pink decorations. Too much yucky pink."

"That's good to know, Drew." Gabe blew out a breath. He didn't exactly relish showing up at the inn, where he was sure to have to face Emma and Mariella if he was going to have a chance to talk to Angi alone. Surely there would be lots of groveling to her friends, which hadn't been part of his plan.

He wanted to talk to her. He'd wasted too much time being a fool already.

"If your game is done, want to drive over to the inn with me?" he asked the boy. "I could use a solid wingman when I apologize to your mom."

"Yeah, I'll go," Drew agreed, then offered a sneaky smile. "But I have to tell Nonna 'cause she's babysitting me. So you're gonna need to talk to her first. And she was even madder than Mom, I think."

"Well played," Gabe muttered, clapping the boy on the shoulder. "Let's go talk to your nonna."

ANGI LAUGHED AT something the mother of the mother-to-be said. A lame joke about how to keep a husband happy when your attention was all on a newborn baby.

The young woman had stared wide-eyed at her mom like she'd made it to adulthood without realizing that her parents must have a sex life, or at least had at some point. Of course, Angi had no experience balancing a romantic relationship with motherhood when she'd had a baby—or ever. Gabe had been the closest she'd come. Everyone in town knew how well that had worked out for her.

"You just gave the fakest laugh I ever heard," Mariella said quietly as she came to stand next to Angi in the threshold between the inn's formal living room and the kitchen.

"It doesn't matter. Nobody's paying attention to me."

"Emma and I are," Mariella countered. "She's worried about you."

Angi lifted a brow. "And you?"

"To be honest, I'm irritated that you let a good one go."

"What was I supposed to do, beg him to stay?"

"It's not unheard-of. Gabe Carlyle looked at you like you hung the moon and the stars. Do you know how precious that is?"

The image of the adoring way Dylan Scott had gazed at Carrie a few weeks before Christmas outside the town hall popped into Angi's mind. She remembered wishing for somebody who would look at her like that.

The difference was Gabe had turned away.

"It's too late now. He's gone. Clearly he didn't have any problems taking his adoring eyes off of me."

"He was going through a lot with his witch of a mother

in town." Mariella's voice went tight. "You've got a great mom, Ang. You can't possibly know what it's like to grow up feeling as though you're a burden to the person who's supposed to care about you most in the world."

"Gabe knows that his mother's problems had nothing to do with him." Angi said the words with conviction because she needed to believe them. She needed him to be the villain because it was the only way she felt she had a chance of healing.

"Don't be so sure. Our parents play a big part in teaching us what it's like to feel love and whether we deserve it or not." Mariella gestured to the pregnant mother who was being feted by her female family members and friends. The sophisticated blonde's gaze turned wistful. "When a negligent parent's words and actions tell you you're worthless, it's a lesson that sticks even when you grow up and know better. Trust me."

"I don't want to talk about Gabe right now. This is a new year. A new start for me." She couldn't keep talking about Gabe; otherwise, she was liable to embarrass herself and burst into tears. She had cried way too much in the past two weeks, even though so many other parts of her life were going well now.

Despite the fact that Angi had walked away from their partnership, Emma and Mariella been thrilled by her return. She'd transitioned from the restaurant to the inn with a glad heart, knowing she had her mother's blessing.

It made her wish she'd told her mom how she truly felt months ago. Which made her wonder what would have happened if she'd told Gabe about her feelings before his mother had come to town and infected him with her emotional poison. Maybe Mariella had been right, but Angi didn't know what to do about it now. Gabe was gone. She'd learned from his grandmother's attorney that he wasn't taking calls or returning messages.

He'd truly left her and Magnolia behind.

Her attention shifted as the front door opened and Andrew walked into the room. The look on the boy's face as he took in all of the bright pink decorations that filled the space would have been comical in another circumstance. Angi's choice for a color scheme might not have included exclusively shades of pink, but that's what the mom-to-be wanted so they'd made her happy.

She took a step toward her son. There was no humor to be found in the situation until she knew what he was doing here when her mom was supposed to be watching him.

Then Gabe entered the room behind Andrew, and her heart skipped a beat.

"This should be good," she heard Mariella say from behind her.

Angi was surprised she could hear anything over the pounding in her head. As if there was a tangible shift in the energy of the room, conversation stopped as all eyes moved to Gabe.

Emma stepped forward before Angi could. "Hey, Drew," she said. "We have extra cupcakes in the kitchen if you want to grab one." She switched her gaze to Gabe. "This isn't the time or place."

"I know," he said solemnly, but didn't move.

Andrew came toward Angi with a wide smile. "Hey, Mom. Gabe came back. Nonna yelled at him real good. I'm gonna get a cupcake."

She felt her mouth drop open as her son walked past her and the swinging door to the kitchen whooshed behind him.

Gabe had talked to her mother.

"I deserved everything she said to me." He shrugged. "Even if I couldn't understand most of it."

"Gabe." Emma's voice held a note of warning. All of the women were staring at him.

"I know," he repeated. "My timing is awful, but it has to be now."

His gaze switched to Angi, and the emotion she saw there made her breath catch in her throat. "I've wasted too much time already."

She shook her head, unsure how to respond to that. A twitter of anticipation whispered through the room.

"Oh my gosh, this is just like *Jerry Maguire*," the soon-to-be-grandmother said excitedly. "Are you going to tell her she completes you?"

Gabe darted a glance at the older woman with her bottle-blond hair pulled back in a poufy chignon.

"No." A ripple of disappointment seemed to dash across the baby shower partygoers.

"Although she does," he quickly added, then looked at Angi helplessly. "You do. Complete me. If you want to. I want you to."

"Tom Cruise said it better," someone called out.

"Zip it," Mariella commanded the guest. Emma rolled her eyes.

"I'm sure he did," Gabe agreed. "I should have prepared more. I did prepare. Rehearsed all the way from Tennessee to here." He winced. "It seems I forgot most of it because I'm scared as hell right now."

"Scared of what?" Angi asked, tucking her hair behind one ear and then clasping her hand close when she realized it was trembling.

"That I messed up so badly you won't give me another chance and I'm going to spend the rest of my life with a hole in my heart because you're not there to fill it. To complete me."

"Much better," the mom-to-be said on a sigh.

Angi's attention was fixed on Gabe. "Was that rehearsed?"

"No." He took a step closer. "Just me telling you how I feel, something I should have done long before now. I love you, Angi. I love your fierce spirit and the tenderness you try so hard to hide. I love the way you love your son and how you want to do the right thing for everyone around you and—" he gestured around the room "—that you're making your dreams a priority, too. I didn't think I deserved someone as amazing as you. There was no way you could truly love me when you're this bright light and I've hidden in the shadows for so long."

"I do love you," she whispered, unable to help herself. "But you hurt me, Gabe. A lot."

"I know, and I'll never forgive myself that." He moved nearer again, or maybe she stepped toward him.

Either way, they were close enough that she could feel the heat from his body and smell the scent of his soap and the minty gum he liked. Her knees went weak with longing.

"If you can find a way to forgive me," Gabe told her, "I promise I'll learn to be brave like you. Before I came back to Magnolia, I wasn't even sure I knew how to love. You showed me, and I love you so damn much. Please give me a chance to show you how much."

She pressed her hands to her cheeks, unsurprised to find them wet with tears.

"If you don't take him back, can I have him?" one of the guests called to Angi.

"He's mine," Angi said quietly, then lifted onto her toes to press a kiss to Gabe's mouth. "You're mine."

"I always have been," he confirmed, wrapping his arms around her. "From the moment I first saw you when we were kids. It's always been you for me, Ang."

"I love you," she said again, and then laughed as Andrew joined them for a group hug. Emma led the shower guests in a round of applause, and Mariella whistled her approval. Angi couldn't even bring herself to care that the sweetest moment of her life was shared by her friends plus a gaggle of excited clients.

Her heart was too full for anything but happiness. It felt so good to be tucked in Gabe's embrace again, like coming home. Angi knew this man would always be her home, and she'd go through everything again to end up with Gabe, the exact place where she belonged.

* * * * *

A CAROLINA CHRISTMAS

CHAPTER ONE

THE ACCIDENT HAD happened so quickly, but Bella Hart couldn't stop replaying it in her mind in excruciatingly slow motion. They were the worst few minutes of her entire life, and that was saying something.

The front door accidentally left ajar.

The ten-month-old puppy gleefully running across the yard toward the street, ignoring his panicked owner's calls to come.

The giant SUV headed right toward the animal.

Bella's scream as she followed her four-legged baby into the road.

In front of the massive vehicle.

The squeal of tires reverberating in her ears.

And then...

"Hey."

Tanned fingers snapped in front of her face.

"You okay, Bella? Are you sure I can't call someone?"

She blinked and looked into the brilliant cerulean gaze of Sam Anderson. Blue that reminded Bella of the Colorado sky on a clear winter's day. A bluebird day, the locals called it as they headed for the slopes in the mountain town where she'd grown up. Bella had never liked snow.

Sam was her neighbor in the duplex she rented just outside the small town of Magnolia, North Carolina. She'd gotten a job as a third grade teacher there after graduating from college five years earlier, much to the chagrin of her parents, who were desperate for her to return home.

Sam was also a couple of years younger than her, as hot as any man she'd ever seen—a fact that made him quite popular with the ladies of the quaint Southern town.

He'd also been the one to hit her puppy. Or almost hit. Bella wanted to believe it was a near miss.

The veterinarian who was currently casting Tater's front leg couldn't be sure if there had actually been impact. The puppy had a broken leg but no other sign of trauma.

Bella hadn't been hit. Thank God the brakes on Sam's ancient Land Cruiser seemed to be in good working order.

But she had a nasty road burn on her legs.

She'd been wearing—still wore—a short robe over pajama shorts and a thin T-shirt, no bra. She pulled the fuzzy pink robe closed as she met Sam's gaze.

"I'm fine," she said, hating that heat infused her cheeks as he studied her.

What was wrong with her? She and Sam had been neighbors for nearly two years now and were friends of a sort. Neighborly, anyway. He wasn't her type, despite his physical perfection, and she certainly wasn't his.

Not to mention he'd almost killed her dog.

Could nothing dampen her physical reaction to the man?

"I'm sorry." He sat back on his haunches. "So damn sorry. I didn't see the little guy and—"

"I know." She reached out and covered his hand with hers. An immediate and unwanted spark of awareness zinged through her. She snatched her hand away before Sam noticed. When they'd first met, she'd literally walked into a wall because he'd flustered her so badly.

In addition to his piercing blue eyes, Sam was tall with a kind of natural athletic grace, like there was nothing he couldn't handle. He wore his blond hair cropped and had an easy smile that lit up his whole movie-star-handsome face.

He had to know she had a major crush on him. From what she could tell, every single woman in Magnolia—and a number of the married ones—felt the same way she did.

Pull yourself together, she commanded silently. Maybe the post-adrenaline rush could be blamed for her overwhelming reaction. The letdown had only come once Sam had driven them to the vet's office, where her sweet pup had checked out in good health other than the leg.

According to Dr. Kaminski, the attending vet, Tater's fracture was simple, so the leg could be cast without needing surgery.

"Let's take care of your leg while we're waiting."

"My leg?" she asked dumbly as Sam straightened and walked to the small sink in the corner of the empty break room. The vet tech had suggested she wait in the back instead of the lobby since she was wearing pajamas, a robe and fake sheepskin boots.

He looked over his shoulder and gave her an encouraging smile. The kind he might offer some hysterical woman during one of his shifts with the local fire department. The kind that said, "don't lose your mind on me, ma'am." As if she were on the verge of...

She groaned as she shifted on the chair. Right. Her leg and the burning road rash she'd gotten from hurling herself in the path of his SUV, like she was some sort of superhero who could handle the impact and save her beloved puppy.

Her right leg had taken the brunt of the damage. From about midthigh to just above her ankle, her skin was a patchwork of red and raw wounds, inflamed and bleeding in several places. Somehow she'd become numb to the stinging pain with her mind focused on Tater's injury.

"I'll take care of it when I get home," she said as he moved closer. He placed the bin of first aid he'd brought on the chair next to her and knelt in front of her.

"We should clean it out now. I can handle this, Bella."

Of that, she had no doubt.

"I don't even remember the last time I shaved my legs." She jerked away as he reached for her, then sucked in a painful gasp.

"I promise I won't even notice your legs." His mouth quirked. "I'm going to touch you now, okay?"

"Okay," she murmured, because he sounded so sure of himself. This caregiver side of Sam was one she hadn't seen before, although it made sense, given his line of work. He dealt with people in crisis every day.

And she refused to think about his comment that he wouldn't notice her legs. That shouldn't come as a surprise. Sam had never noticed her as anything but his neighbor and platonic friend. Oh, he enjoyed her stories about the students at Magnolia Elementary. He appreciated it when she made extra dinner and left disposable containers on his porch.

But he dated women who were much different than Bella.

Beautiful women. Fun women. Women her mother would describe as having loose morals for the most part. Sam had made the dating rounds of Magnolia and beyond. Although his social life had slowed considerably in the past few months. Bella didn't know why.

His hands were sure as he gently blotted at the scrapes along her thigh. "I don't see much embedded gravel. Good thing they repaved the road last summer."

"Yeah," she managed, trying her best not to squirm as she watched him work.

"Hey, Bella?" He looked up at her through lashes that made her green with envy. Maybe it was the frame of thick lashes that made his eyes so striking.

"Yeah?" she repeated.

"Don't run out in front of cars, okay?"

"I didn't think," she said as if that fact wasn't obvious. "Well, I thought about Tater, but that's all."

"You love that puppy."

"I do."

He frowned, his brows drawing together. "I'll pay for the vet bills, of course. I can't tell you—"

"Sam, don't apologize again. He got out. It was an accident."

"I should have been paying more attention. It was a long shift, and I was just focused on getting home and to bed."

"I understand. Tater's okay—that's what counts," she added, because she had to distract herself from how much she appreciated the thought of getting Sam to bed.

She watched him work, gently placing antibiotic cream on her scrapes then covering them with a sterile bandage. Oh, he had good hands.

But she wasn't going to go there.

Because Sam wasn't for her.

Did she imagine it or did the air grow heavy between them as he took care of her? His focus remained on her leg—the one he'd told her he wouldn't notice—and a muscle ticked at the edge of his jaw.

She was imagining things. Sam was a firefighter. He must patch people up or handle injuries worse than hers a dozen times a week. He was this close to people all the time, so the strange intimacy of the moment couldn't possibly affect him the way it did her.

He returned the unused supplies to the bin but didn't

stand. He offered her a sheepish grin and drew in a deep breath. "I know this is odd timing," he said, sounding uncharacteristically unsure of himself. "But would you—"

"Tater Tot is ready to go home," a voice announced from the doorway.

Sam straightened in one fluid motion, and Bella turned to the doctor staring at the two of them.

"Is he okay?" she asked, tightening the sash on her robe as she stood.

"He'll be groggy for a bit, but puppies are resilient. He'll be full of his usual energy before you know it." Dr. Kaminski, who was new to the practice and Magnolia, smiled. "He's a cute pup. A real sweetie." As her attention moved from Bella to Sam, she smoothed a hand over her shiny blond hair. "Hi, Sam. I haven't seen you around for a while. We still need to catch that movie you promised me."

"Sure," Sam muttered noncommittally. "Thanks for taking care of Tater, Deedra."

Bella sighed and took a step forward. Of course the female veterinarian would know Sam. She was young and pretty and human, after all. It was as if the universe had sent Bella a reminder of why he wasn't for her.

"Thank you, Doctor," she said to the woman, turning away from Sam. "I'm ready to take my best boy home now."

CHAPTER TWO

Two DAYS LATER, at seven in the morning, Sam turned the corner onto the block where he lived, his pace even and his breath coming out in rhythmic puffs. The sky was just starting to lighten, but he'd gone for an early run when sleep had been elusive.

Before he'd joined the fire department a year and a half ago, Sam had never had trouble falling asleep. It didn't matter if he was at home or on a buddy's couch or in a woman's bed—and that last was the location he preferred the most.

Something had changed since coming to Magnolia. He'd changed. His work had shown him a side of humanity that made him grow up fast. He'd first pursued the job because he liked the fast pace, the risk and the flexibility of shift work. But it was the service aspect that now meant the most to him.

Helping people in times of need humbled him, and the things he'd witnessed as part of his work deepened his commitment to the job. He wanted to earn the respect of his captains and coworkers, at least while he was on the clock. As much as he might want to some days, he couldn't go back to the stupid lug of a happy-go-lucky guy he'd been.

Yet he also couldn't quite let go of that persona, and keeping up appearances was a crap-ton of work.

His heart leaped in his chest as he noticed Bella in the front yard with Tater.

Just thinking about those frantic moments when he wasn't sure his Toyota would stop before slamming into her was enough to make him break out in a cold sweat that had nothing to do with physical exertion.

But the averted tragedy wasn't the reason for his accelerated heartbeat.

That was all Bella—her innate sweetness and easy beauty. He had to admit, it had taken him a while to notice what a prize she was, a quintessential—and literal—girl next door. She had straight chestnut-colored hair that fell just below her shoulders and a slim figure with the most beautiful skin he'd ever seen.

The other day in the vet's office, Sam had felt like a lecher thinking about her softness when he was supposed to be tending to her injuries.

A creeper neighbor was the last thing a woman who lived alone needed in her life.

And Bella was his friend. That was the kicker. She was not only pretty, but she was fun to be around. She didn't take herself too seriously or try to be someone she wasn't. She was at home with herself in a way Sam envied. Like she'd never need to run away or pretend to be a person she wasn't because it's what people expected of her.

He wouldn't ruin a real friendship with physical complications, no matter how she made him feel. Sam had dated plenty in his twenty-six years, but it was all casual. It didn't mean anything. Bella meant something to him.

Tater, who was on a leash, noticed Sam first. The dog barked and hobbled in happy circles.

Bella shushed him and pulled the leash tighter so the dog couldn't jump.

"He's feeling better I see." Sam hurried forward and dropped to the damp ground to accept the puppy's effusive greeting.

"He has no respect for that cast," Bella said, but she was smiling. "Who knew the hardest part of a broken leg would be keeping the dog calm over the next month so he can heal without reinjuring himself?"

Sam chuckled and petted Tater Tot in long strokes as the dog settled. "You really don't have much experience with puppies."

"Tater is like trial by fire," she answered.

The afternoon she'd adopted the dog from Magnolia's popular animal rescue, Furever Friends, had been the first time he'd noticed Bella as more than a friend.

She'd come home with the fluffy, wriggly puppy, and the look of adoration she'd given the dog... Well, Sam was still embarrassed to admit he'd been jealous of the animal.

"He's going to miss you while you're away." He frowned when she let out a huge sigh. "Speaking of *away*, why are you still here? I thought you were leaving early this morning for Colorado."

"I canceled my trip," she said, and looked past him but not before he heard the catch in her voice.

"Why?" he asked as he straightened, wiping the sweat from his brow with his shirtsleeve.

She gave Tater's leash a gentle tug. "I can't leave him with a pet sitter while he's in a cast. That would be too much to ask."

"I'll keep him," Sam offered without thinking.

Bella's soft smile did funny things to his insides. Things he didn't want or need from a woman. "Your shifts at the fire department don't exactly lend themselves to puppy sitting," she pointed out. "Plus, aren't you going to visit your family for Christmas, as well?"

He nodded. "I'll take Tater with me. Come on, Bella. I feel bad enough about my part in his injury. You can't spend Christmas alone. The guilt will be too much."

Her pretty brown eyes rolled heavenward. "We both know guilt isn't part of your makeup, Sam. I'll be fine. Magnolia is so festive at this time of year. I'll walk around downtown and enjoy the lights and decorations. Binge-watch all those shows languishing on my DVR. Have a mini spa day. It will be relaxing."

"Tell me you went to the dance last night." As part of the town's annual holiday festival, the town council had coordinated some big dance at the old textile mill that was in the process of being renovated. There'd been flyers up all over the station publicizing it because the wife of one of the senior firefighters was in charge of marketing for the town. He'd made fun of the event to Bella, only to discover that she was excited about it.

He'd learned that his neighbor loved to dance.

Her smile widened. "I did go for an hour once Tater fell asleep in his crate. You should have seen how beautiful it looked. The guy who's running the flower shop in town helped organize things, so there were these adorable arrangements of winter greenery on every table. It was perfect."

"And did you dance?" Sam asked, unable to resist imagining spinning Bella on the dance floor.

"A little." She gave a small shake of her hips that made his mouth go dry. Ridiculous, since she was wearing shapeless gray sweatpants and an oversize flannel shirt for the early-morning potty break.

"Any slow dances?" He forced a casual tone even as he

questioned his sanity at fishing for that sort of information. But the thought of another man holding Bella—

"Nope." Another sigh. "No one even asked me. I give off too many teacher vibes, according to my assistant principal."

"There's nothing wrong with teacher vibes."

"They're not sexy."

Sam choked a little. He did not want to talk to Bella about sexy.

"I would have danced with you."

"You weren't there," she answered with an arched eyebrow. "Besides, I don't want a pity dance."

"It wouldn't be—"

"Save it, Anderson," she interrupted with a wave of her hand. "I'm sure if you'd been there you would have been occupied—or maybe mauled is a better word—by your legions of adoring fans. Not to mention all those thirsty exes."

"I can't believe you used the word *thirsty* that way."

Her grin widened. "I looked it up on Urban Dictionary to make sure I had the right usage. Too eager to get something or desperate. My knowledge of current slang is impressive, right?"

He laughed, a common occurrence when he was talking with Bella. One he hadn't realized was as important as it had become until lately. "Don't stay here alone, Bell. Come with me to the mountains. My dad and stepmom close down their resort for Christmas every year to accommodate the family." The words spilled out before he thought better of them. "I'll make sure you get your own cabin if you want privacy. Just come with me. I'm only staying a week. It will make me feel better about almost running over both you and Tater."

"There's that reference to guilt again." She gave him an odd look. "Honestly, I didn't think you had it in you."

"I might surprise you with my depth."

"Doubtful," she answered, and he didn't let the sting of that word show on his face. She studied him for a few weighted moments. "But okay. If you're sure your family won't mind? It would be better than a movie marathon, that's for sure."

Satisfaction rolled through Sam like an easy wave. "Are you kidding? My family is going to love you."

CHAPTER THREE

BELLA COULDN'T EXPLAIN why she felt nervous as they drove deeper into the Blue Ridge Mountains on the western side of North Carolina the following afternoon. She and Sam were friends. Other than the other teachers at school, he was the person who knew her best in Magnolia.

Somehow this felt different. She realized that before today, the only time she'd spent with him outside of hanging on the front porches of one of their respective sides of the duplex was the trip to the vet's office with Tater.

They'd never so much as gone for a beer together in the year and a half they'd been neighbors. Not that Bella went for many beers. She spent time at school and took yoga classes at the dance studio in town. Otherwise, she realized now, she was a bit of a loner.

She didn't really date, although she wasn't against having a boyfriend or falling in love. She wanted those things in her life. Unfortunately, most men she knew or met in the small town couldn't compete with her fantasies of her handsome neighbor. Even if he was a serial dater who'd shown no romantic interest in her, despite his revolving door of casual girlfriends.

It was for the best, she told herself. Bella had no interest in casual hookups and hated that Sam obviously thought he had nothing else to offer.

From what she'd heard through the grapevine at school,

most of the women he'd gone out with had the same opinion of him. He was a good time, always easy with a laugh or ready to make a woman feel beautiful. But no one seemed to expect more of him.

Bella would, which was just one more reason they wouldn't be a match.

Other than in her daydreams.

"It's only a little farther," he told her, his eyes trained on the curving road in front of them.

"This area is beautiful," she murmured, pressing her fingers against the cool glass of the passenger window. "It reminds me in some ways of Colorado, although the trees are different."

"And there's not much snow."

"And no craggy peaks or gobs of rich tourists."

"I promise it will be fun without all the trappings of a Colorado mountain town," Sam told her, his voice grave. "For you, anyway. Like I said, my family will love you."

She cut him a look and noticed that his jaw was tense, his fingers gripping the wheel like a lifeline. "Isn't Christmas with your family fun for you?"

"Sure," he agreed too readily. "It's loud and festive and always something happening. My stepmom makes a big deal about every tradition, and with so many kids and grandkids running around, there's never a dull moment."

He gave the appropriate answer, but there was no feeling behind it. She knew Sam was the youngest of five kids, two older brothers and two older sisters. He'd been born eight years after his nearest sibling, and his mom had died when he was in high school.

"You don't sound excited by the prospect of all the Christmas chaos."

"You have a couple of sisters, right?" He slowed as they took a hairpin turn on the mountain road.

"One younger and one older."

"Do you have a certain role in the family?"

"Peacemaker," she answered immediately.

His mouth curved. "That fits you. I'm the baby of the family, and my part is the goof-off party boy. My brothers and sisters think of me as a shallow good-time guy."

She thought about how to respond. In truth, that's how she'd regarded Sam when they first met. He was just too gorgeous, self-assured and easygoing to be regarded in any other way. The first few times they'd crossed paths in the front yard, he'd been all swagger and no substance. He could throw off lighthearted sexual innuendos like it was his job. It hadn't been until they'd known each other for months that he'd shown her there was more to him than a pretty face and a set of chiseled abs.

Although she appreciated the abs.

"You're not a kid anymore," she felt obliged to say. "You've got an important job and plenty of responsibility. Heck, you save lives. Surely they realize you've grown up."

"Not really." He turned onto a gravel road with the painted sign for the Ridgeway Resort greeting visitors. "It doesn't matter. I can be who they think I am for a few days. Good for a joke and a beer. The rest doesn't matter." His laugh sounded forced. "Hell, there's no denying I like beer. Beer and women and football."

"You're also dedicated to your work and the community of Magnolia," Bella felt compelled to point out. "I know you volunteer at the nursing home and with the local food pantry."

"Let's not mention any of that," he said, his voice tight. "They'll only find a way to make fun of me for it."

Bella didn't want to believe that, and her temper spiked in response. Sam wasn't normally the overdramatic type. He could tell her about a call at the station like he'd done nothing more than cross the street. Despite his tendency to play down the serious things in life, there was a depth to him most people didn't see or appreciate. She didn't like that his family fell into that category.

Before she could ask him for more details about them, he whistled low under his breath. Her gaze tracked out the front window, where the log cabins that surrounded a circle of grass had been decked out to look like an old-fashioned Christmas village.

"Oh, wow," she murmured, her heart stuttering. She thought she was going to miss the Christmas finery of her parents' house but couldn't imagine a more festive scene than the one before them.

"Jayne went all out this year," Sam said with a real laugh as he parked the car next to a row of trucks and SUVs.

"It's incredible and—" Bella jumped as the Land Cruiser was suddenly surrounded by a dozen smiling faces.

Tater, who'd been sleeping in his crate in the back, woke up with a happy bark. His tail thumped against the wire side, and Bella felt nerves rise in her chest. This was way different than the subdued holiday she expected at her parents.

"They're going to love you," Sam repeated, like he could read her thoughts. He reached out and gave her arm a quick squeeze, then opened the door of the car.

This big family Christmas celebration was happening whether Bella was ready for it or not.

CHAPTER FOUR

SAM HAD KNOWN his family would like Bella—everyone liked Bella. But he hadn't expected the way she made him feel like he fit into the fabric of his big, boisterous clan without always having to play the role of the clown.

Every time one of his sisters or brothers told a story of his childhood or teenage antics, Bella would immediately counter it with some piece of information he'd previously told her about a rescue or emergency he'd responded to at the station.

To his eternal gratitude, she didn't go into great detail about the calls that had gone badly. The houses they couldn't save or the story of the elderly woman who'd latched onto Sam and bawled her eyes out as his coworkers had failed to resuscitate her husband.

Sam hadn't realized how much he'd shared with Bella over the course of their friendship until he heard her retelling the particulars of his job to his family.

And although his siblings never ceased giving him grief as the baby of the family or referencing embarrassing moments from his past, Sam thought that he caught his father looking at him with a new sense of respect, something he never would have imagined before Bella.

The first two days after arriving, they'd stayed at the resort cabins. There had been cookie baking, badminton games and charades around the fire when the younger kids went to bed. At first, Bella had seemed overwhelmed by the energy of his extended family, although Tater had loved it from the start.

The puppy made immediate friends with the other dogs. His father's ten-year-old golden retriever, Gracie, had bonded with Tater right away and managed to keep the puppy from exerting himself too much, as if she knew he needed time and space to heal.

Bella had soon found her place as well, and Sam got a true glimpse of her gift with children. His sisters both had elementary-school-aged kids. Two boys for Heidi and one of each for Marla. The oldest of their siblings, Brian, had a set of thirteen-year-old girls, Allie and Amara, and even the teens gravitated toward Bella.

To Sam's frustration, so did his single brother, Kyle. At thirty-four, Kyle was closest in age to Sam. He'd been engaged to his college sweetheart for a few years, but that had ended a while ago. He lived in Raleigh, which was only about an hour from Magnolia, although he and Sam didn't hang out other than at family gatherings.

Kyle had always been a bit of a stick-in-the-mud as far as Sam was concerned. His brother had made partner at the financial advising firm where he worked a year ago, faster than anyone in the company's history, thanks to his drive and determination. Kyle and Sam were opposites in almost every way, most of which reflected badly on Sam. He'd liked partying and living life to the fullest, while his brother acted more like a geriatric in the body of a young man.

He was the kind of steady, hardworking, stable man who would be perfect for Bella.

It just about killed Sam, even though he had no right to be jealous. Oh, he was well aware that his neighbor had a bit of a crush on him when they'd first met. But he knew she'd cast aside all thought of him as real boyfriend material once she got to know him. He didn't blame her.

"Uncle Sam, will you put me on your shoulders?"

He glanced down at his eight-year-old nephew, Lucas, a welcome distraction from watching Bella and Kyle together. The whole family had driven down to the nearby town of Ridgeway for the annual Christmas Eve caroling event. From the moment he'd gotten out of his vehicle, women from his past had seemed to materialize one after the other. It was like his own romantic ghost-of-girlfriends-past nightmare, especially because it was happening in front of Bella.

Kyle had been more than willing to step in and lead her away. Sam had needed to physically resist grabbing her and hustling her off to somewhere private without so many reminders of what a womanizing jerkwad he'd been back in the day.

A reputation he couldn't seem to shake, no matter that he hadn't been with a woman in over six months. No dates. No kisses. No nights of mindlessly losing himself in a bottle and a stranger's bed.

His coworkers at the station had caught on to the change in him, although no one made a big deal about it. They were a great group, closer to him than his family in a lot of ways. And it was easy enough to lie low in Magnolia and avoid the bar or phone calls from women looking for a good time. Sam's preferred idea of a good time these days was reading a book and turning off the lights by ten. Ideally after spending a bit of time visiting with his neighbor.

He ground his teeth as Kyle said something to Bella that made her smile. Sam didn't do possessive, but the jealousy that spiked through him shocked him with its intensity.

Bella loved Christmas. She took part in every tradition and activity with unbridled enthusiasm. He still felt bad that she'd canceled her trip to Colorado and wanted these few days with his family to make up for it in some small way.

At least the Anderson clan was never boring.

Holding tight to Lucas's legs, he made his way through the crowd toward Bella and Kyle, who stood near his dad and stepmom.

"Can I get another hot chocolate, Papa," Brianna, Lucas's older sister, asked as she grinned up at Pete Anderson with a mouth already ringed in chocolate.

"Sure, pumpkin," his dad answered, patting her head.

"Marla's going to kill you," Kyle muttered, but Pete only shrugged and then winked at Bella. "What's the use of being a grandpa if you can't spoil your grandkids?"

"I want some, too," Lucas shouted, and Sam lowered him to the ground.

Bella took a step closer to him and the scent of her lemony shampoo drifted toward him. He wanted to drape an arm over her shoulder and pull her close but kept his hands to himself.

"Your family's wonderful," she said, although her smile wobbled ever so slightly at the edges.

"But you're missing yours," he guessed.

She nodded. "A little. I'll call them when we get back. It's two hours earlier in Colorado." She gestured to the temporary ice rink that had been situated in the local hardware store's parking lot. "I love everything about this town. I can see why you feel at home in Magnolia. There's a very similar vibe."

"Except in Magnolia, there aren't a dozen people calling me little Sammy every time I turn around."

She giggled at that, and the sound moved through him like music. God, he needed to get a grip. Maybe it was all the holiday spirit or his heightened emotions being home. Surely he could get ahold of his crush on her. He wouldn't risk losing her as a friend.

"There's nothing little about you." Her eyes went wide as she said the words, like the potential innuendo of them just dawned on her.

Another thing he liked about her was the lack of artifice. Add it to the mile-long list.

"I'm glad you noticed," he answered in his best teasing tone. It was easier to keep it light than to show her his true feelings.

Her cheeks flooded with color, her mouth formed a tiny O and all he could think about was leaning in to kiss her.

Which would, of course, ruin everything. At this moment, Sam couldn't bring himself to care.

Then the choir director, who'd been leading the local high school glee club in carols at one end of Main Street, whistled shrilly into the microphone. Bella startled and they both turned, along with almost every other person at the event, to face the bandstand that had been erected in one of the closed-off intersections of downtown.

"Let's give a big thank-you once again to our talented students," he boomed into the mic, and the crowd dutifully clapped and wolf-whistled. When the noise died down, the man leaned in with a waggle of his bushy eyebrows. "We have a real special Christmas treat for y'all tonight. Turns out that after his concert last night over in Asheville, country star Jake Combs made his way to Ridgeway for the holiday."

There was a collective gasp from the audience. Jake Combs was one of the most popular singer-songwriters on the music scene, well on his way to becoming the next Tim McGraw for country music.

"Oh, I love his last album." Bella grabbed hold of Sam's arm and pressed against him as the people around them surged forward.

"Yeah, he's pretty good." Sam knew the thrumming of his pulse had way more to do with Bella than any famous singer.

The older man continued to laud Jake Combs, and finally got to the part where the country superstar would be performing three of his biggest hits for their gathering and also making a hefty donation to the local food pantry.

"It's amazing," Bella murmured, and then gave a little squeal as Jake took over the microphone.

He said a few words and then invited everyone to celebrate the season with an impromptu dance party before launching into a rollicking acoustic version of one of his biggest hits from the past year, "Boots on the Bedpost."

Sam could feel Bella's excitement and was just about to throw caution to the wind and ask her to dance when he felt himself yanked away.

"Come on, Sammy," his high school girlfriend, Lori, who'd been following him around all night, commanded as she dug her nails into his biceps. "We know how you love to dance."

"Yeah, Sam." Ashleigh, Lori's best friend, who he'd also—regrettably—dated grabbed his free arm. "Let's see you shake those hips."

He felt like a piece of meat being pulled between two hungry animals. In the past, he would have eased into the feeling and the potential of not having to feel anything but physical pleasure.

Now he wanted more.

"Sorry, ladies, I'm spoken for at this particular moment." He gestured to where he'd left Bella standing, and his gut took a swift kick at the look of disappointment in her honey-brown gaze.

She shook her head and turned away. To Sam's chagrin, Kyle had reappeared and, with a casual thumbs-up at Sam, led her in the opposite direction,

And because Sam was a damn coward, he didn't do a thing to stop it.

CHAPTER FIVE

BELLA DREW A thick fleece over her head—a well-worn pullover that had been left on one of the hooks inside the door to the cabin where she was staying—and fastened Tater's leash to his collar.

The sky was dark with a canopy of stars above her. She'd grown up with a wide night sky in the mountains of Colorado, but somehow these stars felt more like a blanket covering the surrounding hills. Even though her hometown was perched at nearly eight thousand feet above sea level, the sky had seemed so faraway. Now she almost wondered if she could reach up and gather the bright points of light in her hand.

Tater tugged on the leash, bringing her thoughts firmly back to the present. It was nearly midnight, and she'd fallen asleep on the sofa as she read a book after returning to the Andersons' resort with Pete, Jayne and Kyle.

She didn't know what time Sam had gotten back or even if he'd returned. There was no doubt he had plenty of options for where to spend the night before Christmas based on the number of women who'd sought him out in town.

Bella was all too aware of his popularity with the ladies. He'd earned a reputation in Magnolia, although she'd noticed that his social life had taken a severe nosedive in the past several months.

Even before that, he'd never brought a woman to spend

the night at the duplex. And since they didn't exactly run in the same social circles, everything she knew about his romantic life in Magnolia was secondhand.

Tonight she'd gotten an up close view of his appeal to the opposite sex. At least a half dozen women had approached him during the caroling event, including the two that had pulled him away when the Jake Combs concert started. Women who'd alternately flirted, then pouted, demanding Sam's attention and gleefully reminding him of their shared pasts with a knowing wink.

It was as if most of the women in Ridgeway had allergies related to Sam. All that winking and feigned trouble catching their breath. Bella had wanted to start handing out inhalers just to calm the panting he seemed to invoke.

She felt like ten kinds of a fool because she'd actually started to believe there might be something special between the two of them. He'd stayed at her side for much of the time spent with his family, making sure she was comfortable and felt cared for. He'd looked after Tater with a protectiveness that melted Bella's heart.

Her stupid, foolish heart.

It was to blame for getting her into this situation. Making her believe there might be something more than friendship or a sense of guilt between them.

But he'd allowed himself to be drawn away tonight without an ounce of protest. His brother had been sweet and asked her to dance, but Bella had feigned being tired. When Jayne suggested taking one of the cars to head home before the rest of the group, Bella had been happy to go along.

Sam certainly wouldn't notice she'd left.

She smiled as Tater rolled onto his back in the dry grass, then glanced up at the sound of crunching gravel.

Her puppy gave a gleeful bark, and she quickly bent to shush him as Sam approached from the main cabin.

He wore the same faded jeans he'd had on earlier, only he'd also added a thick fleece over his denim shirt. The mountain air was crisp, although at the moment heat poured through Bella like someone had turned on the hot tap at the faucet.

"You're up late," he said with a hesitant smile.

"You're home early," she countered.

"Am I?" His smile faded. "I came looking for you when Jake Combs started 'Only Your Love.' Heidi told me you'd left with Dad and Jayne." He drew in a deep breath. "And Kyle."

"I thought I'd catch a ride back. Figured there was no telling when your fan club would let you leave."

"You said 'Only Your Love' was one of your favorite songs. I figured you'd stay to hear it."

She shrugged, unwilling to admit how hard it had been to leave in the middle of Jake's performance. And what an easy decision it was to make because she didn't want to see Sam dancing with someone else. "I've got it on my playlist."

"You know I don't want a fan club," he said, running a hand through his blond hair. It was rumpled, a few loose strands standing up in different directions like he'd been tugging on them all night.

"It's not a criticism," she lied, because she had no right to judge whom he spent his time with or how many women from here or Magnolia he dated. "You're popular, Sam. Those women are only human, after all."

He laughed at that, but there was no humor in it. "Do you like my brother?" he asked suddenly, bending to scratch behind Tater's floppy ears. The puppy leaned into the touch because he was no dummy.

"I like everyone in your family," she said, trying hard not to imagine how it would feel to have Sam's hands on her. A new low, jealous of her dog.

"I'm not talking about everyone." Sam bit down on his lower lip, then looked up at her. "I mean Kyle. Do you like him?"

"Sure. He's nice. A sweet guy."

"Sweet," Sam repeated, like the word was bitter on his tongue. "He thinks you're sweet, too, and he isn't wrong. You two will make a great couple."

Bella blinked. "We're not going to make anything."

"He likes you. *Likes* you, likes you." He stood, paced a few feet away before turning to her again. "A great couple," he repeated, his voice strained.

Blood pounded through Bella's veins like she'd injected caffeine directly into them. The way Sam was looking at her could only be described as… Longing.

Raw and untethered. The kind of look she'd never imagined receiving from any man, let alone the one standing in front of her. As if he were on fire and she was the only thing that could douse the flames.

Impossible.

Incomprehensible.

Undeniable.

She took a step closer to him, her fingers gripping the leash as if her puppy, who was currently occupied chewing on a stick in the grass, was some kind of lifeline to reality.

Except Bella didn't want real life if it would take away this moment.

The desire in Sam's crystal-blue gaze seemed to become almost a palpabe force.

"I don't like your brother that way," she said quietly.

"You should," Sam answered immediately. "He's a catch, whatever that means. Everyone says so. It's all I hear about from my sisters and Jayne when he's not within earshot." Sam put his hands on his hips like he was giving a lecture. "When is Kyle going to settle down with a nice girl?" His voice had gone into a bad falsetto, but Bella didn't smile.

She could barely breathe.

"He's got so much to offer, and we need some more cousins in the family." He let out a long breath. "They never wonder when I'm going to settle."

"You don't know what they say when you're not in the room," she pointed out.

He gave her a bland look. "I know."

"You're younger," she offered. "You have time."

"They've been talking that way about Kyle since he broke off his engagement. I see how he looks at you, Bell. I see how much my family would welcome you into the fold. It would be perfect."

"No." Her heart was kicking against her ribs so hard she thought maybe Sam would hear it. "It wouldn't be perfect at all," she said despite the pounding of blood between her ears. "Because I don't like your brother that way. Not even a little bit, Sam."

"Why not?" he whispered.

She almost laughed at that question. "Do you really not know?"

He shook his head.

"That's how I feel about you." She gathered her hands in front of her as if she needed protection from his response. There was no way she could say more, not without gauging his reaction first. And she was so darn afraid that one sentence was already too much. What if he laughed at her or walked away or, worst of all, felt sorry for her?

What if she'd misread this night or the look in his eyes? Maybe the light from the starry sky had led her astray.

Sam stared at her for so long, she almost started to fidget under the weight of his gaze. Oh, yeah. She'd probably misread it all.

But just as she was about to make a joke of things, he closed the distance between them and pressed his mouth to hers.

CHAPTER SIX

SAM HAD NEVER dreamed of kissing Bella, not in any real way. Yet, at the first brush of his lips across hers, it felt as though she was an answer to a question he'd been asking all of his life.

He deepened the kiss, his tongue sliding along the seam of her mouth. She opened for him, and his knees went weak when she drew closer. His hands sifted through her soft hair and he reveled in the soft moan she made in the back of her throat. Bella might be practical and understated, but she kissed like a woman on a mission.

It was almost too much. His need for her threatened to obliterate every last shred of common sense he possessed.

He'd get back to that common sense part in a second. First, he released her mouth to run a trail of kisses along her jaw and down the graceful column of her throat. His body hummed with satisfaction at the sweetness of her skin and the scent of lemons that enveloped him. She had a tiny beauty mark just above her collarbone, and for the past several months it had tempted him beyond measure every time she wore a shirt with a collar low enough to reveal it.

He kissed that tiny mark the way he'd wanted to and heard her tiny gasp at the same time he felt her pulse flutter. That was just the start of what he wanted to feel from her, but he forced himself to pull away.

Her eyes were hazy as she stared up at him, and Tater

let out a plaintive whine from where he'd come to stand next to her. What did it say about the situation that the dog seemed to have more sense than either of the humans involved?

"Merry Christmas, Bella," he said, and cupped her face between his hands.

She gave him a shy smile that turned his insides to goo in a way Sam would have sworn he was impervious to. "I got you a present," she told him, eyes twinkling.

"I think you just gave me a present."

He could almost feel the heat of her blush and wondered for just the briefest moment, if that color would extend all the way down her body.

It felt like a question he had to have answered.

As if she was answering his unspoken prayer, Bella stepped back and held out a hand to him. "You should probably come in and see what else I have for you."

It was a damn miracle Sam remained standing, based on the fact that his heart stammered and his knees nearly buckled.

He might not be the sharpest knife in the drawer, but Sam was no fool. He'd stopped believing in Kris Kringle or Christmas miracles a long time ago. Still, he took Bella's hand and followed her into the cabin, Tater trotting along, the cast not slowing him down in the least.

When Bella shut the dog in his crate, turned out the lights and led Sam to the small bedroom at the back of the structure, it was like every Christmas wish he'd ever had coming true all at once.

BELLA WALKED TOWARD the main cabin the following morning, her mind and heart a tangle of nerves and hope. Sam had left her bed in the wee hours after lavishing so much attention on her body, she thought she might die from the pleasure of it.

Merry Christmas, indeed. No wonder he was so popular with women, both in his hometown and in Magnolia.

A man with skills like that was quite a rarity, at least in Bella's experience, measly though it might be.

She'd been the one to suggest he return to his room before anyone in his family noticed his absence. As amazing as their night together had been, Bella didn't relish being a topic of conversation for his family on Christmas morning.

Another secret part of her didn't trust that their night together—as special as it was—meant the same thing to him as it did to her. What if she'd been a convenience, an easy, friends-with-benefits way to pass the time.

The front door to the resort's main cabin opened as she approached up the flagstone walk. But it was Kyle who greeted her, not Sam.

"Merry Christmas," he said with a wide smile.

She wished him the same and led Tater into the resort. They entered the kitchen, where Jayne was icing cinnamon rolls while Pete drank his coffee at the large mahogany table. Bella knew Heidi and Marla, along with their husbands and kids, would be joining them later that morning, once they'd all had their private family Santa gift exchanges.

She hugged Jayne and waved at Sam's dad, who wished her a Merry Christmas, then turned his attention back to the sports section of the local newspaper.

"Sam's still asleep," Kyle told her when he noticed her glancing around.

"He'll be up once the kids get here," Pete said, flipping a page and taking a long swig of coffee. "Have some coffee, Bella," he suggested. "We're all going to need stamina for the pint-size tornado that will hit once the rug rats get here."

Bella grinned and headed for the pot on the counter. She got a kick out of Pete's gruff attitude when it was clear he was a pushover for any and all of his grandkids.

"It wouldn't be Christmas without Sam indulging in some random holiday hookup," Kyle observed.

Bella's hand stilled on the coffeepot.

"No need to be rude," Jayne told her stepson. "Sam is obviously maturing. He's different than usual this year."

"Sam might be more discreet," Kyle muttered, "but he's the same as he ever was." He gave Bella a pointed look when she turned with her mug. "Trust me."

"Well, Merry Christmas to you, too, big brother."

They all turned as Sam entered the kitchen, hair tousled and wearing baggy sweats and a faded UNC T-shirt.

"It's true." Kyle placed his hands on his hips. "It's the same little Sammy show we've all seen for years. You might know how to have fun, but you're not a good long-term bet."

"What the hell do you care what kind of bet I am?" Sam demanded.

Kyle turned to face Sam, and the way they stared at each other made Bella think of some old-time Western standoff. She didn't like it one bit—or the worry crawling over her skin that she might have something to do with the animosity radiating between the two of them.

"She's different," Kyle said through clenched teeth. "She deserves better than you."

"Agreed on both counts," Sam answered without hesitation.

Bella sucked in a small gasp of air and felt Jayne shift closer to her. "It's okay," the older woman whispered.

"You're using her," Kyle spit out, his tone disgusted. "Probably because you knew it would piss me off."

Bella waited for Sam to argue. Of course what had happened between them had nothing to do with his brother.

He only smirked. "You must think a lot of yourself, Kyle. More than I would have guessed. Especially when we both know all I have to do is breathe wrong in your hallowed vicinity and it would make your blood boil. Getting under your skin isn't even a challenge."

"You're going to hurt her like you hurt all of them." Kyle gave a laugh entirely devoid of humor. "At least the ones with any sort of heart or dignity."

"They have a good time, which is more than you can offer," Sam countered. "If casual works for Bella and me, then it's none of your business."

Casual. Bella's stomach seemed to turn inside out. It was just what she'd been afraid of.

"What's all this about?" Pete pushed back from his chair, lifting his reading glasses off his nose.

"Who wants a cinnamon roll?" Jayne asked, offering the plate to Bella.

Bella could barely swallow past the humiliation clogging her throat.

"You ruin everything," Kyle said, his voice tight with anger.

"Enough," Pete shouted, but it was too late.

Sam launched himself at his brother, and they both went tumbling to the floor, a rolling fracas of punches and angry grunts.

Tater came running into the room, followed closely by Gracie. The puppy clearly thought the two men were playing a game, and he wanted in the mix. He pounced on the two of them, then yelped when he was tossed to the side and his cast hit the corner of the doorway.

Gracie let out a series of angry barks as she came to nudge the puppy, and Bella wanted to follow suit even though Sam and Kyle stopped fighting.

They both sat up, looking equally guilty, and Sam held out a hand to Tater. "Come here, boy."

"Don't touch him." Bella managed to give the command with a steady voice.

"Bell, I'm sorry," he said at once. "About all of it. You know last night—"

"No." She cut the air with her hand, then bent to scoop up her dog. "I suppose I should thank you for the good time," she said, feeling heat blaze in her cheeks. "But I don't have it in me."

She turned to Kyle. "I don't need anyone to fight my nonexistent battles," she said with a sniff. "I'm a big girl, and I know what Sam is and isn't able to give."

Glancing up from the brothers, she saw Jayne dash a hand over her cheeks, obviously swiping away a tear. Pete offered her a sympathetic shrug, then moved toward his wife.

Bella hurried toward the front door, wondering how she was going to escape the worst Christmas she'd ever had.

CHAPTER SEVEN

"CINNAMON ROLLS MAKE everything better," Jayne told Bella as they sat in the quiet kitchen of Bella's cabin an hour later.

Although the pastries were indeed melt-in-your-mouth delicious, they tasted like sawdust to Bella. She couldn't stop ruminating over the fact that she'd gotten everything she thought she wanted for one blissful night, only to have it ripped from her hands before the glow had faded.

She'd retreated to the solitude of her cabin after the blowup between the brothers. She didn't want to make a big scene or ruin the Andersons' family Christmas, but she also couldn't pretend she hadn't been hurt by Sam's refusal to deny the accusations his brother made.

Maybe she had been just a way to scratch an itch or a casual holiday hookup. She still didn't understand how she'd managed to misread the way he'd looked at her and touched her, the feeling of connection between them as he'd moved inside her.

She refused to believe that Sam felt nothing for her, but what was she supposed to think at this point? The rest of the family had shown up shortly after Sam had driven away and Kyle stomped out the back door.

Kyle had apologized to her for the scene as she'd loaded her bag and Tater's crate into the back of Jayne's Subaru station wagon, and Pete had given her a tight hug and told her she was welcome back anytime. He'd thanked her for recognizing Sam's unique gifts and holding him to a high standard, making tears prick the back of her eyes.

Jayne had offered to drive her back to Magnolia, but at the last minute had asked her to stay for a bit longer. All Bella wanted was to be home again, but she felt guilty for interrupting Jayne's plan for the holiday so agreed to postpone their departure.

It was obvious Sam's stepmom hoped he'd return to undo this mess, but Bella had only received one text. His message had been a simple apology and a wish for a Merry Christmas despite his behavior. She'd responded with a generic Christmas wish to him, unwilling to let him off the hook for his behavior but unable to call him out or ask him for more of an explanation. She wasn't sure she'd want to read his answer.

"Do you think I'm going to have to move?" she asked as she picked apart the fluffy cinnamon roll without taking a bite. "I love my apartment."

"Of course not." Jayne shook her head. "You and Sam are friends, even though now you're friends with benefits or however that works. Friends don't run away from problems. They work through them."

Bella sighed. "It's awful to think about going back to having a crush on him while watching him cycle through other women again."

"I think our little Sammy has gotten that out of his system," Jayne said with a gentle smile. "He's changed. Both his dad and I see it, probably his siblings, too, although it's hard to relinquish family roles, especially during the holidays. He's different, Bella, and not just because of you. But you're part of it."

"He just left," Bella said, feeling miserable. "I chased him away from celebrating Christmas."

"You didn't do anything," Jayne assured her. "And Christmas will still be here when Sam gets back."

"What if he doesn't come back? What if he went to find one of his old girlfriends?"

"You don't believe that any more than I do."

"I wouldn't blame him."

"Of course you would. You care about him, and you respect yourself. You hold him to a higher expectation than the rest of us do. It's good for him. You're good for him." Jayne stood and refilled Bella's mug from the coffee thermos she'd brought over along with the cinnamon rolls.

"He's good for me, too. He makes me see myself in a different way and try new things that help me step out of my comfort zone."

"You balance each other," Jayne agreed. "Sam needs that. I've known him since he was a baby, all the kids. I was friends with his mother before she passed. It was hard on Pete and the older kids, but they bonded over taking care of Sam. I think he likes the idea of making women happy but didn't want to open himself up to being hurt. He's open with you."

"He's also not here," Bella grumbled.

Tater barked when someone knocked on the door a moment later. Jayne raised a knowing brow and smiled.

"They're probably looking for you," Bella said, but she walked to the door with anticipation making it hard to draw a full breath.

She let out a shuddery gasp when it opened to reveal Sam standing on the other side. Tater wagged his tail and tried to lift his cast to jump on Sam, greeting him like he'd been gone for days. Bella understood the feeling.

"I'm sorry," he said without preamble, then glanced past her to Jayne. "I'm sorry for everything. I shouldn't have let my brother get to me that way."

"You didn't deny the things he said," Bella said. His words had hurt her.

"I'm sorry for that, too." Sam frowned, his brows drawing low over his blue eyes. "Last night wasn't casual for me, Bella. My feelings for you aren't casual, but they're scary as hell because I don't have the best track record. And I don't want to hurt you."

Hope sprang to life in her heart, and she pressed two fingers to her chest like she could keep it at bay.

"Can you come out here?" Sam gave her a sheepish smile. "I have a surprise for you."

With an encouraging nod from Jayne, she gathered the puppy and closed him in the house, then followed Sam into the front yard only to stop short.

Jake Combs was standing near Sam's SUV in a Vanderbilt sweatshirt, jeans and flip-flops, holding a guitar and looking nearly as shocked as Bella felt.

"Merry Christmas, ma'am," he said in his slow drawl.

"Um, Merry Christmas." She glanced toward Sam. "What's he doing here?"

"I sort of begged him." Sam ran a hand through his hair.

"I'm a sucker for a good love story," Jake added.

"A love story," Bella murmured.

"The start of ours, I hope," Sam told her. He held out a hand. "The kind where we start as best friends and end as so much more. Would you dance with me, Bella?" It was a simple request, but it meant the world to her.

As if Sam could read the emotions tumbling through her, he took a step closer. "Would you give me a chance to prove that you've captured my heart? Please let me try again. I promise I'll do my best to be the kind of man you deserve."

Allowing hope and love to pour through her unfettered, Bella put her hand in his. Jake played the first chord of her favorite love song, and she danced on the grass with the man of her dreams. But this was so much better than any fantasy. Because it was real, and Sam was hers. Forever, if she had anything to say about it.

"Merry Christmas, Bella," Sam whispered as he placed a delicate kiss on her forehead.

The best Christmas she could imagine.

* * * * *

SPECIAL EXCERPT FROM

H HARLEQUIN
SPECIAL EDITION

*Brian Fortune doesn't think he will ever find the woman he kissed
at his brother's New Year's wedding. So when the search for the
provenance of a mysterious gift leads him into a local antique
store a few days later, he's stunned to find Emmaline Lewis,
proprietor—and mystery kisser! Brian has never been the type
to commit—but suddenly he knows he'll do anything to stay at
Emmaline's side—for good...*

*Read on for a sneak peek at
the first book in
The Fortunes of Texas: The Wedding Gift continuity,
Their New Year's Beginning,
by USA TODAY bestselling author Michelle Major!*

"I'd like to take you out on a proper date then."

"Okay." Color bloomed in her cheeks. "That would be nice."
He leaned in, but she held up a finger. "You should know that since
Kirby and the gang outed my pregnancy at the coffee shop, I'm not
going to hide it anymore." She pressed a hand to her belly. "I'm
wearing a baggy shirt tonight because it seemed easier than fielding
questions from the boys, but if we go out, there will be questions.
And comments."

"I don't care about what anyone else thinks," he assured her and
then kissed her gently. "This is about you and me."

Those must have been the right words, because Emmaline
wound her arms around his neck and drew closer. "I'm glad," she
said, but before he could kiss her again, she yawned once more.

"I'll walk you to your car."

She mock pouted but didn't argue. "I'm definitely not as fun as I used to be," she told him as he picked up the bags with the leftover supplies to carry for her. "Actually I'm not sure I was ever that fun."

"As far as I'm concerned, you're the best."

After another lingering kiss, Emmaline climbed into her car and drove away. Brian watched her taillights until they disappeared around a bend. The night sky overhead was once again filled with stars, and he breathed in the fresh Texas air. He needed to stay in the moment and remember his reason for being in town and how long he planned to stay. He knew better than to examine the feeling of contentment coursing through him.

One thing he knew for certain was that it couldn't last.

Don't miss
Their New Year's Beginning
by Michelle Major,
available January 2022 wherever
Harlequin Special Edition books and ebooks are sold.

Harlequin.com

Get 4 FREE REWARDS!

We'll send you 2 FREE Books <u>plus</u> 2 FREE Mystery Gifts.

FREE
Value Over
$20

Both the **Romance** and **Suspense** collections feature compelling novels written by many of today's bestselling authors.